CI

SANTINO
HASSELL

A FIVE BOROUGHS
NOVELLA COLLECTION

RIPTIDE
PUBLISHING

Riptide Publishing
PO Box 1537
Burnsville, NC 28714
www.riptidepublishing.com

Citywide

Cover art: L.C. Chase, lcchase.com/design.htm
Editor: Sarah Lyons
Layout: L.C. Chase, lcchase.com/design.htm

ISBN: 978-1-62649-664-4

First edition
November, 2017

Also available in ebook:
ISBN: 978-1-62649-663-7

CITYWIDE

SANTINO HASSELL

A FIVE BOROUGHS
NOVELLA COLLECTION

RIPTIDE
PUBLISHING

For everyone who couldn't get enough of Jaiden and the Queens Crew.
This anthology is for you!

TABLE OF
CONTENTS

REROUTED

A FIVE BOROUGHS NOVELLA

CHAPTER
ONE

B eing the only computer-savvy person in my squad was starting to get old.

Don't get it twisted—computers had been my passion since I was old enough to get my pudgy five-year-old hands on the monstrosity of a computer my father had gifted to my mother one Christmas. I don't know what he'd pawned or what hustle he'd done to score a machine that, at the time, had run over three grand, but she'd been thrilled. I'd been pretty psyched up too.

After that, I was balls-deep in computer games by the time *EverQuest* had come out, and was rebuilding my own machines before most of my friends had internet access in their houses. Which was how I'd turned into the go-to for free IT labor for the past twenty goddamn years when it came to relatives and friends.

It. Was. Old.

Especially since it had topped out at a hundred and five degrees today, and the shitty air conditioner in my best friend's home office wasn't doing much more than making noise. My entire body was covered in a sheen of sweat despite the ceiling fan lazily swishing above my head.

I scowled at Raymond's old-as-fuck HP and the components I'd carefully spread out around me. There was so much wrong with the machine that I didn't know where to start. It was full of dust, the fan had malfunctioned some time ago, and his motherboard was so dated that it didn't have the correct slots for the kind of graphics card he wanted. Or enough space for more RAM.

Sucking my teeth, I jerked a thumb at the machine. "Bro, you're assed out. You're going to need to buy an upgraded machine or buy the parts so I can build you one, because you can't upgrade some shit from 2005 with brand-new parts. The motherboard won't support them."

No response.

I blew into the tower, sending dust flying, and waved my hand with a cough. "And considering how disrespectfully you treat your shit, I don't feel like building you a bomb gaming machine just so you can turn it into another dirty piece of junk."

No response.

I glanced up to the sight of Raymond . . . not even in the room. He'd flat left my ass to tinker with his dinosaur. Irritation ran through me as I got to my feet, dusting off my hands, to track my tall, longhaired asshole of a best friend to wherever he'd gone. After his older brother had married and signed over his half of the property, Raymond had taken over the old Rodriguez home with his boyfriend. It looked way different from the dark cluttered place I'd played in as a kid.

Every time I walked around and peeped at their home office, library, workout room, and attic-turned-library, a twinge of jealousy went through me. Not because I was hating on how well Ray had made out for himself over the past couple of years, but because I still felt stuck. I lived in the same cramped studio above a store on Jamaica Avenue that I'd scored after high school, I drove the same hoopty inherited from my grandfather that was going to break down on me for good any day now, and I had the same lack of a love life. That had all been fine a few years ago, but now I was twenty-seven and frankly . . . ready to move ahead.

"Ey," I bellowed, jogging down the stairs. "I swear to God if I walk in on y'all fucking again . . ."

I had no good follow-up remark for that because I'd been promised some of David's bomb spaghetti, and I wasn't leaving until I got fed. Maybe my lack of a fulfilled threat would scare them into compliance. Fear of the unknown, right? Right.

Following the smell of sautéing garlic and onions, I found my wayward friend and his blond boyfriend in the kitchen. They weren't having sex, thankfully, but the sight of Raymond pressed against David's back, nuzzling the side of his face while David chopped vegetables was . . . weird. Not only did David trust Ray to not startle him into lopping off a finger, but it was utterly bizarre to see Raymond so affectionate.

For all my life, Raymond had been the king of back claps—he'd give me pound as a greeting and goodbye, but no hugs. No mushy shit. But right now? It looked completely natural for him to be glued to his man with that soft smile on his face, like they were made to be in that exact position. And they were also absolutely gorgeous together. David smiling in the deep sunlight of the early evening, and Raymond tall and strong with his long hair once again spilling down his back. It was like a Pinterest photo for relationship goals.

Something inside of me cracked, just a little, and I backed out of the room. Unfortunately, my sneaker hit the linoleum wrong, eliciting a sharp squeak, and Raymond glanced over his shoulder. His smile morphed into confusion, and ah fuck—I was busted looking all emo again. It'd been happening frequently over the past couple of months. Even more so in the past few weeks, after I'd finally deactivated my profiles on every dating app and deleted them off my phone.

"Uh, sorry," I muttered and turned to rush out of the room. I lifted my Yankees cap to swipe my hand over my hair, nervous and suddenly antsy to get out of the house. It wasn't going to happen, mostly because they would think I was an idiot, but also because I was still banking on dinner and the only food at my crib was allegedly imported ramen.

Footsteps trailed behind me as I jogged up the stairs to return to their office and Raymond's busted computer. I plopped down on the floor, fully intending to dive back into the part of my world where things aligned appropriately, clicked together when they were supposed to, and made perfect sense, but David slipped into the room. Which, shit. I could tell Raymond to fuck off and he'd be fine with it because he'd been my boy forever, but I couldn't be a dick to David.

"Food almost ready?" I asked, reaching for the canister of air. "Smells good."

"Yeah, Stephanie gave me her recipe. I just pretend it's mine." David lingered by the door before shuffling closer to me. He sat on the floor, looking half Butler and half Rodriguez in tight shorts, but with a too-big sleeveless Nets jersey and Nike slides. "Are you okay?"

"Yup."

"Are you sure?"

"Definitely sure."

David frowned, worrying but not speaking, like he did when he wanted to help but wasn't sure how. I'd noticed him in this spot a lot since he'd moved in with Raymond. He was constantly surrounded by Raymond's Queens squad—the friends he'd grown up with in South Jamaica. We'd accepted David into our little crew, adopting him as if he was fam by proximity, but we all saw how careful he was about overstepping. Not wanting to insert himself too deep, or be too opinionated, because he was still finding his place. It drove me and Stephanie nuts, but I thought it was the reason why Tonya and Angel had warmed up to him.

"All right," I said, relenting. "I guess seeing everyone be all domestic is starting to get to me."

David nodded slowly, those warm brown eyes fixed on me as he probably took apart my statement and put it back together. "Why?"

"Because I'm always the odd man out? It's been like this since high school, D. Everyone doing their thing—dating or getting laid—and me with my thumb up my ass flying solo." I released a humorless chuckle. "You'd think that shit would have changed by now, but it hasn't."

"Why, though? You go on dates. I've seen you!"

It was true. OkCupid and Tinder hadn't been unkind to me, but one-off dates or random hookups didn't do it for me. Sure, I'd get laid, but . . . that really wasn't what I wanted. Anyone could have sex, but sex had nothing on genuine companionship. And I was lonely. I had friends, but there was no one at home waiting for my text or call. No one waiting to light up a room when I walked in.

My brain flashed two faces in my mind, and a shiver ran through me. Nuh-uh. Off-limits fantasy. I corrected myself without indulging in wishful thing: there was no one waiting for me *who would work in the long run.* And I wanted a long run.

"I dunno, man," I said with a sigh. "Something's just always missing when I go out with a someone from OkCupid or whatever. I'll meet a woman who is smart, pretty, ambitious—and we have a good time, but I'm not invested in it because we have no real connection, and I don't know how to . . . make one happen." I shrugged, frowning, wishing I could explain it better. "For me, I either click with someone straight off or I don't. So me dating turns into me buying some woman food and us maybe even sleeping together, but it never goes any further except pointless dates and pointless sex that goes nowhere."

David had folded his legs under him and was fanning himself. He sent a glare at the air conditioner, as if noticing for the first time that it wasn't working. He probably didn't use the room much. It had *Rodriguez Cave* written all over it, if I went by the empty energy drink cans and scattered game cases. Also, the giant Puerto Rican flag being used as a curtain.

"Okay, I'm going to just throw this out there," he said tactfully. "Have you tried dating a guy?"

"Uh." I glanced between him and the door, paranoid. "What do you mean by *date*?"

"Well . . . I know you've been with guys in the past . . ."

Jace kissed all over the column jutting between my thighs, showing it a lot of love. The tip of his tongue ran along every vein, traced the slit, and then went down to my balls.

I bit my fist and kept staring across the room at his husband—Aiden. My gaze flicked to his erection as it pressed against the thigh of his pants. Aiden kept his legs spread wide, obviously enjoying the attention even though he wasn't touching himself just yet. He seemed to have more interest in watching me contort with pleasure as Jace took me down his throat.

"Oh, fuck yes," I breathed. I braced both hands on the back of Jace's head, gently helping him along as I bucked my hips. "Jesus Christ, you can suck."

Across the room, Aiden drained his beer and set the bottle to the side. His gaze was molten, zeroing in on his man slobbering all over the erection between my thighs.

"Can anyone usually deep-throat that big dick?" he asked, voice hoarse.

Heat rose to my face. I fought the urge to jump up and flee the room. I had no idea why my friends knew so much about my slew of threesomes with Jace and Aiden Fairbairn, but I equally had no idea why it bothered me that they knew. When it came down to it, most of my friends were queer. Angel was the last hetero hold out. Why did it matter?

"I've only been with Aiden and Jace." When David just looked at me calmly, waiting for me to add to the statement, my face grew hotter. "There was this other couple I met with . . ."

He leaned in, immediately intrigued. "Two guys?"

"No. A man and a woman." The memory of that crash-and-burn experience still burned with mortification. "They didn't say they were poly, though. So . . . not like Jace and Aiden."

"Oh, so they wanted to try a threesome?"

"Yeah. Or . . . well . . ." I was pretty sure the exact thing had been her man having some cuckold fantasy. "I dunno, it was a sex thing. We met up a few times, but it was just him watching me and her? It was mad weird and awkward at first, but he seemed to get off on it."

"Um. Did *you* get off on it? Because I always had the feeling that you actually *liked* being with two people? Not just participating in a voyeur kink."

He was right. I'd wanted her husband to participate so we could all enjoy the experience together, but he'd just jacked it and watched. Then one day they'd invited me over while he was drinking, and he'd gotten jealous and flipped. Apparently, I'd worn out my welcome, even though I couldn't pinpoint when it had happened. From my perspective, one moment we'd all been cool and the next . . . not so cool.

I didn't know why I was so embarrassed thinking about it since nothing had actually happened except him asking me to leave, but . . . I couldn't bring myself to tell David. Maybe because I'd *known* what they wanted would never replace the connection I'd had with Jace and Aiden the few times we'd slept together after the QFindr modeling shoot, and I'd tried anyway. I was that desperate to replicate the feeling of being wanted and shared by two people.

"It was okay," I said finally. "But you're right, it wasn't what I wanted."

David nodded slowly, frowning. I could tell he had a lot of questions, but he only asked, "Are you open to being with a man?"

"Yeah? I think. I mean, it can't just be a sex thing if—" If I spent way too much time over the past year mooning over the what-ifs with two dudes. "—if I'd consider dating them, right?"

"Do you want to try dating them?" David asked hesitantly. "We can talk about it if you want."

My first instinct was to change the subject, but why? If there was anyone safe to discuss this with without sarcasm and the playful joking of friends who'd known me forever, it was D. I stopped pretending to tinker with the computer and leaned against the wall, stretching my legs out in front of me.

"It's like this. I've always been attracted to women. I always assumed I'd get a girlfriend, fall in love, we'd get married and have a few mini Mendez kids." I thudded my head against the wall lightly. "But I've always been . . . comfortable with admiring a guy's appearance. Like, Angel and Raymond? As a teen, it was hard not to notice how good-looking they were, although at first I chalked it up to jealousy. It wasn't until I realized I, uh, didn't mind looking at their dicks in their basketball shorts, or them all sweaty and shirtless at the park, that I wondered if there was anything else there."

"Sounds familiar," David said, smiling. "Except, for me, I had those thoughts super young. Like when I was in elementary. I thought at first I just wished I looked like the other boys because I was so soft and pretty, and people made fun of me for it."

Frowning, I reached out to ruffle his hair. "Assholes."

"Kids are awful," he agreed, grinning. One thing about David that I loved was how huggable and touchy he was. Me and Stephanie were super affectionate, and it never fazed him. "But forget about me, keep talking. Raymond always knew he was into guys. He said he was just too lazy to hook up with one."

I spluttered out a laugh. "Uh, yeah, sounds like him. But for me, I never had a huge *urge* to try to bone a guy. I just *noticed* them." I swiped my hand under my hat again, cringing when it came back damp with sweat. "Anyway, it's not like I can blame my lack of investment in relationships with women on some low-key desire to only be with dudes. Until recently, I never considered the idea with any seriousness. Like, there was no one I looked at and said, 'Wow, I want to date them.' You feel me?"

"Right," David said, nodding. "Kinda heteroflexible, then?"

"Yeah, more or less. And I only know what that means because I went hunting down variations of queer labels after my second roll in the bed with Jace and Aiden. Obviously hetero didn't apply to me as much as I thought it did. Or curious. But now that I know I'm for sure into guys, I don't know if heteroflexible works."

"You could just go with queer. Plenty of people think that works best for them."

I'd never thought of that, and the suggestion was grounding. After realizing I wasn't straight, I'd felt pressure to pick a label that would define me, but none of them had felt quite right.

"This convo is surreal, D. Those two got me so fucked up. Not just because I had to sit around and think about my bisexuality, but because that's when all this morose shit started. That's why I hooked up with that other couple even though it was weird."

David hummed a bit. "Was it that . . . good?"

Aiden grabbed a handful of my hair from behind and jerked my head back so he could rumble in my ear. "Tell me you like it."

"Bro, I fucking love it."

He kissed my ear, then the side of my face, and back up again, all while steadily rocking against my hip. "I'm about to fill you up, so show me what that ass can do."

"Yes," Jace hissed. "That's what I want to see."

Aiden pushed my face away from him and grabbed my shoulders. He started in on me hard from the start, powering through and obliterating my nerves, as I panted open-mouthed and pushed back on him.

It wasn't enough.

I wound up riding back onto his dick with such force that his hips slapped against my ass loudly in the silent room. He stopped gripping my shoulders in favor of grabbing my hips.

"Oh yeah," he said breathlessly. "Just like that, Chris."

I managed to keep the ass-clapping rhythm until Jace reached beneath me and started again with the earth-shattering handjob. Jesus Christ, they were trying to kill me.

"I'm—"

I didn't even get the word out before my orgasm tore through me like a storm—lighting me up with bolts of pleasure that whited out my vision. Aiden shoved my head down and went harder, his pace punishing, until he rammed in as far as he could go and came with a shout.

"Uh. Yeah. Oddly, some of the best sex I've ever had in my life has been during threesomes," I admitted. "Which, I know that's weird for you to know since some of those were years ago with Steph and Ray, but it's true. There's just something really dope about sharing intimacy that way. Being that close to two other people at the same time is like being in the best fucking sandwich ever. All the giving and taking and giving . . ." I glanced over at David and cringed at his raised eyebrows. "Yeah, I'm going overboard."

He laughed and waved his hands. "No way. I'm just surprised, I guess. You sound super poly for someone who only ever had dreams of a nuclear family."

"Tell me about it. But I guess I only ever assumed I'd have a nuclear family because I come from a Catholic-as-fuck PR family. There weren't any other options presented until recently." I gave my head one last thud for good measure, then peeked at him from beneath the bill of my cap. "Can you give me some sage dating advice to help me out here?"

David snorted out a laugh, his eyes crinkling. "*You* want advice from *me*? Dude. I've been with Ray for almost three years this coming fall, and I am still a ball of jealous rage anytime anyone looks at him twice."

"Because you're a little blond territorial grizzly bear," I said, snickering.

"'Little'! Excuse you, sir. I am taller than you."

I flipped him off without denying it. Mendez folk rarely topped out any higher than five foot eight, and I'd owned that years ago.

"Just give me advice," I pressed. "You may be possessive as fuck, but you got my growly, mean-mugging, apathetic bastard bestie to fall in super-sappy love with you, so you must know some tricks to the trade."

"I don't though," he said. "I mean, I get what you're saying. I've been there. When I was with Caleb, we stayed together only because we thought it made sense, but we didn't have chemistry. It was obvious it was never going to go anywhere." David bit his lip, brows shooting together like they often did when he discussed his past relationship. "And unlike you, who doesn't keep pushing it once you realize a relationship isn't going anywhere, we tried to force it, until we were both miserable."

"Then you met Ray," I said, smiling.

David's face lit up. "Yes. Then I met Ray. And with him . . . I don't know. Whenever I thought about who made me feel happiest, most at home, most *wanted*, it was his face that came to mind. When we were together, it felt right. And I would imagine a future where we were always together, and that would feel right too."

Every word he said pinged in my brain and brought back memories of my trysts with the Fairbairns. We'd only been together a handful of times since meeting at the photoshoot last summer, but each and every one was ingrained in my mind. The way Jace would greet me with a hug and a shy smile, while Aiden looked on happily before kissing us in turn. Lying in bed wrapped up with them while UFC played in the background, Jace asking me questions while Aiden ordered takeout on his phone. The overwhelming feeling of being desired by both and being included in their world every time they'd pleaded with me to spend the night. How easily we'd fallen into a pattern of work and play the couple of times I'd spent the weekend with them. Aiden was often preoccupied with his job even on days he was supposed to have off, but there was never any tension about it when we were all together.

It had been eerie how quickly my brain had supplied images of myself with them for the long term. Me making dinner with Jace after work as we waited for Aiden to stumble home from his increasingly long days at QFindr—the start-up for the queer dating app he'd created with his half brother Caleb and Caleb's boyfriend Oli—then us all unwinding together in front of the TV or with some beer while we shared stories about our days. No one ever feeling left out or forgotten or alone, just three dudes filling all the empty spaces left behind when there had only been two.

It had been so easy to imagine, but it was just a dream. Even though I'd clicked with them in that instant, magical way I so rarely clicked with anyone, I seemed to be the only one imagining that there'd someday be more than sex. It had taken a couple of months for me to catch on, but then I'd realized we weren't going on dates.

I wasn't included in this huge life they had. And they still fucked other people. Regularly.

I'd always known they were open, but part of me had hoped maybe they'd . . . call *me* if they wanted a third. That was the moment when I'd checked myself and started pulling further and further away.

"You're thinking about Jace and Aiden?"

I nodded, scowling.

David studied me, his pale-blond hair a golden halo in the late-evening sunlight streaming through the window. It was easy to see why Raymond had fallen for him when he was like this—thoughtful and quiet and trying to think of the best way to help without pushing too hard. On instinct, I bopped his nose. He smiled.

"Can I ask how the *hell* you got mixed up with those two?"

I fell back against the wall with a huff, thinking about the previous summer. It seemed like a lifetime ago when Raymond had approached me, Steph, and Tonya about the idea of modeling for the QFindr promotional campaign. He'd been so pumped about the plan— for the money and because he was finally owning his sexuality. His relationship. His entire self. Part of me had felt the same, even though I'd still been so confused about what I'd wanted from a relationship. Though some of that confusion had faded as soon as a set of laser eyes had focused on me . . .

"Jace," I said with a fond smile. "He latched on to me at the QFindr shoot like a kid who'd just found a new toy. He had no idea if I was straight or queer, but he teased and flirted and propositioned, and I think he really enjoyed the fact that I joked along instead of getting all freaked out and panicky, you know? Except, then I realized he wasn't joking, and we started texting, then he added Aiden into a group text, and I realized I really fucking liked talking to them both . . ."

David was nodding, his big brown eyes so wide that he looked like one of those Precious Moments dolls. I nudged him.

"Keep going," he urged. "This is good shit."

"Not really." I snorted. "We scheduled a hangout and rescheduled a bunch of times before I finally agreed to go chill with them. Because, like, part of me knew they wanted to fuck, and part of me was still trying to pretend we were just gonna kick it and watch the fight."

"And you fucked," David said helpfully.

"We did both, actually. Had bomb sex, watched the fights, ate dinner, fucked some more." I could feel my face warming as I said the words, which was weird because I wasn't exactly a shy dude, but I'd never discussed sex with David before. It was sort of like admitting to a close relative that I watched hard-core gangbang porn. "Uh, anyways, it was weird because . . . I could feel myself getting too attached in that *one weekend*. Legitimately daydreaming about how dope it would be to feel that content and wanted on the regular, and those thoughts intensified after I hooked up with them a second time. But they're still open, and sleeping with other people, so I backed off because it bothered me. It's not like I was going to ask them to change their relationship and lifestyle for some dude they'd fucked a couple of times."

David cringed. "Chris, you don't know if that's all they think of you."

"But I don't know that it's *not*, either. They never said anything different. Most of all, they never dialed my number instead of going to Liberty X to hit up a sex party. So . . ."

He cringed deeper. "Did you tell either of them you had feelings for them beyond sex?"

"Fuck no. Not everyone is like me and catches feelings after a couple of rolls in the bed." My face burned as I said it, but I knew David wouldn't judge me. "Besides, after a lifetime of growing up and being rejected for other people—namely Ray and Angel—I've learned to cut my losses and run."

David looked so bummed out for me that I pinched his cheek in the hopes I'd get a smile. He did so reluctantly. "You kept seeing them sometimes, though. Why didn't you tell them then?"

"Because it was only whenever we happened to see each other at a QFindr event or at a party."

"Like Caleb and Oli's party around the holidays?" David asked dryly. "When Raymond confronted Aiden like an angry dad?"

I bobbed my head. "Yup. That was embarrassing."

"It was ridiculous. Raymond is so overprotective."

"Yeah, but it's because he's known since we were kids how sensitive I am about dating." Still though, I'd been pissed at Raymond after hearing the story of him cornering Aiden and getting in his face.

Apparently, he'd demanded what Aiden's intentions were toward me, and Aiden had avoided answering. Probably because he'd had no real intentions other than blowing my socks off in a coatroom. "And it's not like Aiden had some impressive answer for him."

"Yeah, but that could be because Raymond literally threatened to punch him. I had to drag them apart." David shook his head and rolled his eyes. "So, that's why you've been so moody for the last . . . three months?"

"Yup," I said, popping the *p*. "I'm just tired of being single, man. Since I was a kid, I'd crush hard for one person and then mope for *ages* when it turned out to be only on my end, then give up and angst. I have a romantic heart, D."

David gave me a high five. "You and me both. But, just so I'm clear, you never plan to tell Jace and Aiden that you have feelings for them? Ever?"

I shook my head, going for a light tone even though my gut coiled. "Not unless something changes. I try to avoid crushing rejection whenever possible. But even if they *did* also have feelings for me, I can't handle being in an open relationship. My self-esteem would drop lower than it already is, my guy."

David sighed slowly. "Yeah, I get it. I'm not secure enough for that kind of relationship arrangement either, even though I am in total awe of people who are."

"Same, but I'm too old to go along with some shit I know would end with hurt feelings and drama. There's zero point. I can be with two people, but I can't be with two people who also want to have casual sex with . . . other people."

"I understand." David reached over to pat my leg, looking fretful and sad for me and the throuple that would never happen. "So, what are you going to do? From what I've heard from Steph, Jace gets swoony when he talks about you."

"He talks about me with her?" The question came out fast and probably reeked of boyish desperation, but it had never occurred to me that they'd discuss me with other people. Not in a "swoony" way. "What did he say?"

David smiled. "I don't know the details, but she was surprised at how smitten he seemed when he talked about wanting to get you in bed again."

The knowledge warmed me. My entire adolescence and adulthood had been full of incidences where people passed me over for my taller, buffer, or hotter friends, but Jace and Aiden had not been shy or subtle about their desire for me. It was nice to know it persisted. Too bad it apparently only went back to us going to bed together.

Maybe he got swoony talking about us having sex again, but I got swoony thinking about his big dark eyes and the way they lit up whenever he was entranced by a book. Because that was a thing he did—read when he thought everyone else was sleeping. Sometimes I thought he didn't sleep much at all.

"Maybe I'll stop actively avoiding them and see where things go, but I'm not going to set my hopes on them to find my brand of domestic bliss." I waved my hand vaguely. "Uh, whatever that brand is."

David nodded, but he looked so *sad* for me that I wanted to smack myself in the head. Way to bring the whole party down.

"You fuckers done being emo?" Raymond called from the bottom of the stairs. "Because it's like two thousand degrees in this kitchen, and I'll be damned if I slave over this sauce by myself."

David and I looked at each other with matching smirks before rising with identical sighs.

"I'm coming, drama queen," he shouted down.

"I'll help," I offered. "Cooking is superior to trying to upgrade his crappy computer in this hot-ass room. Why is it so hot in March, anyway?"

David groaned and headed to the door. "Global warming? It sucks balls. This place is like a furnace in the summer, so I'm dreading summer if spring is already this fucking hot. Not to mention that weird stuff *always* happens during heat waves in this city. I guarantee the next few weeks will be full of drama."

I sure as hell hoped not. The only way to get out of my funk was to go back to basics and enjoy the parts of my life that made me happy *without* complications: computers, UFC, and car rides with my windows down and music up. Anything more complex needed to take a back seat for now.

CHAPTER
TWO

I got the message as soon as we sat down to eat. One ping, then two, then three steady chirps of my phone indicating someone was trying to contact me with the quickness.

"Who dat?" Raymond asked around a mouthful of spaghetti. He hadn't inquired about my mini meltdown after seeing him love on his guy, and he probably never would. He knew I'd let him in on the details if I wanted him to have them. "Tell them to fuck off during dinner."

"You sound like your mother," I informed him, grinning. "She was so pissed that cell phones were a thing when we were kids. She'd make a big pot of arroz con pollo, and then we sat there glued to our shit while stuffing food down our throats."

Raymond smiled, and his gaze flicked to the wall before going back to his plate. They'd left up one of the ornate wooden etchings she'd brought back from Puerto Rico one summer. In exchange, they'd taken down the dozens of crosses.

"We need to invest in a better cooling system," David grumbled. He'd sat back from his plate to fan himself. "We don't have a window unit for every room, and it's so expensive ..."

They launched into a debate over fans versus window units, and the magic of central air, which was a rare find in NYC, while I slipped my phone from my pocket. Caleb Stone's name glared up at me.

Huh.

Caleb: *Hey Christopher.*

Caleb: *I know you worked with us on the QFindr photoshoot, but I'm afraid we're in a bit of a pickle right now, and I might need to hire you for something other than how photogenic you are.*

Caleb: *I heard you're an IT wizard.*

Jesus, Mary, and Joseph. Another fucker trying to use me for my mad computer skills? Although, he'd said *hire* . . .

Chris: *Sure. What happened?*

Caleb: *This heat wave is killing us. We had a power surge, and I think the server racks we keep for the office are fried. The shared hard drives seem corrupted, and everything is a mess. Is it possible to restore the data? We had source code stored there.*

Chris: *You didn't also have it in the cloud?*

Caleb: *:/ No. Oli was possessive of it and afraid of it being hacked or stolen.*

Chris: *Yiiikes. The app still up and running?*

Caleb: *Yes, those connect to servers that are stored elsewhere.*

Chris: *Okay, good. Well . . . I mean, it's hard to say with just that description, yanno? When did this go down?*

Caleb: *We realized the damage . . . now. The last power surge was a few hours ago.*

At six o'clock on a Friday. I'd left work at three today and was usually kept on a tight schedule, so I could imagine that QFindr staff had left already as well.

Chris: *You don't got any emergency IT dudes to come in?*

Caleb: *No. We're still running with a very small staff, and our IT manager is visiting his mother in Florida. Aiden has been filling in for him, but his skills are limited in this capacity, and we're frankly panicking.*

Caleb: *Aiden mentioned that you're basically a walking computer so . . . I was hoping I could entice you to save us?*

I reread the sentence several times, but my gaze kept zooming in on Aiden's name. Given I'd just been moping over him, it was no wonder I was now obsessed with the fact that *he* had recommended me, even though it literally meant nothing. I was the "IT wizard" he happened to know, and that was all. It didn't mean this was some sly way to get me in their office so he could woo me. Which was unfortunate. The very idea of seeing that red-stubbled square jaw and his beefy biceps made me feel funny in my pants. And the idea of us camping out with pizza and beer while I tried to put their electronics back together made me want to smile dorkily.

That was why this was a bad fucking idea. Even after I'd just decided to quit avoiding them and see if something happened, I was already mooning over theoretical hang-out sessions. Not even the sex part of those hang-out sessions. I just wanted to sit with him and chill.

Caleb: *I'll pay you a hundred an hour for however long it takes.*

Chris: *Fuck, dude, I'm not sure that's a normal amount of money.*

Caleb: *That doesn't matter. What matters is fixing this immediately.*

I gnawed on my lower lip. That was decent money if I wound up stuck in their office for more than a couple of hours, but . . . I wasn't sure I was prepared to face Aiden just yet. I needed a few beers and an amp-up speech to tell myself I could either keep it platonic or do sex with zero feels, and both seemed impossible.

Chris: *Uh, how about you get back to me if you can't find anyone else. K?*

Caleb: *Okay.*

I instantly felt like shit, but this was self-preservation. I was good at making big statements about keeping my blah life simple and uncomplicated to avoid the hurt feelings that would inevitably come from ménages with poly folk, but things were bound to get nice and complex if I gave in.

"What's up?" Raymond asked, nodding at my phone. "You're making weird faces."

"Oh. Nothing."

He arched a brow. "So you're just over there having a stroke?"

"Yeah, that's it," I said. "All this heat is getting to me." Ray glared, and I snickered. "Caleb asked if I could swoop by QFindr's office and save their asses after a heat-induced computer issue. I'd probably make a few hundred easy."

Raymond nodded slowly, chewing on a meatball with his brows all bunched together.

"I'm not doing it," I added.

His brows smoothed, and I wasn't even surprised. I'd asked him to back off on the overprotective stuff after his standoff with Aiden at Christmas, but I knew he was still wary of them. Of all of them, actually. Even Meredith, Ashton, and Charles, who were Stephanie's new pals. I'd once asked what his deal was, and he'd flatly said he didn't trust a bunch of rich white people who seemed to be trying to diversify their sex lives with his friends. Honestly? I couldn't blame him.

"You sure? The money sounds good," David said, not catching the hint or maybe not caring. He ignored his boyfriend's irritated look. "Unless you're tired of being the go-to IT guy for everyone."

Leave it to David to be Mr. Diplomatic. Give me a reason for and against the decision without any personal bias, while ignoring the big elephant in the room. I'd probably hash out the pros and cons with him if Raymond wasn't glaring at my phone as he stabbed a meatball with his fork.

"Nah, I'm good." I looked around the table and pushed my chair back. "I'm gonna grab more bread."

It gave me an excuse to avoid their watchful eyes and to get my shit together, because damn, I wasn't used to being this scrutinized. I wasn't used to having anything resembling drama. Out of all of us, I was the most low-key person in the squad, and I planned to keep it that way. So, I got the Italian bread and spent the next hour talking UFC, baseball, and food. By the time I left their house to head to my hoopty, I was too full for how hot it was outside and craving a cold beer.

I yanked the door open, dropped into the ripped leather seat of a Mazda that hadn't seen any love since the early nineties, and turned the key. What I got in exchange was nada. It didn't even stutter. Legit made zero sounds.

I stared at the steering wheel as sweat dripped down the side of my face, adding to my overwhelming feeling of being an overstuffed, overheated mess. A mess with a dead car.

"Carajo," I muttered, slamming my fist against the steering wheel. "Always fucking something . . ."

With my tail between my legs, I returned to the house to let David and Raymond in on my misfortune, got a ride back to my apartment on the Avenue, and then stood in front of it feeling like an asshole. I should have called a tow truck to tow the fucking heap of metal to a junkyard and made a few bucks that way, although one of Tonya's cousins could probably hook me up with a chop shop that would make me more.

There was no way I was going to sink money into repairing it. What I needed was money for a down payment on a new ride. Just like I'd been telling myself to save money for a down payment on another apartment. One off the fucking Avenue I'd been walking since childhood.

With a suck of my teeth and a lot of reluctant rocking on the balls of my feet, I pulled out my phone and called Caleb.

"Thank you so much for coming."

"No prob, man."

Caleb locked the glass door behind us as we stepped into the QFindr office, and I had to pick up my jaw from the floor. I always heard stories about how Facebook and Spotify started, the tale of the original founders and how it was once grassroots, and it was hard to believe because now they were mega corporations, but as I looked around QFindr HQ, I believed it.

The sorta-shitty queer dating app that I'd helped to alpha and beta test had morphed into something used internationally with gleaming glass offices in downtown Manhattan. I'd known it was a big deal when we'd done the photoshoot and my face had wound up on posters on buses and in the subway, but . . . somehow seeing a physical space made it real. When we'd done the photoshoot, they'd still been working out of a smaller rented space uptown.

"You really made out for yourself," I said, trailing behind Caleb. He was wearing a three-piece suit, and I had on basketball shorts and sandals. I did a little tap dance as I followed him, ensuring the backs of my sandals slapped against the shiny floor.

Caleb looked over his shoulder, startled, and laughed. "What are you doing?"

I shrugged, grinning. "Being dumb."

His eyes crinkled at the sides. "You're adorable."

Oh God. That word again. The bane of my entire life. Since junior high, I'd been the adorable one with the cute nose and dimples, the guy a little bit shorter than the rest, who'd been passed over for my giant muscular friends. But I wasn't trying to fuck Caleb, so I just winked and kept following. I did sneak in a couple of more jigs on the way.

The main part of their space was open concept except for larger offices at each corner. I looked around, on instinct, and wondered which office was Aiden's.

"Here we are," Caleb said, leading me to a narrow room.

It was similar to the space we had at my job, where we stowed the racks of on-site servers. Just a narrow, chilly room with a few hard-core terminals that usually did nothing but exist for the rest of the network to access from everyone's individual computers. Except, the last time our servers had seen damage, we hadn't lost anything valuable. Definitely not anything like source code for an app worth millions.

Caleb hovered behind me. "How long will it take?"

"I don't know until I start looking at it all," I said. "I should be able to recover data with software instead of using a clean room, but—"

"What's a clean room?" The worry in Caleb's brow tripled. "That sounds frightening."

"It's a sterile environment for computer parts to be taken apart and worked on. But, like I said, we won't need that."

It didn't seem to matter that I was reassuring him. Caleb was balls-deep in meltdown mode. I could see it in the way he gripped the front of his jacket and gnawed on his lower lip. A little shred of panic hit me, because while I knew the dude, I didn't really *know* the dude. I wasn't equipped to prevent a full-on coronary.

Ugh. I definitely hadn't counted on him sticking around and flipping out the entire time I worked. I knew what I was doing, but doing my job while an anxiety-ridden millionaire bit his nails and stared at me was a setup for disaster. The only times I made mistakes were when people micromanaged me.

But how the hell could I ditch him when he was paying me a hundred bucks an hour to save his ass?

"Uh . . ." I rubbed the back of my head. "So . . ."

"Chris here yet?"

Aiden's voice boomed through the office like he'd spoken through a megaphone. It should have been annoying, especially when each word dripped with the remnants of an old-school Irish American Queens accent that would grate coming from anyone else, but my lips turned up in a smile.

Aiden had a presence like the sun—warm and bright—and he commanded the attention of everyone who had the pleasure of being close to him. It had the same effect on me that'd been there from the start. Wanting to be close to him, to bask in his personality and big mouth and brawn, while also standing a bit taller to make sure he knew I measured up. I had a big personality too.

He strode up to us, and I struggled to keep my eyes on his face. Tough, considering his thick muscular thighs were looking more delicious than usual in a pair of dark pinstriped shorts and his biceps were exploding out of a short-sleeved white button-down. He had on fucking boat shoes, and my mouth still watered at the sight of his muscular legs. But I kept my expression the very definition of unaffected as I jerked my chin at him in greeting, even though looking at him from the neck up wasn't much easier. The last time I'd stood before those big green eyes, broad jaw, and laughing mouth, he'd been gripping the side of my face, ginger stubble rubbing my cheek raw, as he fucked me and Jace played with my dick.

"'Sup, Red?" I drawled, all *no big deal* that we were in the same room for the first time in what felt like months. "What it do?"

Aiden looked me over, a long slow sweep up and down my body, before giving me the same tough-guy head nod. I didn't know if his nonchalance was for Caleb's benefit—who was apparently a real stickler for ethics within their company—or for me, since I'd been ignoring his texts for a while now.

"Shit's not great with this fucking heat," Aiden complained. "The power's been blinking since the temp shot up this past weekend. Thanks for coming."

"No sweat," I said. "Wasn't doing anything, anyway."

"Really?" Aiden slid his phone out of his pocket and glanced at it, still talking. "I figured you'd be going out to the club."

Heh. He thought he was so slick. When we'd first met, my Friday night MO had been to go drinking and dancing and spend a couple of hours flirting with pretty girls more for the fun of it rather than to truly try to get some culo. Even during the stretches of time when all we did was bullshit in a group text, Aiden had found a way to ask whether I'd met anyone on those nights out. I'd thought his apparent possessiveness had meant something, but we'd stuck to the same routine of fucking infrequently with no changes at all, so I'd eventually assumed his interest didn't imply deeper feels.

I shook my head, not bothering to answer, and Caleb kept fretting over the servers. He was too distressed to chastise his half brother for interrogating the IT kid about his sex life, which meant he needed to take his ass on home before he started making me nervous.

"Okay, I'll be real," I told him. "I have no idea how long this will take, but I'm committed to staying late tonight and coming back tomorrow. You don't need to stick around and watch."

"I don't mind," Caleb said. "I'll just worry the whole time if I go home."

Grimacing, I glanced at Aiden. All it took was half a second of eye contact, and he understood. I could tell by the way he clapped a hand on Caleb's arm to wheel him around, murmuring encouraging nonsense in a steady stream that Caleb was too polite to interrupt.

I watched their retreating backs, weirded out and a little turned on. I'd fucked Aiden Fairbairn only a few times in the past year, and yet he could read me like he'd been riding shotgun inside my body all along.

Shaking myself, I turned away from the server room to find something to write on. It was time to get to work and earn my money, not get hung up thinking about sex and two dudes I had no business obsessing over. It was usually easy to shift my brain from the wistful longing of a lonely bastard to nerd mode, and this time was no exception. I came up with a list of everything I'd need to do, and the supplies I might need, because a physical list always did more for me than a mental one.

It wasn't until I finished scribbling did I look up to see Aiden leaning against the doorway. He looked like porn with his muscular arms and bedroom eyes, a big lug from the Rockaways who wanted to take care of me real good even though his method bordered on the right side of rough, but I managed to glance past him.

"Where's Caleb?"

"Sent him home to Oli."

"Appreciate it," I said. "I work better alone, and he was on that next level of worried. Would have paced behind me the whole damn time."

"He would have." Aiden extended his arm to flick the bill of my cap. "What are you gonna do to thank me for saving you from that experience?"

I left my cap skewed sideways and arched my scarred brow at him. If there was one thing to be said about Aiden, it was that he never changed. He knew what he wanted and he'd come at you like a bull to get it.

"You didn't sabotage your own company just to set up some weird-ass seduction, did you? Because I'mma tell Caleb, and that poor bastard won't ever forgive you."

Aiden burst out laughing, eyes twinkling, as he yanked me into one of his big bear hugs. I was a strong dude, but he had so much mass on me that I felt dwarfed once he squeezed. I'd been brought up affectionate, so I felt qualified to say that Aiden gave the best hugs. Second maybe only to Nunzio.

"You always smell so good," Aiden rumbled in my ear. "I could fucking eat you."

I scrambled my way out of his muscular arms and backed away, holding out a wagging finger. It was ridiculous, especially when he began advancing on me like a red-haired panther in his slick biz cas outfit while I slid all over the floor in my chanclas.

"Calm yourself, Aiden. I'm here to work, not to fuck."

"You can do both."

Aiden lunged at me. *Lunged.* Like a cartoon character. Or a horny Batman villain. Laughing incredulously, I spun away from him and took off running through the great purple expanse of QFindr offices.

"I'm going to spank that round ass of yours when I catch you," he called after me. "Fucking brat."

I skidded to a stop by a strange array of standing desks and workout equipment lined up along a wall of windows. He'd loped behind me, grinning broadly, and clearly enjoying my shenanigans. He always did. *They* always did. My refusal to act like an adult eighty percent of the time was ninety percent of my charm.

"We're not fucking, you big orange bastard."

"'Orange'?" Aiden huffed. "Don't be a dick."

"My bad. We're not fucking, you big ginger bastard." I waggled my eyebrows at him. "Better?"

"Much."

Aiden crossed the distance between us in two long strides and grabbed the front of my shirt. He was all over me again, barely giving me room to think or breathe or exist without him touching me. His tongue lashed against my mouth with a wet demand for entrance that I instantly acquiesced to. I slanted my mouth, groaning when he slid his hot tongue inside, and slammed my hips against his as he gripped me tight with his huge hands.

The last time I'd tasted that Aiden flavor of chewing gum and beer had been a couple of months ago at Stephanie's birthday party. The event had been a strange mix of working class and celebutante, with my boys from the block rubbing elbows with her new friends from the Upper West Side. We'd had a blast partying until dawn at her friend Mere's fairy-tale mansion, but it had been Aiden and Jace in the spare bedroom with their quick hands that had really blown my mind. While everyone danced and drank and enjoyed each other two floors below, Jace and Aiden had shared my body.

Aiden pressed his fingers to my lips, trying to shush me, but nothing worked except for him sliding them into my mouth. I sucked messily as my hands shook where they were gripping Jace's shoulders.

He was squeezing me so tight, slamming back on my dick relentlessly, and it was almost too much. Between the feel of being encased by his tight muscles and heat, and Aiden inside my own ass, I was losing my mind. The perfect rhythm I'd managed just a moment ago was a disaster, and I could feel my orgasm approaching.

"More," Jace pleaded, gripping the metal headboard and rocking backward. "Chris, please. Just use me."

Aiden's hips rutted against me in a particularly violent thrust. His groan was muffled as he released, and I imagined him biting his fist. Once he pulled out of me, I flipped Jace onto his back, pressed his knees back, and fucked him until he was shouting and coming without touching his dick.

"Fuck," he whispered, once we'd collapsed in a sweaty pile. A dreamy smile crossed his lips, eyes shut, as I trailed kisses down his face and neck.

"I haven't come that hard since that night at Liberty with the football players."

My entire body went rigid, my heart slamming in my chest. When Aiden chuckled and ruffled Jace's hair, my stomach sank.

Even the memory felt like a kick in the nuts. I hadn't been angry, because I'd known they went to Liberty X. I'd known my experiences with them were random flings. For all I knew, the football player hookup had been months or even years ago. And yet, my jealousy had nearly strangled me until I'd abruptly bailed on them. Cue the lack of returning text messages and avoidance.

I jerked away from Aiden, breathing hard. He didn't get the hint, or maybe didn't notice I was trying to nudge one in his direction. He cupped my face and trailed wet kisses along my jaw, making soft sounds of pleasure as though he was worshipping me with every touch.

"Stop," I rasped. "I'm here to work."

"You can work later." Aiden stopped pawing me only when he realized I was continuing to hold my body away from his. He searched my face, brow furrowed and meaty hands now placed on his hips. "What's wrong?"

"We haven't seen each other in a while." I straightened my hat and took deep breaths, trying to check my pulse as if that would deflate my throbbing erection. Judging by the way his gaze slipped down and stayed, he could see it clearly outlined in the shiny material of my shorts. Like I'd said so many times before—God had clearly taken the inches off my height and added them to my cock. "Maybe we should catch up before we go straight to slanging dick."

"Why not both?" he rumbled, sounding baffled and ferocious. "I've missed you. Especially since you've been scarce in the group text. Couldn't even lure you out with talk of the Diaz brothers fighting or the new PlayStation console."

I wiped my lower lip with my knuckles, avoiding his eyes to sweep around the office, as if some wayward QFindr employee could have seen our make-out session. There was zero chance anyone was around, but chasing phantoms was preferable to looking at Aiden while guilt slunk around the pit of my stomach. It snuffed out my arousal and left me feeling cold.

Now that we were facing each other, I felt like an asshole for bailing on them with no explanation. And for avoiding the texts. I should have explained. I should get over my insecure bullshit and explain now. Or at least after I finished the job Caleb had hired me to do.

"Listen, we should probably talk about all this shit," I said after a beat of silence. "But we need to do it after I fix the servers, and when Jace is here. The three of us being one hundred percent real once and for all."

Aiden had gone from confused to wary and now appeared flat-out alarmed. "All right, well, Jace is on his way."

So much for buying time and gathering my thoughts.

"Why is he even—"

The lights in the office went out, leaving me and Aiden standing next to the window cast in nothing more than shadows and the light from the moon.

CHAPTER
THREE

"**N**ot this shit again." Aiden growled and stalked away from me, heading to the lobby. "I swear to my mother, I do not understand how this building is so fucking fragile due to a heat wave."

"Circuits probably getting overheated trying to cool it down," I said, trailing after him. "What do you usually do when this happens?"

Aiden stopped walking beside the rows of desks, the wings of his brow sloping downward. "Usually it blinks back on. Or we call the super. We haven't been in this building long enough for me to have a bunch of strategies."

We stood in the shadows, quiet and waiting for the power to "blink back on." After a full minute of looking at each other as an odd stillness filled the building, one void of all ticks and hums and chirps of the multitude of electronics that worked in the background of everyday life, it became apparent that there would be no blinking. At least not this fast.

"Goddamn it," Aiden grumbled. "All right, let me think."

He rubbed his forehead, already going overtime on stress while I edged away. It almost seemed like he expected me to freak out, or ask him what to do, and he was scrambling to try to come up with a solution before I could lose my shit. But the darkness didn't bother me none—blackouts in the summer had been a part of life when I was a kid, and that had been in a cramped apartment on Merrick Boulevard. Not some swank office building where the air still held a nice chill, and floor-to-ceiling windows spilled beams of moonlight everywhere.

"Let's just give it a few," I suggested. "And be glad I hadn't already started turning your machines back on. Last thing we need is another dirty shutdown."

"Yeah, that's true."

I had no idea if he knew what I meant, but Aiden seemed happy that I was shining a spotlight on a high point of this new development. Shooting him a grin, I walked over to the window with my flip-flops slapping louder than ever against the floor. Unable to help myself, I did another step routine in the dark.

Aiden's footsteps followed close behind, as did the sound of his warm chuckle. "I love watching you dance."

"Psh, bro, you just like watching my ass."

He came up behind me near the window, squeezing on said ass and digging his fingers into the muscles. I'd been born with a round ass inherited from my mother, and I'd started working out regularly in the hopes that it would resemble less of a bubble, to no successful end. Maybe I was fated to have the kind of ass that made a dude like Aiden moan. He loved biting it right before sliding his tongue inside to eat me out.

My dick twitched, and I squeezed my eyes shut. I was such a mess for him and Jace.

"Did you used to be in a step team?" he asked in my ear, still rubbing my butt. "Or do you just put together routines on the fly while wearing flip-flops?"

"Steph was in one," I said. "So she made me and Tonya practice with her in the park. Dudes used to say I was gay for stepping with my girls, and then Tonya would fuck them up."

"Tonya sounds like a force to be reckoned with."

"She was and she still is. Our neighborhood wasn't the worst, but it wasn't that great either. She and Ray were so quick to throw hands that people learned not to fuck with me or Steph or Angel unless they wanted to get their faces tattooed with their fists."

"Sounds like me and Jace back when we lived in Rockaway."

"I'd kill to see Jace throw down," I said with a soft laugh. "I bet he was fast and mean."

"He had to be."

His voice came out lower, more serious, and I didn't push from there. I rarely did. I knew enough about their horrifying adolescences to have put a lot of it together myself. Drug-addicted parents, murders, abandonment, and stealing to survive until Aiden had finally accepted money from his estranged father, Kenneth Stone.

It wasn't the type of childhood story you asked a friend to tell you. Reliving trauma wasn't fun for anyone. A good person tried to help their friends forget the bad stuff until they chose to unburden themselves. I wasn't about to pry just to satisfy my own curiosity.

Just thinking about the difference between their days in the Rockaways compared to my childhood in South Jamaica caused my eyeballs to shoot through the window to peer in the direction of Queens. I found myself looking at nothing but darkness except for headlights on the street down below. At first it was hard to reconcile what I was seeing with what seemed possible, but there was no denying that the entire skyline was blacked out. "What the fuck?"

"What?" Aiden asked from where he'd buried his face against my neck.

"Yo, A, the whole city's power is out."

Behind me, Aiden became one long frozen stretch of muscle against my back. I could feel the tension building inside of him.

"What? No way."

I pointed out the window, gesturing to the rest of the city and most damningly, the Empire State building without lights in the distance.

"Crazy shit," I said. "This happened in 2003. Whole fucking East Coast shut down, remember?"

Aiden's tension mushroomed and exploded in a flurry of motion as he stepped back and fumbled with his phone. In the wash of silver moonlight, his fair complexion had bleached to a bone color as he frantically unlocked his phone.

"Hey, what's wrong?"

"Jace was on the subway. If the power went out, the trains would stop running." Aiden's voice was full of anguish and worry. His big shoulders had hunched forward as he sucked in deep breaths. "He'll be so fucking scared, Chris. Trapped underground like that? You have no idea what he— *Fuck*, he's not picking up."

With every one of his words, my own heart had begun thumping in my chest. A violent *budum-budum-budum* until it seemed possible that it would quit just like that, twenty seconds after expanding in my chest because I'd felt so at peace with Aiden pressed up against me.

"When did you speak to him last?"

"Fuck, I don't know, Chris." Aiden stabbed a thick finger at Jace's number again, pacing. "Goddamn it. He will *flip*. Have a meltdown."

"Aiden, don't think about that—"

"How can I not?" he roared. "You don't understand. He isn't good with being trapped. Or the dark. He'll literally have a fucking breakdown if he has to walk through a subway tunnel with a group of strangers, man."

The image he was putting in my mind was too horrifying to digest. Jace was a little guy, shorter than me with a slight stature even though his attitude and big mouth were about four times his size. With his long waves of dark hair, rich dark eyes, and dainty features, you'd expect him to be soft, but Jace was quiet and intense from carrying a lifetime of pain on his back. He could also be mean as a viper if you came at him wrong.

I cautiously walked over to Aiden, hands up as he gripped his phone. He was one of the strongest people I knew, but this possibility had stripped him down to terrified bare bones. I touched one of his shoulders, not flinching when his first response was to rear back and tense further.

"Is his phone going straight to voice mail, or is it ringing?"

"What?" Aiden stared at me blindly, still breathing hard. "It's ringing."

"Then he's not in the subway. If he was, he'd have no signal for a call to go through or ring." I squeezed him hard, digging my fingers in. "He's prob walking over here right this second, hurrying his fine ass up with a bag of snacks and a six-pack."

Some of the stress fled Aiden's broad face, and he started nodding slowly although his eyes were so wide I could see the whites around his pupil. I flashed an encouraging smile and jerked my chin at him.

"If the whole city's power is out, you know we're gonna be camped out here for a while. Everything will be shut down, and for all we know, people will start wilding out, thinking it's free rein to act dumb as hell." Wrong choice of a distraction—the words had Aiden staring down at the darkened city once again. I grabbed his jaw and forced him to focus on me instead. "Let's figure out the plan we're gonna pitch to Jace when he shows up and realizes we're all trapped for a couple of hours with nothing to do. 'Cause you know he'll just be ready to get naked and fuck until the lights come back on, instead of coming up with a way to get home."

Aiden guttered out a short laugh. "You're right. He'll know I'm working on one in the back of my mind so he won't have to worry about it."

"Exactly. You'll be stressed the fuck out while he tries to do everything to forget that this whole darkness thing makes him a little uneasy. Which means mad sex."

Aiden nodded, but he was giving me this serious look, one full of half astonishment and half knowing. "You know us."

"Of course."

"There's no 'of course' about it, Chris. A lot of people spend time with me and Jace, but most folks do not get us the way you do." Aiden's eyelids lowered, and he dipped his head so we were eye level. "Why do you think we both want you so much?"

I tried for a snort, a smart-ass laugh. "Because I have a big dick and a nice ass?"

Aiden's breath whooshed out in a warm wash across my face. "You having a big dick and nice ass is why we want to fuck you. You getting us, effortlessly, is why we want *you*."

The words hit too close to home and scattered my senses almost as quickly as they captured my heart. "What does that mean?"

"You really want to talk about it now?" he asked. "Because you seemed to think we should wait for Jace. And now I kinda agree."

We stared at each other for a moment before I jerkily nodded. "Call him again." My voice came out in a gravelly croak. "I bet he picks up."

Aiden unlocked his phone and called Jace once again, but he did it without breaking eye contact. That stare was intense enough to burn a hole through my head, and I was convinced that's what he was trying to do. Imprint on my brain his thoughts, desires, and all the ways he wanted to ruin me with whatever he was about to say. Unless he was going to say the thing I'd been waiting to hear.

It was quiet enough for me to hear the trill of Jace's phone ringing in his ear. It rang twice before the trill was mirrored by another sound, louder and muffled at the same time, coming from the direction of the lobby.

I turned away from Aiden to jog to the front doors of QFindr, smiling broadly once I saw Jace on the other side of the glass. He pounded his fist against the door, and I scrambled with the locks so I could swing it open.

Jace instantly threw himself into my arms, burying his face in my neck and shuddering against me as he sucked in deep breaths. That was when it hit me—we were only nine floors up, but he'd made that trek in the pitch-dark. The slight tremor in his slim body was enough to spell out just how much it had triggered his phobia, so I stroked his back and shushed him as he clung like a little kid who'd just gotten lost in the supermarket. These fragile moments were always the easiest to remember, even after the rarely seen explosions of his temper, which ran wild and hot like fire on a windy day.

"Baby," Aiden breathed, joining us by the door to enclose Jace from the other side. "Why the fuck didn't you pick up the phone? I was worried sick."

Jace tensed. Uh-oh. Wrong question, Aiden, King of Worriers.

"He was too busy sprinting up eight flights of stairs apparently," I said, pulling away. "Man, you must be in way better shape than me. My ass would be about to double over and pass out by now."

Jace went from bordering on irritation at the instant third degree to deflating against Aiden with a little smile. "Ashton makes us go for runs. It's awful. Especially since Mere is a terrible influence with her flask of vodka and chain smoking along the way."

Aiden downshifted from one worry—his husband—to another—his half sister. "Shit, I need to check in with her. Who knows where she gets herself off to on Friday night. Need to call Caleb too, and make sure he got home safe."

"Caleb probably took a cab," I said. "Besides, the power has only been out for like ten minutes. I'm sure everyone is fine."

Aiden shook his head and began jabbing at his phone again, so I let it be and tugged Jace deeper into the office. He looked less shaken but gripped my hand tight enough for his fingernails to dig into my palm.

Cringing, I petted him and drew him onto one of the long couches lining the windows. Jace set down his backpack and the plastic bags he'd been carrying to curl into my side like a puppy trying to burrow into a soft place. I kissed his forehead and eased back on the couch, which was a lot plusher than I'd anticipated. It was in a sitting area that broke up the rows of desks, and way nicer than anything in my own office. If we were going to be stuck anywhere for a few hours, the swanky and hipstamatic offices of QFindr weren't bad.

"What's going on?" Jace asked, frowning out the window. "I'd just gone through the turnstile in the station when the lights went out."

"Not sure, but let's look," I said, sliding out my phone. "Aiden just about lost his shit when he realized you might be trapped underground. Full-on worried papa bear."

Jace glanced in the direction of his husband, watching his strapping form pace near the lobby while speaking into his phone.

"He won't settle down until he knows everyone is okay." Jace chewed on his lower lip, watching Aiden thoughtfully. "I hope he calls his mom and dad."

I did a double take. "His mom I get, but is he even talking to his dad lately?"

Jace shrugged. "Not really. Not since Kenneth forbade them from using trust fund money for QFindr. But . . . Kenneth still checks in with me."

This did not surprise me. From what I'd gathered, Jace had been the mediator between them for years, even though they had hidden the true nature of their relationship from Kenneth for most of that time. Or tried to. Apparently, he'd always known.

"Is his mother still in Long Island?"

"Yup. I wonder if she lost power too."

"Let's do some investigating," I said, opening my phone's browser. I checked CNN, found nothing but normal headlines, and switched to Twitter. I flicked through my feed before checking the trending hashtags, and saw *blackout* as the first one. I made it through a few swipes before the feed stopped loading and my 4G went wonky. "Fuck, baby, looks like this is all over the state and Jersey."

Jace groaned. "I thought they fixed whatever caused this to happen last time."

"That was probably something different, because that blackout affected the whole Northeast. Started in Ohio." I kept trying to load my Twitter feed to no avail, only pausing after Twitter stopped responding in general. Rolling my eyes, I shot a quick text to my squad. *You all good?*

"What are we going to do?" Jace asked. "If the power's out, that means the MTA is gonna shut down. We will literally be stuck in this building for who knows how long."

"Well, we won't be stuck in the building," I said. "You could always head out and walk to Caleb and Oli's if y'all want. It's not like they don't have the room. And I could walk to Nunzio and Michael's spot uptown. They haven't moved into their new place yet."

Jace's generous mouth pursed into a slash, dark eyes fixing on me with the utmost skepticism and annoyance. "We're not splitting up."

"It's fine, for real. It would take less than an hour—"

"Chris, stop. We're not fucking splitting up in an emergency. That's how bad shit happens."

If he were anyone else, I'd have laughed him off and made a few jokes about how a blackout wasn't exactly a zombie apocalypse, and how the city had always been fragile to circuit overloads during times of extreme heat, but . . . it was Jace. So I didn't. For all that my crew and I acted like we were so hard, it was Jace who'd grown up poor as dirt in the Edgemere Houses in the Rockaways with a drug-dealing father and a mother who'd been murdered in front of him at age seven.

It was Jace who'd been used as currency by that same father, until he'd met Aiden's mom—yet another person struggling with addiction back in the early nineties. And it'd been Jace who'd been abandoned by his father only a few months later.

That was as much as I knew about Aiden's and Jace's history. They'd been thrown together by the crack epidemic of the eighties and nineties, raised together from sixteen by a woman who'd had no idea how to even raise one son let alone a kid as wild as Jace had been, and they'd somehow fallen in love. It was the most fucked-up story I'd ever heard, but one that always made me check myself before I belittled one of Jace's seemingly irrational concerns or paranoid questions. The dude had reason to fear the dark and distrust strangers. And Aiden had reason to be so overprotective.

"All right," I said, throwing my arms along the back of the sofa and slumping down. "Then we stay here and kick it. I bet you anything they have a kitchen stocked full of goodies for these spoiled-ass employees.

All my job keeps for us is some stale peanut butter crackers that were probably engineered during the Cold War."

Jace relaxed and turned sideways, throwing one of his legs over my lap so he could cling to me with every limb. "They usually have all kinds of nonperishables and cases of water."

"So we won't starve?"

"No starving," he confirmed. "And I bought sandwiches, chips, and lube from the bodega by the house, so we're covered for dinner."

A laugh started in my belly, manifesting in a silent shake of my shoulders until I was laughing hard enough for my eyes to tear. The way he slipped in lube so casually in that low husky voice of his had me dead, because only he would add sex as part of a three-course meal.

"All right," Aiden boomed, striding back over to us. "Internet is already acting funny, but I managed to get everybody on the horn."

"Who is everybody?" Jace asked. "Your mom? Caleb and Mere?"

"And Clive. They're all at home and sitting tight for the night." Aiden plopped down next to me, his bulky body causing the couch to screech backward just a bit. "And my father sent out a stilted-ass fucking group text asking if any of us need the services of his security team. He's acting like the boroughs could turn into a war zone with the power out."

"Because it could happen," Jace muttered. "People are gonna be left stranded everywhere, and security systems will be down in stores. Also, circuits get jammed with the cell phones and most people don't have access to landlines, let alone a pay phone these days."

"You're just paranoid," Aiden said, waving a hand. "So's my father."

I could sense Jace giving him the evil eye, so I patted them both and changed the subject. "Regardless of what happens outside, our asses are in a luxury office that I hope holds onto the semi-cool air through the night with heroes from the bodega and snacks in the office. We have nothing to worry about except who is sleeping on which couch."

"Aiden has a huge pullout couch in his office for when he stays late," Jace said. "We can snuggle until it gets hot as fuck and I kick both you sweaty assholes off it."

Aiden snorted. "You might wanna just banish me in advance. You know I sweat like a fucking beast."

Jace smirked at his husband and squeezed me tighter against him. "Just me and my boo, then. You can sleep on the floor after we take turns on your dick."

Aiden's eyelids lowered to half mast, his lips curving up in a dirty smile as he likely pictured something filthy enough to turn my penis into a traitor. I was supposed to be having serious discussions with them, not fucking in their office building.

I repeated it in my head, but the words faltered as soon as Aiden reached down to adjust the swollen length in his shorts.

Christ, I was screwed.

CHAPTER
FOUR

The IT guy's desk was the only space not among the rest of the open-concept rows of work stations. He had his own little glass-encased office filled with spare equipment stored in tidy closets and cubbies. It was so clean that it freaked me the fuck out, because every IT dude I'd ever known had preferred controlled chaos to the sterile environment this human being operated in.

While I was not one to snoop on another dude's hardware, I needed space. After scarfing the turkey, ham, and swiss cheese hero sandwich Jace had brought for me (which was made exquisitely because my boy knew exactly how to order), I excused myself to see what I would be working with once the power came back on. Truth be told, I had no idea when the power would be back on. I'd bullied my phone into loading Twitter just enough to see headlines implying it could be anywhere between eight hours to forty-eight hours. Which . . . no. I refused to be stuck here for that long.

The thing people didn't get about New Yorkers was that the city relied on mass transit to operate. Once you took away the MTA, we were fucked. We regularly commuted between boroughs to go to work or sometimes even to go to a certain store. Getting caught out there on the wrong side of the river could leave you temporarily homeless depending on the timing of an emergency. I had little doubt that the streets down below us would be full of people camping out for the night. Or the weekend.

And I was here with Jace and Aiden.

My two suitors who were not shy at all about telling me exactly how and when they wanted me, and my dick wasn't hesitant to respond. My big squishy heart wasn't either. Every time Jace cozied up to me or Aiden went into daddy mode, I got all warm and fuzzy inside. It was time to lay it all out on the table and just talk about it. Tell them my feelings, find out where they stood about me, and figure out where to go from there once and for all. But now that we were *trapped* together, was it the best time? Being an emo mess with nowhere to go hide seemed awful.

Releasing a disgusted sigh, I sat in the IT dude's—Travis—desk and looked around. It was dark as hell in the room with the exception of two candles from the stash Jace had dug up in Caleb's office. Why the man had a hoard of expensive-ass candles in his office was well beyond my comprehension, but they smelled like apple pie so I was all in for this form of lighting.

Travis's chair was far more comfortable than the ratty one I had at work, and he had a way bigger desk. Oddly, there wasn't much on it. No personal effects, no signs of side projects, no gadgets or stress toys to occupy his hands. Just a big blank-ass desk and an iPad. On a whim, I turned it on and was thrilled to see it had 4G and wasn't password protected.

Again, I wasn't usually one to use another person's electronics, but my phone was already more than halfway dead and it wasn't like I could charge it anywhere. Aiden had reassured me that there had to be a solar charger in someone's desk in the office, but I wasn't going to count on that.

I used Travis's iPad to navigate to Reuters, and was thrilled when it loaded faster than my phone. The brief highlight of positivity lasted for only a moment before I loaded an article on the topic and realized the situation was pretty fucking dire. In fact, it seemed to mirror the situation that had happened back in 2003. Several states were without power due to grids that had failed in a domino effect, and it was entirely possible we would be here for a while.

Given the fact that the air had already lost its chill, and I was already sweating beneath my shirt, it was probably a good time to go forage for food in case we were trapped for the weekend. Before going to share my less-than-stellar news with Aiden and Jace, I started to type in BBC.com and was greeted with a dropdown of Travis's recent browser history.

My eyebrows flew up.

The dude spent a fuck-ton of time on Breitbart, an ultraconservative website. There were links to articles over twenty deep. Cringing, I opened his full search history and found a Twitter account. His handle was @deplorablehipster89. Scrolling through his feed was downright scary.

Not only was this dude a down-low racist, but he had homophobic shit all over his Twitter, despite working for a queer company. What the fuck?

"Hey."

I jumped, fumbling with the iPad, and slammed it down hard enough to almost crack the screen. Thank God I'd never been tempted into a life of crime. I had zero chill.

"Uh, you okay?" Aiden asked, laughing incredulously. "What are you doing?"

Busted snooping on his employee. His employee who regularly threatened liberals on social media, used his IT skills to dox them, and appeared to be a radical white supremacist. Instead of saying this, I squinted at Aiden.

He looked at me sideways. "Are you using precious battery life watching porn or something?"

"Uh. No?"

Fuck, why was I so bad at lying? More importantly, *why* was I lying? I squinted at him harder, and a sudden dawning fear bloomed inside of me. What if he knew and was okay with it? What if they *all* knew? What if they aided and abetted and employed trash bigots as long as they were allegedly competent at their jobs? It seemed impossible. They were all queer and liberal as fuck. This wasn't just about a difference in politics. This dude had legit hate speech on his social media. Threats.

There was no way Aiden knew about it.

Aiden's amusement faded to bemusement. He walked closer. "Chris, seriously, you're freaking me out. You didn't just find out this is some sort of terrorist attack, did you? Or a fuckin' zombie apocalypse?"

"No . . ."

Bemusement upgraded to concern. "Baby, are you still wanting to lay down the law and create boundaries? Because I figure that's where you were going before, but I didn't think it was a good move to do that as soon as Jace walked in the door. You know how he is."

"What? No." I brandished the iPad, furrowing my brow beneath my baseball cap. "I just don't want you to think I'm going through your boy's shit."

A little flicker crossed Aiden's expression, the barest hint of a lip curl, that was just enough for me to know he at least had an idea that Travis wasn't all gravy with the queer agenda.

"He's not my boy. And that's a company iPad, not his personal property, so feel free to use it for whatever you need while we're trapped here."

My brows shot up. Travis had been posting hate speech on social media on a company device? I supposed that was the weird gray area of being the IT dude. You checked up on everyone else, but no one really checked up on you. Either way, now didn't seem like the right time to drop the bomb on Aiden about their employee. There were already too many variables that were way out of his control, and it was bound to make him implode with rage.

"How much does this cat get paid to sit in this sweet-ass office and keep y'all's network safe?" I asked, finally removing my hat and tossing it on the desk. "Is it over six figures?"

"Yes," Aiden said slowly, still giving me that suspicious side-eye. "Why?"

"Because I probably get paid about forty thousand bones less to do the same job for a lot more people."

He cringed. "Baby, that's ridiculous. You need to look for something else."

"Yeah, maybe."

"There's no maybe about it," he said, getting all fired up and loud the way he did whenever he was passionate about a subject. "That's below the average for your field. There ain't no kind of reason why—"

"'Ain't no kind of reason,'" I repeated, mimicking his accent with a fond smile. "Bro, it's not like I'm hurting for money." Well, that wasn't *entirely* true. I could use more money, but I wasn't destitute. "I have no kids, no car payment, and my apartment is $1,300 a month. I haven't tried to move on because I'm comfortable."

"Right, and yet I hear a 'but' in your tone." Aiden pressed his palms flat against the desk and looked down at me, brow furrowed. "You may be comfortable, but at the back of your mind, you know you could do better. You know you deserve better. And even if you're okay with not pursuing a career change right now, you know eventually you will."

I raised my hands, brows going up, because honestly—he had me. I had zero surprise that he could read me inside and out. One of the things I'd come to realize about Aiden in our months of texting and our infrequent hookups was that he paid attention. He didn't just talk to me to get my attention or to wait for his turn to speak—he cared, and he responded, and he always gave me advice. After growing up as poor as he and Jace had, the dude was always looking for routes on how his people could be on the come up. And he was always doing that for me.

"I'm not gonna lie and say I haven't been thinking about moving on," I admitted, nudging the iPad away. "I want to move out of Jamaica, and I want a new car, and I need more money for down payments and new furniture. It's just that . . ."

Aiden raised an eyebrow, waiting, and kept waiting even when Jace slipped into the room to stand beside him. He'd already stripped down to his underwear and bare feet, although he was still wearing his threadbare T-shirt. After winding his thin arms around Aiden's muscular torso, he peered at me with a devilish grin.

"What are we talking about?"

"Your old man wants me to get my head out of my ass and get a job making bigger bucks," I said, slouching back in Travis's chair. I didn't miss the way Jace's eyes dropped to my crotch, where he could undoubtedly see the outline of my meat beneath my basketball shorts. "But, y'know, money isn't everything. I like where I work now."

"What if you found somewhere else you liked?" Jace asked, running his fingers along Aiden's front. "With people you like?"

"Heh. Where is this magical place?"

"Here," he said brightly.

I waited for him to explain himself, or for Aiden to tell him it wasn't possible, but they both gave me the expectant look of people who had discussed this before.

"Yo . . ."

Aiden held up his hands, already catching my hesitance with that one syllable. "It was Caleb who mentioned it, sweetheart. Swear to God."

The part of me that easily rankled, that had been raised by parents who didn't like handouts or favors, unbristled. Caleb suggesting it was . . . different. And interesting. He was the most by-the-book person I'd ever met.

"Why would he mention that?"

"Because you're awesome?" Jace detached from Aiden and sauntered over to me. His way of walking almost always caught my attention. He had the type of swagger I was used to seeing on guys around my block, but I didn't typically want to fuck the hell out of them. "He was impressed with the detailed feedback you gave on the app during the beta. He also brought it up when they started looking for staff."

"Then why didn't anyone ever tell me?" I asked as Jace stood between my spread thighs. With him half-naked in front of me, I forgot all about the fact that I'd just told myself to keep the sex at bay, and put my hands on his hips. "This is the first I'm hearing."

"Aiden thinks you'd say no."

"Why?"

"Because you know how much we want you, and he thought you'd think it was his way of trying to lure you into our wicked poly trap on a regular basis," Jace said bluntly. He took a step forward, making sure his legs nudged against my bulge. "Which, I totally am, but he's more ethical."

As my hands found their ways to his hips and slid down his round, firm ass, my thoughts on ethics, open relationships, and hurt feelings fell away one letter at a time. Who could think that deeply when Jace was staring at me like he was daring me to jump him. He arched an eyebrow, and I jerked him against me on reflex as my tongue darted out to swipe over my lower lip.

"If he's the ethical one, then what are you?" I asked, sliding the tips of my fingers beneath the band of his underwear. Behind him, I noticed Aiden watching us with rapt fascination. His green eyes had dilated as I manhandled his husband in front of him. "The horny one?"

"The one who wants to be spread open on this desk so you and Aiden can take turns on me," he said sweetly.

If I had only one way to describe Jace, it would be as a living, breathing temptation. When he looked at me with those flashing eyes and that fuckable mouth, there were no parts of me possessing the self-control to not get up from the seat and move in closer. The remaining letters that had tried to form rational thoughts about standing my ground in the face of fae-looking dudes and their linebacker husbands faded as I stood, pushed him onto the desk with my hands knotted in his long hair, and angled his mouth for a kiss.

He parted his lips with a sigh, pressing his palms down on the glass and arching up to me. I loved the way he offered himself, how he closed his eyes and raised his brows, how he lost himself to the hungry swipes of my tongue, because every time we touched, I went from cautious to desperate for more.

More touching, so I stood between his thighs and ground my hardening dick against his crotch. More of his sexy voice, so I went from tasting the inside of his mouth to tilting his head back so I could suck on his throat to the tune of throaty moans. And more of our missing puzzle piece, so I shot a glance up at Aiden, who was already squeezing himself through his shorts.

It'd been exactly two and a half months since I'd last had both their hands on me, and right now I was more than willing to trade a moment of that heaven for a future broken heart. Sometimes you just needed to feel alive even if it killed you later.

CHAPTER
FIVE

"**I** thought we were gonna keep it PG," Aiden rumbled, watching me from beneath heavy eyelids.

I stepped back just enough to grab the underside of Jace's knees and jerk them forward, sending him flailing down to his back. He hit the desk with a thump and a groan. He loved that rough stuff.

"Screw PG," I said, breathing hard. "Get the lube."

"Fuck yeah."

Aiden spun out of the room to comply. Jace tilted his head backward, long locks of silky hair falling all over the desk, to look upside down at his husband's retreating back.

"It's in the bag on the couch," he hollered, accent running riot now that he was turned on and undone from the shiny package he'd fashioned for himself in his new life. "Hurry up!"

There was no finesse to my game as I ripped off my shirt, tossed it God knew where, then stepped out of my basketball shorts until I was in nothing but a pair of Batman briefs. My dick was trying to punch straight through the bat signal by the time I got Jace naked, and I hoped there was a way Travis the underground bigot would someday learn that a man in DC Comics underwear had fucked the hell out of his boss's husband on his desk.

"You're so fucking hot, Chris," Jace said, glancing up at me from beneath his long lashes. "I love when you stare at me like that."

I pulled him up again, wanting to feel his smooth, hairless body sliding against my bared skin. I ran my hand over his back, feeling the bumps of his spine and automatically finding myself wondering if he was eating enough. *Focus, Chris. You want to fuck him, not take care of him.*

"Stare at you like what?"

"Like you'll die if you don't get your hands on me." Jace grinned when I rolled my hips again, grinding my dick against him. His hair was everywhere, spilling like an onyx waterfall over smooth pale skin. "And like you know your hands belong on me."

"They do."

He'd just closed his eyes, but they slid open again at the words, which was when I realized I'd said them out loud. Damn. For months, I'd bit my tongue and held back on expressing my feelings, and all it had taken was a heat wave and a blackout to melt my resolve to remain silent.

We were in each other's mouths again within an instant, and when I felt the heat of Aiden at my back, it was all complete. He nuzzled the nape of my neck, rocking his own erection against my cotton-covered ass, and dropped the bottle of lube on the table. A jumbo bottle of some cheap shit that looked like hand sanitizer. Leave it to Jace to shop like he was still on an off-brand budget.

"Get these down," Aiden murmured in my ear as he tugged at the elastic of my briefs. "Need to feel those cakes."

I leaned back on him without separating from Jace, and the quickly dampening air hit my dick as soon as it was freed. My erection was heavy against my stomach, the tip a little slick. I bucked it against Jace just once before Aiden was pressed against me again, this time with a palm full of the cheap lube that he smeared over my cock and started jacking.

I moaned into Jace's mouth, breaking the kiss, but he kept sucking on my tongue.

"Tested recently?" Aiden asked in my ear, nipping at it as I fucked into the tight cup of his hand. "You know we do on the regular."

"Ah . . ." There were spots dancing before my eyes as he worked me over, leaving my brain unable to summon a response as my lips trembled. "I . . . Fuck . . . Yeah. Yeah. Ever since . . . you two, I, yeah."

Jace pulled away, his rich laugh filling the room as he lay down on his back with his knees bent and feet propped on the edge of the table. "Translation: I've been testing regularly since I started fucking you two." Jace slid his feet along the edge until his knees were parallel.

Dead-ass looking like a sex acrobat. "And I bet he doesn't raw dog anyone else . . ."

I shook my head, blinking away the dancing spots once Aiden released my throbbing dick. My balls had pulled up so tight it felt like I could come any minute, the pressure mounting in my stomach like a bomb on the cusp of exploding.

"What he said," I breathed.

"That's what I thought." Aiden bucked his hips against me harder, possessively. That one blunt motion screamed *mine*. "You fuck any other guys lately, baby?"

"No. Never. Just you two."

"Fucking right," he said fiercely in my ear.

Later, I'd finally make him explain why he acted jealous when they were the ones who screwed other people on a regular basis. Later. After we all got our fill.

I dragged my tip against Jace's ass, amazed at his ability to remain so still and perfect as he waited to be breached. He was flawless. The most breathtaking person I'd ever laid eyes on. The discolored burn marks on one side of his torso, and the twisted scars on his lower thigh, did nothing to take away from his beauty. All evidence of what he'd come from, but what had not stopped him from getting to where he'd wound up.

"Damn, I—" *love you.*

So close. So fucking close. And I think Jace knew it too.

His eyes grew large, those wide lips lifting into a slight smile. Before he could talk, I slammed my dick into him. Jace's mouth went slack, and he flung his hands out to grab the edges of the desk as I proceeded to fuck that aborted declaration out of his mind. I gripped the undersides of his knees and held them apart, rocking in and out of his clenching hole as he arched into my thrusts.

"Yeah, Chris," Aiden whispered in my ear, his voice low and thick. "Dig him out real good."

A shiver shot straight through me like a lightning bolt, pinging along my nerves and settling in my gut in a way that nearly tore an orgasm out of me. I didn't come in him yet, but the explosion of sensation drove me wild. My fingers tightened on Jace, and I slammed my hips forward in a powerful thrust that sent his back sliding over the desk.

"God, yes." He thudded his head back, mouth gaping in a wet moan. "I love your dick."

"Why do you love it?" Behind me, Aiden undid his shorts. They dipped down until I felt the full length of his thick cock pressed against the seam of my ass. "Tell Chris how that fucking dick feels."

"So big and thick," Jace groaned, rolling his hips up to meet each of my deep thrusts. His voice caught every time I slid into him. "Fills me so good."

"Yeah, he has you split open with all that meat." Aiden's breath was coming faster now. It hitched as he watched my length saw in and out of Jace, moving more urgently the tighter Jace clenched around me. "I can't wait until he fills you up with his come."

"Please." The word was honey on Jace's full damp lips, dripping down rich and sweet. "Please give me your come, Chris. I want Aiden to lick it out of my ass."

A low filthy chuckle vibrated in my ear.

"I love my dirty boy," Aiden whispered in my ear. "I know you do too."

Instead of waiting for an answer, Aiden sunk his teeth into the side of my throat, and my entire body trembled. He knew where to touch me to light me up like a Christmas tree, every sweet spot singing to the heavens that this man could easily turn me into a puddle of sweat, tears, and semen.

It was moments like this when I wanted to talk. To drop filth all over this beautiful boy with the long slim legs and tight body, and describe how good it felt to be buried in his heat. How the combination of his smooth flesh and Aiden's hot mouth had me flying. But I couldn't say those things, because being with them elevated me to a place where words were replaced by sensation. Anything I said wouldn't make sense.

My heart pounded out of my chest every time Jace released a wrecked moan. Exhilaration filled me when Aiden wrapped his arms around me and humped against my ass as I fucked his husband.

"Give him that milk," Aiden murmured in my ear. "I know you have a big load for him, Christopher."

"Fuck, Aiden," I gasped, pounding Jace harder. The edge of the desk bit into my thighs as I drove into him at a pace that was becoming relentless. The sound of our wet bodies slapping together was deafening in the room. "Gonna come so hard."

Aiden reached down to grab my balls just as Jace arched up and clamped his muscles around my length hard enough for me to briefly lose my mind. Fire raced through me and my eyes rolled back. Fuck coming, I was free-falling. I said Jace's and Aiden's names in turn as I emptied every drop from my balls into Jace's tight body.

"Mmm." Jace gazed up at me, panting and smirking. "You busted hard."

I pulled out, sucking in breaths and recovering from the explosion, but still horny as hell. Maybe even hornier because he was so goddamn beautiful when flushed with a post-sex glow.

"Eat that ass," I breathed to Aiden. "While I suck his dick."

Jace flopped onto his back , self-indulgent and smiling as he spread his thighs again. "My men are so good to me."

Aiden dragged him off the desk in a streak of sweat and pushed him down in a tangle of hair and damp limbs onto the thick carpet covering the floor. Aiden knelt, big shoulders hunched forward, and used his fingers to spread Jace's hole open wider. When he began tonguing at it, and my semen, I moaned at the same time as Jace. Good God, these two combined were almost too much for my brain to process. They turned me into a walking, talking hard-on who did nothing but exist to touch and be touched. I'd just come, but I wanted more.

Jace leaned back on his forearms, head tilted. "Lick me good," he said through a gasp. "Taste Chris inside me."

Aiden made a rumbling sound and did something that drew a loud moan out of Jace. I sunk to the floor beside Jace and wrapped my lips around the tip of his erection. He whimpered, and I took him deeper into my mouth, breathing through my nose the more I swallowed.

Sucking dick was more of a new experience to me than ass play. I'd always been into pegging, and had low-key suggested it with several women I'd had sex with in the past, but having a man's meat sliding between my lips was a whole different ball game. It was queer as all hell, and I loved it. God, I loved it. The taste of pre-come, the musky smell of him, the challenge of not gagging, and the knowledge that a couple of inches lower Aiden was drilling his tongue into Jace's freshly used hole—it was unreal.

Aiden sat up and tapped his fingers against Jace's ass. "Think I'm ready to take my turn."

I looked at him from where I was doing my best to make Jace spurt down my throat, and saw that Aiden was stroking himself and watching me with heavy-lidded eyes. He was so damn big. Every part of him from his thick neck to his meaty shoulders to the tree-trunk thighs. A Viking wanting to ravage me and Jace in turn, and that smoldering stare was a definite promise that he'd have my ass as well before the blackout ended and we went back to real life. I clenched in anticipation.

Aiden shoved Jace's thighs apart and rammed into his preslicked ass, powering into a battering rhythm that caused Jace's body to jolt under my mouth. I pressed a hand to his stomach, holding him still, and kept sucking as Aiden went full caveman.

"I love watching you blow that fucking dick," he panted. "Pump it and suck the tip, Chris. Make our dirty little boy nut all down your throat. I know love that taste as much as I do."

Groaning around Jace's hardness, I pulled my mouth up and wrapped my fingers around his shaft. It was slick from my saliva, and my hand was a mess as I followed Aiden's directions, jerking Jace's dick while I suckled the crown.

"Oh . . . Oh shit." Jace's body jackknifed up, but he lay still after I pushed him back down to the floor. "Please. I'm gonna come."

Aiden chuckled, husky and low, and slowed his pace to a steady in-and-out of deep, powerful thrusts that continued to jolt Jace's slim body each time. The combination of us touching him seemed to overwhelm Jace. He went from taunting and smirking to overwrought with trembles as his mouth gaped in a soundless shout. His semen erupted in my mouth, spurting against the back of my throat as I swallowed. He was still coming when I pulled away, so I caught the last bit on my tongue and rose up on my knees to share the leftovers with Aiden.

One of his big hands clutched the back of my head as he sucked Jace's release off my tongue. He was still kissing me when he hit his stride, his breath ripping out of him and hips once again slapping against Jace.

"I want it in my mouth," Jace said.

Aiden broke away from me. "You got it, baby. You fucking got it."

He ripped out of Jace and scooted up, hand flying over his erection and aiming for Jace's waiting mouth. Jace's dancing brown eyes lifted to me just as the first splashes of semen hit his tongue to the tune of Aiden's shuddering moans. Once he was done, Aiden sat back on his haunches, sucking in deep breaths with his eyes squeezed shut.

"Fuck, you two are gonna kill me," Aiden breathed. "Swear to God, my heart is racing."

I laughed and threw myself on the floor beside Jace, who was grinning like a cat who'd just slaughtered eighty billion canaries. He rolled onto his side, and I leaned in for a soft kiss to his lips. Then one to his jaw and another to the tip of his nose.

"You?" I said between each kiss. "Y'all are the ones corrupting me. I'm innocent."

Aiden snorted and swatted my ass. "Yeah, right. You love being in the middle. It's your thing."

He had my number on that one. It *was* my thing. I peeked at him as I nuzzled Jace, grinning and popping my dimples, and was rewarded by a look so fond that my heart slammed against my rib cage.

Jace cozied up under my chin, going in for full cuddle mode as Aiden stood and slid his underwear back on. He was likely going to get right back to the business of cataloging supplies and coming up with a plan while me and Jace stayed on the plush carpet like a couple of kittens. Then he'd coax us to the pullout bed in his office and scavenge for a snack, taking care of us in the way he did without a second thought, even if he wasn't one for postcoital cuddles.

It was all so cozy and made me feel so full and warm that my fear rose to the surface again. My fear of wanting this forever and maybe never getting it.

"How do you think your down-low homophobic racist fuckboy of an IT manager would feel to learn we just screwed in his office?"

Aiden froze as he stooped to pick up his shorts, and Jace stiffened against me.

"Uh . . ." I looked between them, eyebrows rising. "Okay, so this is what happened—"

"Chris, what are you talking about?" Aiden strode closer to me, his face flushing red. "Do you know Travis? Did that motherfucker ever say something to you? Because—"

"Whoa, slow down, killer," I said, laughing. His accent instantly thickened when he was pissed, and his hands had curled into fists. So ready to beat someone down for saying the wrong thing to me. "You're gonna pop a blood vessel. I've never met that dude in my life."

"Okay . . ." Aiden searched my face before swinging his gaze to the iPad. "You see something on there?"

"Yeah," I admitted. "I was trying to look on some news websites and found ultraconservative shit in his browser history, including a Twitter account where he posts all kinds of racist, phobic, and misogynistic garbage."

Aiden's face was starting to resemble his hair color, and I worried that he'd break the iPad when he clenched it with white-knuckled hands. He jabbed one thick finger at it several times, scrolling through what were likely miles and miles of offensive tweets and retweets as Jace watched in confusion.

"Yo, what the fuck is going on?" he asked, pushing sweaty hair behind his ears. "This is the worst post-sex conversation we've ever had, and there have been some doozies."

I tickled his side, grinning when he threw himself away from me as if I'd electrocuted him. Aiden was less amused. After another moment of scrolling, he put the iPad on the desk with a clatter. Even in his underwear with his body still damp from sweat, he was imposing. Tall, broad, muscular yet padded, and so furious that his nostrils had flared. It was probably good for the IT dude that he wasn't in the room.

"It's really that bad?" Jace asked, grimacing.

"It's fucking awful. The shit he spews out onto the internet, things he says to people—it's disgusting. He hides all of that when he's at work and blends in like a . . . like a fucking chameleon. It makes me sick."

"Sorry, dude." I grabbed my shorts and slid back into them, hoping the office had a place I could wash the bodily fluids off me. It was officially hotter than ten dicks in the office, and me reeking of sex wasn't welcome in that environment. "But at least you know now."

"True, because he's getting the *fuck* out of here." Aiden yanked up his shorts and zipped them. "Someone like that won't be representing our company. The fact that he's using a company device to harass people online is the icing on the cake. He is done, and I'd love to see him try to get unemployment. Clive will have fun with that one."

I nodded slowly and watched as he stormed out of the office, stalking directly to the break room. Likely to catalog what supplies we'd have for the rest of the night or, worst-case scenario, the weekend. He might have been enraged, but he was still in full-on survivalist caretaker mode.

"Welp," I said. "That went well."

Jace snorted and slid back into his own underwear. "Let's go wash up. There's a full bathroom in the back."

I nodded and trailed behind him as he left the office. When he grabbed my hand, I twined our fingers together and squeezed.

CHAPTER
SIX

"**W**hy is there an in-office shower?" I asked as we entered the pitch-black bathroom. "Isn't that a little . . . uh . . . extra?"

"Yup, but it was already installed, and all the little yuppies and hipsters use it for when they work out during their lunch break. I don't understand their devotion to physical activity that doesn't end in ejaculation."

I tripped over God knew what and clutched Jace's hand tighter. For someone who was jumpy about the dark, he could see in the shadowed room like a cat. He opened the narrow glass stall and turned on the shower with minimal fumbling, before sliding into the space.

"Get in, but fair warning—the water is *cold*."

"I can take it."

I kicked off my shorts and got inside, wary of slipping and breaking my neck. Not only did I not want to die in the middle of a citywide blackout, but I didn't want my mother to find out that I'd weirdly died naked in a shower in a fancy office building in Manhattan. She'd have so much trouble explaining to my nosy-ass extended family. She'd already made the sign of the cross like twenty times after I'd started hinting that I might be a little queer my damn self.

Then she'd complained that I hadn't snagged Raymond first.

"Scoo," I drawled, leaning against the wall as Jace squeezed a bottle and started soaping me up with his hands. The water was cold, but it felt good on my sticky, overheated body. "Aiden seemed pretty upset."

"Yeah."

"Was he friends with that guy or something? I mean, he took it really personally, and I'm surprised he's so shocked. Then again,

I pretty much expect most well-to-do corporate types to end up as douchebags."

"Me too," Jace admitted. "But I think the real issue is that Aiden never wanted to hire Travis because he got a bad vibe from him, and Caleb was sort of oblivious and did it anyway. Now he's probably super butt-hurt and wanting to rant at his brother. Hashtag sibling rivalry."

"Oh." If I wasn't as nosy as my nosy-ass family, I could have left it at that. But I was. And the idea of Aiden blaming Caleb for this mess bothered me, especially since it would lead to Caleb being indignant and wounded, and then Aiden feeling guilty that he'd hurt his brother. "We should probably calm his big red ass down before he goes off on Caleb. He'll just feel bad if he starts an argument over something that isn't anyone's fault but the asshole IT boy's."

"Mmm." Jace draped his arms around my neck and pressed me against the tiles. The water beat down on us, surprisingly strong. "I love how well you know him. You're so good."

"Yeah, I'm basically a god."

"You are to me. *My* god." Jace kissed me, slow and gentle with just a hint of tongue. "I'm so happy when you're with us, Chris. For the past two months, I sat around and wondered why you ran away, but now it's perfect again."

My heartbeat sped up and my breath quickened. I clamped my hands on his shoulders, staring at him in the darkness, and tried to find something to say. Something to think. A way to respond to this onslaught of brutal honesty that only Jace was capable of. His rawness and inability to filter anything that came to his head.

"What . . . do you mean when you say that?" Cringing at my own vagueness, I girded my loins and tried again. "Do you mean it's perfect because we have amazing sex, or it's perfect because you like being with me as a person?"

Jace snorted. "What do you think?"

"Jace . . ." He kissed me again, deeper this time, and my dick twitched. I gripped him tighter. "Jace, I'm serious."

"Mmm?" His voice was muffled from the way he was mouthing down my throat and sucking on the base. His hands were everywhere, slippery and soapy and gliding over the body I so often tried to sculpt to match Angel's and Raymond's before giving up and drinking a beer. "You can't tell I like you as a person? C'mon."

Okay, still too vague. I sucked in a deep breath. "Look, I'm trying to figure out what we all are to each other. I'm the type of person who . . . who gets in deep when I'm into someone. And I'm into you and Aiden." I pressed on when Jace stopped kissing me to peer up at me in the darkness. "It scares the fuck out of me, because I'm used to getting my feelings hurt and feeling like shit when I'm into someone."

"Chris." Jace laughed softly. "You can't tell we're into you?"

"Yeah, sexually. I know you wanna fuck me. We never really got around to talking about anything else, so I don't know if all these feelings I have are one-sided." There was another long silence, and I rushed to fill it. "Sometimes I could swear you look at me like you adore me the way I adore you. And sometimes Aiden gets all rammy and territorial like he can't stand the idea of me fucking another dude, but . . . then y'all casually drop some comment about all the other people you're hooking up with, and I get confused."

In the shadows, I could see Jace nodding slowly. He sighed and pressed his back against the tiled wall. "Babe, we do adore you. Your sense of humor, your intelligence, how well you fit with us. All of it. And I thought you knew, but I guess I'm so used to Aiden knowing what I'm thinking that I forget you're not there yet."

Yet. He said it as though they were planning a future for us all together. The relief at his words, that the cues I'd thought I'd picked up on weren't just in my mind, was amazing. But still . . .

"Can I ask you another question?"

"Of course. Anything."

"How come you two aren't monogamous? Like, why poly? Why open?"

Jace went back to squeezing soap into his hand. This time, he washed himself instead of me. "Why do you like threesomes so much?"

"I dunno. It's just how it's always been. The best sex I've had has been with two other people at the same time."

"Insatiable," Jace said, his voice low but teasing. "Was it just a sex thing with Ray and Steph?"

Had it just been? An extra-dirty way to get off? Something pornographic to fuel my fantasies? Nah. I shook my head.

"No. I mean, I enjoyed being wanted by them both. And . . . all right, don't tell anyone, but I always suspected Raymond wasn't straight." Admitting it made me feel guilty, because I'd never even told Ray. There was something weird about knowing someone's secret when they didn't want you to. "It all started with him and Steph messing around while I was in the room playing video games or whatever, because they gave zero fucks. Then . . . she invited me to play, and I acted cool and jacked it voyeur-style while he stared at my dick."

Jace remained quiet, and I pictured his face. Eyes wide and rapt with intrigue, his big imagination putting it all together like a GIF from his filthy Tumblr account, or one of the ménage erotic romance novels he loved to read. I kissed his forehead and continued.

"When I finally got the courage to join in, he'd encourage me and Steph to do specific things while he watched, and sometimes I knew he wanted to touch me. I was shocked as hell because he was like . . . everything to everyone. The dude everyone wanted. And I was the dude everyone usually ignored." A low chuckle escaped me. "Sometimes I made sure we got a little contact even though it wasn't much, but like I said—it mostly just turned me on that he and Steph wanted me at all. It turned me on that Steph wanted us both. And . . ." I raked a hand through my wet hair and grabbed the soap for myself. "And I loved being so close to my best friends."

"And with me and Aiden?"

I watched him work his fingers through his hair in the shadows, mindlessly washing himself and then standing under the spray as he shifted around carefully on the tile.

"I don't know how to describe how it feels to be with you and Aiden. It's just incredible. But you're changing the subject, pendejo. Don't try to escape. Why are y'all into this? What does it do for you?"

Jace released a long-suffering sigh. "I hate this question because no one ever likes the answer. They judge us for honesty and being self-aware."

"Tell me anyway. You *always* avoid it when I ask."

"Because I hate trying to explain," he said grumpily. "I've been in love with Aiden since I was a teenager. Since my father abandoned me, and his mother went to rehab and pretty much left us alone to fend for ourselves while she found a better life for herself elsewhere. We started fucking at seventeen, and we vowed to protect each other. To look out for each other. We were each other's everything, and that kind of love is . . . unbreakable. Nothing that would ever fade." Jace raised his arms and let the water hit against his skin, likely rinsing the soap off. "That kind of love isn't defined by boundaries, so we have no boundaries with each other. Our closeness was never built on this idea of monogamy or one of us belonging to the other. We've explored our sexualities together since we were kids and keep doing so now. We're open about everything, including things we want to try with each other and others, and we know no one else would ever steal our hearts so there's no threat in being poly and open."

"So that's all it's about? Exploring?"

"Yeah, that's why we go to Liberty. It's like an adventure. Some people make the most out of their lives by having adventures with travel, and people like us make the most by having adventures with our bodies and understanding our own desires inside and out."

"So, is that—" I wished I could see his face, but I had nothing to go on but his low intense voice. "So, am I an adventure?"

Jace went still, and I instantly hated myself. I hated my insecurity. The same insecurity that bubbled up whenever I started seeing someone new, and I introduced them to my friends for the first time. Wondering when their eyes would skate along Ray or Angel, wondering why they'd wound up with the short, funny one instead of a sexy one. And now, I had two beautiful men interested in me, and my stupid brain kept telling me it had to be for a reason. It couldn't just be me.

It was never just me. It was because I was nice or helpful. Available. Fun.

And now he knew that I felt that way.

"If you mean adventure as in you're someone we see only for fun, to experience something new together as a couple . . . then no. Abso-fucking-lutely not." Jace touched my arm, his wet fingers sliding along my skin. "But if you mean . . . if we're looking at a new stage in our relationship after twenty years of it being us plus casual encounters?

Then yes. We've never even considered having a permanent third except for you."

Permanent.

I had to put a hand against the tiled wall to steady myself. It wasn't what I'd expected. Not by a long shot. I'd fantasized about this conversation, of them saying something similar—that being with me alone was just as exciting as being with others, but doubt hollowed out my briefly full heart.

"Do you really want me to be permanent?"

"Yes." Jace paused briefly, then said, "If you won't get freaked out and ghost on us anymore."

"I ghosted on you because I had no idea you felt that way, and I was too chickenshit to ask. And . . ." Go for it, Mendez. Spill it all. "And because you're open."

"And?" A defensive edge crept into Jace's voice. "You always knew we were open."

"Right, that's why I kept ghosting on you. I thought I was just one of several people who drifted in and out of your lives." Jace grew silent next to me and dropped his hand. I hurriedly added, "Can you blame me for thinking that, though?"

"Yes," he said flatly. "I think it's pretty stupid, actually."

My head jerked back. "How? Seems like common sense to me. You guys have this amazing lifestyle. You have adventures like you just said. I'm just the dude you picked up at the QFindr shoot. Someone to dial up for a booty call or hook up with at a party."

"Chris, what the fuck are you talking about?" Jace's voice was getting sharper and louder. "I just told you we both want you. You're the one who—" I started to interrupt him and he got louder. "I'm serious, Chris. You're the one who ghosts on us after a night or a weekend, and we have to beg you to come see us again. The only reason we're here now is because there was a fucking blackout. If anything," he went on, his low, deep voice in a full-on rant, "*we* are a temporary adventure for *you.*"

The water shut off with a loud squeak of the faucet, and Jace got out with two stomps of his wet feet. He was moving fast, but as soon as I tried to follow, I nearly slipped and had to cling to the shower door to narrowly avoid death.

"Ay Dios . . . Carajo," I grumbled, staggering after him. "Jace, calm down. Why are you getting so pissed off at me?"

He tossed a towel at me, then stepped into the moonlit-streaked hallway to dry off. His lovely face was creased in a scowl, but those glittering eyes didn't scare me. I just wanted to understand why he was angry. And I wanted to make it better.

"Because you're an idiot."

"How?" I asked patiently. "Can you blame me for not knowing where we stand?"

"Yes, I can blame you," he hollered. "You didn't just say you didn't know where we stood. You thought we were just using you for sex and stringing you along. Right?" When I hesitated, his lip lifted in an actual snarl. "And you know what, maybe I can get over that since clearly it's some epic communication breakdown, but now apparently us being open is a deal breaker."

I flinched. "Jace, try to understand where I'm coming from . . . please."

"I am, and I see you being closed-minded. You deciding this whole thing won't work out because we're open and poly."

"What whole thing?" I demanded incredulously. "Babe, I only just found out my feelings are reciprocated. We haven't even started to talk about anything else."

"We're talking about it now." Jace glared at me fiercely. "We want you to be more than a casual encounter. We want you with us regularly. All the time."

"And I'm saying that's everything I've been wanting to hear, but . . ." My voice was close to cracking. Holy fuck, was this frustrating. We were so close. Right on the cusp. And it was already going wrong. "I just can't with the open thing, J. I can't."

Jace balled his hands into fists, naked and unashamed and absolutely fucking glorious in all his fury. "Chris, when we're all together . . . it's like the way me and Aiden are with each other. You fit. Perfectly. And you love that you fit. Because you love us. I know it's not what you planned on in your life, and I know it's not typical, but it's not like we planted the poly seed in your head, booboo. You were poly already."

"Yeah, okay, I give you that, but there's one problem," I said, sharpening my tone the more he pushed. "It's not just us three. It's not about being poly. It's about everyone else in your lives. A week after you see me, you're with other people."

"Because that's how we've always been," he said, voice rising louder. "I would die for Aiden, and he would die for me, and us fooling around with other people doesn't change that. So how the hell would it change us falling in love with and being happy with you?"

"It won't change anything for you, but the idea makes me crazy," I growled. "Gangbangs at Liberty X. Make outs with Clive—your fucking lawyer. Free love and everyone sharing each other, which is great for you, but I don't roll that way."

The lack of response from Jace was damning. The only sound in the room was the drip of water from the faucet, and the very distant honking of horns downstairs and outside. The worst part was that I couldn't clearly see his expression. And when I reached out to touch him, he backed away.

"I get it."

"Jace—"

"It's fine."

He moved out of the beam of light and hurried away, his footsteps slapping against the tile floor before being muffled by the carpet in the hall. I started forward and slipped again, flailing wildly to keep from falling.

"Puñeta," I snarled, stumbling. "Word to my mother, I'm gonna die in a fucking office building tonight."

I snagged my basketball shorts and managed to get out of the bathroom in the dark, squinting so I could find my wayward lover. There were doors upon doors along the corridor leading to the main office space where the moon clearly illuminated everything. There was no sign of Jace, but I spotted Aiden hunched over something by one of the long couches. He was still wearing his underwear and nothing else.

"Hey," I said, walking closer. "Where'd Jace go?"

Aiden glanced up at me from where he'd been fiddling with the antenna to a radio. White noise emitted from the speakers, so he must have found batteries somewhere. "I thought he was with you."

"Yeah, he was but—" I rubbed the back of my wet hair, sighing "—I think I pissed him off."

Aiden looked so astonished that I snorted out a laugh.

"Usually that's my job," he said. "You're the one who kisses it better after I slink off to avoid an argument."

"Yeah, I know, but that was before we fucking—" I waved my hand vaguely, not wanting to rehash the conversation but seeing no way to avoid it. "Look, he told me you both wanted me to be in your relationship."

"Good." Aiden stood up, looming over me in all his linebacker glory. "We do. We talked about it back in the winter."

I stared at him incredulously. "Then why didn't you tell me?"

"At first we weren't sure if you were interested, and we didn't want to pressure you. But we discussed wanting you to be with us in a . . ." He crossed his arms over his chest, watching me closely. "Triad? Throuple? Whatever word you wanna use. We talked about it."

My heart started beating faster again, turning to a hummingbird in my chest as another one started flapping its wings in my stomach. "Bro. You've *never* told me about any such convo."

"Because you didn't seem ready to talk about it." Aiden frowned. "What, you're surprised? C'mon. I thought it was obvious how thirsty we are for you. We've never been like this with anyone else before."

"How should I know how you are with other people?" I demanded. "And why me, then?"

The same impatience that had been evident in Jace's voice crossed Aiden's face. "You know, we talked about this insecure shit before. I know where it comes from, but I thought you were over it. I thought you knew what you had to offer. That you're a fuckin' prize. Anyone would be lucky to have you, baby. I'd get on my knees and beg for you to join us if I thought it'd make a difference."

"I—" Blood rushed to my face, warming me. His tough-guy accent did nothing to change how he was melting my insides. Turning me all gushy and soft, making me want to hug him close. Kiss his big stupid face. Tell him I loved him too. Loved them both. "It's not just me being insecure. I just— Look, you have this whole life, you know? This *lifestyle*. And I don't know how I fit. I don't know what I bring to the table."

Aiden looked at me sideways. "Really? Because that sounds like more insecure bullshit. You bring yourself to the table. Your sense of humor, your affection, your intelligence. The way you know exactly what we need without having to ask. How you prop Jace up when he's down, and know exactly when I'm stressed and overwhelmed and shutting down. When you're with us—"

"Aiden, stop."

"No, you stop," he thundered, slamming his fist against his own chest. "Do you know what it took me and Jace to admit to each other that we both had feelings for someone else? Almost twenty years together, Christopher. And we've fucked a lot of other people, but always with the understanding that our hearts only belonged to each other. We were scared to admit we were both starting to fall for you, but we did. And we talked about it, and we talked about how much we wished you felt the same." Aiden's voice dropped lower. "Because even though Jace and I have *always* been a near-perfect fit, we love each other enough to be able to admit that there's always been parts that are missing on both our ends because we're too much alike in the worst ways." Aiden gestured with a rough hand. "And you've been what's missing, baby. You weld all our pieces together. When you're with us, or just texting us, your *presence* in our lives makes everything . . . better."

He was breathless by the time he finished, and his eyes had gone bloodshot. He squeezed those big fists again. But I didn't know what to say. I felt the exact same way, except for one key thing . . .

"Look," I said, my voice thicker. Which meant tears. God, this fucker had me wanting to cry. Why did I have to be the sensitive one in every situation? "You're right. Okay? I am insecure. But my insecurity *isn't* making me doubt every word you said, because I believe it. I can feel it when we're together, but I thought maybe it was my imagination. Now I know it's not. But my insecurity will not let me be in a relationship, a triad or a throuple or *whatever*, where you all go out on a Saturday night and fuck other people. I'm sorry, but no. I can't."

Aiden moved closer to me, but he didn't touch me. "How do you know you can't? You could try."

"Aiden . . ."

"Or what if . . ." He hesitated, obviously unsure, and looked around the office. "I mean maybe we could . . ."

I sensed him starting to make a promise he probably couldn't keep. Something he hadn't yet discussed with Jace. Some shit that would make me feel hope only to have it potentially ripped away later.

"Look, we need to put this on hold. I know what you're about to say, and you should probably talk to your husband before you say it." Every time we referenced Jace, I found myself looking for him, but if I knew anything, it was that he was good at hiding. "What I'm saying is, don't say you're gonna up and change your relationship just for me unless it's a real promise."

"There's no *just* about it," Aiden said sharply. "We can talk about it."

"Aiden, please, stop," I begged. "For now. Please. You talking Jace into something he doesn't want to do is a one-way ticket towards y'all resenting me down the road. I'd rather keep things the way they are now."

"How's that? Fucking and then you going home? Us seeing each other every blue moon?"

"If it has to be that way." Even saying it hurt. It burned.

"If that's what you want," he said quietly.

"What I want doesn't matter because what I want might not be possible, and I always knew that, which is why I tried to keep my distance. But this is easier than . . . than people making decisions in the heat of a moment and regretting it later." I wiped a hand across my face, hating the way my eyes had gone damp. "Look, I'm gonna try to catch some sleep. Maybe the power will be on in the morning."

Aiden nodded, looking down at the radio again. "I pulled out the sofa in my office. And don't argue, please? Sleep there. Please."

I knew it would kill him if I didn't, so I nodded and headed to his office. I wanted to tell myself he'd been unaffected by the conversation, that I hadn't just hurt him the way I'd hurt Jace, but I could feel his eyes on my back as I walked away.

CHAPTER
SEVEN

I woke up soaked with sweat.

When my eyes opened, it was to the sight of floor-to-ceiling windows spanning Aiden's office, and a sky that was pink and purple with sunrise. It was beautiful, but the bad news was that I'd slept through the entire night and the power still wasn't back on.

I shifted slightly, groaning, and realized the sweaty mass pressed against me was Jace. At some point during the night, my upset little renegade had crept onto the sofa bed and taken up residence under my chin. On Jace's other side, Aiden was on his back with one arm thrown over his face and one leg hanging off the side. He was snoring softly, and looked like an adorable red-haired teddy bear.

Fuck, I really did love them both.

Instead of fighting my way out of the damp bed, I stroked wet strands of hair away from Jace's face. He was so . . . pretty. His wide mouth, long lashes, the small pointy nose, and his pale skin and dark hair. If we were in a video game, he'd totally be an elf. An elf with an emotional thermometer that changed at drastic extremes in no time.

I kissed to his forehead and slid my hand down his bare back, stroking along his spine.

"Mmm," he murmured, eyelashes fluttering. "Hot."

"Yeah, it is," I whispered, my voice craggy from sleep. "Power's still out."

He made a soft sound and opened his eyes a fragment. "Shit."

"Yeah, it sucks."

"Sucks that you're stuck with us? The insatiable poly couple with the open marriage?"

The sleepy clouds drifted away, and I frowned. He'd opened his eyes fully to glare at me with that fierce expression on his face—mouth pursed into a slash and dark brow furrowed. Like he was ready for a fight.

"Don't be that way," I said, keeping my voice in a whisper. "You know I care about you both. It's just . . . me."

"Don't be a cliché."

"I'm not being a fucking cliché, J. I just want to beat my chest and fight people every time I hear about anyone else putting their hands on you or Aiden. If we were together, the entire time would be me seething with jealousy. Why would I damn any of us to all that drama? I'd bring fire and brimstone all the time."

Jace's lips parted, closed, then parted again. "That's the reason you mentioned Liberty X?"

"What else reason would there be?" I demanded. "What, you thought I was just being a judgmental prick all of a sudden?" When he shrugged, those big eyes flitting away, I wanted to shake him. Instead, I turned his chin so he was forced to look at me again. "Dude, I have no judgment about you being open. I don't think you're *insatiable*. I'm just a jealous person, okay? No one's ever seen the extent because I've never been serious with anyone for a long period of time, but it gets bad. So whenever I hear about you and Aiden at Liberty X, it's like a punch in the gut. It *hurts*. And I get really angry."

Even now, I gritted my teeth at the memory of the casual mentions of them being with other people. If I'd been unable to handle it when we were casually sleeping together at random points, there was no way I'd be able to deal with it happening on a regular basis. I didn't have the capacity for an open relationship.

"I may be a big kid," I said, "but I'm grown enough to think about the long term. That shit would cut me up if it was going down while we were all in a relationship."

"It's just touching," Jace whispered. "Body parts going into other body parts. It's just fun. Nobody makes me feel the way you and Aiden do."

"That doesn't change the fact that the idea of another motherfucker touching you, being inside of you—" My nostrils flared. "I'm not an angry person, but it makes me want to hurt somebody, Jace. After Stephanie's party, you made some offhand comment about having fucked some football player, and . . . Yeah. That's why I avoided you guys. I can't stand that level of jealousy on a regular basis. I'm not used to wanting to brand two people with my name and throat punch anyone who looks twice."

Jace shifted against me, pressing his hips against mine, and I felt his dick. Maybe it was hard from sleep or maybe my words were turning him on, but regardless, my body reacted in turn. My morning chubby thickened, and I ran my tongue over my lower lip.

"Makes me want to fuck you over and over until you realize you only need me," I whispered. "And Aiden. Our lips, our hands, our dicks in you. Our come in your mouth. Or in your ass."

Jace moaned, shuddering against me. "Chris . . ."

I rolled on top of him, rubbing our bodies together as he arched up against me. There was too much fabric between my shorts and his underwear, but I kissed along his face and jaw, dragging my tongue along the hollow of his throat, before sliding down to his chest. I drew his nipple into my mouth, and his groan shattered the absolute quiet of the office. His hands balled in the sheets, feet sliding up to bend his legs at the knees with me settled between them.

No one's body had ever called to me the way Jace's did. No one's moans had ever sent goose bumps spreading over my skin. Those moans got hoarser when I licked the scar tissue on his torso, soothing wounds that had been inflicted on him years ago due to neglect.

Aiden had told me the story once, after Jace had fallen asleep between us and we'd shared a few too many beers. How the burns had come from a pot of boiling water when a seven-year-old Jace had been home alone and trying to cook. How the scars on his thigh had come from barbed wire after he'd been chased over a tall gate in a lot by one of his father's many terrifying friends.

I looked up at him as I trailed my tongue along his hairless stomach. He'd gone quiet because Aiden had stirred awake. As I traced Jace's erection through his underwear, they were locked in a passionate kiss. Picture-perfect.

With Aiden present, the fire stirring inside me flared to five alarms. Especially when he glanced down at me with promise in his narrowed eyes. I held the stare as I unwrapped Jace like a present, and kept looking even after I was blowing Jace the way I'd done him the night before. It didn't take long for the salty tang of Jace's semen to spill over my tongue once I slid two of my fingers into his ass.

Aiden pulled away as Jace gasped for air, his stomach sucked tight and toes clawed in the sheets as he came down from his ejaculation.

"You're getting too good at that," Jace said breathlessly. "I came way too fast."

I drew up to my knees and winked. "Told you I'm basically a god. Fastest learner in all the land."

"Damn right," Aiden said, sitting up and giving me a hooded look. "You learned how to milk my dick with that ass pretty fast."

My throat went dry. I dropped my hand to squeeze myself through my shorts, ass already clenching in anticipation. Either they'd forgotten the unfortunate series of conversations the night before, or they weren't going to let it stop them from enjoying our time together. Especially if there was a possibility that it would be our last.

Jace grinned up at me and leaned over to grab something from the floor. Unsurprisingly, it was lube. He might have come to bed mad, but he'd still come prepared.

"I expect a good showing, boys." He watched as Aiden knee-walked his way over the flimsy mattress, getting behind me as I stroked myself through my shorts. "I want to hear Chris get needy."

Aiden wrapped one big hand around my throat. He pinned me to his chest, rocking against my ass, and then took over stroking my length through the shiny material of my basketball shorts.

"How bad do you want me?" he asked, lips pressed to my ear.

"So bad I bought a dildo to keep me satisfied when I think of you," I admitted, closing my eyes as he pumped me slowly. "Not quite the same though."

"Can't replace the real thing. With a dildo or another dick."

My eyes flicked open just in time to see Jace casting his husband a long look. One full of knowing. Yeah, they were thinking this was the end. Obviously they weren't willing to change things for me, after all.

It would have crushed me, but Aiden chose that moment to shove me forward. I was on my hands and knees with my torso aligned with Jace's, my face pressed to his. He kissed me as Aiden yanked down my shorts, his jagged fingernails scraping along my skin.

"This beautiful fucking ass," Aiden groaned. "I dream about it."

I lifted each of my legs, helping him pull the shorts off me, as Jace nursed at my tongue. My throbbing erection dragged against his stomach. I was half-delirious with the sensation of soft lips against my own, the hot wet tongue stroking inside my mouth, Jace's knees on either side of my torso as he rocked up against my dick, and Aiden's hands—those big calloused hands—spreading my ass open so he could lube me up with his thick fingers.

"Love this tight fuck hole," Aiden said, almost to himself. "I'd play with it all morning if I wasn't so fucking horny."

I tore my mouth away from Jace to say something clever but managed a sound that was somewhere between a gurgle and a slutty moan. Every time Aiden pressed his fingers into me, my body locked up to trap his fingers inside. I was that hungry for it. Hungry for something I only ever got when I was crushed between their bodies, because Aiden was right on one thing—no dildo or cock could replace him.

Grinning devilishly, Jace shifted beneath me, sliding down the bed until his mouth was level with my dick, and he pulled my ass cheeks apart for Aiden to take aim. Jace took my dick in his mouth just as the thick crown of Aiden's piece breached me. I leaned forward, hands braced against the back of the couch.

"Ahh . . ."

"Shit," Aiden hissed behind me, his breath tearing out of him in loud gasps. "Loosen up for me, baby. I need every inch inside of you."

My eyes squeezed shut as I tried to focus on the sloppy blowjob Jace was managing and not the burn of the stretch. Regardless of how often I played with myself while at home, I was never quite prepared for Aiden's girth.

With my fingers clutching the back cushions in a death grip, I gently rocked in and out of Jace's mouth, which caused my ass to slide back little by little on Aiden's cock. He gripped my shoulders the whole time, not fucking into me the way I knew he wanted to, giving me the time to adjust.

"Good boy," he said, rubbing my shoulders. "Take all that dick."

I nodded, not knowing why, too lost in sensory overload as I held myself in the exact position to have every part of them touching every part of me. By the time the pressure eased, my stomach was knotted with impatience.

"Come on, bro," I pleaded impatiently. "Just fuck it."

"Yeah?" Aiden's voice deepened when he was turned on, the Neanderthal coming out as he snapped his hips harder and filled me completely. "Like that?"

"Just like that." I pressed my forehead to the cushions, mouth gaping as Jace suckled sweetly on my tip. "Just like fucking that."

Aiden made an appreciative sound, shifted on the bed, and proceeded to impale me on his cock so hard that I saw stars. He paused, sucked in a breath, and then went to work. For the next several minutes, I could only cling to the sofa and release ragged cries as Aiden took me. He was more relentless than rough, rocking his hips in an unceasing pace that caused his dick to drag along my prostate repeatedly.

Tingles spread everywhere in my body until nothing felt quite real. I forgot who I was and where I was, because nothing mattered but the mouth on my dick and the thick length sliding in and out of my ass. I didn't want it to stop, but when Aiden's teeth sank into the side of my neck as he came, the reality of him filling me up set me off as well. Jace swallowed my come down before turning his face away, patting my ass as Aiden panted roughly above me.

"Jace, move so I don't crush you," I said, voice wavering. "I'm about to collapse."

He obeyed instantly, scooting out from under me and rolling onto his side so he could watch me collapsed forward. Aiden lay down on top of me, his big body crushing me and covering me with sweat.

"You heavy bastard," I gasped. "We're gonna destroy this bed."

Aiden bucked his hips against my ass and kissed the back of my neck before rolling onto the other side of me. Once again, I was in the middle. Jace nuzzled my face as Aiden ran a hand down my back. Silence settled over the room, and I closed my eyes. Basked in the caresses and kisses, the humid air that smelled of sex and sweat, and the exhaustion that seeped into my body every time I had an orgasm.

I was nowhere near cutting the cord or sticking to my guns about not getting in deeper, but I couldn't move. It was hot, I was comfortable and sated, and right then all I wanted was to fall asleep between them.

As my eyelids drooped, Aiden whispered in my ear, "I want this forever, kid. So fuckin' bad."

Jace's hand tightened on my hip, but he didn't say anything. Aiden buried his nose against my neck, and I let myself drift back to sleep.

I woke up feeling a mess. Overheated, sticky, and squishy. I was also alone on the bed.

Grimacing at the giant window that seemed to be magnifying the sunlight on me, I rolled off the sofa bed and got to my feet. I had no idea where Jace and Aiden had gone, but the combination of sex leftovers, damp bedding, and a groggy head made me thankful for the in-office shower I'd mocked the day before.

If someone had told me a week ago that I'd be walking bare-assed naked through the QFindr offices to clean the jizz from my body, I'd have asked what they were smoking. But apparently that was my new reality. And judging from the stuffy air, the power still wasn't back on.

I stood under the cold spray of the shower for longer than was necessary, but it felt good against my skin. It was also doing a bang-up job of clearing the spell that had settled over me a few hours ago. All it had taken was bomb sex for my brain to totally betray me, conjuring up dreams of me waking up in Aiden and Jace's apartment to find them making breakfast and waiting for me as if I were a resident and not just an infrequent guest.

I tilted my head against the tiled wall, eyes squeezed shut.

Get it together, Mendez. You know you can't do what they want you to do. Don't let the sex and your feelings trick you into thinking you can.

It wasn't anything different from what I'd told myself in the past. What I'd been telling myself since the winter—over three months ago. My closeness to them had popped into existence nearly from the start, but one weekend in particular had made the direction of my feelings undeniable. Instead of walking into a Friday night of nonstop sex, I'd gone home with Aiden to find Jace in the middle of an anxiety attack. I'd backed off, thinking it wasn't my place to interfere, but Aiden's tension from his work day hadn't helped. He'd tried to soothe Jace's nerves, wound up making it worse, and removed himself from the situation.

Jace hadn't exactly seemed surprised, but I'd sat next to him in the bathtub where he'd huddled, and quietly sung along with the Backstreet Boys song playing on my Sirius XM app until he'd chimed in. After a while, his body had relaxed and he'd snuggled against me until his eyes had drifted shut. I couldn't imagine how much an anxiety attack took out of a person for him to fall into an exhausted sleep the moment it eased, but I'd carried him to bed and tucked him in.

Later, I'd found Aiden in his office with his head in his hands and a bottle of bourbon nearby. For all his strength and desire to be a fixer, he'd looked absolutely fucking helpless in that moment. And the gratitude in his expression, that I'd picked up the slack when it had triggered his own fears in a way that took him to the drink, had made me feel . . . something. Like maybe I had a purpose there besides just fucking. Maybe I could be as good for them as they were for me. Because when I was with them, I forgot that I felt far behind all my friends. I forgot that anything seemed to be missing from my life at all. Because when I was with them, nothing was.

I turned off the shower, thankful for the brief moments when I'd have a chill on my skin and damp hair, before the oppressive heat of the building got me sweaty again. Wrapping a towel around my waist, and marveling that QFindr had better towels for their employees than I had for my own damn self in my house, I padded out into the main area.

Jace was sitting on top of a conference table with a platter of cheese and fruit next to him, and Aiden was sitting in a chair nearby with the radio on.

"What're they saying?" I asked, stopping at the head of the table. "Power coming back anytime soon?"

Jace glanced up at me, his gaze circuiting my body slowly, before he returned his attention to the platter. He carefully selected a cube of cheese and a cracker before stacking a slice of apple on top.

"Staten Island is lit up already," Aiden said. "Everywhere else is still fucked."

"Shit. Any idea when we'll have it back?"

Aiden shook his head, which was when I noticed he was still fixing his attention on the damn radio and not meeting my eyes. "Nah. Could be tonight or tomorrow. The mayor wants everyone to sit tight and stay off the street as much as possible, which is ridiculous. You got tourists sleeping on the street outside their hotels because they can't get into rooms, people stranded because the subways are down, flights grounded—it's a fucking mess."

"Are people tripping?" I asked. "I'm about to head outside to see what I can scavenge from the store."

"Haven't heard any reports of anyone looting," Aiden said, finally glancing up from the radio. "What are you hoping to find outside? We have plenty here to ride it out."

Jace had started watching me again as he slowly ate his platter, likely planning to polish it off before it went bad, but he didn't speak. Which probably meant he had an opinion he wasn't going to cop to. If I bet by the way he'd drawn his knees up at the idea of me heading outside, his opinion was probably for me not to go.

"I'll be fine," I said to him. "I'm just curious about what people are saying."

"You don't have to explain yourself to me, Christopher," Jace said. "You can do what you want."

My eyebrows flew up, and Jace immediately looked away. A flush rose up his neck as he violently chewed an apple, and behind him, Aiden rose to his feet.

"Well, fuck, all right, then," I said, baffled. "Did I piss you off or something?"

"No."

"So, then what's with the attitude?"

"I don't have an attitude," Jace said icily. "I was just stating a fact."

Pushing him when he was this pissed off would never get me anywhere, so I glanced at Aiden with a *what the fuck* look. He shrugged, worry once again in his brow as something a little heavier slumped his shoulders. I wasn't sure what was weighing him down, given he had our blackout all planned and figured out, but seeing them in varying states of distress was alarming.

"What?" I asked, louder this time. "What is wrong with both of you?"

"We talked this morning before you woke up," Aiden finally said. "About you. About what you and I discussed yesterday."

"And that got you all pissed at me?" I demanded incredulously. "Sorry but—"

Jace swung his legs over the side of the table and hopped to his feet. He was striding out of the room before I could finish my sentence. I stared helplessly at his retreating back, and cringed when he shot a glare over his shoulder.

"Wow, what the fuck? All I said was that—"

"You said you can't be with us." Aiden walked around the table and came to stand beside me. He was shirtless but once again wearing his business casual shorts. "We told you we wanted you to be permanently in our relationship, and you rejected us. Us fucking around this morning didn't change that."

My heart leaped into my throat, momentarily choking me as I looked at him sideways and raised my hands. "Whoa, whoa, I didn't—"

"You did."

"Nah, don't twist what I said. I didn't ever say that I didn't want to be with you. I said I wanted to be with you, but not if the relationship is open." I shook my head, lips pursed as I channeled the power of Raymond's mean mug. "You better not have told Jace I said that shit, A. I swear."

"I told him exactly what we talked about, which is exactly what you told him." Aiden ran a hand through his hair, flicking his eyes up to likely track where his husband had gone. "But I also told him that we need to put an end to all of this if it's not gonna go anywhere. We can't be casual with you, baby. Can't keep doing this . . . random fuck around shit the way we do with everyone else. It hurts too much. So I said that to him, and he got upset. With me as well."

It was what I'd been telling myself, even as recent as ten minutes ago, but the finality in Aiden's voice—that tommy-gun-fast accent— sucker punched me.

I'd never get to touch them again. Kiss them. Go to bed with them.

It left me a little breathless.

"And I also told him that we can't keep pushing the subject to try to convince you if your mind is set," Aiden went on. "Especially because . . . I want to offer you a job. Here. I can work with a lover as well as Oli and Caleb can, but not . . . in these circumstances."

"Whoa, wait, time-out," I said again, making a time-out symbol with my hand. "You're going too fast for me, A. You want me to take fuckboy McAltRight's spot?"

Aiden bobbed his head. "Exactly. I tossed around the idea with Caleb a while back, and he was very interested. He just made it clear that he isn't okay with casual sex between me and an employee because of potential drama."

He kept stressing that word. *Casual.* As if anything that had happened between the three of us could be described that way. Like it hadn't shattered my preconceived notions about my sexuality and what I wanted in the future and altered everything in my life. He was trying to be so good right now, but that word was getting me hot.

I clenched my jaw and took another breath. "I need to think."

"Are you interested in the job?"

"Fuck yeah, I'm interested," I said. "But right now I'm more worried about the fact that Jace won't look at me than about a fatter pay check. I need to fix this."

"Why?" Aiden asked incredulously. "He'll get used to the reality. Just leave it alone."

"I'm not gonna leave it alone if that means him thinking—"

"Chris, just stop," Aiden said, voice rising. "I'm not mad at you, and he isn't either. Not really. We understand where you're coming from. It hurts, but I get it, and I can learn to see you every day and ignore how much it tears me apart that this can't work. But it's going to take Jace time to get there. He's mad at himself, I think."

"Why?"

Aiden looked away, eyes downcast. "Because . . . he's always been pretty fiercely protective of our lifestyle. We get a lot of shit for it. He's been shamed for it since we were teenagers, and now I think he's confused and frustrated, so he took it out on you."

"Because I dared suggest he change so we can all be together?" I demanded. "I thought that's what people do when they love each other."

Aiden flinched like I'd punched him. "He does love you, but he's not . . ." He stopped, clearly struggling with his words. "I just think he needs some time."

I wanted to say something mean. Something really shitty about how they needed, or maybe just Jace needed, all of this fucking time to decide whether I was enough for them all by myself, but I didn't. It wasn't just about them fucking other people. Them being open had nothing to do with them wanting to have all kinds of kinky sex. It was about them having lived by their own rules since they were teenagers in a way that worked for them when nothing else had. They'd been poly and open since the conception of Jace and Aiden as a couple. Maybe they didn't even know who they'd be if that changed. And maybe that scared them. Especially Jace, who'd spent years trying to carve out a safe space that wouldn't let him down.

I understood all that, and I still wanted to yell at him. To be angry and bitter that they were apparently completely unwilling to compromise so we could all be together. But maybe it was me who was unwilling to compromise for them? I didn't know anymore. I was asking them to change a relationship that had been steadfast and healthy for years, and maybe that was too much too soon. Maybe I should have tried. Or maybe they could have tried.

Apparently, no one was fucking trying, though.

"Fuck," I said, voice coming out lower. "I'm—I'm just gonna go outside."

"Bab—Chris." Aiden took a step forward, then stopped himself before touching me, frustration visible in every line of his powerful body. "Just give him time. I know we probably seem awful and selfish to you, but this is killing us just as much as it's killing you." He looked helpless and heartbroken. "It hurts for us too, kiddo. It fucking hurts."

"I didn't want to hurt you," I insisted. "I didn't think . . . I don't know what I thought. I was just thinking about saving my own self and not about how hard any of this could be for you guys."

"And you should think about saving yourself. It's just one of you and two of us, and self-preservation is legit. But even though we're strong and have fought through a lot, not much prepares someone for heartbreak."

And just like that, he broke me. My throat closed up and my eyes started to burn. I think he saw it happening, saw tears forming in my eyes, but he didn't stop me when I turned away. He let me go.

CHAPTER
EIGHT

I'd thought the building was muggy, but stepping outside was like jumping into a furnace. It was barely nine in the morning, and it had to already be nearly ninety and humid as hell.

Sweat slicked my back by the time I made it to the corner, and even having showered, I felt grimy in my basketball shorts and T-shirt. I'd sweat through them multiple times already, not to mention all the grinding and humping I'd done while wearing them. I told myself that I'd left the office to search for any potential open stores and not because I needed space.

I kept telling myself that lie even after it became obvious that very few stores were open. There was an ice cream shop on the corner handing out cones for free, and a couple of other restaurants trying to cook and sell food at an extremely discounted rate before the produce went bad, but everything else was locked down. Despite that, the streets were anything but a ghost town.

Folks were sleeping slumped against buildings, curled up on benches, and stretched out on the sidewalks and using newspapers to protect them from the sizzling concrete. It was like déjà vu back to 2003, but that blackout had lasted for days. I prayed this one didn't.

I powered my phone back on after walking two blocks with no sign of a cheap clothing store, and called Raymond. It went to voice mail, but he immediately called me back.

"Where you at?"

Raymond's voice put me at ease. He sounded relaxed, like he'd just fucked the hell out of David and was lazing in bed while smoking a bowl. No crisis. No tension. Just my boy drawling in my ear and demanding to know why I wasn't there kicking it with him. Where he thought I belonged. *Not* with Aiden and Jace.

"Stuck in Manhattan," I said, sidestepping a couple to try to cop some shade under a store awning. "Is David home with you?"

"Yep. Raising hell about being hot, and lying around half-naked with Stephanie."

"Sounds like a party. Where's Angel?"

"Helping out his mom. T-Bone is coming over soon," Raymond said, speaking of Tonya. "Why the hell are you in Manhattan?"

This would be where the conversation got interesting. I usually avoided talking about the Fairbairns with my best friend, but . . . right now I wanted to steer it in that direction.

"I'm at QFindr."

"Why the hell are you there?"

"I decided to take Caleb up on that offer to work on their servers, but the power went out before I could even get started."

Raymond exhaled slowly, and I knew he was hitting the bowl. Envy seeped into my bones. It would be so much easier to cope if I had a little buzz going.

"Why didn't you go to his apartment?" Raymond asked after a beat. "I'm confused."

"He bounced before the power went out, so I'm stuck here with Jace and Aiden, who also live in Queens. So . . . yeah." He didn't speak at first, and I had to give him props for censoring himself. "Look, can we have real talk for a minute? I need advice."

"If it's about them fucking around with you, you know what I'm gonna say."

I groaned in exasperation. "All right, but can you get your head out of your ass for a minute so we can really talk, though?" At the sound of his sigh, I sucked my teeth. "Come on, Ray. They've never given you reason to distrust them except be rich."

"I don't like that Meredith girl either," he pointed out. "It's not just them."

"Yeah, I know that, but it's the same story. You don't trust rich—"

"I don't trust a bunch of people who are suddenly interested in diversifying their sex lives with our squad," Raymond said flatly. "I know I'm making a snap judgment, but all I have to go on is that some rich sexed-up motherfuckers got stars in their eyes after the QFindr photoshoot and all of a sudden decided to start fiending for the crew from South Jamaica. If there's more to it than that, it's not like you've bothered to share the details to change my mind."

He had me there. As soon as he'd gone into overprotective mode, I'd shut down and given zero details. But that had been when I'd thought it was better to avoid the entire situation. When I'd thought I was *capable* of avoiding the entire situation.

"It's not just a sex thing," I said, lowering my voice and glancing around. It wasn't the best area for the conversation. Even early in the morning, it was loud and there were a ton of people starting to stir and wander around looking for answers. I walked back to the building, prompted to give up on my quest by the heat and the influx of humanity. "Look—there's more to it, all right. You know more than anyone else that I've never had, like, a David of my own. Or even how Angel has been in love with Stephanie forever and knows she's, like, the one he wants. I've never had that with anyone."

A clicking sound emanated from Raymond's end of the line, and I pictured him flicking his lighter or tapping nervously. Wondering where I was going with this.

"Do you just want me to talk to David?" I demanded. "Am I inconveniencing your life?"

"No," he snapped. "I'm just worried, man. I don't want you to get hurt."

My irritation immediately crumbled beneath the soles of my flip-flops. If Aiden went papa bear, Raymond turned into a growly pack alpha when he sensed danger.

"They're not using me, if that's what you really think. There's stuff I worry about, but that's not one of them. One hundred percent guaranteed—those two men actually fucking care about me. They want me to be in their relationship."

"How do you know?"

"How did you know David was in love with you before he admitted it?" I asked. "You could just tell, right? Well I can tell with them, and that was before they told me. Which they did. Last night. I know you don't really get the poly thing—"

"Chris, it's not even about that." Raymond cleared his throat and there was a creak, like bed springs or a chair. "Look, I'm not some narrow-minded asshole who freaks out about people with different types of relationships. I'm a fucking bi asshole who's worried that my best friend who has never dated anyone for longer than a couple of months—"

"Come on, man," I said. "I've been with people longer than that."

"No, you have not." Raymond snorted. "It's always some bullshit where you start seeing someone, and then you think they don't like you because you overthink everything and tell yourself it's not gonna work or they're into someone else, so you let them go on their way to save everyone the trouble of drama. Right?"

I didn't answer as I strode to the building. Relief flooded me as the stuffy air of the office building surrounded me. I made eye contact with the doorman, who looked absolutely miserable. He nodded at me, and I paused with my hand still clutching the phone.

"Hey, man, you been up all night?" I asked, taking in the doorman's sweaty shirt and dark-circled eyes. He was probably in his early fifties, built solid like my own dad, but I could tell he was in need of sleep.

"What the fuck are you—" Raymond's voice asked in my ear.

"Not you, pendejo," I snapped. "Pérate." He grumbled something on the other end, but I kept waiting for the doorman to reply.

"All night," he confirmed, wiping a hand over his face. "I'm starving, but I don't want to leave just in case someone needs something. Or an emergency happens, I don't know." He waved his hand, looking harassed but determined. My heart went out to the dude. Very few people cared enough about anyone else to be the last man standing during a goddamn citywide blackout, but maybe his job was at stake if he didn't.

Either way, I had his back.

"I'll bring you water and some snacks," I said. "Also, me and the guys can take turns hanging out down here so you can shower and get some sleep. QFindr has a full shower."

The doorman—Kevin according to his name tag—looked so relieved that he sagged against his post. "Christ, I would love you if you did that, son. That would be incredible."

"No sweat, my guy. I'll be back in a few."

I took off for the stairs, huffing and puffing after the third flight.

"Did you really just interrupt our conversation to be a do-gooder?" Raymond asked incredulously. "Like, I was peaceful here smoking my shit, finally tuning out David's bitching, and you interrupted me."

"Because I need your advice, asshole." I swung out my hand to grab the railing, trying to move fast in the darkness but still managing to stumble every few steps, and explained everything that had happened in the past day. When I finished the story, I added, "You and David always give me the same BS, that you don't know anything about relationships and you just sort of fell together like a miracle of God or fate or some bullshit, but you *still* fell together. I've never fallen for anyone but Aiden and Jace." Seven flights up, and I had to stop, sucking in deep breaths as my lungs burned. God, I was out of shape. "Ray," I said, between gasps. "Can you just stop focusing on how *you* feel about them and just fucking tell me what you would do if you were me?"

"That's impossible because David would murder me if I even suggested the possibility of a threesome."

I was going to stab him. I really was.

"Bro . . ."

Raymond groaned, and the creaking sound made its way through the phone again. I pictured him throwing himself back onto his bed or into his gaming chair, long limbs slack as he went limp with exhaustion at having to think this hard about something he disapproved of so much.

"If I was you, I'd just go up to them and I'd tell them that . . . you want to give it a shot, but not if they're fucking other people. But you need to drive the point home about how good you all can be together, because in the end, that's what this is all about, right? Not just you telling them what would make you happy—it's how you *all* would be happier together. Big-picture shit, you know?"

"But what if they don't want to try—"

"Dude, stop being so scared all the time. Do you know how many times I told David I wanted him, and his punk ass kept being all afraid that he was an experiment? If I'd just said, 'Oh well, guess he doesn't like me,' I guarantee we wouldn't be together now. Fight for them, man. Fight for them, but don't compromise on something that you know you can't handle."

I exhaled slowly. "I wish I could handle it."

"But you can't," Raymond said, his voice growing quieter as he got more serious. "I can picture your face when they tell you they're going to fucking Freedom X or whatever that place is called, and how those big eyes of yours would get all wet and you'd take a deep breath, then try to act all tough, and it makes me want to crack skulls."

A laugh burst out of me, and I walked slower up the remaining stairs. "You're so overprotective. Just like Aiden. Real talk, if you'd both stop with the macho-alpha-dog bullshit, y'all would be friends."

"My friends list is full."

I guffawed my way to the QFindr office, picturing him scowling and moody at not being taken seriously, but I knew he was full of shit. When it came down to it, he'd dig my boys if he'd give them a chance. And he probably knew it too, which was why he was so determined to double down so as to never be proven wrong.

"If you really thought they were that bad, you wouldn't be trying to help me figure out what to do."

"Maybe I'm just tired of you bitching."

"Aiight, grumpy ass. I'm gonna let you go. I have a security guard to save and two beautiful dudes to talk to. Enjoy the blackout and have a lot of sweaty sex with D."

"If he ever stops griping long enough to get fucked," Raymond grumbled. "But, look, on the real . . ."

I turned the door to the office, only to realize it had locked behind me. Grimacing, I rapped my knuckles on the glass loud enough to hopefully draw their attention. Jace appeared almost instantly, and the relief in his lovely face tightened my chest. He worried so much. About everything.

"I know how it feels to get in your feelings and caught up in your insecurity, and tell yourself there's no way someone would want you when they have better options. Or a better life. Or whatever." Raymond paused, maybe weighing his words or maybe wondering why he was saying them despite his firm belief that I needed to flap my wings in the opposite direction of the Fairbairns. "But if you never try to tell them what you need, it's on you, bro. And if they agree to give you what you need, and are happy to do it, and you still back away . . . then you're not giving them the chance to show you what they have to offer."

"I'm just afraid they won't be willing to try even if I do fight for them," I said, dropping my voice to a whisper as Jace unlocked the door. We were face-to-face as Raymond answered.

"Man, if they love you, they'd be willing to do exactly that. And if you don't think they would be able to stick it out, then you've got your answer on whether you should pursue any of this at all."

My stomach twisted in a painful knot. It must have shown in my face because Jace's expression went from relieved to concerned. I shook my head, trying to force a reassuring grin and failing miserably.

"Thanks, Ray," I croaked. "A lot."

"Be good, man. Figure that shit out once and for all."

We hung up as I stepped into the office, but my heart was thumping in my chest at a terrifying rate at the very idea of once again asking them to change. For me. The resounding fear in my already chaotic mind was: *What if they say no?* or *What if they say yes, then regret it?*

I didn't think I could handle being crushed by the reality that they wouldn't consider me enough.

CHAPTER
NINE

Kevin, the security guard, knocked the hell out as soon as he scarfed a meal of two-day-old bagels and beef jerky. He turned on his side, pillow over his head to hide from the sun streaming from the windows, and conked out. His soft snores reminded me so much of my old man that I turned my phone back on just to text my parents some emoji besos and reassure them I was safe.

"I'm gonna go downstairs and hang out at his post," I said, stripping off my shirt that had been reduced to a sweat rag after my treks back and forth up the stairs. "I dunno what to do in case of emergency, but there's a landline down there, I guess."

"I'll go with you," Jace said.

"You really don't have to. I'm pretty much just holding down the fort in case anyone has any questions or any weirdos try to get in."

"Even so, I'll come with you. Just in case."

Behind him, Aiden snorted. "Baby, this isn't *Escape from L.A.*"

Jace nailed his husband with a look so annoyed, I half expected Aiden to burst into flames. "Can you not fucking belittle me for at least an hour? You always do this shit when something happens."

Aiden glared, which was when I realized they were turning into the hot, sweaty, and aggravated versions of themselves after being stuck in the building for going on a day and a half. Maybe we'd go full-on *Lord of the Flies* if this spanned a few more days.

"You can give me that look all you want, but even if you think I'm being irrational, you don't need to be acting like I'm a fucking idiot."

"Okay, whatever, sure." Aiden ran a hand through his hair, glanced at me, then away. "How about we all go downstairs? I want to see if I can track down some more candles and batteries."

I snorted. "Fat chance on that one. All the stores were closed."

"That's why you don't try searching for stores," Aiden said with a wink. "You find the people with the smart hustle, selling batteries and candles on the corner."

Of course he'd be the one to think of that. Of course.

Grinning and shaking my head, I looped my arm through Jace's because he was still staring at Aiden like he wanted to throat punch him, and walked with them to the door. I'd been all worried about silent treatment and awkwardness following our tense conversation, but we'd eased right back into our usual back-and-forth with no need for a stumbling transition.

The thought caused me to pull Jace tighter against me. I dropped a kiss on his forehead, and we headed down into the darkened staircase. If Jace was annoyed by my hot-and-cold shit, he didn't let on. He pressed against my side as we synchronized our steps like a couple of dorks, and he appeared more amused than annoyed by the time we burst into the brightened lobby.

"All right, you two stay put." Aiden pointed at us sternly. "I'm gonna try to charge my phone since it's on its last leg."

"Is it creepy if I say 'Yes, Daddy'?" I wondered out loud, smirking.

He shuddered comically, looking ridiculous with his brawny shoulders straining a too-small shirt he'd probably snagged from Oli's office. The sight of his biceps wanting to bust out of the material had my mouth watering.

"Yes," he confirmed. "Creepy as fuck."

Jace rolled his eyes at him. "Don't take a long time, Mr. Judgmental."

"I won't." Aiden paused in the doorway. "Use Kevin's keys to lock these doors so no one can get in from the outside. Anyone who got stuck here last night should have an ID. No one else gets to come in."

"What if they're hungry or thirsty?" I asked.

Jace smiled, but Aiden seemed exasperated. "Case-by-case basis, hero."

I flashed a thumbs-up and locked him out. After, I sat on Kevin's chair behind his desk and slumped against it, instantly going into a level of *Clerks* bored as Jace hopped up on the desk beside me. He brought his legs up to fold in front of him and studied me.

"I thought you were going to take off," he noted. "Maybe to Michael and Nunzio's."

"I would have told you first. Or at least called."

"I know, but I was still waiting for that call." Jace's expression was a mix between serious and appreciative, his full lips twisted to the side even as he gazed at me and reached out to stroke my hand. "Thanks for not making fun of me about my irrational paranoia."

"I don't think Aiden is trying to make fun of you," I said quickly. "He just doesn't always think before he speaks. And you two have been together so long, he probably thinks you'll know what he means and won't get upset by it." Jace was gazing at me with his eyes half-closed as he gazed at me from under his long lashes. Grinning nervously, I added, "At least, that's what happens with me and my friends. We talk shit to each other so much, assuming it's all jokes and everyone is in on it, until someone gets mad for real. But since we have so much love for each other, there's usually no hard feelings after a few rants in Spanish."

Jace's mouth twitched. "Is that what happens with Stephanie and Angel? She's mad at him a lot."

"Ahh . . . yeah. He gets under her skin, like, on purpose. Kinda like teasing the girl you like but won't actually tell her you like her."

"I'd smack the shit out of him."

I busted out laughing and slapped my hand against the desk. "Yeah, well, in his defense, he's been in love with her since high school but she's always been a solo flyer. Hashtag exploring her sexuality. A lot like you and Aiden, actually. Angel thinks he can't change that about her, and he can't do the casual thing she usually does, so he settles for teasing her and being emo."

Jace turned to face me completely, sliding his legs down to dangle off the desk on either side of me. Leaning forward, he gave me an intense once-over. "And how does he know she won't change for him?"

"Because . . . she's Stephanie. She's happy the way she is. Why should he ask her to change her life because he caught feelings all late in the game—" I caught myself as he leaned closer, his eyes narrowing further with each of my words. Oh fuck. "Uh," I stammered. "I mean, he doesn't think it's his place to ask someone as independent as Stephanie to change her lifestyle just for him. It'd be kinda . . . arrogant."

Jace's lip curled. "Or kinda . . . cowardly to bow out before really asking her if she'd do it. And to leave her hanging thinking she's being rejected because he can't handle her 'lifestyle.'"

Defensiveness reared up in me like a surge of fire, and I sat up in the chair. "'Cowardly'? For real? Look—if Stephanie was into monogamy, or whatever, she could have come right out and told my dude the first time the conversation came up. But she didn't. She let him hang in the wind—"

"He let *her* hang in the wind by opening and closing the topic before she had the time to think about it and say what she felt one way or the other," Jace retorted, voice rising. "Almost as if he thought she was too complicated to bother putting the effort in to see if they could make it work. Which is, again, pretty fucking cowardly and shitty."

We weren't talking about Stephanie and Angel anymore. I knew it. He knew it. And my defensiveness was all about me, and the way my heart pounded and my anger nearly consumed me at the reality that he thought my fears were borne of cowardice instead of self-preservation.

"I told both of you how I felt." I stood up, planting my hands on either side of him, and leaned in so close our faces were nearly brushing. "I made myself clear. I'm just scared."

"I know you're scared, but give us a chance—"

"To do what? I told you I'd be with you if you weren't open, but I got the impression that wasn't a possibility."

Jace frowned. "I needed to think. Would you really feel good about an answer if we made it in two seconds?"

"Honestly?" I inhaled, gathering my courage, and forged on. "I did think that you should have been able to make a snap decision. That you should be able to see how good we are together. That we fit and we work, and it's perfect. But then I thought that since you walked away, and Aiden hesitated, it meant I would never be enough. And then I asked myself whether I'd even *want* you to change your mind if it meant you'd potentially regret it and resent me later."

"Regret it?" Jace grabbed my bare shoulders and jerked me forward, his hands strong and gripping tight enough to pinch my skin. "Look—" He took a deep breath, closing his eyes briefly as if to gather himself. "Look—I told you we've been doing this since we were teenagers, but in all that time we never once met anyone who caused us to feel anything similar to what we feel for each other. We usually don't even have repeat lovers." Jace searched my face, maybe for a sign that I understood or believed him. "You're different. You've been different from the start. And maybe we weren't clear enough, maybe we didn't say it fast enough, but that's because we were also unsure of how you felt about us. And . . . it took a while for us to admit to each other that we're both in love with you." He started speaking faster as he picked up steam, his face flushed and eyes intense on me. "But now, we know what we want. And if you think we'd resent changing anything for you, you're also dumb as fuck."

I opened my mouth to speak, but no sound came out besides a ragged breath. The hope consuming me made everything feel tight, the air around me shifting slowly and reminding me that it was too fucking hot. With Jace staring at me like he could see through me, see into my head, and analyze all the parts of me that were so scared to try to be the one to change their dynamic, I slowly became overwhelmed. With the possibilities, the realities, and all the ways this could go wrong.

"You're killing me, Jace," I said, my voice huskier than it had been a moment ago. "Every time you make me feel like I stand a chance, I tear myself apart bouncing between wanting to believe it . . . and wanting to run away."

"Don't run from me," he whispered, pressing our foreheads together.

My heart did a flip. "Does all this mean you'll try being with just me and Aiden? I know it's a lot, I know I'm making assumptions about how it will be, but I swear to fucking God, I think it will be perfect."

Jace released a stuttering little laugh that sounded half-scared and half-excited. "I do too. It's just that we've always been this way. And I start thinking . . . what happens if there's no adventures and distractions, and you guys realize I'm too . . . *something* to deal with on a regular basis?" He licked his lips and looked down, breath coming faster. "What if it falls apart? Or what if you and Aiden are better together without me? I told you we loved each other enough to know something was always missing, but maybe . . . maybe . . . I don't know. I'm just terrified of things going wrong if I reach too far for what I want. Like I should be happy that I even made it this far and got this much after where I came from."

Protectiveness reared up inside of me and battled with the shock that filled me. Never in a million years had I considered that he'd be afraid that *he* wouldn't be enough for *us*.

"My first response is to tell you that your concern is bullshit." I tilted his head up, forcing him to look at me. "But I know you really mean what you're saying, just like I really meant what I said about being afraid you'll regret it, so I won't. We'll just have to be really fucking brave together and take the risk. Because Jace, we belong together. The three of us. I've never been so certain of anything in my life."

Jace clenched his hands right before he claimed my mouth in a savage kiss. Hard, teeth gnashing, and interrupted by shaky breaths and a darting tongue. I couldn't tell if he was trying to reassure me or brand me, but I slid a hand through his hair and held him in place, anyway. One taste, and I couldn't get enough of Jace with his tempting body that responded so beautifully to mine every single time.

For the second time in two days, I was fucking his mouth with my tongue as he ground against me on top of a desk. But this time, we were doing it in front of the glass doors of an office building. Neither of us cared.

Jace tilted his head back when I kissed down his throat to suck on his Adam's apple. He moaned and jerked his hips forward, pressing his hard dick to mine. I'd had him twice in the past twenty-four hours, but my body responded like it was the first time all over again. As though I'd never had that hot questing tongue delving into my mouth while his restless hands slid down my shoulders to slide around and grip my back, fingernails digging into the skin. Like it was a total shock that we were so hungry for each other we paid no mind to the potential of an interruption as he used his toes to drag down my basketball shorts, then lifted his own hips so he could get his shorts down.

He wrapped both his hands around our stiff lengths. "Is it bad that I am obsessed with your penis?"

"Um." I looked over his shoulder, but didn't really see anything. Not when he was clumsily trying to stroke us both. "We should probably . . . stop."

"Why?" Jace arched an eyebrow, gazing at me challengingly, and found a rhythm so he could jerk us off. "Your dick is already dripping. I think it disagrees."

"It probably does," I said, clearly delirious and giving my penis an entire personality. "But, like, someone's gonna see."

Jace rolled his eyes dramatically. "Okay. Let me down."

"Huh?"

He slid off the edge of the desk, and then dropped to his knees on the floor. I was graced with a single promising look before Jace knelt between my thighs and took me into his mouth. It was way more low-key than him jacking us on the desk, but the feel of that wet warmth surrounding me sent my eyes skittering around the lobby.

Would anyone see us? Come downstairs? Was anyone looking in at us from the outside or were these windows reflective? Making out was one thing, but as soon as he deep-throated me, the way few people had before considering the size of my erection, I'd be a goner. I'd get loud and stupid.

"Jace—"

He slowly took me deeper, the agonizing slide enough for a tremor to start in my hands and my eyes to shut. Jace hummed appreciatively when he had me all the way in, so deep I was somewhat lodged in his throat. My mouth dropped open as he went to work, dragging his mouth up and down with his lips wrapped tightly around me. I wanted to fuck his mouth, but I held still even though my hips were restless and my balls tightening. When Jace cupped my balls, rolling them gently, I spread my thighs open wider.

"Oh yeah," I groaned. "Just like that, papi."

He hummed again, and I reached down to massage the back of his head as he took his time on me. It was driving me wild—the measured plunging of my dick in and out of his perfect mouth—but I could feel my orgasm starting to build. Or at least, it was until he pulled his mouth off with a wet popping sound to flick his tongue into my slit.

"Jace," I said, unashamed of how close it was to a whine.

"All in good time, handsome," he said, voice floating from beneath the desk.

"Fu—"

Footsteps rung out from the staircase, and I froze. Didn't rush to pull up my shorts or drag Jace from out of the desk, just froze in place and stared at the stairway, waiting to see who would come out. Jace, on the other hand, went back to deep-throating me. There was no way he didn't hear the voices now accompanying the footsteps, but since the desk was L-shaped and he was hidden from view, he probably didn't care.

In fact, he cared so little that he took me down deep enough for his nose to press into my pubic hair. A moan ripped out of me, but I muffled it by pressing my fist to my mouth. It came out sounding like a sob.

Two women entered the lobby, looking hot and tired and still wearing business casual outfits they'd likely worn to work the day before. They glanced at me, and I tensed. Jace was sucking me more enthusiastically, and there was no fucking way these women didn't hear the wet sloppy noises. Or notice how red-faced I likely was.

"Any word when we'll have power back?" one of the ladies, with long dark hair, asked. "It's been forever."

Her friend, or coworker, pushed open the door and let the sounds of traffic and loud voices inside. Good thing, because Jace's saliva was everywhere, and he seemed determined to make me come with an audience. My toes curled as he bobbed his head faster, and the wet squelching noise seemed deafening.

The lady did not appear to notice.

"Uh," I said, not pulling my fist away from my mouth. "I don't, uh, actually work . . . here."

She tilted her head and looked around. "Where's Kevin?"

"Sleeping. I'm—" A streak of pleasure went through me, rocking my world and my brain cells. My eyebrows crashed together as I stared at her, feeling guilty and overheated and so turned on I thought I would die. "—just covering for the dude," I gritted out. "Sorry."

"Oh, no problem." She started to back away, eyeballing me. "You okay?"

"Yep." My voice came out strangled. "Just hot."

"Sure as fuck is." She smiled at me, winked, and turned to the door. "I'll let you know if I find anything out."

Holy shit, I thought as the door closed behind her.

Jace chose that moment to slide a finger against my clenching asshole, and I went off like a rocket, releasing spurt after spurt into his mouth. I bit my fist, eyes squeezing shut, but was drawing in frantic gasps of air by the time I unloaded entirely and sagged in the chair.

"Holy shit."

Jace stood up, his lean body dragging against my torso, and beamed. "That was so hot."

I gaped at him, still panting. He laughed, eyes crinkling.

"You're so cute. That blush is everything!"

I shook my head, trying to clear it, and pinched his side. He laughed harder.

"Babe, that lady totally knew someone was beneath the table."

"I know," Jace said, beaming. "And she was totally into it. I want to find her and be her friend."

He twisted around to peer through the glass, and I swatted his side.

"You're bad."

"I know." He turned to me again. "That's why you love me, though. Right?"

I stared at him and his challenging smirk, and knew exactly what he was doing. Trying to make light of all the heaviness that had taken over what should have been a fun and easy campout in the office. Make a joke of his feelings and fears.

"I love you for plenty of reasons. Both of you."

The happiness crossing Jace's face was punctuated by a sudden flurry of sound—clicks and beeps and whirring—right before a rush of cold air blasted down into the lobby.

The power was back on.

CHAPTER
TEN

"We should wait to work on the servers," Caleb said. "The power could go out again for all we know."

"Gee, ya think?"

Caleb glanced at Oli balefully, who'd accompanied his lover to the QFindr office not even thirty minutes after the power had returned to Manhattan. I'd never spent much time around either of them beyond the occasional social function, but they were a handsome couple. Caleb with the silver streaks in his hair and poor attempt at casual clothing with his light-blue polo and blue cuffed slacks with pointy-toe shoes, and Oli dressed like James Dean in all black with his hair slicked back and damp from a shower.

"You really didn't need to run over here," Aiden said from where he was leaning against the wall. He seemed grumpy about the arrival of his half-brother and business partner. "We weren't going to rush into a server surgery after a full night of—"

"Fucking?" Oli guessed, tossing a wink my way.

Caleb glared harder. "Will you be appropriate?"

"Why?" Oli looked from Aiden to me before meeting Jace's eyes. He was stretched out on the floor with his Kindle. "Jace, was there fucking?"

"Lots."

Oli grinned triumphantly at Caleb, and laughed when his lover gave a mournful headshake. For a minute, I was embarrassed. But then I noticed the way Aiden was pushing his shoulders back, all ready to defend himself, and I intercepted faster than a Russian number calling the White House.

"Besides fucking, we found out your IT guy is a bigot Twitter troll. What're y'all gonna do about that?"

The grin was wiped from Oli's face, Caleb's mouth dropped open, and I spent the next few minutes rehashing what I'd found on Travis's iPad. Even after regaling them with all the hate speech, they poured over it themselves until Oli reddened, his eyes narrowing, and Caleb had gone pale.

"I should have listened to you," he said miserably, after turning to Aiden. "You are such a better judge of character than me."

"Yeah, that's why you're with Oli," Jace called from the floor.

Oli flipped off Jace, who blew him a kiss.

"He has to go," Aiden said. "Like yesterday."

"Right. Of course." There was an undertone of anger in Caleb's voice that I'd never heard before. "We'll tell him as soon as he returns from his trip. We'll have his things all packed." Caleb was looking around the room like he was ready to throw the dude's shit out the window. "My God. I'm so embarrassed. How could we have been so oblivious?"

"It's more than embarrassing," Oli said, holding up the iPad. "There are things about us on his social media. About the company."

Clearly, I hadn't investigated that deeply before being interrupted, because all I'd seen was the usual troll viciousness. Now, I frowned. "Like what?"

"He doesn't name us on his time line, but he went off on a series of rants about a queer company raking in millions for doing nothing more than aggregating data to help other queers get laid. And that they pay their 'normal' employees like shit."

"Fuck his hetero tears," Aiden growled. "Little bitch. His salary is commensurate with other salaries in the field."

I nodded in agreement, but something about Oli's tone was off. There was tension in his shoulders that hadn't been there before, and I wasn't the only one who'd noticed. Jace had sat up straight, as if his sense for danger was going off.

"What else?" he pressed.

Oli's eyes flicked between us again, then forced a smile. "There's some more detailed chatter in his DMs about the company, but it's nothing. I'll have Clive look at it on Monday."

"Lawsuit material?" I asked.

"Maybe."

He clearly wasn't going to go further into detail, so I backed off. If there was a potential lawsuit, he probably didn't want to tell us everything, since he likely knew it could get repeated to our growing crew of friends. Jace crawled over to us on his hands and knees, quizzical but less alarmed, before coming to sit between where Aiden and I stood.

"So, does my boo get the bigot's job?"

"Jace," I hissed. "Cállate."

"What?" he asked innocently. "I'm just asking. We know you guys already wanted to hire him."

Aiden reached down to run his fingers through Jace's hair, smiling fondly. "I was going to wait to ask until we get the servers and the firing sorted."

"Guys," I muttered. "Chill."

"Why wait?" Jace got to his feet and draped himself all over me, smiling. "If you hire Chris as soon as possible, douche-canoe will be out the door and Chris in his spot to take care of the servers while on salary. I'm basically an HR genius."

I covered my face with my hands, but peeked through my fingers to see Oli smiling slightly, despite his obvious preoccupation with the iPad, and Caleb nodding seriously.

"Chris, you were my original choice for this position. Would you be interested?"

My eyebrows shot up. No interviews or résumés? Was this what happened when you had connections? "Seriously?"

"Absolutely. I'm not very good at jokes. You're highly skilled, have several years of experience, professional anytime I've worked with you whether it was about testing or the shoot—"

"Dude," I said, interrupting him. "I'm standing here in gym shorts, and I spent the night screwing your brother and his husband in your office. I'm not exactly professional."

The blood rushed to Caleb's face, but he bravely continued. "Right, well, that is certainly unorthodox but given the situation . . ." He gestured vaguely, maybe reaching for an explanation. "Well, it wasn't as though it was a work day."

Jace snickered. "You're so cute, Caycay."

He was, but I was hung up on . . . everything. My mind was going at a hundred miles an hour because as soon as the words had left Caleb's mouth, I'd realized that I really did want the job. The glass cube with the sleek furniture in the fancy purple office with the shower and workout equipment. The queer-friendly environment where I'd get to see people I genuinely liked every day. Where I'd get to collaborate with them on something innovative and cool. Replacing a racist-ass fuckboy was the icing on the cake.

"I want the job," I said quickly. "But I need to give my current job notice. I can't just walk out after all this time."

"See?" Caleb beamed. "Professional."

I held up my hands to thwart him from going off further. "There's more." Looking over at Jace's thrilled expression, then Aiden's quietly proud smile, my heart thrummed in my chest. I thought about what Jace had said in the lobby, what Aiden had said earlier this morning, and Raymond's drawl in my ear. "What if—" I stammered. "What if . . . I'm with . . . one of my bosses? How does that work?"

Aiden straightened.

"What do you mean?" Caleb asked, cocking his head. "'With'?"

Oli looked at his lover with exasperation. "Darling. Really? *Really*?"

Caleb blushed again. "Oh. I get it."

I couldn't help it. I burst out laughing. I kept laughing when Jace pulled me into a lamprey hug, and when Aiden hovered by my side as Oli dragged Caleb away from us.

"Let's give them a minute," Oli said, walking farther down the hall. "And we'll work something out," he called back to me. "After all, I'm fucking the founder."

Caleb said something chastising to him, but by then I was burying my face against Jace's neck as Aiden put a hand on both our shoulders.

"Christopher, are you sure?" he asked, low and serious. There was almost a warning in his tone. "Or are you talking about the casual—"

"We were never casual," I said sharply. "Not for a few months, anyway. So quit saying that shit."

"Agreed." Jace looked up at us. "But can we take this time to nail down what *with* entails while all three of us are here?"

My heart had been slamming into my rib cage as soon as I'd blurted it out to Caleb and Oli, but as my two men looked at me with hope and trepidation written all over their lovely faces, calm washed over me. They were nervous because of me. They were waiting for me. I wasn't the only one who was desperate for this to work.

"For me, it means . . . no more random booty calls or sexy weekends. It means we're together. For real. Sleeping together, eating together, spending time together for more than just fucking . . ." Aiden was squeezing my shoulder so hard I thought he would crush the bone. I took a deep breath. "But . . . I can't do it if y'all are fucking other people. I know it's what you've always done, but I don't have your history. I haven't been through more than half a lifetime being confident that you two love me like you have with each other."

Jace jerked me against him, hugging me so tight it was hard to breathe.

"You already know what I think. I want us to do this."

Aiden, who'd not been prepped on that part of our lobby hookup, moved his hand from me to clamp both on Jace's shoulders. The hope that filled his face matched what I'd felt as soon as Jace had said the words downstairs.

"God," he breathed, closing his eyes for a minute. "You have no idea how this feels."

"How what feels?" I asked, looking into Aiden's eyes over Jace's shoulder.

"The relief." He shook his head slowly. "Are you both sure? I want this so bad, I'm fuckin' afraid that it's a dream."

"It's real," Jace said. "He's ours. We're doing this."

The word *ours* lit me up like the sky on the Fourth of July. I smiled, big and dorky, and for the first time, I felt no doubts. No fears.

A smile spread over my face. "Can we celebrate with booze and food and sex and UFC? It's fight night."

Aiden pulled me and Jace to him, grinning his rakish grin. "We can do anything you want. But you may have to slow me down because I'm ready to cab it to South Jamaica, pack your shit, and bring you home."

"Let's start with the job," I said, laughing even though the possibility of someday living with them nearly caused my heart to explode. "Then we can figure out everything else."

"Okay, but your lease is up in July," Aiden said. "So, y'know. Fate."

"And . . . how do you know that?"

"I keep track of the important things in my men's lives. And I've been thinking of you that way for quite a while."

I sagged against Jace, but Aiden moved around us to sandwich me between them, propping me up. Between the feel of his strong broad chest at my back and Jace's slight form pinned to my front, I felt complete.

This was real.

This was really happening. To me.

"This isn't some kind of fucked-up fever dream induced by the blackout and heat wave, is it?" I asked suddenly. "Because that would be really messed up."

Jace burst out laughing. "No, Chris. It's real. We turned the electricity back on with the power of a public blowjob."

This time it was me snickering slightly hysterically.

"I missed something," Aiden said. "Something I really didn't want to miss."

"We'll tell you later," I reassured him. "After we talk to Caleb and Oli. We have plenty of time."

Jace grinned up at me as Aiden kissed the back of my neck.

"That we do."

GRIDLOCKED

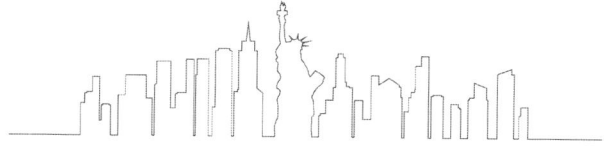

A FIVE BOROUGHS NOVELLA

CHAPTER
ONE

"**Ms.** Stone is staring at you again."

Stavros and I had managed to get through the entire evening without exchanging more than a few pertinent words regarding the security of the space the QFindr crew had rented for their "pop-up" event. It was an old factory in Industry City that they'd fashioned into something that looked, to me, like a purple Apple Store. There were two bars, one on either end of the loft, and an open space for dancing and mingling if people chose, but there were also rows of glass platforms with smartphones hooked up so people could sample QFindr's newest app—QFindr Plus.

I didn't even know what the app did.

"Maldonado."

"I heard you." I kept my focus on the crowd, and the couple of rando dudes who seemed more interested in talking to each other and people watching than sampling the app. "But I'm not interested in what Ms. Stone is doing."

I expected Stavros to leave it at that. He had about fifteen years on me, was probably the most physically fit person I'd seen outside of the military, and wore his longish light-brown hair pulled back in a severe knot. He was a serious-looking guy. A no-nonsense dude uninterested in shooting the shit. It should have been perfect, and yet here we were. Talking.

"Did she say anything to you?" he asked.

"No."

"Then why does she look like she wants to cut your throat?"

I shrugged. "Holding a grudge, most likely."

There was another pause. Then, "Over what?"

Finally, I met his dark eyes. "Because about a year ago I made her squirt, then left her sitting on a dressing room table with her underwear around her ankles." He stared at me, and I lifted my chin. "Does that answer your fucking question?"

We stared at each other for a long moment, then he swung his gaze back to the milling crowd. Satisfied, I did the same. The two guys had disappeared into the mass of people, but a quick scan allowed me to locate them again in the middle of the room. They had joined the people near the platforms and were finally using one of the phones. Or at least pretending to use them. I didn't know why something about them put my back up, but I wasn't one to ignore my instincts.

"So, I take it she didn't know you would be here."

I shot Stavros a long, exasperated glance. "I don't really like talking to people."

"Neither do I."

"Then what's with the cross-examination?"

He didn't look at me as he replied. "When a business or individual hires guards from Redline Security, Redline asks them to send a detailed evaluation of the services rendered. And since she is our point person, *she* will be doing the evaluation."

"And?"

This time, he was the one giving me an impatient glare. "And I want to make sure my file isn't tarnished because you fucked the woman who will be filling out the evaluation."

Ah. Hadn't thought of that one.

Stavros's curiosity had turned into outright irritation at the prospect, and guilt kicked in. It was only my third assignment with Redline, a company that I'd already decided I hated due to the blatant sexism of the higher-ups, but Stavros had apparently been at the nightmare agency since he'd left the military ten years ago. In my opinion, working a decade and hitting a glass ceiling of forty thousand a year wasn't exactly a retirement plan, but whatever. According to a couple of the older guys at Redline, that kind of thinking made me an entitled millennial.

Double middle fingers up to them too.

I found Meredith standing by one of the floor-to-ceiling windows looking like an absolute goddess. If Athena had leaped from

Zeus's head, Meredith must have jumped out from one of his lusty daydreams. She was distracted and talking to a catering person, so I took the opportunity to drink her in.

She had her usual red lipstick and heavily lined eyes, but her hair was longer than when I'd seen her last—curls hanging down nearly to her waist and golden blonde at the bottom while darker closer to her scalp. I knew there was a word for that type of color, but it was beyond me. I went to the same barber as Angel and Chris, and my hair was cut short with a hard part, a fade, and racing stripes at the sides.

My eyes dropped from her face to the rest of her body, and it took everything in my power not to bite my lower lip. Her dress defied gravity. The neckline plunged to her waist, and her breasts seemed to be supported by magic alone. She was already quite tall, and the combination of the short hem of her dress and the sky-high heels made her legs go on forever.

Those legs had been my undoing over a year ago when I'd first seen her on the QFindr cruise. She'd been wearing a ragged tank top and torn-up shorts, and I'd spent the better part of dinner picturing myself shoving her thighs apart so I could go down on her while she squirmed and moaned in that sexy voice of hers. I loved her voice. She sounded almost hoarse, like she'd been born smoking three packs a day, but it turned me on.

Months later, after I'd agreed to model with the rest of my squad for the QFindr photoshoot, I'd had her dress hiked up around her waist and my fingers plunging in and out of her pussy, and her wild, hoarse cries had gotten me almost as hot as how hard she'd gushed.

"Eye-fucking her probably isn't the best way to get back into her good graces."

I glanced at Stavros, who still looked unimpressed with me and the entire situation. Maybe he'd be giving me a bad evaluation of his own. Somehow, it didn't bother me. He had a reason to be a pillar of salt.

"Normally, I'd be pissed off by your nonstop commentary," I said. He arched a dark brow. "I figured you were."

"Well." I redirected my attention to Meredith again. "Most of the men I've met at Redline would have asked me for visuals or threesomes, and I'd have had to rip their nuts off."

"Most men are scum," he said. "It was pretty brave of you to assume I'm not."

"I figured you wouldn't be interested in being scummy in that capacity since you're gay."

We gave each other another silent stare down. I prided myself on the fact that he cracked first.

"How'd you figure that one out?" he asked, going a bit gruffer.

"You have linked gender symbols tatted on your middle finger."

Stavros smirked, and I went back to ogling Meredith. Unfortunately, she wasn't where I'd left her. She was right in my fucking face. Some armed guard I was turning out to be.

"Ms. Stone," I said, making my voice even and formal. Respectful or whatever. One thin blonde brow rose as Meredith's ice-blue eyes slowly slid down my body, taking in the black suit I wore. I knew I looked good, but the flush that spread up her chest and over her face made it clear she thought I looked *really* good. And she wasn't shy about wetting her lips, even if the gesture was subconscious.

Stavros cleared his throat, and her gaze jerked to him. There was no sign of embarrassment. She just smiled politely before focusing on me again.

"Do you need anything from us?" I asked, wishing she'd go back to her goddamn party. The closer she was, the more things about her I noticed. How her lips were a perfect cupid's bow, upturned slightly even when she wasn't smiling. The hint of a tattoo beneath the gravity-defying plunge of her dress. How she had to have taped her breasts in place, because everything stayed just so even as she moved. "Or did you just want to stare at me?"

Her lips curled down.

Stavros gave me a look that made it clear he hated every bit of my soul. I didn't blame him, but I couldn't handle her. Not this close to me. I already felt hot beneath the suit and long-sleeved white button-down I wore beneath. Before I'd had this blonde temptress standing here fucking me with her angry blue eyes, the industrial fans had done a good job of keeping the heat wave outside the building where it belonged. Meredith was a walking-talking heat wave in and of herself.

"I don't need anything from you," she said clearly and coldly. "I don't even know why you're here."

"You hired Redline to do the security."

"I know that, *Maldonado*. Because Caleb told me to. He's overreacting to some petty shit on social media."

Actually, it wasn't petty. After being handed the assignment, we'd been informed that a request for armed guards had been made by QFindr for every event going forward due to upper management having been doxed online, and escalating threats made by 4chan trolls after Caleb, Oli, and Aiden had fired their former IT person. Most people would brush it off or will the situation away, but from what I'd heard of Caleb Stone, he didn't take such things lightly. I didn't either.

"He takes safety seriously. I commend that."

"Good for you," she said, sarcasm thick in her tone. "But that's not what I meant. Why are *you* here. Why would you take *this* job?"

"I was assigned this job," I shot back. "I'm here in a professional capacity. I was under the impression that it was the same for you. Clearly, I was mistaken."

Her eyes widened, and Stavros stepped forward.

"Ms. Stone—"

Meredith turned and walked away, moving faster than I would have expected in the spiked heels. Her back was stiff, hands balled into fists.

"You fucked that up," Stavros said, voice low. "Fix it."

I ripped my eyes away from her ass to sneer at him. "She had it coming. I don't give a fuck about her attitude problem."

"I do. Maybe you have bigger plans than Redline, which is all fine and dandy, kid, but I don't. This is my job. And I take it seriously."

I inhaled slowly and turned just in time to see Meredith disappear out of the showroom. Beyond the space, there wasn't really anything in the building except deserted hallways, empty floors above them, and a couple of somewhat-functioning bathrooms. The place was eerie, and watching her go into the gloom prompted me to jerk my head at Stavros before following Meredith.

On my way, I swept the room for a sign of the two dudes I'd been keeping an eye on. They were nowhere to be found. I breathed a sigh of relief right before it morphed into the sharp edge of paranoia.

I quickened my stride, then picked up the pace further when I stepped into the silent corridor.

The building was boiling hot without the arsenal of fans QFindr had deployed in the large room. It had topped out at over a hundred degrees for the eighth day in a row, and I was fucking sick of it. Although, at least there hadn't been anymore blackouts. Or there better not be any more. This would be a really shitty location to be caught in the pitch-black.

If there was one thing I hated more than a crowded room with low visibility, it was an empty building with enough doorways, corners, and staircases for someone to get the drop on me. On a regular day, I didn't suffer lingering effects from my time overseas. I wasn't jumpy, I didn't have nightmares, and I wasn't haunted like some of the others I'd served with. But what did remain was a wariness about being caught off my guard. I had no idea why that wariness was sinking into my bones here, at a goddamn party for a queer dating app, but it was being triggered by two corny-looking white dudes with undercuts. I wasn't going to ignore my instincts even if there was a chance I was overreacting.

I glanced over my shoulder, moving more cautiously, and approached the bathroom at the far end of the hall. There was no line, which I credited to the fact that no one at the pop-up event was drunk enough to want to be in this creepy-ass factory alone.

Except Meredith.

"Mere," I growled, yanking the heavy door open. It shut slowly behind me. "You in here?"

The interior of the bathroom was just as grim as the hallway. Low flickering light, sinks that had probably been installed at the turn of the century, and the same dirty-looking concrete. When Meredith stepped out of a stall in all her shining wet-dream glory, I had to bite back an urge to drag her the hell out of this dreary-ass place.

Instead, I leaned against the door and crossed my arms over my chest. "Everything okay?"

Meredith sneered and turned to wash her hands. It wasn't even a sneer. It was more of a sulky scowl.

"Don't act like a kid," I said impatiently. "You have Stavros sweating that you're going to give him a bad eval."

"Why the fuck would I do that?" Meredith turned off the water and shook her hands, sending water flying everywhere as she glared at me. "You're the one pissing me off."

"How the fuck am I doing that?" I mimicked. "All I did was show up for work."

"Uh-huh. Yep. That's all you did, Tonya. Showed up for work."

"If I offended Her Highness in some other way, Her Highness should spell it out for me," I said, bored of this back-and-forth. "Because I'm getting tired of the side-eyes and stank looks every time we cross paths."

"And I'm tired of you treating me like shit," she shot back. "You are the meanest person I've met in the past year, and it makes me furious. So furious that I can't shake it off and get over it like I do with just about every other asshole in my life."

In the space of fifteen seconds, she'd insulted me multiple times, and yet she was the one standing there looking aggravated. I wanted to laugh, but instead I pushed away from the door and crossed the distance between us. She immediately dropped her arms from where she'd folded them over her chest. A flash of uncertainty flitted across her face, but she didn't back up. Instead, she lifted her pointy little chin and arched an eyebrow.

Something about her bratty defiance just . . . turned me right the fuck off. Scoffing, I said, "Explain how I treat you like shit."

"You ignore me." At my blank stare, Mere swallowed audibly. Then she licked her lips, shifting in her heels. "Pretend I don't exist."

"What should I do instead?" I couldn't hide how incredulous I was, or the way my voice sounded louder and harsher than I'd meant it to be in the empty bathroom. "Bow down and thank my lucky stars that Meredith Stone, queen of Page Six, ex-lover of Ruby Rose—"

"That was *one* night six months ago," Mere protested. "Besides, how do you know about it? Keeping tabs?"

I briefly clenched my jaw before continuing. "—and best friend to the famous Ashton Townsend, let me touch her little pink pussy? Nah. That's quite all right."

This time, all the blood rushed to her face, and I couldn't tell if it was from embarrassment or rage. "Just because you hate where I come from doesn't give you the right to treat me like I'm nothing.

And just because you think I'm Miss Rich Bitch, and you're Mis—"
she stumbled over the title, uncertainty swamping her again. "Um.
Whatever. Fuck you, is my point."

My mouth quirked. "What were you going to say?"

Mere looked away. "'Miss Alpha Vet,' but I wasn't sure if you
prefer *miss* or *mister*, so I stopped. I'm sorry."

Without thinking about it, I grabbed her chin and made her meet
my eyes. She was gnawing on her lower lip now, squirming in her tight
little dress. I stepped closer.

"I go by either. Or you can call me Sergeant if you want to be cute
about it."

"I'm always cute," she snapped.

I rolled my eyes. "This is why I fucking ignore you. You're always
doing the most and dying for attention. Making a big show of ice
grilling me, so everyone in the vicinity is all up in my business, asking
what I did to you. You have no chill, and it makes me tired."

She cringed, shoulders hunching forward. "Fine. Sorry. I'll never
look in your direction again."

It was the perfect opportunity to say, *Cool, glad to hear it,* and walk
the fuck out, but I didn't. Her flip-flopping between sassy immaturity,
and bashful insecurity was starting to tug at my interest. I wondered
how much of her attitude was an act. Or a shield she threw up when
she was feeling unsure of herself.

"Why does it matter if I address you?" I asked, lowering my
voice so it hopefully sounded less irritated. It was hard. I'd been born
with my bastard father's harsh tones, and I had to work to not sound
aggressive. "We fucked once. Almost a year ago."

She sucked her lower lip into her mouth and said nothing. I took
another step forward until there was barely any space between us, and
I didn't miss her sharp inhale. Or the way her eyes briefly closed when
I put a hand on her waist.

"Talk." I dragged my thumb over the sheer part of her dress,
feeling her smooth skin beneath. "Last opportunity."

Mere shivered but wrenched her gaze up to my own. There was no
challenge in her eyes this time. Just agonized desire. "I want another
chance."

"To do what?"

"To convince you to not walk away." She lifted her hands, letting them hover on either side of my shoulders, before she slowly touched me. "To show you that I can ruin you just as badly as you ruined me."

"Oh my God." Mere threw her head back, strands of blonde hair sticking to her damp gaping mouth and spilling over her shoulders. "Please, please, please . . ."

I held her thigh to the side with one hand, and with the other, I slid my fingers in and out of the wet heat between her legs. With each thrust of my index and middle finger, she fell further apart. The shining picture-perfect version of her unraveled into someone wild and needy, someone who didn't give a damn about the fancy dress or hours' worth of makeup the crew had put on her.

She just wanted to get fucked. And she didn't care that people outside the door could probably hear the wet sound of my fingers driving in and out of her.

"Oh . . . like that." Mere's brows scrunched together and disappeared into her messy hair. Her lips quivered. "Don't stop doing it just like that," she pleaded, voice hitching into a wail.

I smirked as her body locked up, and it took every bit of control in my own body not to kiss the hell out of her when she came—soaking her thighs, the bits of fabric hanging down from her dress, and my fingers.

My nostrils flared, and I jerked her against me so hard her hair tumbled forward to curtain both our faces.

"So show me."

CHAPTER
TWO

Mere was kissing me before my brain could catch up to my loins and remind me this was a bad idea.

This was work. She was trouble. We weren't compatible. Her attitude drove me nuts. And Stavros was going to get me fired.

I reached up to bury my fingers in her curls, intending to yank her away from me even though I'd invited her to my mouth, but instead I cupped the back of her head and slicked our tongues together. She tasted like cigarettes, which should have had me recoiling but didn't. I was almost glad there wasn't any sugar or rosé on that naughty tongue of hers. Just Marlboros and trouble.

I sucked on it to make sure I wasn't missing anything, as if I could read her intentions by keeping her in my mouth, and was rewarded by a sound that was half growl, half helpless moan. Like she didn't know if she wanted to be the aggressor here or the one, once again, spreading herself open.

Mere backed up, drawing me with her, the perfect give-and-take. She wanted to be spread open all right, but it was on her terms this time—her reeling me in instead of staring at me with smoky eyes and waiting for me to make the first move, like she had last time. When her ass hit the ancient sink, she hoisted herself up and drew me between her thighs, all without breaking the kiss.

The many reasons why this needed to end were repeating in my brain, but I ignored each one. My hand found its way to her plunging neckline, and my fingers moved over the sheer fabric that barely hid three-quarters of her small round breasts. I traced my fingertips downward and rolled them along her nipple. Her thighs tightened around me, and she pulled away with a low gasp.

I kissed down her chin, latching on to the side of her neck as I gently caressed her breast. Considering the shiver that tore through her, you'd think I was rubbing her clit. Maybe I should.

Maybe I would.

"Tonya . . ."

She smelled so fucking good. Not like perfume, but something subtler. Bodywash? Moisturizer? I licked down the column of her neck to investigate further, and finally let my fingers slide beneath her dress. Her nipple was pebbled, and I wanted it in my mouth.

Mere's fingers dug into my shoulders. "We should stop."

Three little words, the same three words that were supposed to have been my own mantra, sent everything screeching to a halt. Awareness seeped into me, and all of a sudden, the reality of how warm and wet I was irritated me. She'd ruined me with barely any effort at all—guiding me out of my better judgment with only a few uncertain looks and a huskily spoken offer.

I stepped back, wiping her lipstick from my mouth as she slid to the floor with a clack of her heels. She was blushing so prettily that I couldn't stop watching as she tugged down her dress, tucked her breast away, and messed with the long loose ringlets of her hair.

She was trying to become picture-perfect yet again. For some reason, that bothered me too. Why did people need personas and masks? I had no idea what the real Meredith was like, or which parts of her were more dominant once she wasn't putting on an act. A flash of irritation went through me at the thought, and I backed away.

"I'm not playing games with you," Mere said, meeting my gaze at long last. "I know it probably seems like I was trying to prove a point. To tell myself that you wanted me, or I could get you to do something even after you spent a year ignoring me."

That was exactly what I'd thought. It was why anger had replaced lust as soon as I'd blinked the stars out of my eyes—I couldn't tell what she wanted or which version of her wanted it. I didn't say that, though. I just gave her my dead expression, the one that drove Stephanie and Chris nuts, and waited for her to explain.

Mere looked in the mirror, examining her makeup. The red had smudged on her mouth and onto the pale skin around it. I watched her try to fix it, licking her finger and wiping before using one long nail to scrape at it, and I didn't miss the way her slim hands were trembling or how she glanced at me from the corner of her eye.

"But there's something about you that gets under my skin, and if we let that go any farther . . . I'd have lost sight of why I'm in this shitty fucking factory and begged you to eat me out regardless of which guests could hear." She gave up on her lipstick since the red still stained her skin, and turned to me. "And then I'd get fired."

My eyebrows shot up, and I forgot to be irritated at the direction this had all gone in. Even now, as she fiddled with the hem of her dress and clearly tried to figure out a way to position her body as we faced off, I could feel my resistance to her crumbling. Maybe she'd start acting like a seventeen-year-old again, and I'd remember what a dumb-ass plan it was to fuck a spoiled heiress.

"Fired? Your brother owns the fucking company, Meredith."

"Right, he owns a third of it, and he made it clear that if I can't be professional, I won't remain as the brand ambassador." She huffed out a little breath, fondness and irritation all balled into one scrunch of her nose. "I doubt the brand is . . . 'CEO's sister gets tongue-fucked in the toilet during QFindr Plus pop-up event.' I mean, I'm just guessing."

A laugh left my mouth before I was ready to contain it. Meredith's eyes got huge, which made me laugh more. How was it possible to be this annoyed and amused at the same time? She had to be into some low-key brujería shit.

"You look so beautiful when you laugh."

I abruptly stopped laughing. "Thanks for ruining it."

She rolled her eyes. "You're so prickly. How do you manage to date anyone?"

"I don't." Way to lead her into another line of annoying questions, T-Bone. Yeah, it was time to get the fuck out of this bathroom and far away from her. I was not myself when we were in close proximity. "I'm going back to work."

Turning on my heel, I strode out of the bathroom and into the sweltering hallway. There were a couple of people heading toward the bathroom from the event room, so I gave Meredith mental props for having more willpower than me. There was no way word wouldn't have gotten around had someone walked in on me with my face buried between her thighs.

But she would have tasted so fucking sweet.

Meredith's knees had drawn in and pressed together, light tremors wracking her body as she came down from her orgasm. I watched her try to piece herself back together, taking deep breaths and blinking at me. Her legs went slack, and I slid my drenched fingers out of her. She hissed out a breath when I traced her swollen folds with my fingertips one last time before pulling away.

"Fuck." Her voice was even lower and throatier post-sex. "I don't think I've come that hard in ages."

The ache between my legs intensified, and fire licked upward from there. A whole mural of filthy images passed before my mind as she sat there leaning back on her hands, damp and gorgeous and still possessing a hungry look in her eye. Not an ounce of shame that the entire production crew and likely our friends had heard her moans, the way she'd said my name like a fucking prayer. The way she'd begged me to fuck her while rubbing frantically at her own clit.

A spasm went through my fingers. My heart sped up.

Then, a knowing smirk, a cocky one, spread across her lovely face, and she arched a brow. "I can't wait to tell Ashton that I fucked the hot Marine."

The words were ice-cold water all over me. She reached out to grab my arm, but I coolly took a step back.

"I can make you come just as hard," Mere said. "If you get those pants down."

"Nah. I'm good."

Mere cocked her head, confused, and I turned around right after sucking her wetness off my fingers. If I were on death row, I'd request to taste her for my last meal, but I wasn't. And I was nobody's fucking conquest.

I walked out without a backward glance.

Meredith's heels clicked against the floor behind me as we returned to the event room, but I didn't look over my shoulder. I was too busy reminding myself of why I'd backed off the first time. Stephanie and Chris had vouched for her more times than I could count, Stephanie ever since they'd become partners in crime, and Chris since hooking up with her half brother and his husband—Aiden and Jace. Although, hooking up didn't seem to be the right description anymore.

He'd just told us that he'd be shacking up with them as soon as the heat wave broke, and that we could save our wise-guy comments for moving day when he'd put us to work helping out. Figured he'd get into a throuple with some rich guys and still want to do all the manual labor. Couldn't even splurge when his pair of husbands were offering.

"Can we talk after this is over?" Mere murmured as we stepped through the door. "Please."

"If we have time."

She didn't look convinced, but she returned to her side of the room and I went back to mine. Stavros had moved, but he was easily visible in his black suit amid the guests who were all dressed for summer in a hot-ass factory. There were enough pretty girls in short, lightweight dresses to fill about eight thousand fantasies, but this was work, so I didn't see them as anything but potential issues.

"You handle it?"

"Yeah," I said, coming to a stop next to Stavros. "You're fine."

"Good." A pause. "Your zipper's down."

My hand shot down before I remembered I'd never unzipped. Stavros laughed silently, and I glared.

"Funny. I didn't touch her."

"Then why are you wearing her lipstick?"

Christ, this guy wouldn't give me a break.

"Man, you got your promised A-plus eval, right? Get off my back."

We glared at each other for a moment before he snorted and returned to his bored observation of the crowd. "I appreciate the effort, kid. I need this job, as sad as it is."

I didn't know what was sadder. The awareness that I might be stuck at Redline with him for the next however long to commiserate about being stuck there, or the fact that I didn't really have anything else I'd rather do. I settled for finding Meredith in the crowd, and watching her drape those long lovely arms around someone else's neck. I was sure it was a friend, but I still wanted that person to die.

"Do you have a girlfriend, Maldonado?"

"Do you have a boyfriend, Mr. Never Shuts the Fuck Up?"

"I'm married."

"Well, good for you. I hope you have an easy future divorce."

Another of his *what an asshole kid* snorts. Then, "If you have no one waiting at home, a pretty blonde with a boatload of cash seems like a solid plan."

This time when I glared at him, I meant it. And I kept glaring until he got the hint and held up his hands in surrender. No personal talk. No small talk. Just two queers who were stuck together because Redline hadn't wanted to send any of their hetero guards to the queer event.

Yeah . . . both Stavros and I were gonna need to get the hell out of there.

The rest of the event dragged out, but I made the rounds, checked the exits, and learned the function of QFindr Plus. It was an actual dating app instead of an app that aggregated the results from dozens of other dating websites. The original QFindr app would pull results from QPlus as well.

I had to admit that Caleb, Oli, and Aiden were probably making bank. As cranky as I was, the event was cool in a yuppie sort of way, and Meredith was a great hostess. She smiled so much that her face likely ached by the end of the night, and I noticed that her movements slowed after a while. Like a toy winding down. It probably took a lot out of her to maintain her sassy attitudinal flavor of a personality for long periods of time, but the guests loved it. And the press loved her too. I noticed a specific journalist, a lady with a half-shaved head and tattoo sleeves that rivaled my own, hovering near Mere more than seemed necessary.

It irritated me. And I was irritated that it irritated me, but it burned that I could easily picture them together. Mere liked her women forceful, take charge, and Tatyana Rush of the *Village Voice*, or where the fuck ever, seemed like she'd be up for the job.

Yeah, I wanted her to die too.

When everyone cleared out and it was time for the cleaning staff to file in, I quit staring her down and turned to Stavros to figure out when we were released from duty. We'd check the perimeter, sweep for anyone remaining in the building, and then dip once the clock struck twelve.

Sounded good. My head ached from a near constant subconscious clench of my teeth, and I needed to get laid. Staring at Meredith's legs all night had me in desperate need for a three-hour sexual encounter, and it couldn't be with her. I wouldn't be her alpha Marine, and she wouldn't be my rich army candy. Whenever people were immediately assigned stupid-ass titles based on assumptions, it usually meant my time would be better spent somewhere with less trouble.

Meredith left while we were clearing the building, which should have been a relief but wasn't. The thing in the back of my brain, that craggy paranoid voice, didn't like that she'd left alone after her brother had demanded the event be saddled with protection all night.

"I'm gonna take off," I told Stavros. "We have ten minutes, but I need to catch my ride."

"You're good, kid."

Stavros winked, like he knew who I was chasing after.

We said our goodbyes, amicable despite our bickering, and I speed walked to the freight elevator. My heart was thrumming in my chest, adrenaline coursing through my veins. I reminded myself over and over again to stop being a stereotype—to stop living in the headspace where I spent every waking moment expecting something to go wrong. But I'd carried that worry since I was a kid, since my mother's smacks and my father's closed fists, and it had heightened after multiple tours overseas. Usually, when I felt like something would go wrong . . . it did.

Which was why I was prepared for it when the elevators opened and I saw one of the motherfuckers with an undercut pinning Meredith against the wall while the other one pawed through her purse.

Usually, an icy calm settled over me once my awful gut feelings panned out. *Okay*, I'd tell myself, *she's going to hit you, so brace for it.* Or, *He's going to challenge you, so put your fucking fists up.* And lastly, *We're surrounded. Handle it.* But seeing that big meaty hand crushing Meredith against the wall? It sent me into a blind rage.

I blinked once and felt myself moving forward.

The next time I blinked, Fuckboy A was unconscious at my feet with a crushed-in nose, and I looked up to find Meredith clocking the hell out of the guy who'd promptly lost his shit at the sight of me unleashing holy hell onto his pal.

He wasn't ready for my right hook catching him in his jaw, so he spun oddly, slammed into the wall, and then took off at a dead sprint down the street. I immediately launched myself after him, but Meredith wrapped her long arms around me and yanked me back against her dress.

"No," she panted. "He might have a weapon."

I didn't remind her that I was armed. She was shaking like a leaf against me, her teeth chattering, and her voice sounding all wrong. Thick with tears. With fear. With Fuckboy B having vanished, and his buddy bleeding and unconscious on the floor, I turned to Meredith and cupped her face in my hands.

She was chalk white, eyes wide and damp, and her lips were pressed into a thin red line.

"You okay, mama?"

"Yes." Her voice cracked. She shook her head. "Can you hug me, please?"

Goddamn, but that request almost broke me. It was a little too familiar. A little too much like me back before the scar tissue had sealed me into something hard and impenetrable.

I pulled her against me with one hand—letting her press her face against my neck and cling like I was the only thing that could anchor her to the world—and ripped out my phone to call the police with the other.

CHAPTER
THREE

Meredith had shrunk in on herself as she stood by one of the squad cars in a wash of blinking lights with her arms wrapped tight across her chest. It felt like a billion degrees, especially since I was still running on adrenaline in my bullshit suit, but I could tell she was shivering. Shivering, blocking out the questions being aimed her way, and focusing entirely on me.

Those big blue eyes of hers hadn't shifted away since I'd gently released her from my arms, smoothed hair back from her damp face, and gruffly snapped, "Yes," when the cop asked whether I was her boyfriend. He'd stumbled all over himself after getting a closer look at my face and writing down my name, but I wasn't in the mood to educate people on why I never bothered to "correct" people because there was nothing to "correct." If they wanted to understand me not having a binary gender, they could get on the fucking internet like everyone else.

The important thing was that Fuckboy A had been carted off in an ambulance while cuffed to a stretcher, that Stavros had rushed down to assist in snooping out any lingering paparazzi looking to exploit the situation, and that Meredith was okay. Well, she had red marks on her upper arms and neck that would inevitably turn to bruises, but she was alert. Even so, the sight of her injured to any degree just about sent me chasing the ambulance so I could kill the already-unconscious dick-bag, but I didn't.

If the military had taught me anything, it was how to channel my anger into something productive. Like robotically answering questions while trying to convey an *I'm-here-for-you* vibe, even though I was wearing an expression that probably belonged on a convicted murderer. I didn't have a resting bitch face. I'd been born looking like I was ready to knock everybody out.

"I don't need to go to the hospital."

Mere's low-pitched voice barely made its way to me over the sirens and the noise of traffic, but I heard it. And I knew she was deliberately talking loud enough for me to hear. They'd questioned me repeatedly, asking me specific questions about descriptions since I'd been keeping an eye on the two clowns for the entire night, but they'd finished with me a while ago. Mere seemed to have been less able to give viable information due to being shaken up, and now she was obviously ready to go.

Ready to go with me.

I pushed away from the light pole I'd been leaning against, suit jacket over my shoulder, and walked to the squad car. The cops didn't stop me. In fact, they seemed to like me. Like we were all in on something together, but I had no fucking clue what. Maybe they thought I was cool because they thought I was sleeping with a semifamous person. Weird how even random beat cops knew the last name Stone. Or maybe they read the tabloids she always wound up in.

"If she says she's fine, then she's fine," I barked, coming up to them with a glare that spanned the width of the East River. "The hospital will be a fucking zoo right now with paps waiting to take her picture, and she doesn't need that shit in her life. I can take her if she needs it."

One of the officers stared at me like she wanted to argue, but between my glare and Mere's refusal to even dignify her continued requests with a glance, she gave up.

"Call the number on this card if you need to add any information to the report," one of the cops said, handing me a blue card. "The case number is on it."

I nodded and once again didn't correct the assumption that I was her significant other, or her fucking caretaker, or whatever they were acting like I was.

When I tried to offer the card to Mere, she shook her head. I tucked it into my pocket. "Okay, what happens next?"

"An investigator will be put on it and will likely contact you," he said, finally turning to Meredith again. "They'll put together a case, and give you all the information about what happens next. If we pick up the other guy, you'll have to identify him."

She stiffened at the words, and I put an arm around her.

"I'll go with you if it comes down to it." The words were out of my mouth before I could rein them in, but the grateful look in her eyes calmed my nerves. I glanced back at the cop. "So, we don't have to do anything else?"

"Not unless she remembers something, or you have to take her to the hospital," the cop repeated. "Other than that, someone will get in touch with you."

I nodded and stepped back, pulling her with me. She didn't say a word, not even to drop some sass bombs about how quickly they'd put her in the role of "helpless woman" and me in the role of "dude worth talking to." I hadn't spent a lot of time around her, but I knew enough about her personality to identify this silence as atypical.

It wasn't until Stavros had whisked us away in his dark Lincoln, did she clear her throat.

"Sorry. About all of that."

Stavros looked in the rearview mirror, frowning but not speaking.

"What are you sorry for?" In my head, the question was incredulous, but out loud, it sounded sarcastic. Fuck, why couldn't I communicate like other people? "There's nothing to apologize for."

"I acted like a fragile flower. Let you do all the talking." She licked her lips, glancing out the window with her brow furrowed and red mouth turned down in an unhappy frown. "I'm not like this. I'm not helpless. I'm—"

"You knocked the fuck out of your attacker and made him bleed with bare knuckles, ma. I know you're not a princess."

Stavros's gaze shot up to the mirror again. "No shit?" he asked, a smile in his voice.

"Dead-ass," I confirmed. "She's tough."

Stavros nodded his approval before fixing his attention on the road again, navigating to her mansion on the Upper West Side. I squinted out into the darkness before realizing Meredith was watching me again. And, fuck, she was so pretty like this. Not smirking or taunting or challenging me to some weird sexual duel. Pensive and quiet, her hair pulled back and shadows crossing her high cheekbones and delicate nose.

I swallowed hard. "You sure you're fine?"

"I'm fine," she said softly. "Thank you."

There was more to say, namely apologizing for claiming to be her boyfriend and taking charge of the situation like a dickhead, which was likely why she'd gotten the impression I thought she was helpless. However, that wasn't a convo I wanted to have in front of Stavros.

I let her hold my hand until he parked in front of her home. She mumbled a thank-you to Stavros, pressed a fold of bills into his hand, and then stood out on the sidewalk with her arms wrapped around herself.

"Call me tomorrow, kid," he said to me. "I have a weird feeling about how all that went down."

"Yeah, me too."

I jerked my head in a goodbye, shut the door, and turned to her after he'd driven off. She was staring at the mansion like she'd never seen it before, which gave me an opportunity to do the same since I really hadn't. Stephanie had gone on and on about the prewar row house and how shocking it was that a seven-bedroom mansion was tucked away on a normal New York City street, but her description hadn't prepared me for the reality. It had a limestone front, gold-and-black doors, and was at least four or five stories high. What really struck me, though, was how old it appeared to be. It was serious old-timey New York shit.

"Kinda ridiculous, right?"

Meredith was giving me that look again, uncertain and shy. The one that made me want to press her up against that big black-and-gold door and kiss her until she forgot this shitty night.

"This entire night is ridiculous," I said.

"I meant my house."

Frowning, I asked, "How do you figure?"

"Well, it's gigantic, and I literally live here by myself since my mother moved to the Hamptons to get drunk in closer proximity to a beach. You probably think—"

"Stop." I paused, trying to temper my sharpness. "Look, don't do that, okay? I'm not stressed over your money. I'm fine with my status.

No need to fall all over yourself insulting your house and your job and your family to make me feel like I can relate to you."

She cocked her head, one brow going up. "So, you're saying you can relate to me in some way?"

"Fuck no."

Meredith released a choked laugh. "Why do I like you so much? You're such an asshole."

I shrugged, grabbed her forearm, and tugged her toward the house. "Because I'm sexy."

"And super modest too."

Snorting, I tried to haul her to the door, but as soon as we got closer, she froze. It was like her feet had become rooted to the ground. When I flicked my eyes to Mere, I saw that her face had gone ashen.

"What?" I demanded.

"I . . ."

I turned, putting my body between her and the door. For the second time, I cupped the sides of her face and stared into those huge blue eyes. She seemed fucking *terrified.*

"What is it, Meredith? Tell me."

"The guy—" Her throat worked as she swallowed, breath coming faster. "Fuck, Tonya. He—he knew me. He was there, not just to case the event, but . . . he knew *me.*"

"Explain. Tell me everything."

Her eyes flit around us as if she was expecting someone to come out of the shadows. "I'd blanked it out or something. Fuck, how did I not tell them?" she babbled. "It just came back to me, the guy, the one who ran away. He said—he said, 'I've been following you since Ninety-first. Gotta love a rich dyke who still takes the train.'"

Holy fucking shit. This definitely was not a random case of two opportunists wanting to rob the recognizable socialite at the heavily promoted pop-up event. Nah, this was about her being a Stone. About her working for QFindr. It was related to the doxing.

"I'll call that number on the card," I said. "And your brother can come over—"

"No," she said quickly. "Please, no. I don't want to see anyone right now."

"Meredith, I can't leave you here alone—"

"I don't want to be here! They know where I live, Tonya." Panic seeped into her voice. She clutched me tighter. "Can't I go home with you? Please?"

"To Queens?" I asked incredulously. "You could get a hotel—"

"Please just let me come with you. *Please.*"

She looked so absolutely desperate that it broke my heart. I smoothed hair out of her face again, and all my prickly parts retracted when she leaned into the touch. Goddamn, but this girl was starved for affection. Even from a pissed-off former Marine who'd spent the past year pretending she didn't exist.

"I don't live alone," I warned. "I share a place with Angel."

"I know."

Of course she did.

Meredith went quiet after that, and this time it was me who grabbed her hand. We walked without speaking to catch the B train near Central Park, and sat on the old wooden bench on the platform in grim silence until the train screeched into the station. We huddled together by the door until we could switch to the F train at Rockefeller Center.

The trains were emptier than usual but nowhere near deserted. So when we sat together on the colorful seats as we rode into Queens, we got some attention. My legs were sprawled in front of me, white dress shirt partially undone, and I was slumped down with one arm extended behind Meredith. By now, I'd draped my suit jacket around her shoulders, and she was turned toward me, face pressed against my chest and long hair hiding her profile. She'd taken off her high heels at some point, and they were in the seat beside her.

I upgraded my Subway Glare to an I'll Fuck You Up glare, but didn't actually say anything when I caught a girl with a rainbow tote snapping a picture on her phone. If I was going to trust anyone to not sell us out to a magazine, it'd be someone repping the rainbow flag. Maybe she just thought we were a cute couple.

We kinda were.

CHAPTER
FOUR

The station at Sutphin Boulevard and Hillside Avenue was basically never quiet. People were always hanging out at the store or walking up and down toward the LIRR or Jamaica Avenue. I glanced at Meredith, wondering if she'd ever come to this side of the river, and raised an eyebrow at how the bustle relaxed her.

Instead of turning inward, she stood up straighter and was looking around curiously. Now that we were away from Manhattan, the Mere I'd come to know was once again making an appearance.

"If you think I'm showing you around the neighborhood, you're wrong."

She shifted closer to me, a smile playing on her lips. "Aw, come on. What kind of boyfriend doesn't give the grand tour?"

Discomfort clenched my chest. I cleared my throat. "Yeah, so, about that . . ."

"It's fine, Tonya," she said quickly. "I know you were just saying whatever to get them off your back. I'm kidding."

She looked a little mortified that I hadn't reacted well to her coyness, but I never reacted well to it. Ever. Instead of answering, I grabbed her hand again.

"Okay, so, a tour." I jerked my chin to our left. "Over there we got Popeyes and the liquor store, which is hilariously called Ho's."

Meredith snickered. "My kinda place."

"You calling yourself a ho?"

Those slim shoulders rose. "I own whatever bullshit labels people sling at me just because I like to fuck."

Damn, no wonder she and Steph were homegirls. Smirking, I nodded across the street as we walked. "Over there is Maloney's, which is a decent bar. Pretty much the only bar I'll fuck with."

"The only bar at all?" she asked, eyeballing the dive. "You don't ever go anywhere else?"

"I don't like crowds, or music, or dancing people."

Meredith shook her head, another tiny smile on her face, and kept looking at the bar. Maybe she was wondering if we should go in and have a drink, but I'd have to tap out on that one. Now that the adrenaline had run its course, I was drained. The comedown from a rush tended to be brutal.

"T-Bone," someone hollered from the front of Maloney's. "Who's the blonde?"

I squinted into the darkness just enough to make out a couple of older dudes who'd been kicking it in that exact same spot since I was in high school. I was pretty sure they were bus drivers and worked a late shift, but they always had some extra shit to say to me.

"Too hot and young for you," I shouted back.

He yelled something back in Spanish, a pretty crude description of what I should do to Mere once I got her home, and I flipped him off. I couldn't stand people.

"Sometimes I wish I was fucking invisible," I muttered, and walked faster, dragging her behind me. "Hurry up."

"Why? He's just talking shit."

I looked at her, surprised. "You understood what he said?"

Meredith gave me a haughty look and tossed her hair. "He said to enjoy eating my pussy. I frankly think it's a great idea."

Good God, she was a trip. Shaking my head, and trying not to smile, I finished my half-assed tour by pointing out the civil court house taking up the majority of the block across from my building, and hiked the four flights upstairs. She jogged up in her heels as if she were rocking Jordans. Her legs were probably ridiculously strong. I fantasized for a hot minute about them wrapping around me, before unlocking my apartment door to another unwelcome sight.

I stood framed in the door with Mere behind me, looking over my shoulder. Picking up on my downturn in mood, she tensed and put her hands on my shoulders. I stiffened, and she squeezed.

Angel was standing in the living room with a tall, broad dude who had always reminded me of Aaron Hernandez—in looks and temperament. Victor Quinones was Stephanie's bad-ass little brother, and had terrorized the neighborhood for our entire adolescence. The number of times he and Raymond had beaten the fuck out of each other while Stephanie stood there hysterical and trying in vain to pull them apart had to be in the dozens. Just the sight of him, even when he turned to me with a calmer and steadier expression than I'd ever seen on his scarred face, turned my stomach.

My lip curled. I looked at Angel. "Why's he here?"

Angel had the decency to look abashed as he ran a big hand through his dark-blond hair, but then his gaze fell on Meredith. When she walked around me to slip into the apartment while casting nervous looks back at the shadowy hallway, his eyes went wide. "What the fuck? Are you okay?"

Her hands instantly went up to the red marks on her neck. "Yes. Sorry. I was robbed by some homophobic stalkers at an event where T happened to be working. I'll go if I'm—"

"You're not going anywhere." My voice came out in that low aggressive rumble again, but I couldn't help it. Not with Victor standing in my house for unknown reasons. If I had fur, it would all be standing on end as I tried to make myself look big enough to take on this bastard. "My room is down the hall. Bathroom is across from it. Borrow anything you want."

Meredith hesitated, but the relief slumped her shoulders. "Thanks."

I nodded and watched her walk to the bedroom. When I realized Victor's big brown eyes had also dropped to her ass and legs, I stepped forward.

"When did you get back from Chicago?"

"Today." His voice was different. In the past, he'd spoken every word like a challenge. Even the most innocuous ones had been laced with some low-key disrespect. But now, he seemed . . . soft-spoken. He had his hands in the pockets of his sweatpants, and there was no sign of the former drug dealing, thieving motherfucker who Steph had shipped off to live in Illinois with their uncle three years ago. "I finished Job Corps."

"Good for you. Why didn't you get a job back in Chicago?"

"Because I wanted to be here. With my sister."

I stared at him incredulously, but Angel interjected quickly. "It's just for a few days, T-Bone. Stephanie asked if it was okay."

The anger slid from me as quickly as it had arrived. I wasn't about to help his dumbass without Steph's consent. After giving him another ill once-over, and Angel a narrow-eyed *we'll talk later* stare, I went down the hall. Meredith wasn't in my room, but I heard the water running in the bathroom across the hall. Thankfully, Angel was the cleanest dude I'd ever met—like legitimately cringed at the sight of a mess—so I knew everything would be on point.

Which, why did I care, anyway? This wasn't a date. She just didn't want to be alone. And because I'd gone all America Chavez on the scumbag with the undercut, she seemed to be seeking comfort from me. Or protection. Odd, since I was pretty sure if it came down to it, she could protect herself.

Even with that rationale in mind, I looked around my bedroom with critical eyes. I'd been on the lease with Angel for years, but while I was active in the Corps, the apartment had been his to turn into a pretty bomb bachelor oasis. I'd told myself, for the past couple of years, that I would deck out my room to look as fly as his, but all I'd managed was a platform bed and new sheets from Ikea, a full-length mirror that leaned against the wall, and an enormous backlit graffiti pop wall piece of the Puerto Rican and genderqueer flags wrapped together. Michael Rodriguez, Raymond's brother, had given it to me for my twenty-first birthday—basically proving that Rodriguez peeps were the best peeps on Earth.

Bad-ass art aside, there was nothing else in the room. Not even a TV. I couldn't tell if it looked all cool and minimalist, or if Meredith would take one look at my room and think I was some kind of psycho for having zero possessions.

Shaking my head, I stripped off my clothes, tossing the suit in the laundry basket shoved into my closet, left my chest binder on, and threw on a white ribbed tank and pair of basketball shorts. I needed a shower, but I wasn't about to wander around in a fucking towel while Victor's ass was hanging around.

My door opened, and Meredith walked in wearing a pair of my old silkies—the green booty shorts Marines had once worn during PT—and a black tank top. It was too small for her, so her breasts were straining against the stretchy fabric.

"Really?" I asked, not hiding the way I was looking her up and down. "Really, Meredith?"

"What?" She tossed her clothes in a careless pile by the window and tied her hair back in a loose ponytail. "You said I could borrow something."

"You're a walking thirst trap."

A gleam shone in her eyes, but she just rolled her shoulders and moved closer to my bed. Her hair still reached almost to her ass. When she walked, the tip swung like a pendulum right at the small of her back. She was clearly trying to hypnotize me into bad decisions.

"It's disgustingly hot, and you're surviving on fans. It was this or the boob tape and thong I was wearing under my dress. Your choice, T."

The other option sounded pretty damn great.

"I don't know how people wear thongs," I said, sitting at the head of the bed with my legs sprawled in front of me. "I could barely stand those fucking silkies. I felt like my ass was out."

"There's nothing else I could wear under that dress that wouldn't show." Despite all her brash talk, Meredith lingered at the edge of the bed like a nervous cat before climbing in beside me. She extended her long legs and crossed them at the ankles. "I thought you were taller than me."

I shot her an incredulous look. "How? You're tall as fuck."

"I dunno. You just... seem bigger than you are? Like your presence or something." A flush rose up her neck, spreading onto her cheeks. So pretty and kissable, I had to ball my hands in the sheet to keep from putting my hands on her. "Look, these are the things I think about."

"My presence?"

"Yes." She inched closer to me and rested her head on my shoulder. "I told you, there's something about you. Even before the dressing room incident, I was kind of obsessed."

She smelled like heaven and her skin was silk under my callused hands. She probably needed the kind of gentle treatment I couldn't give, but she was panting for it anyway. When I sank my teeth into the side of her neck and slid my arm around her front, fingers sliding down into her underwear, she moaned so loud everyone in the studio likely heard the throaty sound.

"I want you so bad," she whispered. "You don't understand how much you turn me on."

I licked the place I'd bitten, hoping there would be a mark, and rubbed her clit faster. My fingers circled that spot as she trembled, and I pressed myself against her back tighter when the heat between her thighs grew slicker.

"Don't stop," she said, a desperate edge working into her voice. "Make me come."

"Then get on the table. And spread your legs."

"We should call your brother. And the number on that card."

Meredith sighed. "Can't I just be here with you without involving other people?"

"Yes, but you need to report that this is connected to the harassment, and you also need to tell your brother to give the rest of the staff a heads-up that there are people stalking employees with the intent to harm them."

"Oh fuck."

Meredith was crawling to the edge of the bed in an instant, and reaching for the phone in her bag as she leaned forward on her hands and knees. The hem of the silkies rode up, showing the curve of her ass. I wanted to press my face against it, lick her every single place that mattered, then shove my tongue deep into her.

Was it normal to be this horny in the middle of an emergency? I legitimately had no frame of reference for this, but my concern about the safety of her and the QFindr staff wasn't taking away from the fact that the sight of her ass in the air had me clenching and wet.

Rubbing my hands over my face, I slid down until I was on my back, and tried to think about something else. Like the fact that two men had tracked Meredith down, and one of them was still out there. That it was starting to look like a hate crime. That the media would turn it all into a circus.

And beyond that, Victor was back in town, staying in my apartment, and giving off the vibes of a reformed dick-bag criminal. I needed to talk to Stephanie about what was going on. The boy had been a total hellion, and their lack of functioning parents had created a situation where she'd been the one in charge of wrangling him. And he'd given her hell.

But on the opposite side of the token, he'd defended her fiercely. They were both pretty ride or die when it came to standing up for each other, even if he'd always done something stupid to bring her nothing but stress.

The apartment was quiet, so maybe he'd gone out with Angel to give me and Meredith some privacy. If they were that thoughtful, I'd be shocked.

"Are you going to tell Dad?"

The way she'd said *Dad* pricked my ears. I sat up, looking down at the long stretch of her body lying flat against my bed with her face turned to the side so she could hold the phone. The relaxation of only a few minutes ago had gone, and she was tight with tension. Without thinking about it, I ran my fingers along her spine, then repeated the motion in a slow caress.

"Yeah, I'm listening," she said haltingly. "I just don't see the point." Another pause, a low sigh, then, "Okay. I'm sorry I didn't call you sooner." There was a longer pause before Meredith said, "I'm in Queens. With Tonya. She's taking good care of me, Caycay."

After a second, Meredith ended the call after a sincere-sounding "I love you too," and tossed the phone onto the floor. She rolled onto her back, and my hand wound up resting against her stomach.

"Is it okay to call you 'she'? I should have asked."

I dragged my fingers along her stomach, pressing down lightly before dragging them up again. She didn't react, but her body was thrumming. "I can go either way."

"No preference at all?" she asked.

"No. I'm good. If I feel disrespected, you know I'd let you know."

Mere nodded slowly, her eyes going hooded. "Right. You'd just walk out of the room and ignore me."

My mouth quirked, but I didn't take the bait. "Following Steph's and Chris's lead is a safe bet in general. I've been friends with Chris since he, Ray, and I were little."

"And Stephanie?" Her tongue swept out, dampening her lower lip. "When did you two get close?"

"Junior high. We used to make out in the locker room at school, and the other girls would watch."

"That's all? Preteen smooches?" she teased, wiggling her eyebrows. "I heard otherwise . . ."

"We used to play around some. Experimenting." Which was partially how Victor had gotten all up in my grill one day about a decade ago. I'd slept at her house after a rough night at my own, and he'd walked in on a hard-core finger-banging session. He'd dragged me out of the bed, accused me of trying to turn his sister into a lesbian, and I'd brawled with him. Then Ray had shown up and had round two. "We always got caught, so we quit it. It was just for fun, anyway."

She nodded slowly, eyes narrowed, and I could almost see what she was thinking. Maybe wondering if Stephanie was my type. Visually, the only thing they had in common was height. She was tall, thin, pale, but with a sun-kissed tan, and had gold hair. Stephanie was tall, curvy, dark-haired, and the same bronze skin as her idiot brother.

"What did Caleb say?"

Mere seemed to snap out of her thoughts, and frowned. "Stavros had already filled him in. My phone was turned down, so I didn't see the million calls Caleb had made to me after we got off the train. He was worried sick, and said we all need to meet ASAP to get a more intense security plan in action." Another of those long pauses, like she was thinking of what to say and how to say it to avoid a response she didn't want. "He was relieved I'm with you."

My brows shot up. "Why's that? He doesn't know me. He barely knows anyone in my area code."

"He knows enough." There was some fire in her when she said that, like she couldn't stand for anyone to even imply anything bad about her brother. "He loves Chris. Like *adores* him."

"The only people who don't adore Chris are the kind of people who hate kittens."

"So, monsters, then," Mere said, choking on a laugh.

"Yeah, pretty much."

"I'm sure he'll love being compared to a kitten."

He'd fucking hate it, but I'd grown up with him acting as my walking, talking Chester Bear, keeping me warm and comforting me even before I'd realized I'd gone cold enough to shatter into splintering pieces.

"What else did Caleb say about me? You're holding back."

Mere ran her tongue over her lower lip. "He suggested I ask if I can stay for the weekend. Here. With you. To lay low until the other guy is caught. He thinks you'll watch out for me."

"'Lay low,'" I repeated. "He used that phrase?"

"Yeah, well, you see, my big bro is kind of a dork."

I smiled. Not even one of my shitty ones. A big smile, one just for her and her dorky brother, because seeing her talk about him was sweeter than I'd expected. And it didn't fit the image I'd crafted in my mind, no matter how many times Stephanie had sung her praises.

"You can stay here and lay low." An image popped into my mind. Early-morning rays of sunlight already suggesting another satanically hot day, my internal alarm clock jolting me awake and finding all those long willowy limbs twined with my sinewy ones. Her hair everywhere, our sweat causing skin to slide together. Her breasts pressed against my side, because she'd undoubtedly curl into me and I always slept on my back. "I'll sleep on the pullout in the living room."

"Isn't that guy sleeping in there?"

I cast a baleful glare at the door. Fucking Victor.

"I've slept on worse places than my own floor."

"Floor?" Meredith stared at me, astonished. "T, are you that scared of my pussy?"

Choking on another startled laugh, I shoved one of her knees.

"Well, if you're not scared, then we're sharing this bed." She raised her eyebrows in a challenge, but it wasn't that coy taunting shit again. It was more like a dare to come up with a rational suggestion. An impossible request. Everything that sprung to mind, including leaving my own apartment to sleep at Ray and David's, was ridiculous, since I was supposed to be . . . taking care of her. An idea that made me feel things I seriously had no business feeling, considering the massive brush-off I'd given her not five hours ago.

"I have a suggestion."

"This should be stunning," I said dryly.

"You bet your sweet ass it is." She extended her legs, and the silkies slid further up her thighs. "How about this—we fuck right now, get it out of our system, and then we move on?"

The glance I gave her was mean. I knew it even before she flinched and looked away, temporarily flailing in rejection.

"Is that how it usually works for you?" I asked. "Fuck someone enough times to quench your thirst and move on?"

"Well, T, not all of us can move on after a little finger fuck. Some of us aren't machines."

My ego rose up, ready to fight. I leaned closer, and put a hand on her thigh. My fingers brushed the inside, soft skin over sleek muscle.

"A 'little finger fuck,' huh? You gushed all down your thighs and all over my hand, ma. I could smell you on me for the whole train ride home."

Meredith swallowed hard, but didn't look away. She wet her lips again, a nervous gesture more than one meant to tempt me, but it did anyway. Now that it was all in the air, that the memories were rushing back in full video instead of sporadic bursts, I couldn't stop thinking of things I'd do to her if I gave in. If I tried to "get her out of my system."

"If you think I came hard from your fingers," she said softly, looking at me from under her lashes, "imagine how wet I'd get from your tongue."

CHAPTER
FIVE

The words hung in the air like a magic spell, slowly infiltrating my armor and seeping into every pore until the wick on my desire ignited. I shifted on the bed, half straddling her legs as I finally allowed myself to blatantly feast on her body. She was showing a lot of smooth tanned skin, but there was still so much I hadn't seen.

Her nipples. Her belly button. The *stay nasty* tattoo an ex-boyfriend had told a tabloid she had on her pelvis. The glistening pink between her lower lips.

Mere started to speak, probably to say something obnoxious that would obliterate the humidity of our combined lust, so I pressed the rough tip of my index finger against her mouth. She exhaled against it, her breath warm and damp, and shivered when I moved the digit lower. Increasing the pressure, I dragged my finger down her chin, along her throat, and to the collar of the borrowed tank top. I tugged sharply, just enough to see the tops of her breasts and kept pulling until the deep cuts of the arm openings gathered in the middle to reveal the curved sides.

Meredith shifted under me, already undulating at the slow tease of being exposed, and groaned softly when I hooked my pinkie and thumb in the material on each side. The tank top bunched in the middle of her torso, revealing each breast fully. Her nipples were deliciously hard, protruding out, all waiting to be tasted.

I leaned closer for a lick, got addicted to that one taste, and then sucked hard.

Mere's hand rose to toy with her other nipple, writhing against the air like the stifling heat in the room would give her some relief, but she bit back the sounds straining against her mouth. I could still hear them though—aborted moans and husky sighs.

I surveyed her body again, and my breath came faster. She was flushed all over, and her lips were parted as she gazed up at me with eyes already dilated and wild with lust. She'd slid her legs up the bed and bent them at the knee, spreading wide and offering what she knew I wanted. What she wanted me to touch.

As hungry as I was, I could wait. We could both wait. Getting her out of my system meant I needed to do everything I'd fantasized about in the past year—after every event when we'd shared breathing space, and I'd forced myself to ignore her eye-fucks and heated glares.

Leaving the tank top trapped between her breasts, I slid my hand down to the flimsy green material of her borrowed silkies and gathered them in my fist. They pulled taut, pressing against her sex.

"So wet already." I pulled tighter, eliciting a sharp gasp. "I can see it through the shorts."

"Tonya," she said roughly. "I—"

Whatever she'd been about to say transformed into a loud appreciative moan when I bunched the material of the shorts the way I had her shirt. The crotch bunched between her pussy lips, causing the material to get wetter as I dragged it along her slit.

"Oh fuck." Mere eased onto her back, her hair fanning out as she reached back blindly to grab the foot of the bedframe with one hand. She clutched one of her breasts with the other, running her thumb over her nipple. "God, Tonya."

That voice. That throaty voice all wrecked with lust and saying my name . . . It took a lot not to just shove my face between her thighs and stay awhile. Take my time with that delicious meal. But I didn't. Instead, I dragged the twisted fabric of the silkies along her slit, feeling my lips part and my breath quicken the wetter the fabric got. When they were drenched, along with my fingers, I shoved the fabric to the side and leaned forward.

"Lick me," she pleaded. "Please?"

"Not yet."

"*When?*"

"When you're a complete fucking mess."

Meredith shuddered violently, arching up again, but she went to pieces once I pressed my index and middle finger to her clit. I rubbed them over the little nub, in a slow tease at first, and then faster once she began writhing in earnest. I panted harshly, mouth ajar, looking between her pussy and her face. She'd tilted her head back and was squeezing her breasts, mouth gaping as she tensed up.

"Yeah," I whispered, transfixed by that beautiful face creased in ecstasy. I knelt between her spread thighs and slid two fingers inside of her, pushing them in as far as I could reach while using my other hand to torment her clit, rubbing faster. "You're so hot like this, Meredith. When you're so fucking turned on you can't run your mouth."

She made some sound then, maybe it was supposed to be a word, but it was more like a guttural exclamation. Oh yeah, she was close. Her body jolted and her hands flung out, making to push up, maybe even pull away, but she didn't. Even as her thighs began to tremble like it was too close. Too much.

I flicked my eyes between her sex and her sweat-covered body. The sheen of dampness on her skin caused the *stay nasty* tattoo to gleam in the low lamplight.

"Tonya—" She spilled over my fingers. The shocked cry she released had to be heard on Sutphin Boulevard, but I didn't stop. I kept fingering her, loving the sloppy sound of my fingers in all that wetness, and loving how loud she got. "Oh fuck," she wailed. "Oh my God."

Her thighs clenched together as she returned from that high, and she flopped back against the bed. She sucked in deep breaths, her stomach caving in with each inhale, and lay there like she was dying. Or like she'd died. She only moved again to kick off the soaked silkies. The tank stayed on, but it was twisted around and clinging to her torso and breasts.

I sat back on my haunches, sucking my fingers clean, and watched her from beneath my lashes. She did the same. The crackle between us had me sweating, a trickle down my spine, my shirt sticking to my skin and my basketball shorts damp everywhere but especially between my thighs.

"Can I see the rest of you?" she asked softly.

Without pause, I ripped off my tank top, leaving only my chest binder, and kicked off my shorts, leaving only boxer briefs. I tossed the clothes to the side and looked at her again, smirking at the sight of her parted lips and hungry gaze.

"Your body is so incredible." Mere rolled onto her hands and knees with hair spilling over her shoulders. She crawled over to me like that, chest brushing against the bedding and bare ass in the air, and gently pressed her lips just beneath where my binder stopped on my midriff. After glancing up at me, she kissed over my abs. "Just like how I imagined."

"How's that?"

"Strong," she whispered against my navel. "Lean and muscular." She put her hands on me, dragging her fingernails down my sides, over my hips, and then massaged my thighs. "God, your thighs are so hot. You're fucking perfect."

Mere was being so worshipful and adoring that my stomach flipped, then tightened into a knot. I grabbed the front of the tank top and dragged her up for a kiss. There was no hiding how hungry I was for her, the breathless moan I released as soon as her tongue was in my mouth, or the way my heart pounded out of my chest. And she just melted against me, arms draped over my shoulders as I explored her mouth. It went on until I had to rip away for a breath, and by then my body was raging. Hot and clenching with need, my own sex so fucking wet I was tempted to touch myself.

Instead, I sat on the floor, my back against the side of the bed, and tilted my head back so I could look up at her.

"Turn around and ride my face."

Mere's cheeks went bright red, but she hurried into the position as her breathing once again picked up. Within seconds, she was on her hands and knees, and faced away with her slicked folds positioned over my face.

From this angle, I could see everything. The hairless hood of her sex, the shiny pink of her labia and the glistening skin inside. The smell of her was what sent one of my hands into my own underwear while I clamped the other onto her thigh. I pressed my index finger to my clit just as I jerked her down so her pussy was against my open mouth.

She tasted as perfect as I thought she would. Tangy and delicious, something I could survive on for a lifetime if I had a choice between it and anything else. I dragged my tongue between her lips, giving her a slow tease of what was to come, and rubbed myself faster when the tremors started in her thighs.

"Fuck, Tonya."

Apparently, that was her new favorite phrase. She said it over and over as I worked on her, sucking her clit into my mouth, then tracing designs over it with my tongue. She writhed on me when I circled her clit with the tip, released a sound like a sob when I did it repeatedly, then clenched up when I opened my mouth over every exposed surface of wet flesh to suck again.

Meredith dropped to her forearms, appearing unable to support herself on shaking hands. The sounds that came out of her made zero sense—a combination of wild cries and incomprehensible pleas. A few times she jolted away from me, but I yanked her back. I was too greedy to give her a break just yet.

She started grinding her pussy against my mouth, zero shame as she rolled those hips and rode my face. The sound of me eating her filled the room again, and I rubbed my clit faster. If I'd thought ahead, planned this better, I'd have brought a clit stimulator to keep me company, something to buzz just right as I lapped her up. I hadn't though, so I settled for my own fingers, and was already on the edge.

"Lick my clit," she pleaded. "Fuck, please. Please, baby."

I obeyed, mostly because I knew that tone. It was the same tone she'd had on that dressing room table, the precursor to her coming all over herself.

Mere slipped down lower on the bed, her torso crushed in the messy sheets and her ass held up just enough to keep from smothering me. A high-pitched keen filled the room, and I jerked my fingers out of my underwear so I could have both hands on her. I slapped one ass cheek, then pulled them apart, licking her with the thick flat of my tongue before going for broke with another firm suck.

She cried out sharply, saying my name over and over, and arched away from me. She came on my mouth and chin, and nearly went into convulsions when I shoved my tongue into her hole one last time for good measure.

I drew away, licking my lips and smirking. She was fucking wrecked. Face pressed into the mattress, body heaving as she panted, and clutching at the wreckage of the bedding. Thinking she was done, I pulled myself on the bed beside her to finish on my own, but Mere looked at me through her hair.

And holy hell. That look. Half-deferential and half-accusatory. One hundred percent sexy.

My smirk widened.

Mere sat up, wobbling a little, and turned to me. I didn't move, sitting with my back to the headboard and my legs once again sprawled in front of me, wondering what she would do.

My girl didn't disappoint.

She straddled me, yanked my hair back so she could lick her own wetness from my face, and reached down to slide her finger over the top of my underwear. I was already on the cusp of an orgasm just from having had her pussy in my mouth. When she crooked her fingers up inside me and rapidly fucked them in and out as her thumb flicked over my clit, I stood no chance.

I came with a hiss and a low swear, arching my back and closing my eyes as she kissed the base of my throat. My hips jerked up, stomach cramping from the force of it, and my toes curled in the sheet.

Mere slipped her fingers out of me, but kept kissing me, both of us a mess of bodily fluids. I tangled my fingers in her hair, unable to pull away, and kissed her harder. Like if I could jam my tongue farther into her mouth, I'd be closer to having her out of my system.

When she finally broke away to suck in a breath, and I leaned in to follow that mouth before it could go too far, it was clear that she wasn't.

CHAPTER
SIX

I woke up covered in sweat and aching from hunger pains.

It took me a minute to catalog everything that was going on in my bed. Sheets were a total mess beneath me, everything was damp, and there was a tall, beautiful blonde clinging to me. I was on my back, and she was tucked up against my side with one thigh thrown over my front and locked around one of my legs. Her hand was resting on my stomach, and her face was shoved against my neck. She was also completely naked. So was I for, that matter. I'd stripped down and removed my binder during round three.

This was usually the part when I wondered what crack I'd smoked to allow another human being to sleep in my bed. It didn't make me nervous, but it made me . . . uncomfortable. The idea of someone being this far in my space, of potentially waking up and catching me unaware, usually put me on edge. It wasn't like I thought a hookup was going to knife me in my sleep, but I presented myself to people a certain way, and I couldn't get myself back together if some random woke up before me. And I didn't like that. The only people I trusted enough to catch me sleeping were the people in my squad.

Except, Mere didn't feel like a random. And she'd seen me in all stages of undress and ruin the night before. We'd fucked three times, then she'd fumbled in the dark for the bottle of water I'd snagged from the kitchen between rounds, and finally collapsed in exhaustion, snoring softly.

I'd honestly expected to lie in the dark as she knocked out, but as soon as I'd closed my eyes, I'd been gone. My body hadn't been that relaxed in a while. Even now, I felt rested. Disgustingly sticky and overheated, but rested. Peaceful.

I lightly ran my hand along the side of her face, smoothing sweaty hair away, and cringed at the dark bruise on her neck. Anger heated my blood, and a red streak of protectiveness boiled it, as I traced the bruise.

"Mmm." Her eyes slid open, dark circles lining them. "Get up?"

"Nah. Go back to bed."

"'Kay."

She dead-ass rolled over and went right back to snoring. Not even quiet this time. I snickered and got out of bed, stretching and cracking my back, before grabbing my towel with the intent to go to the bathroom. I took one last look at her, the rounded globes of her ass, those ridiculously long legs, and had to force myself to leave the room instead of waking her up with my tongue.

The shower helped to clear my head. We'd fucked. A lot. But that had all been an attempt to get each other out of our systems or some bullshit. It hadn't worked, since I was getting turned on just thinking about the way she'd come all over my dick after I'd put on my harness, but that had been the purpose. Even if we'd—or at least I'd—failed.

I dried off, trying to think about whether I'd wake Meredith to call the police department to update them on what she'd remembered, or do it myself, and returned to the room. She was still on her belly, face pressed into my pillow, and still snoring.

After throwing on a jersey and fresh shorts, I padded down the hall in my bare feet. I found Angel and Victor in the living room watching ESPN. They were both so tall that the room felt dwarfed with the added bulk of Victor's muscular tattooed body, but I just jerked my chin at him instead of glaring.

"There's food," Angel said without looking up from the TV. "Victor got egg sandwiches from the bodega."

"Nice. Thanks."

"Got one for your girl too," Victor said in that low rumble. "I'm sure she's starving."

Realistically, I knew they'd heard us fucking. There was no way they hadn't. The apartment wasn't that big, and Meredith was loud. And her loudness had made me get loud, even when I'd described a number of filthy things in increasingly filthy ways. But I'd forgotten Victor was here. Angel had no leg to stand on about sex noise.

Back when he and Stephanie had been screwing on the regular, I'd pretty much heard every thrust. The time she'd first pegged him was ingrained in my brain.

"I'm sure she'll be hungry once she wakes up," I said.

Victor stared at me, I stared back, and Angel watched ESPN.

"I feel like I should shake your hand," Victor said, going for a smile. "Or buy you a cigar."

I snorted. "I'm not talking about this with you."

"You don't have to. I'm just saying. Damn. She must have been really—"

"Shut up, Victor," Angel said, still scowling at whatever was flashing at him from the giant television. "Before you piss us off."

"My bad."

I didn't know what was more shocking. His compliance, or the fact that he complied without a sneer. Whatever had happened in Chicago had changed him. A lot.

I found the egg sandwiches in the kitchen, grabbed two and more water, and returned to my room without any additional convo. Meredith was still asleep, so I ate my sandwich and called the number, filling them in on the knowledge that her attacker had both targeted her and called her a queerphobic slur, and the fact that she was bruised enough to probably warrant a doctor's visit.

The cop told me the case would be assigned to an investigator today, and that Mere should expect a call if they needed her. It sounded a little too dismissive for me, and I couldn't help but wonder whether they'd be making a bigger deal of this if it had been Ashton Townsend who'd been attacked.

Protectiveness reared up again. Where the hell was it coming from? Just yesterday, I'd been annoyed by her presence. Not just annoyed. I'd been infuriated by the constant reminder that this grown-ass woman was going to sulk and pout every time we saw each other just because I hadn't treated her like a queen. I'd hated the entitlement. The expectation that I'd worship her. And the notion that she'd seen me as something to check off her sexual bucket list had gotten me hot in all the wrong ways.

But now . . .

I didn't know. I didn't know *why* there was a *but now*, but there was.

I sat on the edge of the bed next to her and shook her shoulder. "Hey. Wake up."

She moaned again. It sounded so close to one of her little sex sounds that my body reacted to it. Damn, she had me acting like a lust-crazed teenager. My mouth pulled to the side as I walked my fingers up her spine.

"Meredith. Wake up before I shove my fingers in your ass."

Her lips curled up in a wicked smile. "Is that supposed to scare me? I love anal."

"Of course you do."

Her eyes slit open. "Was that judgment?"

"No. A complete lack of surprise."

"Hmmm." Mere eyeballed me for a minute before she rolled onto her back. She was completely unselfconscious about her nudity. "You should get one of those double penetration deals for your harness. I'd lose my fucking mind."

Christ, this woman woke up with filth on the brain. Heat spread through me at the mental image she'd put in my head.

"I thought we were out of each other's systems," I said, shifting on the bed. "We tried pretty hard to make that happen last night."

That cupid's bow mouth turned down, and the wings of her brows snapped together. "You're not serious, are you?"

"Was that not the purpose?"

The sheets crumpled in her fists and that flush climbed her skin. She swung her legs over the side of the bed, looking hurt and mortified.

"Can I use your shower? I'll go after that. I'm not riding the train to Manhattan smelling like sex."

I frowned. "Meredith."

"What?" Her voice was sharp as she fussed with her hair, trying to tie it back in a tangled knot. "Whatever, I'll just call a Lyft."

The combination of her taut back, the bruises, and the hurt in her voice prompted me to grab her hand and tug her back to the bed. I expected her to resist, to sulk and stomp and storm out dramatically, but she didn't. She let me pull her down to the bed beside me, and looked at me with apprehension.

"I said we'd tried to get each other out of our systems. Not that it worked."

Relief slumped her shoulders. She groaned and threw herself back onto the bed, covering her face with her hands. "Holy fuck, T. You've totally bewitched me. I'm not even kidding. I'm like . . . a mess when it comes to you."

Instead of answering, I shoved her sandwich at her. She peeked up at me, then sat up to eat, still naked.

"I know you don't want to hear it," she said around a mouthful of bread, egg, and cheese, "but this isn't just a sexual fixation. The idea of you dismissing me again made me feel like bursting into tears. It was ridiculous. I'm so sprung."

She was watching me closely as she waited for a—likely negative—response. I didn't rise to the occasion. Instead, I traced the bruises on her arms. They were shaped like handprints and fingertips.

"Do you think I'm weird?" she pressed. "Because I like you so much?"

"Yeah."

Mere glared at me. "Well, I think you're weird for not liking me. I'm attractive, smart, I smell good—"

I snorted.

"I'm a good kisser, I'm *amazing* in bed, and I have my own job and house. Also, I'm already friends with a bunch of your friends. I'm such a good catch."

"Are you done campaigning?"

"No. Not until you tell me why you don't like me."

She looked so serious and determined, that I couldn't help another fond smile. She scowled in response, and I leaned in to brush our lips together. Mere immediately hummed and parted her lips for some tongue, and I wasn't strong enough to deny her, although I ended it after only a moment.

"You want honesty?" I asked against her lips.

"Yes. Brutalize me."

Shaking my head, I sat back on the bed. "Fine. I've wanted to fuck you since the QFindr cruise. I thought you were gorgeous and sexy, and I loved that you didn't follow the dress code at those stupid dinners." Mere's brows flew up, but I kept talking. "Usually I'm fine without sex for long periods of time, but I went home and found a blonde chick to screw just to satisfy my craving for you."

"I—" She shook her head slowly, seeming to have trouble coming to grips with this information. "Did it work?"

"Hell no. Not until I got you on that table at the photoshoot, months later. And right after, you pulled that bullshit about bragging to your friends about fucking the Marine."

Mere's face reddened. "I was just being dumb. I didn't know what to say."

"You always have something to say."

"But not to you! I was a disaster, and you were calm and cool and wouldn't even speak to me."

"Because you're not my type," I countered. "You just seemed like some spoiled rich white girl who had nothing in common with me."

Her face was starting to resemble a cherry. "Is that not still the case?"

"Maybe it is, but at least I got to see other sides of you." Pausing, I thought back to the night before and even this morning. "You're way stronger than I assumed you were, brave enough to go through some shit like that and be honest about how scared you were. How you didn't want to be alone. You may think that made you look weak, but I seriously can't stand people who have too much pride to ask for help." She was still giving me that skeptical little pout, so I chucked her chin. "Put it to you like this, ma—I like that you say what you mean. I think you're smart and funny. You don't give a shit about what other people think. You made me smile, for fuck's sake, so, yeah, safe to say I like you better now than I did twenty-four hours ago."

Mere pulled the sheet up to her chest, staring at me from the mess of her tangled hair.

"But if you go back to all of that taunting and cocky shit, and making it obvious that you *expect* people to fall for you, I'm out." I jerked my head at the door. "I don't do well with entitlement or spoiled people. Or people hitting on me just to prove they can fuck the tough Marine. Because believe it or not—people acting like I'm some alpha soldier conquest fantasy pisses me off more than anything else. And it happens every time I get with someone."

Meredith flinched. "I'm sorry. I had no idea. I was just trying to be cool so you wouldn't realize . . . how much I was feeling you."

"I know that now," I said. "But in that moment, it got under my skin. The reason I've been single for so long is because girls I got with between overseas tours *always* came at me with that vibe. Like I was a check on their bucket list. Or they wanted to act out some weird fantasy or fetish. I'm not here for it."

"I'm really sorry," she insisted. "I swear."

"And I believe you, mamita. I just want to stress that you may not be like anyone else I've been with, but that type of attitude is a dime a bullshit dozen." Mere had begun nodding again, watching me carefully and crumpling the sheet in her hands, so I brushed my fingers against her knee. "You get it?"

"Yes. But . . . why didn't you just say that instead of totally writing me off?"

"Because before last night you were just a piece of ass, and I had zero reasons to explain my thoughts to you."

For a second, I wondered if I'd gone too far, but she'd asked for brutal honesty. I smiled a bit to soften the blow. Or at least tried to make my face look like the face of someone who wasn't deliberately trying to be a dickhead. It must have worked, because Mere leaned in, planting her palms on the mattress and letting the sheet fall to her lap. Her mouth turned up into a little smile, but she bit the side of it, and was so fucking cute that I wanted to devour her. I hadn't been this thirsty for someone in a long time, but I hadn't been pursued this way in a long time either. Most people just wanted me to fuck them so they could brag about it on social media.

"So, am I not just a piece of ass anymore?"

I tilted my forehead against hers. "Yeah, you are. But a more likeable one. One I wouldn't mind taking out for a pizza or something."

"*Out* for a pizza?" Mere made a face. "We could just order one and stay in your bed, and avoid all the annoying people."

"Now you're turning me on with all that antisocial talk."

"I knew being a curmudgeon was the way to your heart." She nudged her nose against mine, grinning and looking ridiculously giddy. "So does that mean we can hang out beyond the parameters of me *laying low* for the weekend? We don't have to tell anybody. It could just be for us . . ."

I knew we'd been leading up to this, but I hesitated. She caught on and squeezed my hand, hopefulness causing her lips to purse and brows to smoosh together. Part of me expected her to get annoyed that I wasn't jumping at the chance, but part of me wondered if we were just caught up in some sex haze.

"I'm not proposing, asshole. I just want to have a Netflix and chill with you. Like, when I'm not traumatized and you're not in protective mode."

The guardedness eased, but before I could respond, I heard a loud knock on the front door. Meredith instantly tensed, and I squeezed her shoulder.

"Could just be Ray or Michael coming to check up. I bet this shit was on the news."

She relaxed, just marginally. "Maybe I should shower."

"Do it. Borrow whatever you want. I'll try not to instantly ruin your clothes this time."

It looked like she wanted to say something dirty judging by the gleam in her eye, but she wrapped herself in the sheet and hurried across the hall. I smacked my cheeks, trying to blink away the aforementioned sex fog that was leading to some kind of bizarre infatuation, and went out into the living room.

Instead of finding my two favorite dudes, I found a white man in a suit. Angel was leaning against the wall in his work uniform, one eyebrow raised and a look of complete dismay on his face, and Victor was dressed for the gym—both a complete contrast to the man in the suit.

Suited Dude's eyes fell on me and did a slow circuit once, then again, before he slowly nodded. Was it approval? Understanding? I had no clue. However, a hint of recognition just about knocked me over the head once I really paid attention to his features. The same silvering pattern at the sides of his light-brown hair, slate-gray eyes, same square jawline . . .

I pointed at him. "Kenneth Stone."

His eyebrows shot up and a smug little smile crossed his face. "Yes."

Angel blinked, unimpressed. "Who?"

"Mere's father," I said. "Though I don't know why he's here or how he got our address."

"I have my sources," Kenneth said, as if that weren't a ridiculous thing to say.

Angel gave me the most dead-eyed stare he could muster. "I'm going to work. Call me if you need anything."

He took off carrying his utility belt, and then it was just me, the man Mere apparently liked to compare to Robert Durst, and fucking Victor. Victor leaned against the counter with his arms over his chest and stared Kenneth down. My first instinct was to think he was being nosy, but his stance read as wary.

Huh.

"Your daughter's in the shower," I said. "But I'm curious as to why you came all the way to South Jamaica instead of sending a car for her."

"Because I didn't come to talk to my daughter. I came to talk to you."

Shit, was this the part where it turned into some weird standoff, and he told me to keep my callused military hands off his bespoke kid? I scowled, squaring off.

"Why?"

"Because I saw the surveillance footage of you taking down my daughter's attacker, and it intrigued me. I looked into your background and saw you're a decorated Marine. Recently left the military and went to work for Redline Security—a rather shitty company that is more fit for mall security than personal body guards. I'm not sure what my son was thinking when he hired them." Kenneth paused, letting that sink in, then added calmly, "I wasn't sure what someone as competent and talented as you was thinking when you went to work for them."

"I was thinking that I needed to work," I said sharply. "Why is any of this relevant to you?"

Kenneth looked me over again. He clasped his hands in front of him. "Because I want to offer you a job."

CHAPTER
SEVEN

Victor snapped to attention before I did. Mainly because I couldn't do much more than eyeball Kenneth in extreme skepticism. He smiled at me, the tiniest upturn of his mouth, almost as though he liked my wariness.

"What kind of job?" Victor asked.

"Security." Kenneth didn't look away from me, not even to take in the small apartment or to glance at the hallway in an attempt to locate his daughter. The daughter who'd been attacked only hours ago. "In the past couple of decades, I've put together a strong security team made up of the best in the industry. Former military, intelligence agents, private military professionals, and so on. I handpick them, contract them with full benefits, and pay higher than anyone in the industry."

"How much do you pay?" Victor piped up, as if anyone was talking to him. "I just finished security training and certification in Job Corps, and average pay for a guard is pretty fucki—damn low. Like thirteen bucks an hour when you start out."

"Depending on experience, you could earn upward of six figures a year. For someone with less experience, I would still pay double what you just quoted."

Victor's eyes bugged out of his head, but I continued to survey Kenneth coolly. It wasn't unheard of for the mega wealthy to want their own team of private guards—one of my Marine buddies was currently making seventy bucks an hour working for a movie star. And from my own research about the Stone family, research done after Meredith had refused to leave both my daydreams and late-night fantasies, Kenneth Stone was worth about ten billion. He could afford to spend a couple mil on security.

"How big is your team?"

Kenneth's little smile grew, and for half a second he reminded me of Meredith when she was being knowing and cocky. He liked that I was asking questions. I was performing as he'd expected and wanted.

"I employ ten full-time guards. More during events."

"What kind of trouble do you anticipate getting into with an army of personal security guards?"

"I don't anticipate trouble. The purpose of my team is to circumvent it with risk management and threat assessment for me and my executives." There was a slight pause and finally, Kenneth glanced around as if searching for someone else. "And my family as needed."

Ah-hah. I wondered how long he'd known about the doxing, if he was familiar with the lawsuit QFindr was currently pursuing against their former IT manager for making private information public, and whether Caleb had turned down Kenneth's offer for additional protection and gone with Redline instead.

And now I wondered, given the actual attack on Meredith, if the situation had changed. Were they accepting Daddy's help? I sure as fuck would. The very idea of sending Meredith home without constant surveillance . . .

"If you already employ ten guards, why are you looking for more?" I crossed my arms over my chest. "Adding to your stable for a specific reason?"

"I think you know the reason."

"I'm gonna go out on a limb and assume the threats against QFindr staff," I said.

"Specifically, against my three children."

I didn't know what to make of a man who sounded like he was swallowing something sour while acknowledging his three grown children but was still planning to spend several hundred thousand dollars to protect them. I'd picked up on Mere's animosity for the guy the night before, just by the way she'd mumbled the word *dad*, so there was clearly more to this story than a father wanting to protect his spawn.

"What else do you know about me?" I asked. "Did you do a full background check?"

"Not as thorough as I'll do if you end up accepting my offer."

"You know I'm queer, then?"

"I know you've slept with my daughter in the middle of a photoshoot, if I go by the rumors," Kenneth said flatly. "I know your social media says you are genderqueer."

He said *genderqueer* like Donald Trump said *Latino*. As if it was a word he'd never heard of and was having trouble pronouncing. My lip ticked up, but I smoothed my expression again.

"And you're willing to hire a genderqueer Latinx person who has 'slept' with your daughter?" I asked, going full asshole with air quotes.

"Why wouldn't I?" he demanded, an edge working into his tone.

"Because I'm willing to bet the rest of your team is full of white cis hetero bros with military tats. The kind of douchebags who drop racial slurs like it's a normal part of conversation, and who have zero problems profiling."

Across the room, Victor smirked as the smugness fled Kenneth's expression.

"I understand why you'd make such an assumption, but you're wrong."

"I guess we'll see," I said. "Although I'm still confused as to why you'd come here to talk to me. Just because I whooped some fuckboy's ass on a surveillance video?"

"And because my daughter, who inherited my tendency to trust no one and make myself vulnerable to even fewer people than that, sought protection from you. And you took care of her."

Ah-hah. Maybe he'd been talking to Caleb. I had no other ideas as to how Kenneth Stone would know Mere had been with me or that I had "taken care of her." The phrase dug far beneath my skin. It was fucking infantilizing.

"Meredith can take care of herself," I said sharply. "If you saw the video, then you know that."

"I know she can fight, but she isn't a trained professional." Kenneth slid his hands into his pockets. "And who knows what else may be coming."

The words sent a chill running up my spine. He was right. Maybe nothing else would come of this, but it was equally possible that this attack against a well-known queer person would embolden others. All it took was one strike for the masses to team up and lash out, especially if Mere's attack became a media circus and her would-be robbers were crucified. Which, if I went by the air of vengeance coming off Kenneth, he'd bribe whoever he had to in order to make sure they were. Who knew how many other homophobes and stalkers would crawl out of the woodwork?

"I can't be Meredith's guard," I said finally.

"Why?"

Because it was a conflict of interest. I wanted to potentially date her, not fucking work for her. Technically, I'd be working for Kenneth, but it was still too close for my comfort. Not to mention how personally invested I was in her well-being. The next time someone put a hand on her, I was liable to rip their throats out, not just knock them out and wait for an arrest.

"What's going on?"

Meredith's voice jolted me. I looked over my shoulder to see her standing in the archway coming from the hall, wearing a pair of my basketball shorts and a ribbed tank top. Her long mass of hair was wet from the shower, and her makeup-less face made her look younger.

I swung my gaze from her to Kenneth, and did not miss the way he zeroed in on the bruises on her neck and arms. There was the briefest flaring of his nostrils before he smoothed his expression once again.

"You need to go to the hospital," Kenneth said briskly. "Even if your injuries aren't severe, there needs to be a record—"

"Okay, I already planned on doing that today, but what were you talking to Tonya about?" Meredith walked farther into the room, distrust etched into every line of her lovely face. "And why can't you call before randomly showing up to someone's house?"

Kenneth's cheek clenched. "I apologize if I interrupted."

Meredith's jaw dropped.

"I wanted to check in on you. I've already spoken to your brother this morning. He's increasing the security at QFindr, and plans to meet with the rest of the staff about the details we discussed over the phone."

"Why would he discuss—" A realization dawned, and Meredith huffed out a slow breath. "Let me guess, your security guys will be shadowing us?"

He inclined his head. "Do you take issue with that? You always got along with the team. You would bring them dessert whenever we went out to dinner."

"That was years ago," she muttered, still stink-eyeing him. "But no, I actually don't have a problem with that for now, as long as I don't have to go back to that enormous mansion alone."

Huh. Shocker. I'd expected her to scream and stomp her feet about being assigned a guard by the infamous Kenneth Stone. Who she seemed to hate.

"So, why were you talking to Tonya?"

Victor looked from me to Meredith to Kenneth, and he was so into this fucking soap opera. I wanted to kick him out, but I had a feeling he'd push back on my request, and I wasn't going to argue with him in front of these people.

"He offered me a job with his security team."

Meredith's mouth tightened at the sides. "Okay, so you told him you're not interested, right?"

The pause that stretched out had the capacity to ruin moods, days, and potential future dates. I ran my tongue along the inside of my lip, weighing my words and watching storm clouds gather over her blonde head.

"Right?" she pressed.

"Let's talk about it later," I said. "Without an audience."

For the second time, Meredith's jaw dropped.

Kenneth slid his hand from his pocket and extended a business card. It was glossy and embossed, most likely bearing all the appropriate contact information for the devil, but I took it. Even with Meredith seething beside me.

"Can I get one of those too?"

Any other time, I would have smacked Victor in his big head. Now? I was a little grateful for the seemingly random request.

"I don't have a military background like Maldonado," he said, deep voice louder than necessary in the small room. "But I'm certified."

"A lot of people are certified," Kenneth said.

"Yeah, but a lot of people haven't lived shoulder-to-shoulder with cold-blooded criminals." Victor raised his eyebrows, unapologetic and showing the brashness I'd come to recognize in his youth. "I have. I know how they think."

I was fully expecting Kenneth to dead-eye him and walk out the apartment door without a backward glance, but he extended another of his Satan cards. Then he walked out the door.

"Tonya, can we talk? Please."

Dragging my gaze away from Victor, and wondering whether he'd stuck around because of some sixth sense for cash opportunities, I focused on Meredith and realized she was pissed. Whether her ire was directed at me or her dad, I didn't know, but I nodded.

"I'm taking off," Victor said. "I'll be back tonight."

"Thanks for the update on your daily agenda."

He scoffed at me and left, dressed for a day of nothing useful in Nike slides, shorts, and a sleeveless shirt. I wondered what the fuck he even did with his time besides encroach on my conversations with billionaires.

"You're not really going to work for my dad," Meredith said as soon as the door shut. "Please tell me you took his card just to be polite."

I walked around the bar into the kitchen and put the card on the counter. It glared up at me, gleaming under the fluorescent lights. Frowning, I flicked the light off so there was nothing but the bright morning sun streaming into the apartment.

"Tonya." Meredith's voice rose the more impatient she got. She stalked me into the kitchen and moved closer until she had me backed against the counter. "Can you please answer?"

"I don't have an answer for you."

"How? *Why?*"

I leaned against the counter, elbows on the edge. "Because this is the industry I want to work in, and what he's describing sounds like the type of move that would never happen for me at Redline."

"You don't know anything about his security team," she insisted. "You're considering this after a five minute convo?"

"I'll consider it more seriously after I do some research. And you said yourself—the guys he has on the team aren't bad. Coming from you, that's glowing praise."

Her face flushed red, nostrils flaring the way his had a few moments ago. "He's a dick," she gritted out. "And has spent most of his life ignoring my existence. I do not want him in my business."

"That makes him a bad father. Not a bad boss."

I'd known it would be the coldest take even before she gave me the most appalled and betrayed look she could muster. I made to put a hand on her shoulder, but she shrugged me off and took a big step backward.

"Meredith—"

"I'm gonna go."

She abruptly turned, wet hair nearly slapping me in the face, and stalked back toward my bedroom. I followed close behind, irritation sweeping me as I watched indignation gather in her shoulders.

"I thought you were staying for the weekend."

"I was, but now I'm not."

"Thanks, Meredith, but that was obvious," I said flatly. "Where are you going?"

"To Caleb's or Aiden's houses. Or Ashton."

"That's fine, but are you only going because of the tantrum you're having, or did something come up while you were getting dressed?"

Meredith froze with her back to me, then she sucked in a breath so deep it was almost like she'd just been under water. She turned, eyes blue slits and finger jabbing at my chest.

"Don't talk down to me. I'm not having a tantrum. I'm upset."

"You stomped out of the room because you didn't like what I had to say." I pushed her finger away. "That's a tantrum."

"I walked away because I had nothing positive to say to you in that moment, and I'd rather remove myself from the situation than tell you off." Mere ran her hand through her damp hair, squeezing. "What you said was—"

"It was true."

"No, it was fucked up. And heartless. My parents suck. I was invisible. I still am unless my mom needs a drinking buddy and can't cougar her way into a suitable date. And my dad? Forget it. He only acknowledges me on a holiday. Until I apparently get hurt. You have no *clue* what I've dealt with when it comes to my parents."

"And you have no clue what I went through with mine," I replied, keeping my voice even despite my desire to snap at her. "Because we've only been on speaking terms for about fifteen hours, and there was no reason for me to start dropping bombs about my homophobic mother who encouraged me to move out at sixteen so she wouldn't have to deal with the shame of having a dyke daughter, or the way my father would challenge me to fights since I wanted to 'act like a man.'"

Meredith blanched. Her hand came up to her throat before shooting back down to her side. "I'm sorry."

"I don't need you to be sorry. My point is that we don't know a thing about each other. We've fucked a few times, but we've never been out together. For all I know, we won't know each other in a few months." There it was, that harshness. I could feel every sharp edge of the words taking shape in my mouth, but I couldn't soften them. Because they were true. "Look, ma, I like you, I do, but—"

Meredith put up both hands this time. "Just stop."

I grabbed her forearm and pulled her closer to me. "Let me talk, okay? I'm not writing you off, but I am trying to be real." Apprehension colored every inch of her face. Or maybe that was the heat already steaming up my room as the fan ineffectually swished above us. "Unless you tell me that he abused you and your brothers, or your mother, or that he is corrupt and a fucking monster, why should I not even consider an opportunity to double my current salary with decent benefits? He'd be paying me to look after you or your brothers. Or Chris, who might also be on the shit list since he took the white supremacist dude's spot. And he doesn't have a billionaire family to have his back."

Meredith closed her eyes and took a long deep breath, then another. By the time she looked at me again, I was starting to wonder if she was having a fucking asthma attack.

"You're right," she said. "You should consider it. We barely know each other."

It sounded shittier coming from her. They were my words, but I hadn't meant them the way they now sounded. "Is this a deal breaker for us getting to know each other better?"

"I don't know." Meredith knelt to gather her belongings from last night, cringing at the dress and heels. "Would it matter if I said it was?"

"Wow, can you not do this?"

"It's a reasonable question." She stood up, dress bunched in her arms. "There's no point in me answering you if it wouldn't make a difference. Your mind is set, and I don't know whether mine is as well."

Holy shit, this was driving me up the wall. I brought my hands to my face, rubbing my palms over my eyes to prevent myself from saying something else harsh. This was why I was single. Why I infrequently slept with people a few times, maybe went on a couple of dates, and started from scratch all over again. I didn't know how to deal with someone else's expectations of me when I was still unsure of what I wanted from myself. How could I make my choices based on a person who might not even be around next week?

The room got very still around us until I could hear nothing but my creaky ceiling fan and music playing somewhere down the block. Meredith wet her lips, shifting from bare foot to bare foot. Her nerves were setting in again, and she was practically twitching under my serious stare.

"Do you need me to call you a Lyft?" I asked.

She looked down. "I can do it, but it'd be nice if you lent me some shoes."

"I can do that."

Meredith turned away, mumbling about finding her phone, and I stared at her back, wondering whether this was really our first and last morning in my bedroom.

CHAPTER
EIGHT

"I thought you were shacking up with Meredith for the weekend." I sent Chris a withering glare from where he stood by the counter in Raymond and David's kitchen. It was a tradition that when we weren't gathered at the Rodriguez house for UFC fight nights, we came on alternating weeks for Sunday dinner. Typically it was the usual crew—me, Steph, Angel, Chris, and Ray and David—but this week Michael and Nunzio had showed up as well.

"Can we not talk about Meredith?" I asked around a mouthful of pork chop. "I just want to gorge on all this food in silence."

"Why? Did you run her off already?"

Angel released a long-suffering sigh. "Chris, man, you never shut up."

"I don't," Chris agreed. "That's why y'all kept me around this long. Comic relief."

"I bet Jace and Aiden like you for a lot more than comic relief," Nunzio said, winking from where he was dishing out the bomb carbonara he'd made. He and Michael had teamed up to make an Italian/PR meal that made no sense but was fucking delicious. "I heard there were some other reasons why they're trying to get you to move in two weeks after polying up . . ."

"My winning smile and tendency to make breakfast?"

"I was thinking more along the lines of a big di—"

Michael covered his husband's mouth with his hand. "Please don't. I don't want to hear about their sex lives."

Raymond snorted into his plate. "Says the dude who used to fuck on the couch while I was home."

They all bantered back and forth, so I kept eating my food, chugging beer, and avoiding Stephanie's increasingly pointed stares. I knew she and Mere regularly Snapped and texted, and I *knew* she'd heard the story. Or some version of the story. But unlike Chris—

"No, but for real, what'd you do to Meredith?"

I slammed my beer down. "Damn, you're like a dog with a bone, Christopher. I didn't do shit to that girl. What, did she go crying to her brother?"

"Nah, I pretty much figured you were mean to her for one reason or another." He shrugged unapologetically. "Am I wrong?"

"Yes."

"Okay, then what happened?"

I didn't like his challenging tone or the way everyone was suddenly looking at me with interest. Maybe silently betting with themselves about whether or not Tonya Had Been Mean. If I wanted to be reasonable, I couldn't blame them for the concern. As I'd told Meredith, I had a long history of shitty interactions with girls who'd only wanted a fetishy hookup instead of a date. And when I'd realized they were casting me in a role, or trying to position me in a certain way because of a fantasy, I would cut them off.

Sometimes, I was too harsh about it though. Stephanie had been cautioning me for years about crushing hearts. She'd made the case that I was one of the few out people in our neighborhood, which had brought a lot of attention from young queer girls still figuring their shit out.

But why the hell did I have to put up with being a goddamn test subject? Or an experiment? Or again—an *experience*? It had taken me years to accept my identity, and I was sick and tired of people trying to twist who I was to suit their desires.

It was part of the reason I'd been attracted to Meredith from the first look. Bullshit aside, she clearly knew exactly who she was and what she wanted. I loved that confidence.

Although, apparently I wasn't above being Mean to her either.

Which, what the fuck ever if I had been. I hated how everyone went around expecting me to go out of my way to use kid gloves all the time. It was more efficient to make my point in the bluntest way possible and keep it moving. "Being nice" was bullshit. And everyone expecting me to "be nice" all the time was some misogynistic bullshit.

They didn't stop staring even when I internally ranted for a solid thirty seconds. But when Michael, my big brother from another mother, raised a concerned eyebrow, I broke.

"Her father saw the surveillance video of me going HAM on one of those dick-bags—"

"I saw it too. Was pretty sexy."

Raymond reached out to shove Chris. "Cállate, fuck-face."

He held up his hands.

"*Anyway.*" I rolled my eyes as hard as I could and kept going. "He saw the video, thought I was a badass who had the potential to fit in with his security team, and offered me a job."

Stephanie dabbed her mouth, making it obvious she'd already heard this tale. I scowled at her.

"How much would he pay you?" Michael asked, leaning on his elbows. "Benefits?"

"He said he gives full benefits and someone with my experience could probably make almost a hundred grand. I'm thinking less since I don't have a lot of actual bodyguard experience, but even seventy or eighty is nearly double what I make now." There was a pause, and I shoved a finger at Stephanie. "Your brother copped his card as well."

Again, she just nodded and took a demure little drink of her beer. I snarled at her, and the dimple in her left cheek appeared. Brat.

"That sounds great to me," Raymond said, pushing his plate away and rubbing his stomach. "What's the problem?"

"She hates her father," David guessed.

"Yup," I said. "So she wanted me to not take the job, I said I'd think about it because it was a good opportunity, and she dipped."

A sea of blank faces stared back at me. Well, I'd already bitched to Angel for a solid evening after he'd come home sore and grumpy from a day of climbing poles to fix wires.

"Wait." Nunzio was tempering his words as he usually did, probably trying to see this from multiple angles to figure out why this would be so monumental to Meredith. "Why does she hate him?"

"She said he and her mom ignored her, and she doesn't want him in her business." I slouched in the chair, realized I'd subconsciously mirrored Raymond, and kicked him under the table. "But it's like them ignoring her doesn't stop her from living in their mansion and living off her trust fund, right? Why should it stop me from taking a job I'm interested in that would potentially let me keep an eye on people I care about?"

Michael and Raymond were nodding, but David and Chris cringed.

"Did you . . . say it like that?" David asked carefully. "In those words?"

Defensiveness reared up in a monstrous wave. I could tell I was glaring solely by the way David began to fiddle with his fork, but he held eye contact.

"No, not those words exactly," I said.

He slanted his big brown eyes away. "Uh, well, maybe that wasn't the best route to go."

"What should I have done? Lied to her? Told her I was going to give up a job opportunity for a girl I'd spent *one* night with?" Each word caused the cringes to spread across the room except for Raymond and Michael, who were the best people in Queens. Clearly. "Fine," I growled. "What should I have said?"

"You could have made it about yourself instead of her," Angel said. "Even if it's really about you not thinking shit with her is gonna go anywhere deep, you can just . . . not say it. And talk about what you need."

"Oh, is that what you do when you blow someone off?" Stephanie examined her nails, arched eyebrows somewhere near her hairline. "Interesting."

Angel instantly shut up and closely examined his empty beer bottle. If I was in a better mood, I would have laughed. They'd been sleeping together off and on since the QFindr cruise over a year ago, back when Michael and Nunzio had first gotten engaged, and they couldn't seem to get it together enough to reach the next level.

"Nice try, but I explained what that job could do for my career." I replayed the convo in my head, frowning. "Mostly."

"Who cares?" Raymond asked around a mouthful of pasta he'd snagged from David's plate. "Like you said, is she giving up that dumbass gingerbread house she lives in on the Upper West Side? Or going to get a job that didn't come without family connections, instead of living off nepotism and her asshole parent's money? No. Sooo..."

Stephanie rolled her eyes at him. "You're such a dick just for the sake of being a dick."

"No shit, Sherlock. It's part of my charm."

She glared, and he flipped her off. They were not helping me. Then again, I hadn't asked them to. But now that we were on the subject, I hated that my whole "a job is more important than us sexing" speech might have left her feeling disposable. Or like I hadn't taken her family issues seriously.

If I replayed her words and the way she'd said them, it reminded me of the way she'd lashed out at me following that photoshoot. I could still hear the sound of her voice when she'd accused me of hurting her and pretending she didn't exist. Was this a pattern in her life? People getting something from her, or not, and then forgetting she was alive?

Damn. *Damn.*

I could practically picture her turning in on herself, or maybe having taken a Lyft back to her house to be alone rather than stay with anyone. Licking her physical and metaphorical wounds like holing up in her bedroom with the security system turned on.

I looked at Stephanie. "Did she go home yesterday?"

"I think so. She sent me a Snap, and her bedroom was in the background."

I exhaled through my nose. Just fucking great. The guilt that swarmed me was suffocating in its intensity, but I tried to keep an even expression.

"Change the subject," Michael said finally. "Tonya can bring it up again if she wants to."

Everyone instantly listened, partly because he'd used his teacher voice, but mostly because all of us still kind of looked at him and Nunzio as the dads of our crew. Even when we were all younger, we'd listened to them like they were our authority figures—something I'd desperately needed while spending as much time as possible outside of my own house.

I'd gravitated to Raymond in school, sensing something about him that felt too much like family to ignore, and I'd had the same closeness with Michael (the first person I'd come out to as genderqueer), then Nunzio. Now, as I looked around the kitchen after they went right back to making fun of each other (Michael threatening to cut off Raymond's ridiculously long hair and David glaring at him; Stephanie pointedly ignoring Angel, who was poking her; and Chris grinning into his phone as Nunzio peered over his shoulder), I wondered if we'd all gravitated to each other and had instantly felt so close to each other because of our queerness. Well, Angel was straight, but he was the most stone-faced ally you'd ever ask for. Ride-or-die hetero.

Contentment briefly soothed my frayed nerves and worries, but it didn't last. I walked home alone after Angel lingered around to talk to Stephanie, and tried to go to sleep in my overheated room. It was truly sweltering even after ten, and the fan and open windows produced nothing more than a hot breeze.

I tossed and turned restlessly, overly conscious of the fact that I'd yet to change my sheets and that I could still smell Meredith on them, and wound up turned on and irritated at midnight. Getting off to thoughts of someone I'd potentially hurt wasn't really revving my engine, and neither was the idea of watching porn. Lesbian porn tended to be fucking tragic on all the free websites, so I usually went with my imagination. And images of Mere.

Fuck.

Now that I was actively trying not to think about her, I couldn't think of anything else. And I didn't know why. Sure, she was beautiful, smart, and funny when not being a diva, but . . . weren't a lot of other people? Why was she the one keeping me up at night and haunting my dirty dreams for a year now? Why did I always end up creeping on her Instagram or checking up on her relationship status?

And more importantly: why did it kill me that I'd never get to figure all of that out? For a hot minute on Saturday morning, I'd been excited about the idea of dating her. Something I hadn't done with someone I had actual interest in for year. Maybe since before my service. And now that excitement was gone, and I was once again tossing and turning in my bed. Alone.

Monday morning started with a massive email from Kenneth Stone's lawyer, which included a boilerplate contract and a line about them being open to negotiation. Reading it, especially pre-coffee, was like reading an ancient language.

I forwarded it to Chris so he could get feedback from Aiden, who apparently sent it to the QFindr lawyer Clive, and I got a curtly bulleted email about the pros and cons of the contract.

The pros were relating to the fact that there was a clear-cut explanation about how overtime was paid, a hefty benefits package that required me to pay zip with no deductible, and no morality clause. The details about health insurance alone were enough for goose bumps to spread all over my body. I knew it was likely because I could potentially be injured while guarding Kenneth's old pasty ass, but Redline's benefits package wouldn't even cover a trip to my PCP until I paid six thousand bucks.

The cons weren't that bad either. There was a nondisclosure agreement I had to sign that Clive found questionable if I observed any illegal activities; he wanted more specifics on expectations relating to overnight service and travel; and he thought I should be higher on the salary schedule due to my extensive military service.

All in all, it was as good an opportunity as I'd thought.

I wanted it. I wanted it like I'd wanted to re-enlist with the Marines over and over again. The very idea of it made me feel like I had a purpose again. A real shot at doing something I cared about for decent money, and this time close to the people I loved.

But if I signed it right now, I knew my chances with Meredith were out the window. And that ate at me. If I reacted this strongly to losing the chance to get to know her better, who knew how intense things could be if we actually managed to get anywhere.

"Fuck."

I blindly reached for my phone, realized I didn't have Mere's number, and settled for an ineffective Instagram direct message.

Tonya: *How are you doing?*

It was late, and I didn't expect her to respond, but shockingly my phone pinged only a moment later.

Meredith: *I'm okay.*

Tonya: *Why didn't you tell me you went home?*

Meredith: *It's fine. Chester is here. One of the guards on my dad's team.*

Tonya: *He's there 24/7?*

Meredith: *No, they were here in three shifts. I'm starting to feel stupid with all of this manpower being used on me.*

Tonya: *That other guy is still out there though.*

Meredith: *No, he got picked up earlier today.*

Tonya: *For real? That's great. Are you sure it's him?*

Meredith: *Well, I don't know. I'm hoping his friend sold him out, but I have to meet with an investigator tomorrow.*

Tonya: *Want me to come?*

She stopped responding. I wondered if it was because she didn't want to see me or if it was because she did. Not knowing kept me up for the rest of the damn night.

I woke up covered in sweat, sunlight streaming into my face, with the contract on my mind. I was almost positive I'd had a dream about going to the precinct with Meredith to talk to the investigator only to have the damn cop start quizzing me about the contract's clauses.

A quick glance at my phone showed Meredith had never replied, and that it was seven in the morning. I had no jobs assigned today, which wasn't entirely shocking—I guess Redline just saved me for queer events—but I stumbled into the kitchen to find coffee. Instead, I found Victor in a suit. He looked like a gang member about to face a judge.

"Where the hell are you going?"

Victor jerked his thumb at the already-brewed coffeepot. "Stone's office."

I froze with my hand on the handle of the carafe. "You serious?"

"As a fucking heart attack, sis." He jerked at his tie. "Seems too good to be true, but I have nothing to lose, right?"

"Yeah. Especially if you getting a job with him means you getting up off my couch."

Victor smirked. "Go get yourself dressed and come with me. He's just having a preliminary meeting with me, but you're pretty much guaranteed a job if you really want it."

I hesitated and dropped my gaze to the coffeepot. My mind still hadn't made a decision about what to do, which was a pretty big indicator that I was more into Meredith than I'd let myself admit before this weekend. The usual me would have already moved on this, but here I was—dragging my feet. Over a girl. I lived my life pretty much trying to never do shit that would later leave me regretful and full of shoulda-couldas.

Frustration choked me and turned me off everything. Even coffee.

"Let me get dressed," I said finally. "I can at least talk to the guy."

Maybe he'd know which precinct Meredith was at.

CHAPTER
NINE

Compared to Victor's suit, I'd already felt bummy in my too-much-fabric-for-ninety-eight-degrees outfit of jeans and flannel, but I felt like a complete slob once we stepped foot into Stone Capital. It was one thing to abstractly know someone was rich, but it was another to see evidence of it.

The place had marble floors—or at least floors shined to a marble finish—windows with stained glass, giant paintings with golden frames, and all the furniture was plush and velvety. It was also completely silent except for the receptionist. I felt skeptical that real people worked in these opulent conditions. I'd constantly worry about messing something up.

I ran a hand over my hair, glancing around as Victor spoke to the receptionist, and was glad the place seemed so vacant as we were led to a small conference room. It looked like a hotel room but minus a bed and plus a giant wooden table.

"Let me talk to him first," I said once we were sitting side by side. "I'm not staying for long."

Victor shook his head. "You're being dumb."

He was right, but I still glared at him until he resumed his close observation of the room. Back in the day, I'd wonder if he was scoping the place to see what he could steal. Now, I just wondered if he was picturing himself working for a man who had an office like this. I honestly couldn't see it, but Victor had only been back for a few days, and my most vivid memories of him involved violence against my friends, and him hanging out with people who were now sitting in Rikers. As I studied the tattoos climbing up his thick neck, and the face that looked far younger when not gnarled into a glare, I wondered how many of those same friends could have changed for the better had they had the same chance Steph and her uncle had given Victor.

"Stop looking at me," he griped.

I snorted, which was when the door opened. I got to my feet and Victor followed half a beat later. Kenneth entered with a gorgeous woman with mahogany skin and a close-cropped haircut.

"Good morning," he said, looking between us. "This is Shonda, my lifeline."

"His executive assistant," Shonda said, sitting down with a tablet. She was all business in a way I appreciated, and now I wondered if that was why Kenneth had kept smiling and nodding at me during our first meeting. I had the same kind of no-nonsense lack of interest in wasting time with pleasantries. "I only had Quinones down for this meeting."

"I only came to ask Mr. Stone a couple of questions," I said. "If that's okay? I'll set up a separate meeting at another time."

"We can set it up now." Shonda set a small portable keyboard in front of the tablet and clacked at the keys. "I have an opening for—"

"Thanks, but I haven't made a decision on what I want to do yet, so I'd rather wait."

Shonda pursed her lips and said nothing.

Internally cringing at how tacky I was being, I looked over at Kenneth. "Can I have two minutes of your time? Separately?"

He stone-faced me, and I couldn't blame him for it. I'd party crashed hard, and I was making Victor's preliminary meeting about me. Grimacing, I shot Victor a look.

"Sorry, Vic."

He raised his hands, and I had to pick my jaw up off the floor. Yeah, he'd changed.

"Two minutes, Sergeant Maldonado," Kenneth said, and turned to step into the hall. I thought he would lead me to his office or somewhere more discreet, but he simply crossed his arms over his chest. "Speak."

"Do you know which precinct Meredith is meeting the investigator at?"

His head jerked back enough to betray his surprise, but he just as quickly shifted to staring down his pointy nose at me. "That's what you wanted to discuss?"

"That's most of it." Nerves shot through me, spreading beneath my skin, but I held his gaze and kept my chin up. I'd bet he was used to people who feared going toe to toe with a billionaire hedge fund manager in a sharp suit, but that was before he'd faced off with a Maldonado. "She should have someone with her besides a bodyguard. She's tough, but that was scary shit, and she needs support. That doesn't make her weak."

"I didn't say it did."

"You're not saying much of anything." My words were flinging at him, bullets full of bad attitude and impatience, so I tried to dial it back. Put myself in his shoes and think of how I'd react if I were him, and some punk-ass twenty-seven-year-old in ripped-up jeans had stormed my office, interrupted a meeting, and was now demanding answers. If I were him, I'd have thrown my ass out. I rolled my shoulders and adjusted my stance. "I'd be very grateful if you helped me to support Meredith. We'd planned to go together, and I'd like to follow through."

"Why didn't you call her?"

"I don't have her number."

"Even though you—" Kenneth stopped and looked close to clutching his pearls. He cleared his throat. "Is this why you're debating not taking my offer? Because you want to have a relationship with Meredith?"

"Maybe." I looked around, lowering my voice. "And maybe I want you to tell me why I should work for a man who has such a bad relationship with someone I might want a future with."

The condescending down-the-nose stare returned. "If this is your approach to a job—"

"It's not. Trust me on that. But this isn't exactly a normal situation, Stone. You came by my house unexpected to make an offer after I got out of bed with your daughter. And she proceeded to walk the hell out of my apartment like I'd told her I was considering a job as a necrophiliac gravedigger." His lips twitched, and I moved closer, dropping my voice again. "Look, I don't know why you want me on your staff—"

"You're a decorated Marine who served multiple tours in Afghanistan. You earned a Navy and Marine Corps Commendation

Medal for heroism in combat. There were stories about it in the news. And as I said before . . ." He glanced at the door to the conference room before returning his steady stare to me. "Meredith's judgment says a lot about a person."

"So, does that mean I shouldn't take the job because she hates you?"

Judging by the clench of his jaw, Kenneth wasn't used to people coming at him hard and direct. He blinked at me slowly, pursing his lips and then obviously trying to relax his face before speaking again. "My relationship with my children is, to be blunt, fucked. I saw them as miniature versions of me and was frustrated when that turned out not to be the case. It wasn't until very recently that I realized I was wrong." When I continued to watch him, he added, "I don't talk about my family with anyone, let alone strangers, so that should show you how invested I am in acquiring you."

"But why me?" I demanded. "There's a bunch of former Marines looking for a job."

He exhaled through his nose, resembling a pissed-off bull. "After I looked into your background, following my viewing of the surveillance tape, I realized you identified as queer. Then I realized you're connected to my son's . . ." I watched him struggle to describe who Chris was to Aiden, and relished every moment, "my son's other significant other." His nostrils flared again. He didn't have the vocab or the understanding, and I could not help but privately enjoy his struggle even though I appreciated his effort. "I specifically want a set of guards who my children would be comfortable with, so Shonda suggested I look for people who are, as she put it, queer. I took the suggestion in the hopes that Caleb and Meredith would accept my assistance."

"What about Aiden?" I couldn't help but ask. "Don't you want him and his fam to be safe too?"

"Yes, but his husband actually speaks to me. We get along perfectly well."

My eyebrows shot up but instead of asking how the hell he had a good relationship with Jace, of all people, I said, "If you're still looking for new people, there's a guy I work with at Redline who might interest you. Also former military and openly gay. His name is Stavros."

"Thank you for the recommendation, but am I now pursuing him instead of you?"

I shrugged, still torn on the answer, even though the idea of being hired to personally provide protection to people who mattered to me sounded pretty fucking great.

"I'll let you know. Now, *do* you know what precinct she's at?"

I left his office in midtown and practically flew to the R train to Brooklyn. The train came quickly, but I still couldn't seem to get to the precinct fast enough. Realistically, I knew Meredith would be fine. I knew it was entirely possible that she'd glare at me and ask why I'd bothered to show up at all, or maybe even be confused at my mixed signals. But it was also possible that she'd been serious that night, and that she'd actually felt safe with me. Some people didn't value their word, but I'd grown up knowing it was all I had.

After shoving my way through the crowded subway and sprinting up the stairs two at a time, I stripped off my flannel shirt, balled it in my hand, and ran to the station without once stopping for air. I knew it was ridiculous, I was being really extra in a way that was cringeworthy as hell, but I tended to have a sense about these things. Right now that sense was telling me to haul ass so I could see the girl who might someday be my girl.

I stopped in front of the precinct, breathing hard, and looked around. There were cops lingering on the steps, but there were also paparazzi snapping pictures across the street. It wasn't the kind of side show that would have gone down if Ashton had been the one inside giving a statement, and I was glad for it. I had no idea how that kid functioned when there was always a camera up his ass.

I climbed the steps, steeling myself to go into a place that usually put me on edge, and nearly barreled into Meredith as she stepped out. She dropped her purse, eyes going wide, and reared back.

"Holy shit!"

"Sorry," I said quickly, picking up her bag. "My fault."

"No, it's fine." She put a hand to her heart and took a deep breath. "I'm just being ridiculous and jumpy."

"You're not being ridiculous. You have a right to be jumpy."

Meredith's mouth tipped up, and her gaze skated over my sweaty outfit. She wet her lips and looked away, squinting down at the car waiting on the curb. It was a black Lincoln with tinted windows, and I bet one of her dad's people was inside. It was confirmed when she grimaced a little.

"I guess you have a ride," I said dryly. "Sorry. I wanted to be there for you and dropped the ball."

"You didn't. I was the one—" She broke off and glanced at the cops lingering nearby. They had mostly stopped talking, and I wondered if they were actually all up in our business instead of talking about whatever cops talked about. "I was the one who didn't answer you. I was being childish, I know."

"No. Well, maybe."

Meredith smirked and pressed the tips of her fingers against my shoulder. "Gotta love the brutal honesty."

"It's one of my best qualities," I deadpanned.

"I agree." Meredith walked farther down the stairs, hesitated, and grabbed my hand. "Is that invitation to talk still open?"

"Of course."

A giant soundless exhale escaped her, and she beamed like it was Christmas morning. It was so bright and infectious I couldn't help returning her smile, or pulling her to me to brush my lips to her cheek, photographers be damned.

"Your car or my, uh, subway?" I asked in her ear.

"I could ask Chester to drive us to Queens?"

My mouth ticked up. "We can go to your place, Meredith. Unless you don't want to for a reason besides trying to placate me."

"God, I can't get away with shit with you."

She dragged me to the town car and practically threw me into the back. Only when she got in behind me did I notice the bright-yellow, and incredibly thin, dress she was wearing with her big boots.

"Chester, can you take us to South Jamaica?"

Chester glanced in the rearview mirror. He looked at me, seemed confused, and then frowned. "*Where* in South Jamaica?"

"Um . . . wherever the F train stops on Sutphin Boulevard?"

"Just drop us by the civil courthouse on Sutphin," I said. "We can walk from there."

He gave me another skeptical stare, and I knew for damn sure he wasn't going to just let us wander away. Meredith seemed to know too, because her well-formed mouth sank into a frown. I didn't know what part of this was getting to her, but I assumed it was having to be shadowed by someone who already wasn't too thrilled with driving her around. He was also looking at me like I'd just busted into the car thinking it was a dollar cab.

"I thought you said these guys were nice."

She shrugged. "They were when I was little. Now, my father is forcing them to be my chauffeur and they're salty."

In the front seat, Chester rolled his eyes without responding. Either he knew Meredith well enough to know engaging in a petty argument would get him nowhere, or he'd known her long enough to let her comments roll off his back.

"I guess that's why my father is trying to hire more staff." Mere nudged me with her knee. "Anyway, I'm just irritated in general. I do wish you'd been in there with me, because I kept forgetting shit. Maybe they'll talk to you next?"

"Probably. Or we can go back together."

Her hand found mine, fingers sliding together. "They didn't tell me all the details because they're still investigating, but the second guy was picked up at his house in Staten Island."

I scoffed. "Figures."

"I know, right?" Meredith shook her head. "The cop, Detective Henson, didn't say it outright, but I think the guy's friend had to have turned him in, unless they identified him some other way."

"If they tracked him through surveillance cameras to a car or something, they could have. But I know literally nothing about criminal investigations and something like that would probably take longer than two days."

She nodded. "Yeah. But he's in jail. I identified him and gave the investigator all the details. I don't know how long they'll be locked up, because they could get bonded or whatever, but . . . there's an actual investigation and everything, which makes me happy."

I nodded, forcing a smile for her even as my brain sprinted ten steps ahead to a thousand what-if scenarios. What if someone else decided to use that information to target her? What if someone else decided to rob her or her house now that her address had been made public? What if those dude's friends decided to avenge their now-jailed buddies?

What if people decided to lash out at Chris, who'd found the evidence on the guy's laptop? Or Mere's brothers? Or Jace—the dreamy-eyed guy who looked like an anime character?

"Hey, what are you thinking?" Mere leaned in, concern creasing her face. "You got that serious mean mug again."

"Sorry."

"Don't be sorry. I can just tell you're not exactly walking on sunshine at the news."

"That's because I'm a cynic with a huge chip on my shoulder." One glance up front at Chester showed he was driving, eyes on the road, but something about his body language made it clear he was all up in our convo. "How long are you going to have this guy driving you around? I'm sure he was taken off some other kind of duty, right?"

Chester nodded without speaking, and Meredith inclined her head. "Caleb wants all of the QFindr execs to have full-time security until this situation dies down. Right now we have an entire forum of trolls plotting against us, trolls who have our personal information and addresses, and the situation is close to spiraling. So . . ." She looked down, eyelashes shading her eyes. "Caleb and Aiden both agreed that using Dad's team is for the best."

"Do you agree?"

She raised a shoulder slightly. "I guess. I don't like him, but this is for the best, right?"

I watched her cautiously. "You tell me what's best. This is about your life."

Meredith rubbed her thumb over my knuckles as if she was trying to massage the scar tissue away. "I think we should be safe. Especially now. And that my personal feelings about my father aside, utilizing his force is smart. And . . ." She cleared her throat and looked up, meeting my stare. "And I think, if you want to, you should consider that job."

"Why the change of heart?"

"Because I was having a kneejerk reaction, a series of them, without really thinking it through. It's not like you'll be golfing with the man," she said, causing me to snort. "Besides, I'd love it if you were my guard."

"Uh, no. Not gonna happen." I shook my head empathetically. "This isn't a Whitney Houston movie, ma. No blurring the lines at work."

"But we'd get to spend so much time together, plus so much sex."

"Right, plus me being distracted by wanting to fuck you nonstop when I'm not wanting to go homicidal on the next fool who looks at you wrong."

Meredith batted her eyelashes at me. "That was so romantic."

"Yeah, that's as much as you're gonna get from me, so I'm glad it touched your heart."

She laughed, and upfront even Chester snorted. I pulled her in for a half hug, relief fanning out over me in an unfamiliar way. I hadn't been this emotionally invested in a girl in a while. Then again, I hadn't had someone look at me the way Meredith looked at me in a while. She wasn't deterred by my hard-ass exterior, sneers, or cold attempts to drive her off. She somehow bypassed all that in a way that no one else had ever done, or tried to do, before. I didn't know why I was so special to her, or why she was so special to me, but all of this special shit had to lead somewhere good, right?

"I want to kiss you."

"So do it," she said. "Right here in front of Chester." I kissed her forehead, and she scowled. "That's *it*?"

"Until you fully explain your change of heart, yeah."

"Fine. But let's wait until we're at your place." Meredith tilted her head onto my shoulder and curled against me. I was all hard angles, but she acted like I was the most cuddly person in the world. "Unless Angel and Victor are there . . ."

"Shouldn't be."

"Good. We can talk, but then I want makeup sex."

Upfront, Chester sighed. I just laughed.

Thankfully, Angel really wasn't home when we got there. His day tended to depend on cancellations and emergency visits for technician support, and I did not have the mental capacity for an audience. There were few times when I could interact openly without my guard up if there were people watching.

There was a difference between talking to people and talking in a way that ripped me open and left me bare, and I'd never been good at that. Even as a kid, the idea of answering a question when called on in class had fucking paralyzed me. The idea of being wrong, and being ridiculed for being wrong, had been terrifying. Why would I open myself up to that? Why would I open myself up to anyone but people I trusted one hundred percent?

I flipped the locks and tossed my keys on the counter.

"You want anything?"

Meredith shook her head. "Can we go to your room?"

"You sure? It's not the most visually stimulating."

She snorted. "I'm not here for a light show, T."

Shaking my head, I kicked off my shoes by the door and led her to my room. The bed was still unmade, and she hesitated at the foot of it. Her long fingers trailed along the messy sheet, and I wondered if she could remember our night together as vividly as I could.

Judging by the hazy way she looked at me, with her teeth catching on her lower lip, she did.

I grabbed the front of her dress in my hand and tugged her to me, loving how she came with no resistance at all. I loved it even more when she slanted her mouth for me and let my tongue in to play, lashing at her in hot wet strokes as she pressed her body to mine. My hand found its way into her hair, my other one shooting up her dress to clutch her ass, but she did nothing more than hang onto me as I tongued her breathless.

As a teenager, I must have kissed hundreds of girls as I'd claimed my status as one of the few out studs of our high school. Kisses should not have had the ability to power through my body armor and explode through my nerves, but these did. Because these were kisses I'd fantasized about for a fucking year. Even when I'd resented her and hated myself for fixating on her, I'd wanted it so bad.

"What is it about you?" I rasped against her lips. "I've been wanting this since that fucking cruise, and every time I touch you, I just want more and more. And I don't think I'll ever get enough. You have no idea how weird this is for me."

She panted against me, hands sliding up to curve over my shoulders. "What? How ridiculously intense every little touch is between us?"

"Yeah." I jerked her harder against me and flicked my tongue at her lower lip. "That."

Meredith rubbed her breasts against me, undulating like a ridiculously sexy wave. "I think they call it being totally infatuated and in love at first sight. People just don't usually simmer over it for a year the way we did, Sergeant."

My body clenched up at the use of my title, from my abs to my pussy. My fingers became clawed in her soft skin, eyelids lowering.

"Fuck, I like that."

Her lips curled up, gaze full of knowing. "What else would you like, Sergeant Maldonado? You know I'll follow any order."

Damn it, this wasn't what this little jaunt to my apartment was supposed to turn into. We were supposed to be having serious conversations to avoid repeats of earlier bouts of anger and silent treatment, but all I wanted right then was to bend her over and play with her until she came all over that cute little dress. I didn't want her to just say my name. I wanted her to scream it. To sob it. To fall apart while her body opened for me and got wet for me, as she begged her sergeant not to stop.

"Keep the dress on," I whispered. "I want to see how badly I can ruin some more of your clothing."

An actual shiver went through her, and then her eyes opened wide like she'd just had a revelation. "Few people can get me wet from words alone."

"Then you've been screwing the wrong people."

I pushed her down onto the bed, nodding to indicate she should scoot back. She did, which was when I realized she was still wearing her boots. She hadn't taken them off at the door. The picture of her sitting against the headboard with a soft cotton dress up around her waist and old chunky boots still on her feet was something I wanted ingrained in my mind—her looking like a biker someone had forced into an Easter dress.

"You're gorgeous." Her rosy skin turned a deeper shade of pink, and I couldn't help another smile. They weren't so rare around her. "People must tell you that all the time."

"Those people aren't you."

"What's the difference?"

She thudded her head against the headboard. "You only say things when they have an actual meaning. Most people give compliments because they think they're supposed to, or because they want something from the person on the receiving end."

"Bleak," I noted, kneeling on the edge of the bed and inching closer to her. "Maybe I'm saying it because I want to lick your pussy."

"It already belongs to you, Sergeant." One of those cocky smiles appeared, but there was no resenting it, because she knew exactly what to say to set my blood on fire. "Like I said, you could do whatever you want to me. I *want* you to do whatever you want."

I walked my fingers up her legs, watching the way her thighs automatically inched wider apart.

"Funny, because on Saturday it seemed like you'd ghost on me if I did something you didn't want."

Meredith jolted upright just a little, even as I continued my slow investigation of her smooth skin. "Do we need to talk about that now?"

"Yeah. We do."

"Why?" she whined a little, pillowy lower lip pushing out in a charming pout. "Serious conversations are one of the leading causes of vaginal droughts."

I twisted my mouth to the side to avoid laughing, but she caught the motion and winked.

"It's like this." I crawled forward again, not stopping until I was kneeling between her legs and forcing them to remain splayed around me. "I want to touch you. All over. Know every inch of that body you spend so much time shining to a polish. And I can't be that close to you, and know you that thoroughly, when there's a big. Fucking. Problem. Looming just over the horizon of our orgasms."

"Holy shit, a Marine and a poet." Meredith put a hand over her heart, but then flopped to the side in a heap of willowy limbs. "Okay, fine. I'm sorry. I have a tendency to want to skip straight to pretending nothing unfortunate ever happened."

"I get that, and in some cases that's probably okay. For example, if we start dating and I get pissed at you for leaving your hair all up in my drain, I might bitch one time without needing a thorough discussion a few days later."

Meredith put her hands on my hips. "So dating and sleepovers *are* in our future."

"If we can get through this convo, I sure as hell hope so." I leaned in for another quick kiss, because her mouth seriously was irresistible. When she pushed herself against me, parting her lips for a brief hint of tongue, it was a struggle to sit back on my haunches again. "I know it seemed like I took your past with your father lightly, and that was a dick thing to do."

She blinked at me and her hands tightened around me. "I wasn't expecting that."

"Why not? It's true. If someone had ever tried to brush off my shit with my parents and act like it was no big deal, I would have flipped on them."

"Maybe so . . . but it's a different situation. I can admit that." Meredith shrugged and rolled her eyes up to the ceiling. "The stuff with my parents is complicated, but it's not— I don't hate them. I really don't. I just hate how cold they are. But the older I get, the more I realize they don't know any other way to be, so they couldn't even learn from each other when they were together."

I resumed rubbing her thighs, liking the way she almost always shivered just a bit under my palms. For someone who looked so delicate, she enjoyed a bit of roughness. The thought spurred me to press down harder, slide my hands up higher.

"Keep talking," I said softly.

"Stop distracting me," she said with a smile. "A couple of years ago, I realized I'd almost started to become like them. Judgmental and heartless."

"Yeah? What changed?"

"The company I kept." She looked down then, eyelashes shading her big blue eyes. "I spent more time with Oli, Aiden, and Caleb. Then I befriended Jace and reconnected with Ashton. And oh God, Charles and Stephanie. I *love her*. And she calls me out so much, which I need."

I could see that. Easily. My lip curled up at the mental image.

"You never fucked my homegirl, did you?"

"No." Meredith made an offended face, then smiled. "She wouldn't let me."

I couldn't help it—I laughed. For as much as her smug entitled attitude had pissed me off, I loved how honest she was about who she was and what she wanted.

"But anyway, my father—I just hated the idea of him being in my life any kind of way without me choosing it. And then I talked with Stephanie, and she reminded me that he would be in your life. Not mine. And that was your choice. Not mine. And that me putting the weight of my grudge on you wasn't fair."

"Right, so you couldn't figure that shit out yourself?"

Meredith thwacked my side. "Come *on*. I'm just now recovering from being a prima donna asshole. Sometimes I need to be reminded that I'm not the center of the world. Eventually, I'll be better at consistently checking myself." All traces of joking left her expression, and she pushed herself up onto her elbows. "I swear I'll be better."

"I'm sure you will, if you were already trying to improve yourself before meeting me. I'd have some doubts if it was just to get in my pants."

She snorted. "I don't *just* want to get in your pants. I want to get in your bed. And your shower so I can clog it with my hair."

This time I didn't fight my laugh, and I didn't stop myself from leaning in for a longer, slower kiss. One that let me taste every inch of her mouth and draw out soft little sounds that translated to restless shifts of her hips. I kissed down, dragging my lips over her chin before making my way to her throat, all while covering her hands with my own to hold them in place.

"I love the way you touch me, Sergeant Maldonado." Her breath hitched when I eased down, sliding my mouth over her dress and between her breasts. "I used to fantasize about it. Try to figure out how you'd be in bed."

I laced our fingers together and pulled until she was flat on her back, and smiled at her gasp. She bent her knees, causing the dress to slide up her thighs and expose the light-gray underwear she wore beneath.

"And how'd you think I'd be?"

"Just—" She gasped again, louder this time, when I pressed my mouth against her pussy through the thin fabric covering it. "Just like this."

"You haven't seen shit yet, ma."

Her hips lifted, thighs spreading wider. I took the offering and traced every inch of her with the tip of my tongue. The folds hiding her clit and the outline of her lips with the same painstaking slowness. She jutted her hips up again, seeking more, so I gave in just a little by pressing my tongue down harder.

She arched her back, moaning beautifully for me, and I pulled back with a smile. I loved how flushed she got, pink turning to red when she was turned on. Not to mention the way her nipples poked through her dress.

"Don't stop," she said, pleading and firm at once.

"Wasn't planning on it."

I rubbed two fingers over her slit and moved them up and down. Slow, then, at the first hint of dampness through the fabric, I sped up. Another noise tore out of her, a deeper moan. Wanting to hear more, I rubbed faster, teasing her clit on each upward slide.

"Yes," she whispered, breathy and already sounding far gone.

I looked up, expecting her to be watching, but found her head tipped back and her hands busy. She'd yanked the dress up so it had caught near her neck and was toying with her nipples. Rubbing them at the same pace as my fingers. When I moved faster, so did she, and soon she was writhing on the bed and twisting them.

My body throbbed in response, and the sensation intensified once I returned my attention to her sex and realized her light-gray underwear was soaked through.

"I love how wet you get."

I leaned down just enough to touch my lips to the patch of fabric, sucking on everything I could, My body clenched at her taste. I was rewarded with another of those throaty groans, so I pressed her legs up and back until her sweet spot was perfectly displayed and positioned for me to devour. After one last glance up at her—just to see the utter delight of Meredith watching me with keen desperation, biting her lower lip as she gripped one knee to her chest and continued to toy with her breasts with the other—I moved her underwear to the side.

Goddamn, what a sight. She'd opened up for me, and she was drenched, clit swollen. I gave it a light slap with my fingers, and she released a huffed giggle.

"No laughing," I said from between her legs.

"Oh, this is serious business. Yes, you're right."

"Super fucking serious."

I showed how critical this situation was by sliding two of my fingers into her hole and leaning up to latch my mouth on to her nipple.

"*Fuck.*"

Her cry had to have transcended the ceiling and broken through the walls, but she got louder as I steadily slid my fingers in and out, up to the knuckle. With my fingers in deep, my thumb swiping over her clit in a circle, and my lips sucking her nipple into my mouth with pressure that was likely close to painful, her agonized moans turned to ecstatic shouts.

Meredith arched her back, trying to ride my fingers, and clenched around them tight. With a soundless gasp, her body jackknifed up and she came as I kept fucking her, the wet sound of my plunging fingers and rubbing thumb deliciously obscene in the quiet room.

I grinned wickedly when she collapsed on the bed, gasping for breath with her eyes squeezed shut. The cocky part of me expected her to give me a dazed smile, but Meredith's eyes snapped open and she fumbled her way to a sitting position. With slightly uncoordinated determination, she pushed me onto my back and crawled to the edge of the bed.

"Jeans off, Sergeant." She licked her lips, eyes ablaze. "And can I use your harness?"

My stomach flipped and my hands stilled on my belt. "Fuck yeah, you can."

She grinned but kept studying me. "Why'd you look surprised?"

"Because the girls I bring home usually want *me* to fuck *their* brains out and assume I have no interest in getting in return."

"Well, those people live in a narrow world filled with stupidity, stereotypes, and assumptions leading to bad fucking."

"Hey now. My fucking is never bad."

"Uh, duh. But clearly they weren't giving you everything you wanted in return."

Meredith hopped off the bed and removed her dress, tossing it to the side so she was standing in the middle of my bedroom in nothing but underwear that had been reduced to a wet rag, and a bra that looked more lace than solid fabric. She went to my closet, clearly remembering where I stored my harness and assortment of toys from our marathon sex session a few nights before.

There was something indescribably sexy about watching her slide into the harness and adjust it. She bit her lower lip when I began slowly rubbing my clit.

She prowled toward me, cupid's bow lips turned up into a filthy grin, and climbed onto the bed. She caught my legs under the knees, dragging me closer to her, and rocked forward to drag the tip of the dildo along my slit. I watched with rapt fascination, unable to stop myself from jerking my hips closer to her. When she angled the tip to my slicked entrance and slid slowly inside, I fought the urge to close my eyes.

I wanted to see her fuck me, hips flexing forward and hair hanging around her as she moved faster and jerked her hips with more intensity. I loved watching the veiny silicone slide into my pussy and come out coated in my wetness. It wasn't even the act of being penetrated that turned me on so much—it was all those details.

I dropped a hand to my clit again, and rubbed hard. No teasing, no drawing it out, I moved my fingers over my clit so fast that my elbow pinged from the angle.

"You're so beautiful." Meredith was breathing erratically as she fucked in and out of me, sweat trickling down the sides of her face and dampening her hair in the now-humid room. "You said I was wet, but you're making a total mess, baby."

"Oh fuck." My back arched, hips slamming onto the dildo. I grit my teeth, eyebrows hiking up, but kept watching. "Don't stop."

She said something else after that, something dirty and fond, but it was lost to the roar in my ears. A sound exploded out of my throat, half-panicked and half-overwhelmed, and I planted my feet onto the mattress harder. The orgasm hit me so fast, and with so much power, that I couldn't stop crying out. A continuous series of hoarse shouts escaped my mouth, and I didn't stop rubbing myself until the pressure against my swollen clit was almost painful.

I fell back on the bed much the way Meredith had earlier, and finally shut my eyes. It burned to breathe, likely because I'd been holding my breath, and it took a long moment for me to get myself together. She was right—I was a mess. Wet and probably flushed, chest heaving, but I also felt turned inside out from the intensity of my orgasm. In the past, I'd have stumbled out of the bed to get myself together in the bathroom. Now, I just exhaled slowly and blindly reached for her.

"That was really gorgeous," she whispered in my ear, raining kisses all over my face. "Like, the prettiest orgasm I've ever seen."

I shook my head at the absurdity. "There's something wrong with you."

"It's so true. I'm pretty sure I look like I'm in my death throes when I come."

The laugh that burst out of me bordered on hysterical, and I couldn't tamp down on it the way I usually could. My shoulders shook as she cuddled up to me, still trailing kisses all over me.

"Stop making me laugh," I groused, wiping dampness from my eyes with my forearm. "You're ruining my style."

"I ruined your vagina too. Might have to go inspect it later."

"Meredith."

She snickered and pressed her face against my neck. "Okay, I'll stop being goofy. I'm just ridiculously happy right now. And kind of hoping I get to spend the night."

I wrapped an arm around her, tightening her against me. "You absolutely get to spend the night."

"Mmm." Meredith kissed me, gentle at first and then deeper. When our tongues touched, I had to pull back or we'd end up fucking again right now. "You know, if I spend enough nights, Chester could go do whatever Chester usually does since I'd be staying with my bodyguard on the regular."

I swatted her ass. "I'm not going to be *your* bodyguard. It's a conflict of interest."

"Oh?"

"Yes."

"Because you want me to be your . . . girlfriend?"

She'd said it teasingly, but I shrugged. "Maybe."

"'Maybe,' she says." Meredith sighed tragically, but judging from the acceleration of her heartbeat against my sweat-damp chest, those two syllables had made her happier than the orgasms.

"Fine," I said. "I want you to be my girlfriend." Her response was a huge smile, but I kept talking before she could interrupt. "But I'm really not going to be your bodyguard. Seriously, Meredith."

"Okay, I get that." She propped herself up with her face against her hand, still beaming. "But you're going to be *someone's* bodyguard at QFindr. You're taking the job for sure?"

I rolled onto my side so I could fully face her, putting a hand on her hip and stroking it with my thumb. "I'm strongly considering it."

Meredith held my gaze and nodded without a flicker of resentment or bitterness in that lovely face. "If my father's an ass to you, I'll murder him."

Snorting, I smoothed my hand up to the small of her back. "Thanks, but I think I can handle it. I kind of got in his face today, demanded to know why I should work for someone whose own kids can't stand him."

Meredith's jaw dropped. "Are you serious?"

"Uh-huh. I expected him to kick me out on my ass, but he fucking *explained himself to me*. He was obviously pissed off about it, but he said he'd been *wrong* for being a shitty dad." She continued to gape. If we were in a cartoon, her mouth would have slid down to the floor. "He also said the reason he wants to hire me is because his hot assistant, Shonda, suggested maybe folks at QFindr would feel more comfortable having other queer people constantly shadowing them."

"I'm sorry—" Meredith shook her head. "I'm, like, mind blown. He admitted to a fault?"

"Yeah, but considering he hasn't said it to any of you, let's not get too excited. He's still an ass in my book."

"I know. But, Jesus, at least he's aware of it. Wow." Meredith settled onto the bed, eyes still round. "I have to tell Caleb."

I jerked her closer to me. "Later."

A smile curved onto her face again. "Later, huh? Does Sergeant Maldonado want to cuddle?"

"Don't ruin the vibe, Meredith."

"Okay, no vibe ruining, but on one condition."

I waited, watching her make a serious face, and fighting the desire to kiss it off her.

"No calling other women hot."

"Oh my God." I laughed again, burying my face in her neck. "You're ridiculous."

"I will *fight* someone," she said. "With fists."

"Instead of dueling pistols?"

"Exactly."

"No need for all that. You have no competition." I wrapped my arms around her, and she stilled against me, curling against me like she belonged. The fan swooshed above us, stirring the warm air and adding to the drowsiness settling into my bones. My eyes grew heavy, but I didn't fall asleep before saying, "I haven't wanted anyone to be my girlfriend in a while."

"So I'm special," she murmured.

"Special," I confirmed. "And mine."

DERAILED

A FIVE BOROUGHS NOVELLA

CHAPTER ONE
ANGEL

Raymond: *You're really not coming?*

Angel: *Really.*

Raymond: *Wow son. Thanks for leaving a dude high and dry over here*

Angel: *Wtf are we going for anyway? I don't know these people. Why do they want us to be present for their engagement party?*

Raymond: *I know them both, dumbfuck. Caleb is David's ex*

Angel: *Yeah. The one whose nose you broke that one time?*

Raymond: *That was mad long ago*

Angel: *Lmao. Two years is mad long?*

Raymond: *Two and a half.*

Angel: *Uh-huh.*

Raymond: *Anyways . . . and Oli is . . . . . Idk some kinda friend when David is in the right mood for it. Also Tonya's new woman, Meredith, is Caleb's sister*

Angel: *You forgot that one of Chris's new men is Caleb's half brother. What does that make Chris to Caleb?*

Raymond: *Idk . . . what does that make him to Tonya?*

Angel: *Brother-in-law? This is complicated.*

Raymond: *Who gives a fuck. The point is them getting engaged is a big deal round these parts because our whole crew is all intertwined with their whole crew. According to David, we're "basically family"*

Angel: *"According to David." Whipped af.*

Raymond: *You the one watching Stephanie get dressed like a fucking creeper*

I glanced up from my phone to see what Stephanie was doing. Applying a third layer of something on her already flawless skin, and holding up the bottle to her phone's camera where it was propped against her mirror. I hadn't realized she was doing another "get ready with me" recording thing. She put them on Instagram a lot, and I watched them because she was beautiful and the big smile she flashed at the end could bring me to my knees.

Angel: *How am I creepy? She puts the videos on Instagram.*

Raymond: *Yuh . . . for people who want to use the products she uses, cockhead. Not for thirsty cable techs. And now you upgraded to being in her house while staring at her like a pervert*

Angel: *No, I'm not. I'm talking to some jackass who's about to be surrounded by corny rich people at an engagement party by his damn self.*

Raymond: *W/e, I'll get high before we go.*

Angel: *You're a bad friend.*

Raymond: *And you're a dry ass bucket of thirst*

I shoved my phone into my pocket and slumped lower on the couch. Stephanie's furniture consisted of hand-me-downs, but they were comfortable as fuck. I thought about taking a nap while she made herself all shiny, but wound up watching her again.

In the time it had taken me to bitch at Raymond, she'd finished with her face and eyes and was now applying deep-red lipstick. My gaze caught on her mouth, plush and wide, and kissable. When she finished and gave her hair a flip, grinning at her phone, I was still watching.

"Okay, so—" Stephanie broke off when she caught my expression. One of her brows arched up. "Don't be looking at me like that, fresco."

"Like what?"

"You know what." She stood up and brushed bronze-colored powder from her silky robe. "I'm going to get dressed. Are you really wearing jeans and a Yankees T-shirt? You look—" She traced my shoulders and biceps, pursed her lips, and then sighed. "Well, you don't look suited for a fancy engagement party, anyway."

"That's good. Because I'm not going."

I regretted saying it as soon as Stephanie's face fell. Her brows drew together, and genuine disappointment dampened her shine.

"You said you'd go."

"Changed my mind."

"But you said you'd go with *me*." She put her hands on her hips, hurt quickly turning into irritation. "What the fuck, Sharky?"

She always called me Sharky when she was mad. It was an old-ass nickname, one I'd outgrown years ago along with my *Jaws* obsession, and had finally gotten almost everyone to stop calling me. Except her when she was mad. Or Ray when he wanted to be annoying.

"Listen—"

"No, you listen, pendejo. I'm going to be the only one there without a date—"

I looked at her incredulously. "You serious? *All* of our friends will be there. It's not like you're some shrinking violet withering in a fucking corner alone."

"Our friends will be there with their significant others." We stared at each other, me stubbornly silent, and her getting steadily more pissed off, before she waved a hand at me with a suck of her teeth. "Vete p'al carajo—"

She stalked into her room, every step punctuated with a "puñeta" or "coño," but kept the door open. I followed her, freezing in the doorway when I found her in underwear and a bra. The robe was in a puddle at her feet.

"Sorry—"

"You always do this," she said, picking up where we'd left off and jabbing a finger in my face as if she weren't wearing a bra that only covered half of her breasts. I kept my eyes on her face, intently focusing on how her makeup leveled up her already-stunning beauty, instead of how obsessed I tended to be with her nipples. "You say you'll go somewhere with me, out in public, and then you back out at the last minute. What am I, some embarrassment?"

"What? That's fucking ridiculous."

"Oh really?" She put her hands on her hips again, looking like a pissed-off Victoria's Secret model who was about to shove her foot up my ass. "Even before we started fucking, you acted like you couldn't go anywhere alone with me."

"Bullshit," I said, pronouncing each syllable clearly. My voice rose, matching hers, both of us trying to out-mean each other. Business as usual as soon as we'd included sex into the friendship equation. "Made-up bullshit."

"Like the time we were supposed to go to a Knicks game, because my uncle gave me tickets, and you told me to take Chris?"

"I don't like the Knicks."

Her jaw clenched. "Or the time I asked you to drive me to Manhattan in that storm, and I had to beg you to actually *go into the store with me.*"

"It was a sex store."

"*And*? Are you afraid of dildos? You're a bigger dick than any of them, sooo . . ."

Why did she have to be funny even while telling me off? It was awful—I wanted to laugh at an insult aimed at myself. Instead, I crossed my arms over my chest and glared back.

"I wasn't comfortable going into a sex shop with you," I said stubbornly. "And you know why."

"Oh please. Like you were going to *give away the fact* that you were attracted to me? As if I didn't already know?" Stephanie scoffed and rolled her eyes at me so extravagantly, she needed to win a medal in ocular Olympics. "Besides, you wound up watching me fuck myself with that new vibrator the same night, so . . ."

"Yeah, nena. Show me how you use it . . ."

Stephanie met my gaze dead-on, sweat dampened and breathing hard as she stopped fucking herself and let the slicked vibrator remain inside of her. Her lip curled up into a challenging smirk.

"Then show me your dick."

My heart skipped a beat. I palmed myself, squeezing it through denim. She didn't move an inch until I fumbled with my jeans and revealed my hard-on to her in all of its throbbing glory. Her eyes fell half-shut and her lips parted as if she wanted it in her mouth, and I nearly lost my mind.

"Touch it," she whispered. "It's only fair."

My eyes immediately flicked to the side table that contained her stash. She had really good shit, and that vibrator had been our first step to her helping me explore the world of sex toys. We'd spent that entire afternoon and evening flirtatiously teasing each other about trying out some of her stuff until it had gone from teasing to tense, and in the middle of the night something had changed.

After I'd asked why she had such a big collection, she'd mentioned some of them had been gifts from girls she'd fooled around with, but admitted she'd bought most because she loved trying out new things. And because I'd been deliriously turned on by that point, I'd asked her which things.

Cue the object of my desire since high school explaining how hard she could make herself come. I'd stared at her in a silent plea to show me what she was describing. She'd done it without needing me to speak, because she was never afraid of making mistakes or reading a situation wrong the way I was.

I'd already wanted her more than anything, but us getting ourselves off while staring at each other had sealed the deal. There'd been no going back from there. Later, she'd randomly send me a picture of a new toy she'd procured, or I'd send her a Snap of a Fleshlight or prostate massager that I wanted, and we'd hook up to fool around, watching and not usually touching.

Things had changed when we'd started touching. The playfulness had intensified, and by the time we were regularly having sex, it seemed to be all we ever did. Text about fucking, fuck when we saw each other, and then . . . the tension had filled all the spaces around the fucking until there was nothing else but sex and anger. Anger about there only being sex, about me not wanting to tell anyone about the sex, about me never asking her to go anywhere but my bedroom . . . And me never explaining that I was in fucking love with her—had been since high school. The problem was that I knew she wasn't in love with me, and I wasn't down for the level of self-destruction that went along with us pseudo-dating. Which was why we'd stopped sleeping together.

Mostly stopped.

Now, we tried to act like friends. Friends who talked about our mutual interests, our days, the job at the cable company that my entire family assumed I hated even though I loved it, and her frustration over busting her ass as a paralegal without getting a raise in two years. But none of those conversations stopped us from eye-fucking each other while we had them. Or us casually touching each other, finger grazes leaving behind the residue of lust.

"Did you die just now while standing here?" she demanded.

"Unfortunately no, so I still have to hear these dumbass accusations."

"You dramatic asshole. Just forget it, Angel. I should have known better, anyway."

She turned away, dark hair falling over her shoulder to cover her back like a silky curtain, and walked over to her vanity. It was messy with jewelry and makeup, notes written on the mirror in pink lipstick, but it was controlled chaos. Usually, anyway. Now, she seemed irritated by the clutter and shoved things around with jerky movements.

I came up behind her and put my hands on her bared shoulders. "Nena." When she ignored me in favor of hyper-focusing on her bottles of perfume, I squeezed. "Nena, look at me."

Stephanie looked into the mirror, remoteness casting her expression in indifference even though I could see through that mask. When she didn't protest, I eased closer, pressing my chest to her back. Her fingers balled into fists, and she closed her eyes when I gathered her hair to slide it over her shoulder. She was so soft, just like I'd always known she would be, way back in ninth grade when I'd begun hanging out with her and the guys on the regular.

Even then, I'd been infatuated. Obsessed. I'd been quiet around her at first, but had done anything she'd wanted before she'd thought to ask. Grabbed her a seat in the crowded cafeteria, carried her backpack, bought her loosies at the store because I'd looked older, helped her with her Spanish homework because it was all we'd spoken at home for years whereas she and her brother weren't as fluent. Braided her hair while she read our English homework aloud, because she was better at analyzing texts.

And I'd hated her parents for leaving her and Vic all alone. Loved Vic like he was my own brother because it had hurt her to know everyone else loathed him. Hid him in my fucking apartment the night of the shooting, away from both the cops and the shooter. That was when he'd gone from scary-tough-guy Vic to scared-kid Victor who'd agreed to be sent off to Chicago to avoid ending up like his dead best friend.

I would never forget how hard she'd cried at the airport. Not because she would miss him, but because she'd been so relieved. And how she'd told me she loved me for being there when no one else was, for buying the ticket because all her money went to tuition and rent. That moment was etched into my brain even though it wasn't the kind of love I'd wanted from her, but still.

Still.

"Angel."

I blinked away the memories and refocused on her, seeing her half-shut eyes and parted lips, and realizing I'd been caressing her arm with my face pressed into her hair.

"Stephanie." Her name sounded thick in my mouth, padded by a decade's worth of longing. "I'm sorry I always let you down these days. You know I hate being that guy."

She tilted her head back against me, observing, quiet, giving nothing away. "Then apologize."

"I'm so—"

"Without words."

My heart nearly beat out of my chest, slamming into her back, and my dick chubbed up almost instantly. "I thought we weren't fucking around anymore."

"We're not fucking around," she said softly. "You're apologizing, and then I'm going to the party by myself."

My hands slid along her arms, trailing down to settle on her waist. I didn't break eye contact, and didn't move farther, until she turned to face me and pulled me against her. Unspoken permission to touch her body. I leaned in, desperate as always to kiss her, but wasn't surprised when she turned away.

"I'm not redoing my face."

"Harsh," I said, kissing the side of her neck instead. "Considering this is my last chance to kiss you."

"That was your choice."

She wasn't wrong. We'd pushed and pulled each other for the past year, her initiating, then me, her putting a stop to things when it got too intense, then me calling for a finale when my feelings had escalated into jealousy and spiraled out of control. Me eyeballing Raymond for dancing with her on a cruise ship had been a serious red flag that things were getting out of control. I'd dragged her off and fucked her mean and hard until she'd come on my dick, as if that had meant I had any ownership over her. God, I was an idiot. Everything was mortifying in retrospect.

"I want your mouth," I said against her throat. "Come on, nena."

"No." Her voice was losing its cool unaffected factor the wetter my kisses became, openmouthed along her neck, then over her clavicle. "You can kiss something else."

My dick thickened fully, throbbing in my jeans, as she pressed her hands to the top of my head and pushed me down. I gave no resistance, sinking to my knees, and stared up at her as she watched me. I didn't look away when I hooked my fingers on the sides of her skimpy underwear, dragging my fingers along her thighs as I knelt.

When she was standing in front of me with nothing more than her bra, I grabbed her hips and guided her back against the vanity. She took the hint, sitting on the edge, and spread her thighs open with her heels propped against the lower drawers.

I dragged my teeth over my lower lip, while rubbing the inside of her thighs. I wanted to kiss every part of her, from her mouth to her breasts, over her soft stomach, then down to her pussy. Try to make her feel, with my touch, how much I cared about her, even though I always said the wrong thing. Let her know that I wanted her to be with me if she ever decided being with one person was her thing.

But she didn't want all that right now. She wanted an apology, which meant she wanted me to give her an orgasm—something I was actually good at.

I leaned in to kiss the hood of her sex, pressed her lips apart with my thumbs, then kissed her clit. A breath whooshed out above me, and her fingers went into my too-long hair, right before I went full steam ahead from worshipful to flat-out nasty—how she liked it. I tongued her pussy the way I would have done her mouth, until my saliva was everywhere and her clit was swollen.

There was a clink of her bracelets as she ran her fingers through my hair, tugging and clawing through the strands. When she yanked harder, her breath gusting audibly, I began tracing *I'm sorry* against her clit with my tongue. Then I traced *I love you*. By the time I got to the last letter, she was writhing.

"Angel." Her voice went high, and she ground against my face. Her thighs tried to clench together, but I held them apart. "Baby . . ."

I loved it when she called me that, so I thanked her with three fingers in her hole as I made out with her clit, alternating between sucking and licking. I could taste her instead of my own spit now, and I finger-fucked her relentlessly until she went from gripping my hair to leaning back against the mirror with her legs spread wide open.

"I'm gonna come," she panted. "Oh fuck, I'm gonna come so hard."

I lodged my fingers inside of her, crooking them while sucking on her clit.

"Angel—"

She broke off with a loud cry, her hips jolting as she came all over my fingers, giving me even more to lick up. The trifecta of her filthy mouth, her taste, and the feel of her juice all over my hand was enough for my body to rebel against me. My dick was trying to burst out of my jeans, pulsing in a way that meant wet spots, but I didn't touch myself. I'd wait until I was home, and whack it all by my lonesome.

Stephanie whimpered when I slid my fingers out of her and sat back, her eyes squeezed shut. She'd melted against the vanity, legs slack and hanging down as she held herself up with taut arms. She didn't open her eyes until she regained control of her breathing, and until her trembling lips stiffened back into forced indifference.

"How's my face?"

I smirked. "Still on point. I figured you use that extra-strength stuff to prepare for such unexpected emergencies."

A laugh burst out of her, she tried to quell it, and then laughed harder. I joined her, wiping my arm across my mouth and wondering how I'd survive the walk home with her taste in my mouth and her smell all over me.

"You're so dumb," she said, sliding off the dresser.

"Yeah, but am I forgiven?"

Stephanie shrugged, smile fading. "Yes. I was mostly joking about all that. I don't know."

She hadn't been, but she was better at being cold with me when we weren't touching. She always gravitated to affection after we fucked. Something I knew wasn't typical with other people she messed with. A fact that had briefly deluded me into thinking she wanted to be monogamous. Which, she'd made quite clear, she did not. Ever. With anyone.

"Do you ever wonder why we can't get along like normal? Like David and Ray?"

"Or Chris, and his guys? Or Tonya and Mere?" she asked slowly.

"Yeah, but all of them got together during this same hot-ass month. I can count them as our relationship goals after the summer—" I broke off as her eyes widened. Because I was out here telling her I wanted what they all had. With her. "Uh, yeah, let me let you get ready."

"Okay . . ." Stephanie grabbed her robe and put it on, looking away. "I'll see you, Angel."

"Yeah. See you."

After a quick pit stop in her bathroom, I booked it down the stairs of her three-story walk-up like the end of my aborted sentence was chasing me.

CHAPTER TWO
STEPHANIE

I spent over fifty dollars for an Uber from Jamaica Estates to Caleb and Oli's penthouse in the Financial District, and I had no regrets. The idea of taking the hot, crowded subway during rush hour while it was ninety-eight degrees was bad enough, but I knew I wouldn't make it from here to there without a bevy of catcalls that would end with me getting in someone's face. It was not the day to trifle with a Quinones.

My driver, Marcel, rolled up in a shiny black Suburban as if he were picking up an entire entourage, and promptly drove me toward Manhattan in complete silence. He also played a nineties R&B station on Sirius XM, and I wound up relating really hard to Mary J. as we went over the bridge.

Humming turned to singing, and I only realized I was hitting M.J. high notes when I caught Marcel looking at me in the rearview mirror.

"Marcel, have you ever had a lover who acted mad undercover? Because I think Mary knows what she's talking about."

He shrugged and made a seesaw gesture with his hand.

"I hear you, boy," I said, nodding.

The song switched to Fat Joe and Ashanti, a clear omen that I was meant to be in this giant vehicle. I needed to unwind, but nothing helped. Even the blast of arctic air from the vents weren't helping. I could still feel Angel's hands on me, his *mouth* on me. I could still see those green eyes looking up at me as he knelt between my thighs. Feel his fingers digging into my flesh as he got more and more into tasting every inch of me. He'd probably been so hard . . .

I squeezed my thighs together and exhaled slowly. It shouldn't have happened. I was an idiot, and now I was the one sending him confusing signals, which was what I always accused him of doing. He'd say he was cool with being fuck buddies, then hulk out as soon as another person glanced at me twice, then I'd say it was friends with bennies or platonic friendship, right before getting mushy and affectionate. We'd both been going back and forth like this for months, and it was starting to become too much.

We toyed with each other so frequently that I couldn't keep up. It was why he'd recently suggested we stick to platonic friendship. Fat chance of that. And it wasn't even *him* who initiated us fooling around half the time. Earlier, I'd known I was doomed as soon as I'd glanced up in the mirror to catch him watching me. My breath had caught, because he'd been giving me *that look*. The look he gave me when he thought I wasn't watching. The one he'd been giving me since high school. It conveyed a lot more than lust, and it often caused butterflies to explode in my stomach.

I'd known him for ten years, and he could still make me nervous with nothing but a glance. If I was like several of my high school friends, I'd take that as a sign that we were meant to end up having a big Catholic wedding ending with adorable one-quarter Italian, three-quarters Boricua kids popping out right after the honeymoon.

But I didn't, because signs were bullshit, and that was *not* my dream. Even without the wedding and the kids, I wasn't here to get caught up with a guy just because he managed to look like sex in torn-up jeans and a thin gray Yankees tee when he wasn't fronting like he couldn't manage to be around me in a public setting. Getting caught up wasn't my life plan. My goal was to only depend on myself, just like I'd been doing since I was a kid. Focusing on me, and me alone, and not changing things to fit another person, had allowed me to put myself through college, get my own place, and feel successful without anybody's help. At all.

We pulled up in front of the gleaming tower that housed the penthouse, and I could not deny that I felt deliciously fancy. It was a nice change after I'd spent the entire day hunched over my desk at work, making magic by transforming bits and pieces of information into a narrative that would get one of my boss's clients a hard-won O-1 visa. In my heart of hearts, this would be the assignment that showed him I deserved a raise. In the bitter reality, I was going to stay stuck at twenty dollars an hour unless I found another job, which was undesirable since I loved his practice.

"Thank you," I said to Marcel. "I'll give you five stars for not speaking."

He nodded at me. "Thanks. Cheer up."

I slid him a side-eye as I got out of the car. "Don't tell me what to do."

His laugh was cut off by me slamming the door shut. My fancy feeling vanished in the humid night air, and I speed-walked into the building. It wasn't the first time I'd attended one of Caleb and Oli's parties, but I was struck by the glitz every time. Comparatively, it made my large-for-NYC one-bedroom apartment in the Jamaica Estates look like a hovel. This place was . . . unreal. A fantasy. Something I'd never conceived of, let alone wanted. While I loved visiting the world of penthouses or mansions with the Stone kids, I still liked going home to my cozy place above Hillside Avenue.

The doorman nodded at me in greeting as I crossed the lobby, and I checked my reflection in the elevator once the doors closed. I didn't look even remotely as messy as I felt, and my white dress was still unsullied, so I considered it a win.

Taking a deep breath, I stepped out of the elevator and . . . found myself face-to-face with my brother. I went from feeling put together to internally flailing, because I wasn't ready to see Victor this frequently. Or to face the memories that had come rushing back ever since he'd returned from Chicago. My childhood, *our* childhood, had remained safely tucked into the back of my closet for the past several years, but he was forcing me to confront it solely by being in the city.

"What's good, Steph?"

I blinked, looked around, and then went back to staring at him in something that likely resembled panic. He'd been back in town for two weeks, and my stomach still sank every time I saw him, which was why I was keeping my distance. It wasn't that I was avoiding his hulking, muscular, tattooed self—it was more that I casually tried not to speak to him. I'd done enough of that three years ago before forcing him to go to Chicago. Upon his return to New York, I'd begged Angel and Tonya to let him crash for a week until he got a place together. Seeing him was bad enough, but having him in the house with me where we'd inevitably ruminate about our absent parents ... It seemed like a nightmare.

"Why are you here?" I asked, more sharply than I'd intended.

He raised one shoulder. "Meredith invited me."

"... Why?"

Victor snorted. "Trying to suck up to Tonya by being nice to her squad?"

"You're not in her squad," I reminded him. "Only Angel likes you."

"Yeah, because he isn't a dick. Unlike Raymond."

The way he said Raymond's name put me on edge. Even as reformed as Victor claimed to be, with his button-down shirt hiding his gang tats, and his voice a little lower and less confrontational, the aggression poured out of his mouth at the mention of Ray. It took me back to the time when I'd been terrified of them crossing paths, convinced they'd kill each other one day. The hostility he'd had toward Raymond had never made any sense to me. He'd fixated on Ray. Gone out of his way to provoke a guy who'd been my best friend since junior high school. Even now, I didn't get it. Just the mention of Raymond had been enough to set Victor off.

"Don't worry, sis. I'm going." He ran a hand over his hair. "You here with Angel?"

"No," I said sharply. "Why would I be?"

He gave me a weird look. "I dunno. I thought you were hanging out or whatever."

Hanging out or whatever was his awkward brother way of saying he'd thought we were sleeping together.

"We're not in a relationship, if that's what you're implying."

"I'm not implying nothing. I kinda figured you'd end up with a woman by now, to be honest." It was so out of left field that I just stared at him and waited for an explanation. He snorted out a laugh. "You used to get more girls than me."

He was right. Between Tonya in her white ribbed tank tops and baggy jeans, and me with my name chains, gold hoops, and skater outfits, the teenage girls around Kings Park hadn't really stood a chance. Her open queerness had made me feel comfortable coming out about my bisexuality early on. And I couldn't deny that I'd crushed on her for mad long before realizing neither of us were willing to risk our close friendship for sex. Not to mention that she hadn't shared my disdain for monogamy.

"Because I'm flyer than you."

"No doubt. Maybe that's why you fit in so well with this crowd." He glanced over his shoulder, brows twitching together. "You really like these people?"

"They're not bad," I said. "You should give them a chance if you plan to work for Kenneth Stone."

"That's the only reason I showed up." Victor brightened visibly at the mention of his prospective job, and I softened. Sometimes I needed a reminder that he had no reason to change if I kept holding the past against him. Watching him smile shyly at the mention of a real job was a good reminder, and it calmed the part of me that wanted to reject the reality of him standing in front of me. "Caleb is a nice dude. His man too. They introduced me to the other peeps who work for their company, because apparently he's been talking to his father about me doing security at their office."

"I can't believe this is necessary." The memory of Meredith's bruises, of the entire story, chilled me to the bone. It hadn't just been a random robbery—someone had hunted her down. The two guys were apparently sitting in Rikers, and would be for a while after pleading guilty for various crimes, but like Caleb said—who knew who else was out there? It awed me that Caleb exercising his right to release an employee for spewing hate speech on social media had resulted in the exact audience of that hate speech . . . teaming up against them. "That guy Stavros is Mere's guard, right?"

"Yuh. And T-Bone and one of the more senior dudes, Chester, keep an eye on Chris, Aiden, and Jace."

"Caleb and Oli?"

Victor shrugged. "Some dude named Sean."

"What about Clive?"

"The slick-looking lawyer cat? I dunno. Oli mentioned he'd taken off early and seemed pretty mad about it."

I was willing to bet he'd dipped after a run-in with Michael and Nunzio. Three years later, and the guy still wasn't over Michael. It was exactly the kind of life-ruining heartbreak I wanted to avoid. Well, the exact kind of emotional dependency. As put together as Clive looked, the man was broken after losing the man he'd loved. Probably still loved. That would never be me.

"Thanks for the update, Vic. Turns out you're pretty good for gossip."

He snorted. "See you later."

I kissed him on the cheek, and he surprised me by pulling me into a tight bear hug. My throat closed up, and I tensed against him. The last time we'd embraced had been before the gang shit and the fighting and the trouble he'd brought to our door. It'd been during the days when we'd secretly lived alone in our crummy basement apartment, after both our parents had left and never returned. Even the night at the airport, when I'd shipped him off to Chicago, he'd been hard and cold and empty as he turned away with ghosts in his eyes and the world on his shoulders. A shudder went through me at the memory of that awful night, and Victor let me go.

Hugging him back would have been the right thing to do. Or I should have at least explained that it wasn't him who had repulsed me. I was put off by memories of our awful parents and how they'd torn each other apart until drugs had been more important than their own kids. I was disgusted by their relationship because it had been a fucking crime against us both. But I couldn't speak, so I watched him quickly head for the staircase instead of taking the elevator.

This night was not going as planned.

A security guard I didn't recognize allowed me into the penthouse, and I made a beeline for the bar that had been set up in the dining room. It was Caleb and Oli's engagement party, which meant I needed to find them, but first I really needed alcohol. Thankfully, I found Tonya and Raymond camped out in the corner, trying their best to blend into the shadows in the dim lighting. The sight of them being their normal selves grounded me.

"Nice outfits, friends." I sat beside Tonya, gesturing at their sneakers and formal jackets over nonformal shirts. "Did you call each other?"

"We're both just similarly brilliant at fashion," she deadpanned.

Raymond scoffed. "I did call her to ask what she was wearing, though."

More of the heaviness left my shoulders. God, I loved them. Of course they'd have the power to act as my personal life vests when I was close to drowning in confusion and stress. Leaning over to Tonya, I rested my head on her shoulder and waved at the bartender.

"Ketel One on the rocks?"

"Sure thing."

I watched him make the drink, adding a cute little wedge of lime. There was something about his olive complexion, dark eyes, and tall willowy build that reminded me of Charles. I missed our fabulous dancer friend, but he still wasn't back from his contract on a Carnival cruise ship. Things were off when he wasn't around, because he was the happy middle ground between my Queens-ness and Mere's Upper West Side swag. Charles was everywhere and everything. He was also one of the few people I spoke candidly with about my fear of monogamy and putting all my faith in one person. Considering his abusive asshole of a sometimes-boyfriend, Charles always advised me to stick to my guns. He regretted getting in so deep with his boyfriend. Regretted that he had such a hard time walking away.

"So, what's happening?" Tonya asked knowingly once I had my drink. "Stressed?"

"Somewhat. Work is frustrating me, among other things."

She nodded, not taking those serious eyes off me. "Where's your man?"

Oh my fucking God. It never ended.

"He's not my man."

"Angel flat left us," Raymond said. "He's probably home watching ESPN and memorizing stats for his wack fantasy sports shit."

"It's not wack," I protested. "It's actually really interesting. He explained it to me one time."

They both stared at me blandly.

"Shut up."

Raymond snorted and went back to his beer, but Tonya looked at me closer. Somehow, I knew she could tell something had happened. That there was a ripple in the fabric of my unflappable exterior, and Angel was the cause. Well, part of the cause.

"You two doing okay?" she asked shrewdly. "I heard he was at your house."

"Hmm." I took a slow sip, wincing a little, and set the glass down. "Well, he made me come really hard right before I called my Uber, and then I sent him home with an edict that it was the last time we'd fuck around. For real this time."

They both gave me the same identical unimpressed face.

"Don't you two say that shit every third Sunday of the month?" Raymond wondered. "That's how it seems."

"I think it's seasonal," Tonya said. "Every three months they get mad and stop sleeping together, make everything awkward for the crew for a while, and then fall into bed again."

"Or fall into my bathroom," Raymond muttered. "I will never forgive you for desecrating my new sink."

Glaring at them, I took a bigger sip and slammed it down to the make-shift bar. "Well, I'm *so sorry*. Not everyone can meet adorable teachers and fall into domestic bliss with actual houses and refinished bathrooms, *Raymond*. Or . . ." I pointed at Tonya. "Fall for a gorgeous heiress who has spent every day of the past two weeks in your bed instead of at her equally gorgeous mansion."

"What can I say?" Tonya shrugged. "She prefers Queens to the Upper West."

Raymond made an impressed noise, as if this somehow made Meredith cool in his book all of a sudden. I rolled my eyes.

"Regardless, her being a perma resident in your bed is why Angel has been at my place so much. He thinks it's awkward that he can hear how wet she is when you're—"

"Calm yourself, mamita." Tonya's expression had morphed from unimpressed to irritated. "It's not our fault you two are the most complicated people ever. You don't need to start talking shit."

"I know." I drained the glass and set it down again. "I'm sorry. I'm just frustrated and confused."

"Confused about what, though?" Raymond pointed the mouth of his beer bottle at me. "Steph, he's been wanting you for years. You seemed like you finally noticed he's a piece of ass and returned the sentiment. Why's it such a big deal for you two to just get together?"

"Because I don't *get together*. Never have. Never will."

"You'll never . . . get with someone you like? Have sex without cursing each other out because you're both trying to pretend you're not sprung?"

Tonya punched Raymond in the shoulder. "Stop being an ass."

"I'm not." He rubbed his shoulder. "I'm just saying, I don't get it. I'm genuinely confused."

I struggled with how to explain it, but I usually avoided full-on discussions about it. Once you tell someone you'd rather die single than ever depend on another person to keep you happy, or to keep promises, they assume you're pathetic or defeated. Since I wasn't either, those pitying comments led to me wanting to punch them in the face. Also, I hated explaining since it would inevitably lead to me using my shit-show of a family as an example. I generally tried to avoid talking about my past at all costs.

Meredith and Charles had been the first people I'd discussed my relationship aversion with in depth, because they were more like me about sex and dating. But even then, I'd loathed going into too much detail. I wasn't ready to go there with anyone other than my oldest friends. Maybe Jace, because his life had been similar to mine in some ways, but he didn't seem to want to talk about his background either.

Besides that, now Mere was a card-carrying member of Club Monogamy as well.

"It's not him," I said finally. "I mean, we drive each other nuts, but it's because we both want something neither of us will let the other have."

"Yeah, you want to fuck him and casually date while being besties, and he wants to carve his name into your ass," Tonya muttered.

Raymond said nothing, but that was likely because he agreed. Angel being into me had become Angel getting irrationally jealous several times. It was another reason why we'd started fighting. I'd reminded him of what we were and what we weren't, and he'd gotten pissed and bitter before checking himself. It was a cycle I didn't know how to break.

Sometimes I wondered whether we *could* work if we just got out of each other's way. In my weakest moments, when I missed him so much it hurt, I *wished* it could work. Even if it wasn't me. Or who I'd designed myself to be.

There were times when I pretended I trusted other people enough to invest my whole self into a long-term relationship. Those fantasies had even led to me telling my coworkers that I had a vague fiancé after one too many irritating questions about my single status. In this work-fantasy, my fiancé was Angel. I imagined he'd moved into my apartment, that I woke up next to him, watched him fold laundry because he was fucking meticulous, and that we cooked together while the UFC fights played in the background. That we had amazing sex every night. Sometimes in the morning too. That I wasn't afraid of my feelings for him, and that he trusted me not to disregard his. That we were functional.

"Uh-oh!" Chris's voice boomed across the quiet room, jerking me out of my pity party. "What's this?"

I turned on the barstool to see Chris sauntering over to us, looking absolutely adorbs in a dark-purple suit and backward Yankees cap, with his phone in one hand. He set it to record as soon as he slid over to us.

"What's up, QFindr fam? This is ya boy Chris Nasty Mendez doing the rounds at the Stone-Buckley engagement party, and I've just found my whole squad chilling in the cut, acting like they don't know nobody."

"Chris, what the fuck are you doing?" Raymond asked wearily.

"Vlogging. Obviously. As QFindr's newest, and breeziest, IT master, I've assigned myself the role of chronicling all-important QF events. But anyway, let me introduce the faces of last summer's QF promo campaign." Chris aimed the camera at me. "This is my girl Stephanie, looking quite entrancing in some Versace—"

"Chris, this is from Express."

He snorted. "Well, all right, you guys see me out here trying to elevate my homie, and she wants to stay at the mall, but it's cool. Good to be true to yourself."

I covered my face with my hand to muffle a laugh as he turned the camera to Tonya.

"And here we have Sergeant Maldonado, looking sharp in some fresh retros on—"

Tonya snatched his phone.

"Hey!"

"No recording without my permission." She stopped the video and handed it back, not looking anything close to apologetic. "I've deleted all my social media, so why would I want to be recorded live? I'm being discreet for a reason."

"Oh good point. My bad, T-Bone." Chris dragged her into a big hug, grinning when she returned it, and then leaned against the bar. "I'll resume recording later and make sure to do a thorough examination of Raymond's man bun."

"Stay away from my hair, man."

"Nope. Did you know there's a giant poster of you with your hair like that in a conference room at QFindr?" Chris guffawed at Raymond's horrified face. "It's so true. It's the best part of every morning meeting. You looking all cute and mad and like a Tumblr search result."

"I'll break in and vandalize it," Raymond said grimly.

"Bad joke considering the threats they've had," I said. "Just deal with being pretty."

He scowled deeper, and I ruffled his hair.

"I wish things were always this chill." I signaled the bartender for another drink. "Or that Angel would come be chill with us instead of icing himself out."

"He's just a homebody, Steph," Chris said, always the mediator. "It's not even the people here, it's parties in general. Can you remember the last time he went to a party for someone on the block?"

"Well . . . no," I admitted. "Okay, maybe not everything is about him ignoring me. Us."

"It's not. You're just mad self-absorbed." Chris winked. "For real, though. If we ever did something really cool, like a group road trip or a trip to the beach or some outdoors shit, he'd be right there planning every detail with T-Bone. Getting all survival man on us. But shit like this?" Chris waved around the penthouse with the professional lighting and staff, and the guests of honor not even anywhere in sight because there were so many people. "Not his scene. And not the way to get him to kick it with us, since we're forcing our new friends and their fancy-ass lifestyles on him."

. . . And there it was.

I was worried about not changing myself for anyone, including Angel, and yet I was continuously trying to force him into outings and situations that specifically made him uncomfortable or that he wasn't interested in.

"Now I feel like an ass," I muttered. "Maybe I'll call him."

"Leave him alone with ESPN or Discovery Channel for the night," Tonya said. "And go say congratulations to Oli and Caleb before you get drunk."

"Good point." I hopped off the barstool and smoothed down my white dress. "How do I look?"

Raymond flashed a thumbs-up without looking, Tonya nodded her approval, and Chris said, "Would look better if you'd said it was Versace."

I laughed, but it faded as soon as I turned and spotted Angel across the penthouse. I'd just seen him an hour ago, had had his face between my legs an hour ago, and yet the sight of him stopped me in my tracks. He was wearing a black button-down with the sleeves rolled up, and a pair of dark-wash jeans—not exactly formal—but I wanted to drag him into the bathroom by a handful of his dirty-blond hair.

Instead, I smiled and tried to come to terms with the fact that I had it bad.

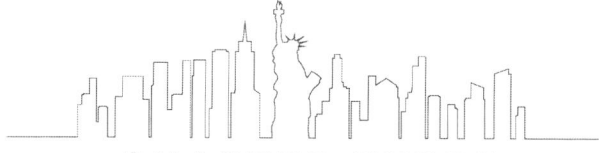

CHAPTER THREE
ANGEL

J ust as I spotted Stephanie, Meredith appeared in front of me. I was always cordial to her, because how could I not be? She and Tonya banged the hell out of each other down the hall every night when they weren't mooning over each other in front of Netflix in the living room. She also always greeted me like a long-lost friend. Kisses on the cheek, a big hug, and a huge smile when I hugged her back.

"You came!"

"Well, how could I not after you laid out an outfit for me?" I asked dryly. "Thanks for the shirt."

"Tonya picked it out." Meredith's voice tended to lower when she said Tonya's name. I couldn't tell if that meant T-Bone's very name was enough to turn her on, or if it was some effect of new relationship giddiness. I wouldn't know, considering I'd never had a relationship last longer than a couple of months. Women I spent time with tended to catch on quick that my feelings were . . . elsewhere. "She has good taste."

"Always has," I agreed. "Where is she?"

"I think she and Ray are holding down the bar, which is awesome." Meredith rolled her shoulders, glancing around the thickening crowd. "I have a feeling I'll need a refuge soon. Playing hostess is tiring. I expected way fewer people. When Oli suggested I invite the whole staff of QFindr, I didn't think they'd all seriously come."

"Guess that means they really like your brothers," I suggested mildly, looking around. "Or they're just here for the food and booze."

Meredith snorted out a laugh. "Maybe both."

Stephanie sidled up to us, eyes locked on me. "Hey."

"Hi there." I slid my hands into the pockets of my pants, acting cool. We played the weirdest games, if that was even what this was anymore. The sex came easily. Everything else? Us shuffling our feet like two school kids at a dance when we weren't pissed at each other. "Where're the grooms-to-be? I brought them a card."

Meredith gave me another of those enormous smiles and a half hug. For a second, I saw Stephanie's face change. A microcentimeter eyebrow raise, dark eyes dropping to Meredith's grasp on me, and she stood up straighter. I ruffled Mere's hair like she was my kid sister, she made a horrified sound and latched on to Steph instead, and everyone relaxed.

Weird. Fucking. Games.

Steph had to know Meredith's interest in me went as far as her interest in Chris—a friend, or something closer to a family member, to people now in her life. And yet Stephanie's first instinct had been territorial. I could see her checking herself now, squeezing Mere and comparing their similar dresses, snickering about Mere's dress being Versace, but . . . I'd seen it. And man oh man, if it didn't pump me the fuck up to know she got those irrational moments of possessiveness too.

"Mere," I said calmly. "Where's Oli and Caleb?"

"Oh sorry. They're upstairs messing with the computer. Apparently a work thing came up." Mere shook her head. "At their fucking engagement party."

"Work never stops." I nodded at her and started to retreat. "I'll catch you—"

"I'll go with you," Stephanie said. "I haven't said congratulations yet."

We turned from Meredith to walk the weird spiral staircase up to the second floor, and I refrained from touching Stephanie.

"You look gorgeous," she noted casually. "As usual."

I snorted. "Thanks."

"You just need to accept that you're a beautiful man and quit scoffing every time someone brings it up."

"I'm not being fake modest. I just know I'm no Raymond."

Stephanie grabbed my wrist, frowning. "You're not. You're Angel. And you're beautiful."

Don't kiss her, León. Don't fucking touch her.

"Thanks, nena."

She smiled, and we found Oli and Caleb hunched over an iMac in a big glass office. Their house was like some shit out of a movie. I couldn't believe it was real, let alone that people I was vaguely acquainted with lived here.

"Knock, knock," I said, looking between them. "I'm not staying long, but I wanted to say congrats and give you a cheap card I picked up from Rite Aid."

Caleb straightened, grinning like someone had brought him a box of treasure, and walked over to shake my hand. I immediately liked him more. Maybe it was old fashioned, and too much of my grandfather in me, but I loved a strong handshake.

"Thank you for coming. I'm so glad to see you."

I nodded, watching as Stephanie hugged him, then gave Oli a half hug as he kept glaring at the screen. "Hello you two," he said, finally spinning away to stand. He looked Stephanie over, then me, one dark brow arched. "I'm not sure I appreciate how many devastatingly sexy couples there are at my engagement party." I opened my mouth to correct him, but Oli kept talking. "Soon-to-be husband, we need uglier friends."

Caleb flushed a little at the title and smoothed the lapels of his jacket down. I immediately noticed a shiny black band on his ring finger. If that was his engagement ring, I liked them even more. "There's no such thing as ugly, darling," he said to Oli. "People just look differently."

Oli gave him a dull look, but I couldn't help a smile. I never got the chance to interact with Caleb much, but I had the feeling he and I would be on the same page about a lot of shit. I had a hard time sitting with the Meres and Jaces and Charleses of the world, hearing about their sex lives in gory detail, but Caleb was all right.

I waved my envelope at him, and he snagged it, beaming. Inside was a card that said: *Congratulations. Shit just got real.*

Caleb's smile widened, and he showed it to Oli, who laughed delightedly.

"Thank you both."

"Oh, that was—" Stephanie halted when I gave her the *I put your name on the card, estúpida* look. "Angel picked it out."

"I was thinking about giving you a $5 Amazon gift card, but times are hard."

"Oh, we didn't want gifts," Caleb said quickly. "No awkward registry or anything. I hate presents."

Oli made a handjob motion. Stephanie winked. "I'll send you a fun link later for a new purchase you can make yourself."

"Oh really." Oli rubbed his chin. "Is it from my favorite store? That sells my favorite machine?"

"Yup. There's a new model." Stephanie's grin turned naughty. "I'm saving up for it."

I looked between them, mystified, but judging by the splotches of color on Caleb's face, they were talking about something sex related. Of course.

"Put it on your registry," Oli advised. "If you two ever decide to make shit get rea—"

Caleb's eyes widened. He laughed awkwardly and abruptly enough for Oli to catch on and clam up. Caleb was definitely my dude. The quiet ones were always the most observant.

"I was joking," Oli said quickly. "I just like teasing them about being together because they're very aesthetically pleasing." He gave us his cat-that-ate-the-canary smile. "And I'll save the fucking-machine talk for later. For when me and Steph and Jace can discuss the pros and cons . . ."

He said other words, but my mind was stuck on *fucking machine*, and now my gaze was stuck on Steph.

I had an absolute obsession with making women come. It was partially why we'd delved into all the sex-toy talk after she'd dragged me into that store. Just listening to the matter-of-fact discussion she'd had with the sales person about intensity of orgasms depending on which type of toy, and which could make her gush, had destroyed me. I'd stared at her, and fantasized about seeing her bring herself to that state, for hours afterward.

Now, I was fantasizing about her and a fucking machine. There were entire porn subcategories dedicated to people being plowed to kingdom come with those things, and as weird as it was, it did it for me. Watching a woman lose her mind as she was fucked relentlessly by a dildo, or even imagining a woman using it on me . . . Not just any woman of course. Just this one.

I cleared my throat and snapped back to reality just as a random dude walked into the room. I had no idea who the hell he was, but he looked like an older and douchier Tom Hardy.

"Scott." Stephanie did a double take, looking between the Hardy look-alike and Oli. "Wow. You two know each other?"

Dirty thoughts were cleared away, and I hyper-focused on the new guy. He was bulkier than me, but strong, and wearing a suit that looked like it'd been tailored just for him. His silver hair was slicked back, and he had on fucking cuff links, but his expression was the picture of awkward. Half-hearted smile as his gaze flicked between us like a panicked animal. This was not a guy who loved small talk.

"Scott DeFrancis is my brother-in-law . . . twice removed?" Oli tilted his head, and I saw the internal trigonometry at having to figure out his own familial relations. "Basically, he's the brother of my sister-in-law. My own brother wants nothing to do with me, but oddly enough his in-laws think I'm great. Very active on the QFindr social media pages."

"Got it." Stephanie was still eyeing Scott like he'd just wandered in off the street. Then she glanced at me, but she had a weird look on her face, and that weirdness spelled reluctance. She did not want me to meet this person. "Scott is my boss. He's the, um, DeFrancis of Berger & DeFrancis."

"Uh-huh."

I stared at her hard, waiting for her to introduce me, and watched that panic grow. What the fuck? There was absolutely no way Stephanie was banging her boss. She had too much integrity. And besides that, she'd often complained about the inequity of salaries, and how her fellow paralegals and the legal assistants irritated her by obsessing for years over her not having a boyfriend or girlfriend. She'd never once said anything to imply . . .

But it wasn't my business. She did not belong to me.

I pasted on a half-assed smile and held out my hand. He had a limp, damp handshake.

"I'm Angel León. Nice to meet you, man."

Scott nodded, cocked his head, and then awareness sparked. "Oh, you're Stephanie's fiancé."

I stared. "What?"

Beside me, Stephanie's face was flaming. She seemed close to exploding right there in the glass-encased office as Caleb and Oli looked between us in confusion. They, wisely, didn't speak.

"Stephanie's fiancé," Scott awkwardly clarified. "We don't, uh, well, that is, I don't talk about personal things with my employees, but—" Holy fuck, would he ever get a sentence out? Stephanie appeared ready to melt into a puddle of humiliation on the floor. "She said she couldn't come to the company retreat in Lake George next weekend because she had plans with her fiancé. Angel."

The effort to not crack a smile was monumental. This was stupid. I knew it was stupid. She'd thrown my name in the fray at work to keep them off her back. It had nothing to do with some actual desire to ever be engaged to me. But even so . . .

I wrapped my arm around her shoulder and pulled her in with a shit-eating smile. "Gotcha."

Across from us, Oli was also turning red from an obvious effort not to laugh. Caleb looked like he wanted to die from secondhand embarrassment.

"Um . . ." Stephanie shuffled besides me. "Right . . ."

"But you know what, Scott?" I dug my fingers into Stephanie's arm. "Those plans may dry up. Is it too late for her to go along?"

Oli had taken a sip of his drink and choked. Stephanie gave me a hateful glare. I kept smiling at Scott.

"No, not at all. We're going to have cabins, do team-building activities, and there will even be a hike." Scott listed these activities as if in theory they were awesome, but his voice barely made it to *semi pleased to be participating*. "There are a lot of couples going, so you're more than welcome to attend. We still have one room available."

This time it was Stephanie who brightened like her wattage had suddenly received a boost. "Well, *we* might just take that into consideration, Scott. My Angelito loves outdoorsy stuff."

I kept my mouth sealed into a smile even as I saw this plan backfiring. Caleb took pity on us and whisked Scott into a conversation about what type of law he practiced (immigration law), before going off on a glowing review of Clive Baptiste, their QFindr attorney, and the recent legal efforts to obtain subpoenas for the social media accounts that had participated in doxing them.

As awkward as I felt with Stephanie glued to my side while she practically vibrated with the need to kick me in the nuts, I paid attention long enough to glean some details. Apparently, the legal process was slow but steady, and it could take a year or two to confirm the identities of the people behind the cyber threats, since they had to wait for subpoenas from various social media and email platforms. However, Caleb and Oli seemed confident that their suspect would eventually be caught. Considering the doxing had caused Meredith to be physically assaulted, I fucking hoped so. Even though everyone seemed chill, I had not missed the not-so-discreet armed guards by the door when I'd entered the loft.

"Hey, Angel, I forgot Raymond wanted to talk to you," Stephanie piped up about five minutes in. "If you guys will excuse us . . ."

She dragged me away from the office, halted by the stairs, and then made a beeline for what I could only assume was Caleb and Oli's bedroom. She shoved me inside with enough force to make me stumble, and shut the door behind her.

"What the fuck, Sharky?"

"What?"

"What?" Her voice reached a higher pitch. "Why did you say I'd go on that stupid retreat! Have you missed the parts where I complain your ears off about how my coworkers are irritating to work with, let alone be on a three-day retreat with?"

"I did not, but . . . I also didn't miss the parts where your primary complaints were related to them always clucking their tongues about how you're single. And now . . ." I smirked, "you're not anymore. Apparently you're engaged."

That blush covered her face again. The desire to kiss her nearly consumed me. I had to shift my attention away from her and surveyed the bedroom.

"Angel, I only said that because—"

"I'm not stupid. You said it because of all their annoying questions about your love life." I studiously avoided meeting her eyes and kept visually snooping. "I don't think you actually enjoy pretending to be mine."

Stephanie made a sound beside me, but I ignored her. That comment was supposed to have been dropped in a lighthearted manner, but my chest had hollowed out as soon as I'd said it. So I avoided meeting her eyes and studied the elegant but understated bedroom before noticing a device in the corner. A device that could only be . . .

"Holy shit, is that the fucking machine?"

I moved closer without thinking, eyeballing the apparatus. It was aggressively . . . mechanical. It kind of looked like a tripod for a camera, but with a big dildo attached to it. I didn't touch it, but I could easily see how it could be adjusted for height and different positions. The visualization instantly turned to me adjusting it for Stephanie.

"Fresco," she murmured, coming up behind me. "It's so easy to tell when your mind has gone down into the gutter."

"How could it not?" I licked my lips as she put her hands on my shoulders. "So, you're saving up for one, huh?"

"Mm-hmm."

"Let's get engaged for real and put it on a registry like Oli said."

She burst out laughing in my ear and wrapped her arms around me, hugging me to her chest. "Seriously, papi. I'm sorry I put you in a lie without telling you. I really was sick of them always giving me sad looks and worrying about the status of my womb and ring finger."

"They want you to have kids?" I made a skeptical face even as I stared at the dildo. "For what?"

"*Right*?" Stephanie squeezed me tighter. "This is why I used your name. You get me."

Uh-huh. Not because she liked me. Nah, couldn't be that.

"Go on the retreat." I turned away from the machine so I could look at her. "I know you only like being around us or your new friends, people who get you, but trust me—you'll benefit from going along."

She wrinkled her nose.

"You know you have to play those games to get ahead sometimes, Steph. We talk about this shit all the time with Ray and Tonya. How they are physically unable to be fake and go with the motions, but you can. You're charming. Schmooze them into kissing your ass and giving you a raise."

Groaning, she said, "I guess that's true. But . . ." She bit the side of her lip, searching my face. "Would you go with me?"

"Uh . . . I dunno . . ."

"Please?" Her hand tightened on me. "It's going to be blazing this weekend, and Lake George will be nice. It's cooler there, and you'll get to do outdoorsy stuff."

"While pretending to be your fiancé." At her nod, I said, "And you don't think that will muddy the waters? The we're-no-longer-fucking waters?"

"No. Why would it? Just . . . be there with me, and we'll act like how we always act." She smiled, as if any of this made any sense. "People always assume we're together, anyway."

I wanted to shake her. I really did. But I could deny her nothing, so I nodded. "Let me see if I can switch my day on Saturday."

She drew me into a hug. "Thank you, Angel."

I hugged her back, even though this was going to be a mess.

CHAPTER FOUR
STEPHANIE

My reactions to the Lake George trip were giving me continuous cases of whiplash. I smacked myself for perpetuating the stupid I-have-a-fiancé-named-Angel lie for over a year, then I was pleased with myself for not jumping out the window in mortification after being busted, but then I'd been thrilled by his response, and ultimately mystified by the turn of events.

We met up with the rest of the firm at the crack of dawn on Friday morning, boarded a charter bus, and promptly sat next to each other in dead silence. It was over a three-hour drive to upstate New York, I was undercaffeinated and unfed, wanted to do nothing other than listen to my music in peace, and because Angel was my fucking Patronus, he did the exact same thing.

At some point, I leaned my head against his shoulder, closed my eyes, and woke up over an hour later to find myself burrowed into his side. He'd put an arm around me and was watching sports clips on YouTube as if this was all the most natural thing in the world.

Because I was half-asleep, and caught in a fondness spiral, I looked up at him with what was likely a sickeningly sweet smile. He flashed a tiny one of his own, light eyes hidden behind aviators, and kissed my forehead.

My stomach fluttered. I reminded myself we were pretending.

"Go back to sleep," he said.

I did. Or at least, I closed my eyes and tried to stop thinking about how good he smelled, and how solid he felt against me, for several minutes before dozing off again.

The next time I woke up, it was for a pit stop. It was around ten in the morning, and I felt vaguely more alive, so I stumbled off the bus to stretch my legs. Also, to greet my coworkers now that I was more of a human being.

For the most part, they were okay. Just irritatingly "helpful" about my personal life. It was almost as though they thought it was their duty because I was the youngest person in the firm. If some of my own friends didn't get my lack of interest in relationships, there was no way I was going to try to explain it to colleagues.

I waved half-assedly, joining their group in the shade. Scott was in the store with Angel and Melanie Berger—the other attorney at the practice—but everyone else was either still on the bus or mingling. Scott's wife Ryanne and Melanie's husband Daryl were chitchatting about their own lives (corporate attorney and stay-at-home dad), but the other paralegals and legal assistants were bitching about the heat. As usual.

I leaned against the side of the building, fanning myself, and watched as Marshawn showed off a backpack that came with tubes and huge jugs of water for him to drink on a hike, as Kip and Corrigan (who looked like they'd sprung from the same yuppie fountain) took selfies for a Snapchat story. Marisol, the bad-ass legal assistant who basically ran the company, sat on a crate and ignored us all.

There were people still on the bus, significant others and the antisocial office manager, but this was my work crew. As semiannoying as they were, I sometimes liked them. I even liked some of their significant others, except for Kip, who rapidly cycled through girlfriends and still managed to somehow evade the "poor you, single person" talks.

"Hey, Kip," I said. "The lady on the bus—is that Veronica?"

His fake tan turned crimson "*No*. That's Dee. Dude, keep up with the program."

"Dee? Like the letter?" Marisol's contempt was obvious even without a tone. "Hmm."

Kip made a face at her. "Be nice. I just met her last week, and she's hot as fuck."

Good God. Although, did I have room to judge? I was dragging my on-again off-again fuck buddy around pretending he was my fiancé. Who cared if Kip was taking a Tinder hookup on a work trip?

"Your Angel is hot," Corrigan piped up. "That one picture you showed me did him no justice."

It was a good time to demure and take the attention off my situation, but I grinned. "I know, right?"

"And he's getting you coffee and breakfast without you having asked," she went on. "My boyfriend won't even brew a pot if we're going to be home together all morning. He makes one K-cup for himself."

"Your boyfriend—" Marisol stopped talking and smiled. "Is a very nice man."

Marshawn cracked up, and Kip snickered. Everyone knew the stories of Corrigan's irritating boyfriend and his immature ways. It was weird talking about it while he was in the bus a few feet away, though.

"Angel's a sweetheart," I agreed, instead of going on with the comparisons. "But we probably should hold off on canonizing men for doing more than the bare minimum, right?"

Corrigan rolled her eyes, but Marisol held up her hand for a high five. I turned it into one of Chris's complicated handshakes. By the time Angel reappeared and offered me a large coffee and an everything bagel with cream cheese, I was in a much livelier mood.

"Did you get anything for yourself?"

He held a Red Bull. "I'll be fine."

"We'll share my bagel." He shrugged, not disagreeing, and I impulsively kissed him on the cheek. "Thank you, baby."

He stared at me like I was a mutant. Well, that was how it seemed to me. Everyone else probably assumed he was simply stoic.

We boarded the bus again, and I twisted in my seat so I could face him while we ate. My knee rested on his thigh, and once we were done, he put his hand on it. His thumb dragged along the curve of my knee as he went back to his phone. I kept watching him.

Over two hours into this charade, and already I was wondering how this would play out. Either we'd have a great time and it would be us goofing around for three days while punctuating sentences with endearments, or . . . it would be awkward. We'd get caught up on what we were, or weren't, versus what we were pretending to be. He'd get in his feelings and retreat emotionally, or I'd get defensive about having to do this at all, and we'd bicker. There was already a tiny voice at the back of my mind hissing at me to stop enjoying this so much.

"Stop thinking so hard."

I looked up to find Angel was studying me. He'd shoved his sunglasses up into the tangle of his blond hair.

"What are you talking about?"

He raised an eyebrow. "We'll have fun. Stop worrying."

Why did he have to know me so well? "I'll try."

"Hopefully you don't get poison ivy again." He paused, then raised his voice. "That rash was all up your—"

I put a hand over his mouth as his eyes twinkled. Leaning in, I pressed my mouth to his ear and murmured, "If you start teasing me with fake stories, I'll tease back."

"Try it. It's pretty difficult to embarrass me."

Poor sweet summer child. I smiled and said, "Thank you for breakfast, querido," before brushing our lips together. He turned to stone, so I did it again. And since everybody had returned to their music and their phones, and nobody was in the seat beside us, I slipped my tongue into his mouth.

He made a sound so low only I could hear it, but that faint moan caused me to clench up. The feeling intensified when he kissed me back, hungry and demanding, until my pulse was rocketing, and I was struggling to keep my hands to myself. I should have known better than to think we could *just* kiss without me wanting to escalate things.

"You behave yourself," he murmured against me. "Or this is gonna be a lot harder."

I couldn't help it. I dragged my fingers down to his crotch, and ran one along the erection clearly showing through his jeans.

His eyelashes fluttered, and he shifted on his seat. "Bad."

"I will be if you don't behave *your*self."

Angel shrugged casually despite the wood he was sporting. "We'll see."

ANGEL

That should have been my cue to stop teasing her, but I didn't. I couldn't help myself. As immature as it was, I got a kick out of it every time she flushed or grumbled or glared me down like she was going to punch me in the dick. I also wanted to know what she'd do to get revenge.

A couple of hours later, we established ourselves in the lodge the two attorneys had rented. An entire lodge. There were six bedrooms, but Marisol and the office manager were sharing one, and Marshawn and his wife claimed the huge pullout bed in the study. I had a feeling it had something to do with the proximity to the hot tub right outside on the deck. Very smart man had done his research.

I teased Stephanie the entire time. About her pausing in unloading to drink water, about make-believe vacations we'd taken together where she'd acted like a princess, and an off-the-cuff story about a time when she'd nearly drowned. It was all complete bullshit, but everyone got a kick out of it and the way she'd smack my ass or the back of my head in response.

I personally got a kick out of the glint in her eye. That glint—it was a warning glint. She was gonna get me later.

So far, everything was gravy except for the fact that we'd wound up next door to Kip and Dee. They'd regaled us with an edited version of their Tinder hookup on the bus, so I was dreading sharing a wall with them.

"No couch," I said to Stephanie after we'd dumped our duffel bags in the room. "I could pretend to pass out downstairs every night."

She gave me a stank face. "So they think we don't like sharing the bed? No."

Snorting, I stripped off my sweaty shirt and tossed it on the bed. "Do you care if they think we're not fucking?"

"Yes. They think we're some idealistic couple. I plan to milk this appearance for all its worth if you quit being a pain in the ass."

"Aw." I grabbed her arm and pulled her to me, enclosing her in a sweaty hug. "My poor, poor fiancée is so touchy. Doesn't want me sharing the details of our fake-ass vacation mishaps from years past, making this dumb lie more believable."

"It's not dumb." She laughed as I squeezed her, not protesting when I nuzzled the side of her neck. This was dangerous. "They really think you're some amazing guy."

"Based on what?" I asked against her skin.

"Beats me. And Corrigan thinks you're so fine. I'm liking the response."

"Huh." I kissed her on the cheek and pulled back as a weird feeling moved through me. "Glad I'm living up to whatever standards you set for the version of me you'd actually be in a relationship with."

I turned away before I could see whatever expression crossed her lovely face at my extra-ass passive aggression, but I did not apologize. And she didn't comment. An awkward silence filled the room as I changed into a clean shirt and she semi-unpacked.

"Ready to go down? I think they're grilling for lunch."

She nodded quietly, and we went downstairs to rejoin the others.

It took thirty minutes of foot shuffling and weak jokes about half the group only knowing how to use Seamless or Blue Apron, and the other half pointedly looking away because they weren't about to cook for their bosses, for me to step up and get the grill going. Did I want to cook for strangers? No? Did I want to eat? Yes. But most importantly, watching their incompetence made me want to punch them.

The lodge came stocked with everything we needed. Apparently, Scott had called ahead and had requested the fridge be filled with items that all the staff and their plus-ones had requested. The guy was awkward, but he seemed to want to show his employees a good time.

The lodge was stunning. Now that I'd walked around and checked the entire place out, I kept trying to figure out how much it had cost and had no idea. There were several bedrooms and bathrooms, a stocked bar, stocked kitchen, a giant pool, a fire pit, grill, deck, multiple sitting rooms, and several outdoor seating areas. There were plenty of places to snag a private moment if someone wanted it.

But despite dropping a likely exorbitant amount on the place, Scott lingered nearby, looking guilty, as I took control of the food. I shooed him away, advising him to go play cards, and promptly appointed Brandon, Corrigan's lazy-ass boyfriend, as my sous chef.

"I don't really cook," he explained, gazing wistfully after Marisol, Corrigan, and Stephanie as they headed to the pool. "I told you, I just order Blue Apron."

"My dude, Blue Apron delivers raw ingredients." I wiped my forearm across my head, squinting at him in the sunlight. Lake George had a nicer breeze going than the city, but it was still blazing. "Do you close your eyes and wish real hard for it to turn into a meal?"

On one of the wooden deck chairs, Marshawn cracked up around his beer bottle. "I like you," he said to me. "I knew Steph's man had to be cool."

"Oh yeah?" Again, I stripped off a shirt that had been reduced to a sweat rag, and stood there in my jeans and flip-flops. Why hadn't I thought to change into some basketball shorts? Oh right, because I wasn't trying to scandalize anyone with my dick print. "Why's that?"

Brandon sullenly chopped vegetables for me to roast after the meat, glancing between us silently. Maybe he'd be silent for the whole weekend. In the few exchanges we'd had since entering the house, I wasn't real impressed with him. He found things to bitch about that were basically made up.

"Because she's awesome." Marshawn looked at me like this should be obvious. "She works the hardest of any of us, to be honest. Finishes her work in half the time, and not because she's rushing. She's just quick. Scott adores her."

"Really." I shifted my gaze to the canopied lounges where he'd gone to play cards with Kip, his wife, and Daryl. "Then why won't he give her a raise?"

Marshawn snorted into his beer. "Good question, man. I'll tell you my thoughts on that at another time."

Judging from the sharp edge of his smile, and his quick glance at Brandon, the conversation would happen when we were alone. A flare of irritation went up in my chest before I snuffed it out. Now was not the time for me to start having an attitude with her boss. She could handle this herself. Stephanie had never needed a white knight.

"Anyway, she's a great person to have in the office. And a good leader. She knows so much that sometimes Scott has to ask *her* questions."

A swell of pride replaced the fire from a moment ago. I smiled, looking over toward the pool, where she was sitting on the edge in some kind of short gauzy cover-up. "She's amazing."

"And hot as hell."

My gaze swiveled from Stephanie to Brandon, and I realized he was staring at her too. My emotions were ping-ponging all over the place, and *jealous motherfucker* lit up with a thousand dinging sounds. "Yeah, it's real hot out."

Brandon blinked at me, confused, but my ice grill must have told him all he needed to know. He dropped his head and went back to chopping vegetables. It was now my mission in life to son him for the next couple of days. Maybe it would distract me from my masochistic desire to rile Stephanie up.

Then again, probably not.

CHAPTER FIVE
STEPHANIE

"**S**o, how did you two meet?"

The question caught me unexpected after spending the majority of the day in the sun and pool, then a few hours of eating and drinking beer. I was in that warm, full, and slightly buzzed state that had allowed me to curl up next to Angel on a chaise lounge as a cool breeze whipped off the lake. It had seemed perfectly acceptable to doze off with my head on his chest as he absently stroked my hair while paying attention to his phone. Now, I realized people had been watching us. We were the picture of a couple in love right down to the constant casual touching.

Self-consciously, I sat up a straighter, but there was little to no bonus room on the lounge. Getting distance would require me to suddenly get up, which would make me look like a freak.

"In high school," Angel said. "I worshipped her and she let me help her with her Spanish homework."

"Um, excuse you, I helped you with English." I poked his side. "And you were dating Crystal."

He rolled his eyes the way he always did when I mentioned Crystal—my high school nemesis. "Yeah, that was senior year. We met way before that."

I also wasn't sure they'd officially been dating. Judging from the stories Crystal had loved telling me and my other friends, it had sounded like they'd had nonstop sex. Those same stories had driven me nuts. Even now, I was mad at her for talking about everything from his dick size to the way he'd loved going down on her. My rage had been the epitome of hypocrisy considering *I'd* also made out with Crystal dozens of times in bathrooms and staircases all over school.

We'd been fine until she'd set her eyes on him. Mostly everyone in the school had understood that I had an unspoken thing for Angel, except for her. Well, and except for him. He was oblivious to this day.

"Okay, fair, but," I said to our audience, holding up a finger, "it was the Crystal thing that made me realize someone else would have him if I kept dragging my feet."

Angel looked at me, surprise clear on his face, but it was Corrigan who leaned in for a juicy story. "So competition caught your attention?"

"Uh, I guess? Now it sounds cliché." I wrinkled my nose but couldn't deny it was partially what had happened. Crystal had made it sound like Angel wanted to ravish her nonstop, and he probably had. She was gorgeous. In my freshman and sophomore year, *I'd* wanted to ravish her nonstop. She was thick and brown and beautiful with a head of curly hair that had transfixed me. But, I'd also noticed she was the type to catch feelings, whereas I'd always liked flying solo, so we'd quit fooling around.

Way later, after she'd started college, I'd thought she and Raymond would make a good couple, but . . . Ray's apathy had caused her to give up. I didn't blame her. "So, in high school, Angel was very low-key, didn't date much, and mostly hung out with me and our other friends. Then all of a sudden he had this whole passionate relationship, and I remember wondering why it had been her to spark his interest in that way and not me. They were only together a couple of months, but still. I wondered."

"Because Stephanie wasn't interested," Angel told them with a scoff. "Literally zero interest."

"Friend-zoned," Brandon muttered behind his drink.

I nearly died laughing at the flat look Angel aimed his way. They had a weird dynamic that I'd noticed as soon as everyone had gathered to eat. Interesting as in, Brandon spoke and Angel stared at him like he was an idiot. Then again, the whole picture of Angel holding down the grill and producing seriously delicious food while standing there like a walking thirst trap with no shirt on had been . . . amazing. I hadn't been able to stop watching him.

Lots of people grilled. I grilled all the time at Ray and David's house. So why was seeing Angel being the only competent dude in this group turning me on? It was super pathetic, but I'd stared him down the entire time I was eating my burger. No wonder my coworkers kept prying into our fake relationship.

"First off, friend-zoned is not a real thing," Angel rumbled next to me. "It's called someone not wanting to fu—be with you romantically. That's just how life goes. Some people want you. Some people don't. In Stephanie's case, she didn't want me until a . . ." He cocked his head and glanced at me with faux sheepishness. "When did we get together, nena?"

Across from us, Corrigan had hearts in her eyes at the endearment. I almost felt bad for her. Brandon was apparently so unromantic that Angel just acting like himself made her think he was a deity. "Three years ago," I said. "Three years ago on August fifteenth."

Next to me, Angel went still. My heart slammed into my rib cage at the thought that he would recall that day. The day he'd bought Victor a ticket to Chicago and held me as I sobbed at LaGuardia Airport. The way he'd stroked my hair and promised to check on my brother, to do anything he could, to be there for me no matter what, since no one else in my family would be. I'd told him I loved him, and he'd said it in return. I'd never forget those three whispered words as he held me to his broad chest. Or his promise to never let me down.

It hadn't seemed like a romantic thing so much as us trying to find comfort, but in that moment, Angel had meant so much to me. He'd been my fucking hero. After that is when I'd started wishing, hoping, he'd openly look at me the way he looked at me when he thought I wasn't paying attention. That he'd touch me. Kiss me. I'd fantasized about it, even though I knew I wouldn't be able to give him what he wanted. A relationship. Tradition. The happily ever after that the rest of our friends had.

"Well, you two are beautiful together," Ryanne said, smiling. "You'll have such gorgeous babies."

I sighed inwardly. Angel shook his head.

"Nah, I'm sterile."

Ryanne's eyes went wide. "Oh my God, I'm sorry."

"Nah, it's fine." Angel shrugged, grinning his slyest grin. "I'm pretty happy to just be with Steph."

This time I went still. As tingles shot through me, intensifying when he kissed my forehead, I had a sudden urge to get distance from him and the lie I'd created. Instead, I went back to leaning against him and smiled.

Two more days.

ANGEL

Sleeping was a nightmare.

The only times Stephanie and I had shared a bed in the past had been during our on-again stages. We hadn't necessarily always knocked out after wild banging, but I'd been comfortable with her next to me. I'd known we could touch each other if we wanted. That I didn't have to suppress my attraction or instinct to cuddle up to her.

Now, as we lay awkwardly in the queen-sized bed with less than a bible's width between us, I was overly aware of her presence next to me—the warmth of her body, the feel of her arm pressing against mine, and every time she sighed or shifted in her sleep. I lay awake for over an hour, staring at the ceiling or out the window.

I dozed off and what seemed to be moments later, a sound snapped me out of the light sleep. My eyes cracked open, and I found myself staring at the window again. There was no telling what had jolted me, but—

Something bumped the wall behind me. The sound was punctuated by a muffled moan.

I'd expected this as soon as I'd seen Kip and Dee barely able to stop groping each other at every rest stop and then in the pool, but damn. Sighing inwardly, I closed my eyes, determined to not let it keep me up. It was a plan set to fail because I was now focused on what was going on next door. Every thump, moan, and louder cry worked its way into my brain until my body was tense and the lick of my arousal began to grow more insistent.

After a tormented five minutes, I chanced a look at Stephanie. She had one hand pressed to her eyes as she bit her lip. Definitely not asleep. I dragged my gaze down her body, since she was a weirdo who slept without covers, and couldn't help but notice the way her other hand was splayed on her abdomen, fingers flirting with the band of her little shorts. Her thighs were also pressed together.

The lick of arousal widened and swallowed me whole.

"How long have they been fucking this loudly?"

Stephanie dropped her hand from her eyes and huffed out a long sigh. "Like thirty minutes? I have no idea."

"Huh. Didn't think he'd have the stamina."

"Judging from her encouraging comments, he's been fingering and eating her out for an eternity."

I stared at her shadowed profile, grinning. "I can't tell if you're mad or jealous."

"Both," she muttered. "She sounds like she is genuinely enjoying this, and her voice is hot as hell. Now I'm horny and irritable."

My hand twitched with the urge to slide it down and cup my growing erection. Instead, I nudged her with my elbow. "Just close your eyes and pretend you're somewhere else."

"If I was somewhere else, I'd already be on orgasm number three."

She sounded so fucking grouchy that I imagined she was oblivious to how hot she was getting me. That was just Stephanie. Blunt. No filter. Talked about sex the way other people talked about sports or music.

"You're that turned on by those two fools?"

"Not *them*. Just . . . the sound of a woman enjoying herself really does it for me." She shifted again, fingers still dragging along her waistband.

I rolled on my side, trying to keep my attention on her face and not the way her body looked in the moonlight.

"She could be the most annoying person ever, but knowing she's probably on cloud nine as someone spends their time *really* turning her out is like . . ."

Her voice was getting lower, her fingers now toying with the waistband. She shifted again, wetting her lips, eyes closed.

"What's it like?" My own voice came out in a husky scrape that she responded to with a deep breath.

"It just jump-starts my imagination. I start wondering what they're doing and then picturing it—not *them*, but . . . other people. Another woman on her back with her legs spread open, but not like . . .

poised and pretty and clean. She's sweaty, hair tangled from her own hands and her partner's, and her pussy is so wet."

Stephanie's breath hitched, but she kept teasing her waistband even as she subtly arched her hips. My dick was a fucking stone column. I ignored it and covered her hand with my own, sliding her fingers down into her shorts. I withdrew just as she found what she wanted, and watched with rapt fascination as her head fell back, thighs slid open, and her fingers went to work beneath the cotton.

"Keep talking," I whispered. "How wet is she?"

"Soaked." With her free hand, Stephanie squeezed her breast through her tank top, then rubbed her palm over it. Her eyebrows drew together as the motions got faster, the sound of her fingers sliding over her own flesh loud in the quiet room.

"She sounds like a mess." I moved closer, speaking into her ear without touching her. "Tell me what she's doing."

Stephanie shuddered, her hips rocking against the bed. "Rubbing her clit. Pretending it's someone else's fingers."

The game we were playing flipped without me even thinking about it, and I pressed against her side so she could feel my dick. "Someone who's gonna turn you out the way that girl next door is?"

"Yes. Fuck yes. I want it so bad, Angel."

"Tell me what you want." I pushed up her tank top, rubbing the smooth skin of her stomach and panting at my hand's proximity to the heat between her thighs. "Describe it. Every fucking detail."

Her lips moved, but no words came out except for a rough moan punctuated by the increasingly wet sound of her touching herself. "I want someone to play with me," she panted. "Push me down, yank my legs apart, and do whatever they want to my pussy until it's swollen and sloppy just from them using me like a toy. Making me come hard over and over until I can barely think."

"Fuck yeah, Steph." I gave in, grabbing my dick through my shorts and squeezing. "Tell me how to make you come the first time."

"Keep rubbing my clit. Fast. Like—just like that. And then, oh God—" A spasm went through her, and she sucked in a deep breath. She arched into her hand, muffling back a series of moans, and then squeezed her thighs together again. God, I loved watching her come. "*Fuck*."

Stephanie's hand stilled, but she didn't pull it out. She lay there, breathing hard, and continued squeezing her breast. I kissed the side of her face, trailed down, and then nudged her hand away so I could shove the tank top up further and run my tongue over her nipple. She hissed out a breath.

"Feel better?" I asked against her damp skin.

Next door, the party was raging. There was a consistent thumping now, but that was the least of my concerns. Stephanie's body was an inferno against me, and there was growing tension thrumming between us. She swallowed audibly.

When she didn't answer, I put my hand over where hers was beneath the cotton. Even through her shorts, I could feel how wet she was. They were damp. "Does this need more?" I asked, rubbing my fingers along her hand.

"Yeah . . ."

I moved her hand with mine, and was ridiculously jealous of her fingers when she dragged them along her slit. "Is that what it needs, nena?"

Stephanie released another tortured moan, arching up against me so I was forced to press against her harder.

"Or do you want something in this tight little pussy?"

"Yes," she breathed, eyes opening to train on me.

"Your fingers, maybe . . ." I trailed off, running my tongue over my lower lip as she gazed up at me with wild eyes. "Or did my bad girl bring something else to fuck herself with? Just in case she couldn't sleep and needed something to come all over?"

Stephanie's mouth turned up at the sides. "In my bag."

I leaned over her to reach into the duffel bag still sitting next to her side of the bed. We were briefly face-to-face, and I took the opportunity to lick her parted lips. I sucked the lower one into my mouth, then kissed her messy and breathless as I rooted around in her bag. There was an interior pocket, and in there I found a glass dildo instead of her favorite vibrator.

I knelt between her thighs, staring down at her in a way that I knew had to be filthy. "Trying to be sneaky?"

Stephanie arched an eyebrow. "Didn't know if I'd need to get off on the low."

The idea of her masturbating when she thought I was sleeping, or sneaking off to the bathroom to do it, drove me wild. My nostrils flared, and I reached down to grab my dick again.

"Take your clothes off."

She did it with no pause, flinging her tank top somewhere and then kicking out of her shorts. Laying before me, she bent her legs at the knee and let me see every part of her—the heavy breasts, wide hips, thick thighs, and the wet mound between them. I gave her the dildo, watching her fingers wrap around the base. She dragged it along her slit, and I squeezed myself harder.

"Let me see your dick," she whispered.

I shoved my shorts down my hips and let my cock rest in my hand. It was heavy and throbbing, pre-come already gathered at the tip. I stroked myself as she teased her clit with the head of the dildo, and found myself subconsciously rubbing the head of my own cock against her entrance. The need to fuck her consumed me, and I started a steady jerking rhythm. When she finally slid the dildo into her hole, I was fucking my hand wildly.

With her knees pulled back, one hand rubbing her clit as the other drew the dildo in and out at a slightly frantic pace, she was the picture she'd described earlier. Sweaty and wild and shameless. Her brows were wound together again, mouth gaping.

"Fuck it harder," I panted, hand flying over my shaft. "And tell me how it feels."

"Amazing." Stephanie's hips jolted, and she spread wider, sliding it in deeper. "God, Angel, my pussy feels so good."

"It's hitting you deep?" I hunched over her, one hand pressed against the wall behind us as I jerked with the other. "Nailing that good spot?"

"Yeah, right there, baby." Stephanie closed her eyes, like she was lost to the feeling, to whatever weird fantasy we were creating. "Yeah, *there*. Please, Angel." Her thighs began to shake. Her lower lip trembled.

Fireworks cracked through me at the sound of her breaking, anguished voice. I angled the tip of my dick against her ass, teasing the hole. Just the idea of fucking it while she used the dildo sent me into a meltdown.

I came so violently that I shouted, deep and loud enough to be heard through the wall. The orgasm took hold of me, sending my hand flying over my pulsing dick, as ropes of semen splattered her thighs and her exposed ass. When she was a total mess, I leaned down and shoved her hand out of the way so I could rub her clit with my fingers coated in my come.

She cried out my name as she came, her body jerking up against me and the dildo as she kept fucking herself even as she got wetter and stickier. When she finally pulled it out, she was shaking from the force of her orgasm and looked so beautifully ruined that I instantly covered her face in kisses.

Stephanie wrapped her legs around my waist and forced me down on top of her, our bodies sliding together in the mess we'd created. After we came up for air, I crushed her to the bed with my body, loving how she kept her long limbs locked around me even then.

"You have a couple minutes," I whispered in her ear. "And then I lick my fiancée clean just so we can make another mess."

CHAPTER SIX
STEPHANIE

The next morning, it was a struggle to keep my eyes open, and my body was literally numb.

Not only had Angel done exactly what I'd described—made me his plaything until I was reduced to a shuddering rag doll—but he'd . . . surpassed my expectations. There were times when I'd wondered how couples could stay together forever and never get bored of each other sexually, but he'd shown me just how many cards he had up his sleeve. Specifically, the playing-with-my-butt-while-fucking-me-with-the-dildo card had given me a nearly embarrassingly powerful orgasm that had put me into a coma.

I still wasn't sure if he'd gotten off again.

And he'd never slid inside of me himself. His self-control was on another level. Now, of course, he was casually making scrambled eggs for everyone and talking sports with Marshawn and Scott as if he hadn't kept me up all night causing my eyes to roll back in my skull. Meanwhile, I just wanted to nap. With him. Or eat breakfast and then go back to bed and watch TV or nap.

We should have blown off the retreat and just stayed in my apartment all weekend with the AC on.

The thought jolted me, and I turned away. Only twenty-four hours of pretending to be a couple, and my brain was already tricking itself into thinking we could behave this way all the time. It wasn't just the sex I was sprung on—I'd known we were ridiculously compatible in that regard. It was the way I wanted to show him off to my coworkers—*Look, he's beautiful, smart, and competent!*—and how my thoughts kept skewing to this idea that our mini vacation would be much better minus the other people. Even though this was all supposed to be an act.

I tried to turn my attention back to the dumb game everyone in the living room was playing. It was supposed to be a team-building activity to come up with our vision of an amazing working environment, but had turned into everyone lazily discussing the broken facilities at the firm. I could tell by the look on Melanie's face that she hadn't intended it to turn into a bitch session, but there was no saving it now.

Somewhere between a complaint about the copy machines and the lack of paper, Dee caught my eye. Her lips spread in a little smirk, but I kept my face neutral. Part of me wanted to be mortified that Kip had probably heard us, but a larger part of me did not care. Everyone was acting normal, except me and Dee being smug as hell. Although I'd planned to be a lot less obvious about how smug I was.

We went through the motions of the next few hours without me being particularly excited about any of them. There were more games, swimming, a break for lunch, and then Scott announced that he and Melanie would be holding one-on-one meetings with us after we ate so *we* could give *them* feedback on the firm. Coming on the back of the morning's first activity, where everyone had lodged complaints, it seemed like a bit much. Then again, maybe they were worried about staff retention. There had been rumblings from a couple of people, me included, about potentially finding a job elsewhere. I just hadn't known those conversations had reached Scott's ears.

My bemusement must have been clear, because Angel nudged me.

I stood as Marisol followed Scott and Melanie into the little library first, and gestured Angel to follow me. He got up, and I grabbed his hand, tugging him outside onto the deck.

"I'm going to talk to him about the raise," I said quickly. "Or is that a bad idea?"

"I think you should do what you think is best." Angel glanced down at our still-joined hands and squeezed. "You know what you deserve."

"Fuck. I know."

I let him go and ran my hands through my hair, stressing over the potential conversation. In all actuality, I knew exactly what to say, and I knew how I wanted to say it. The problem was that employers tended to respond a lot differently to me being direct and speaking my mind than when men did. And I knew if Scott had the wrong response, my mental seesawing over whether I should find another job would weigh more heavily on the side of leaving.

Angel wrapped his arms around me, squeezing me just enough for me to relax against him. He kissed my forehead, one hand rubbing my back. "You got this, nena. These cats wax on about how amazing you are. How you're a leader, and you know everything about everything."

I looked up at him, and saw the same pride in his face that I'd felt after watching everyone fawn over him. The satisfaction of everyone knowing that the person you cared for was wonderful and deserving of praise.

Something in me cracked, and the splinters widened when he ran his fingers along the side of my face. I'd known him for so long, and had wanted him for so long, but for the first time, my heart thrummed in my chest, the vibrations spelling out very clearly that I loved him.

Angel's brow puckered. "What's wrong?"

I closed my eyes and took a deep shuddering breath. "Angel . . ." He waited quietly, and his hands slid away from my arms. One look at him showed the clouds forming over the brilliance of his smile. He knew me so well that just by my tone, he could predict what I was about to say. "Baby," I said, trying again.

"Don't call me that." The gates had slammed shut, and his affection was gone. I hated how his face hardened, how his eyes went blank. "There's no need to say anything else, Steph."

He started away, and I grabbed his wrist. "Please, just listen."

"Why do I have to listen to you reject me? I know what you're gonna say."

"No, you don't," I hissed, moving closer until I was crowding him.

"So, you weren't going to tell me we need to ease up on acting like a couple because you're worried I'm getting the wrong idea?" Angel raised his eyebrows, making a smart-ass face at my pause. "Yeah, that's what I thought."

My chest constricted, but I couldn't find the words to explain how I felt in a way that wouldn't hurt him. And the hurt was so clear even as he defaulted to his tough-guy expression—his mouth set hard and that dead-eyed stare. It was such a harsh punishing difference from the way he'd gazed down at me moments ago.

"Can we talk after all of this shit is done for the day?"

He shrugged, already looking past me. "I don't see what there is to talk about. I'm not gonna screw you up here. I'll stick to my role in front of everyone else."

I squeezed my hands into fists. "And when we're alone?"

Angel's gaze flicked down to me. "I won't bother you until you want me to make you come."

It was a punch straight through my chest, so painful that I had to turn away or else he'd see the wound he'd just inflicted. It wasn't even the words. It was the fact that he'd said them deliberately to make me feel like shit.

"Go talk to your boss, Stephanie." His voice came out scratchy and hoarse. "He won't let you go without a fight."

My eyes narrowed, and I jerked around as accusations filled my head and my mouth. Was he trying to say Scott wouldn't let me go, but *he* would? I couldn't help but think he wanted me to react to the statement. So I didn't.

"We're really fucking shitty at this, Angel," I said, voice clogging.

"At what?" he demanded, defensive again.

I jerked a hand between us so sharply I nearly hit him. "Everything."

His cheek clenched. "No, nena. We're fucking shitty because we both know what we want from each other and won't let ourselves have it."

"You don't understand," I said. "You never have."

Angel scoffed. "Believe me, I get it."

He walked away without saying anything more, and I wanted to scream into the fucking mountains until my voice echoed. The worst part was that I couldn't chase him. Couldn't demand he listen, or that he use his goddamn words and speak. *Really* speak. Stop skittering away when faced directly with this conflict, or bowing out of a fight before it began. But then again, maybe he wasn't willing to. I wasn't even sure if I could blame him.

For the next thirty minutes I sat in one of the large arm chairs in the living room and stared outside. We were supposed to be getting ready for a hike, and I was already trying to figure out how to get out of it. The idea of being stuck around everyone for an extended period while having to be "on," as I was internally screaming, would make me want to dash myself down to the rocks.

To prep for my inevitable plea to not go on the trek, I told Marisol that I wasn't feeling well, and she didn't press me too hard. The mood of everyone coming out of their meeting with Scott and Melanie was light, but I couldn't focus enough to plan what I'd say. My thoughts were scattered, and I was frayed.

All of this had been such a bad idea.

I felt Angel's eyes on me when I walked into the library to meet with Scott and Melanie, but I ignored him. Maybe that would be how I'd get through the next night and day.

I schooled my face into calm neutrality and joined them at the circle of soft arm chairs and couches in the corner.

"I think it's great you guys are doing this," I said. "It feels more valuable than a feedback ticket put in a box on your door."

"We want you to feel heard," Melanie said. "It's important to us that the staff here looks at Berger & DeFrancis as a home."

I nodded, looking between them. "Why?"

They blinked at me. Scott flushed a bit, obviously not having prepared an answer to something that should seem obvious.

"We value a consistent team," Melanie said. "And we want to keep the team we have for the long run."

I nodded slowly, sitting up straighter. "That makes sense."

Melanie looked at me, waiting, like she knew I had a lot more to say.

"I love working for you both," I said, surprised at how honest it felt to say. "I love what you do—what we do—and every time one of our doctors gets their H1-B, or the rare time we get an O-1, I feel like I've accomplished something. And it feels good to believe I played a part in positively impacting someone's future."

A slight smile danced on Scott's face before he smoothed it away.

"I know that sounds idealistic, but for me to have continued working in a place with such a low glass ceiling, those feelings were important to me."

Scott frowned. Melanie did not.

"Why do you see it that way?" Scott asked finally, rumbling in his Long Island accent.

"Because despite the praise I do get for my work—which I'll add is important because other bosses I've had never acknowledged their employees . . ." I rolled the words around in my head, "it's been made clear that my skill and work ethic won't allow me to advance salary-wise, and that's a difficult pill to swallow. So while I love the fact that you acknowledge our work, and you organized this trip, and your desire for longevity, I can't really pay my bills with those things."

The words fell into the room and were met with a stilted silence. They looked at each other, then Scott said, "Thank you for letting us know."

For the second time, I wanted to Fucking. Scream.

"I want to work here," I said. "That wasn't a subtle hint that I'm looking at other jobs, or a heads-up to start seeking a replacement. You wanted me to share my thoughts, and I did. And actually, I have more."

"By all means," Scott drawled.

I didn't want to turn on him, but his tone was tipping me in that direction. "I can't help but think that you'd be responding differently if it were Kip in here discussing this. And I trained him." Inhaling through my nose and then exhaling slowly, I looked them square in the face and word vomited all over them. "I can't help but wonder sometimes if you don't consider my salary, or my hard work, as seriously as the people with spouses and families, because you assume a woman my age, who's single, would be more willing to put up with being underpaid. Maybe you even assume that single women aren't worth as much investment because we're less tied down and therefore less predictable because you think we might pick up one day and relocate for some man once we get hitched. It's partially why I said Angel and I were engaged."

At last, they responded with real emotion, even if it was nothing more than Scott looking at me sideways, and Melanie doing a double take.

"So, you're not . . ."

"We're involved," I confirmed. "But I exaggerated because the culture in your firm is very geared toward men or married women with families, and I felt like I needed to belong to get ahead. And I *want* to get ahead here, which is why I made that choice."

Scott was looking like he'd just swallowed a handful of nails, but understanding had fallen over Melanie's face like a curtain.

"I'm sorry you felt that way, Stephanie," she said. "You'd be considered an equal part of the team regardless of your relationship status or orientation."

It sounded like something straight out of an HR manual, but I knew Melanie. If she hadn't meant it, she wouldn't have said it at all. She'd just have denied, denied, denied.

"We'll be discussing raises as the busy season draws to a close," Scott put in gruffly. "So don't start looking for other jobs just yet."

"Like I said—I'm not."

A *yet* hung in the air, but I felt positive about the meeting once I walked out. I let the feeling, and my relief that my thoughts and desires were finally in the open, bolster me. Maybe I'd go on the hike after all.

ANGEL

I packed a tent and a sleeping bag because I intended to spend the night in the campgrounds that ran along the trail instead of at the lodge. I'd already wanted to do it, but the desire had grown over the course of the afternoon. Regrets and bitter thoughts were running riot in my head, and I needed to clear them out. To be away from all the people, Kip and Dee especially, and maybe get some space from Stephanie.

Except, of course, as soon as I planned to do it alone, I began imagining how dope it would be to lay out at night and look at the stars with her. To kiss her under the moonlight. Make love to her with no one around to leer at us the next day, because I was still mindful that these people were her coworkers. It wasn't us fucking in one bed while T-Bone and Chris slept a few feet away on a cruise ship.

We started out the hike not talking to each other, and attached ourselves to different groups to avoid even walking together. We didn't go very far or hike for very long, but after a while, the feel of being outside and not forced into a room with a bunch of people eased my nerves. Everything uncluttered, and I replayed my conversation with Stephanie, and thought I'd been an asshole to get so uptight.

It was plain as day to anyone that I adored her, and she'd likely been about to remind me that this was all an act. And you know what? She was right. It was some purely selfish shit to be resentful over *my* feelings expanding due to all the supposed playacting while hers didn't. She didn't owe me anything, and it was stupid to think this retreat would change her mind.

My eyes drew to her as we walked, and the way she was staying off to the side instead of with the rest of her colleagues. She was unreadable, which was normal when Stephanie was in a bad mood. The first time I'd realized she was good at shielding herself that way had been when she'd come to my house for dinner when we were sixteen and had flatly told my mom that her own parents had left, and she didn't know when or if they were coming back.

My mother had freaked the hell out, and had even offered to let Stephanie stay with us instead of having an "aunt" look after them—a claim that was mad suspect since I'd thought her only functional relatives had moved away. There had been a fragment of a moment where Steph had looked at us in astonishment, and hope, before she'd realized my mother's invitation had not extended to Victor. The shutters had slammed down on her expression again.

The memory of her shutting down right before my eyes, and me being powerless, clung to me. It also prompted me to catch up with her quick, long-legged strides.

"Hey."

She glanced at me. "Hi."

"Can we talk a sec?"

"About what?"

I tried to smile. "How I acted like a dumb fuck?"

Stephanie drew to a stop, letting the rest of the group get farther ahead of us. Only when their voices faded did she turn to me fully, her fingers wrapped around the straps of her book bag.

"Why do you say that?"

"I got mad because you were about to remind me this was just a game, and I shouldn't have." I chewed on the inside of my cheek, watching her watch me, and hoping her mask would crack. "And I said some fucked-up shit."

"Yeah, you did." She crossed her arms over her chest. "That little comment about how you'll just stick to making me come or whatever? We don't have to fuck anymore at all if you're going to think and say shit like that. Don't try to imply I'm using you for your glorious cock."

I cringed and looked away. "I'm sorry. Really. I never meant it that way. I was just being a little bitch."

"Okay, but that doesn't answer my question. Do you feel that I'm just using you for dick, and that is hurtful? Because if so, we can one hundred percent go back to being strictly friends."

"Is that what you want?"

"*Angel*." Stephanie grabbed my chin, forcing me to look at her. "Stop trying to act like some prince, always making it about me and my wishes and you pleasing me whether it's in bed or otherwise. I want to know what *you* want."

I sighed slowly, but didn't pull my face away from her tightening grasp. "Stephanie, sometimes I would rather be single for the rest of my life if it meant I'd still get to touch you even once a month. There has never been anyone for me but you, anyway. Every woman I was ever with knew that. Even in high school." Her hand dropped. I didn't look away. "I know that makes me sound like a loser, because it's been so long and I'm no closer to getting over you."

She didn't immediately respond, and I swore softly under my breath.

"This is why I keep my mouth shut. It just turns into me dropping some desperate shit on you, and making you feel all pressured. I don't mean to do it, but you have to understand, nena, I've loved you forever. I know you don't feel the same way, and I'm not mad about it. Fuck, sometimes I wish I'd fall for someone else just so this could—"

Stephanie grabbed the back of my neck and dragged me into a kiss. I didn't think twice before slanting my mouth and deepening it. Maybe a day would come when this desperate ache for her would fade, and I wouldn't rush into trying to satisfy it so constantly, but that wasn't today. During times like this, I didn't think I would ever stop needing her. Even after all these years.

"Angel," she said, pulling away just enough to breathe against my mouth. "I meant what I said that day. Three years ago in August."

I pulled back farther, searching her face. "We said a lot of things that day."

"I know. But I said I loved you, and at the time I didn't mean it romantically, but . . ." She dropped her gaze to the ground between us, hands balling into fists. "I do love you. For the past year, I felt like I couldn't admit it to myself without feeling like I was betraying my principles. But I do. And that's me being honest."

There was an unspoken challenge in her voice, a *now it's your turn to be honest*, but I could barely process it. I was too busy struggling with her confession. The idea of her loving me the way I loved her. Of what that could mean but might not mean, because of course my fucked-up brain was immediately cycling things through the gray scale of cynicism.

I took a deep breath, put my hands on her shoulders, and said, "Anything I say right now is going to be over-the-top mush that might scare you off this fucking hike, so . . . how do you feel about camping with me tonight? Just us with no one to witness our conversation but the moon and stars."

Stephanie's gaze shot up to me again, and she barked out a laugh. "God, you are ridiculously romantic sometimes. You'll make some girl really happy someday."

After only a second of hesitating, I grabbed her hand and started walking again. "Maybe someday it will be you."

CHAPTER SEVEN
STEPHANIE

As we finished the rest of the hike with the group, walking close enough to occasionally bump each other but otherwise quiet, I became terrified. Regardless of the burst of bravado-infused affection that had inspired me to tell Angel about my feelings, there was still part of me cowering.

It wasn't that I regretted telling him the truth. What I regretted was opening Pandora's box of emotional discussions without an idea of what I wanted from him. Because that was what confessions were all about—one person vomiting up their feelings to another person in the hopes that their feelings would be met with a specific response. Why else would anyone fling those words into the air like emotional confetti? But I had no idea what I wanted from him. I wasn't even prepared for a conversation past what we'd already talked about. He was in a great mood, but I was as conflicted as ever. It would have been wiser to stay quiet, but his sweet confessions had drawn out one of my own.

And I truly did love him. So fucking much.

I glanced at him repeatedly as we walked, but he just flashed me a smile or poked me in the side. As if everything was normal. Except it wasn't. My mind was spinning, my heart pounding, and I had no idea what I was going to say during our campout. Not only because I wasn't set up for this, but because I hated camping.

By the time the rest of my coworkers returned to the lodge and Angel and I made camp alongside one of the tiny peninsulas dipping into the lake, the cooling air blowing off the water had marginally calmed me down. It helped that Angel didn't dive into the relationship topic as soon as we were alone. He was more interested in meticulously arranging the tent, the one blanket and sleeping bag he'd brought along, and the minor provisions.

"I can't believe you know how to camp," I said, watching him build a little fire. "Were you a Fresh Air Fund kid?"

"No. I watch a lot of *Survivorman*." Angel sat in front of the tent, facing the fire, as the sun continued to sink below the horizon. "I don't really like animals and nature, but I like being alone. You don't get much more alone than when camping."

I pointed across the lake where I could see dozens of people frolicking. "Not so alone."

"Yeah, wise ass, but they're tiny specks in the distance and not here talking my ear off." Angel gave me a wry look. "We can go back if you don't want to do this."

"Who says I don't want to?" I plopped down next to him in front of the tent. "I'm outdoorsy when necessary," I informed him when he snorted. "It's just usually not necessary."

"Smoking pot at Baisley Park doesn't really count."

"Ha ha." I swiped his little bag of goodies, and a grin swept across my face like a brisk wind. "You were going to make s'mores by yourself?"

"Fuck yeah. That's comfort food right there. I used to make them on the stove when I was little."

I could so easily picture mini Angelito standing at the stove, glaring at a burner and trying to figure out how to melt the chocolate without burning himself. I bet he'd have taken it so seriously.

"You're adorable sometimes," I said.

Angel snagged the bag and pulled out the graham crackers. "What am I all the other times?"

"Somewhere between a pain in the ass and a sexy bastard." I removed the rest of the ingredients. "Do you think it's too hot for s'mores?"

"Don't be closed-minded."

Man, he was taking this seriously. It was charming enough for my fear to dial back a little more, and I was able to relax. With my legs stretched out in front of me, a cool breeze blowing my hair away from my face, and the sky turning purple and orange the farther the sun sunk, it was perfect.

"Jerky, cheese, and water for dinner, with s'mores as dessert." Angel shot me an apologetic glance. "Not very gourmet."

"Angel, we're gonna be here for one night. We'll be fine. I'll gorge on graham crackers and marshmallows."

"That's my girl."

Angel shoved a long stick of jerky at me and stretched out on the ground, leaning on his forearms as he stared across the lake. The breeze whipped his dark-blond hair around, tangling it and sometimes covering his eyes. I itched to smooth it away or tie it back in a small knot, but settled for watching. He was so serious as he contemplated the water and the families in the distance. Was he thinking about going for a swim or had his thoughts drifted completely away? There was no way to know, but I wished I could read his mind.

"So we gonna talk about this?"

The question jolted me. Apparently telepathy was unneeded tonight.

I ripped off a tough piece of jerky, chewing with difficulty, and looked out at the water myself. "We can talk."

"You said you wanted honesty."

Nodding, I said, "I did. I do."

"Cool." Angel shifted his attention from the water to my profile. I could see his intense gaze in my peripheral vision. "Then I honestly want to know what changed your mind."

The chunk of jerky caught in my throat, but I swallowed noisily. "What do you mean?"

"I mean you've been saying you wanted to be friends with benefits for months. Saying you prefer it to anything else. Never once did you admit to having feelings for me besides friendship or sexual attraction. I thought you didn't like me in that way. Or . . ." When I raised my eyebrows, a sheepish expression crossed his face. "There were times when I *did* think you felt the same way I did, but you'd always pull back. I wondered if you didn't want to be in a relationship with a guy."

My jaw nearly dropped. "What the hell? What does that have to do with anything?"

"Because . . ." The sheepishness turned to outright reluctance. "I noticed in the past the only times you even seemed close to dating, it was with a woman. So, I wondered if you preferred women but still liked to fuck guys—"

"Angel," I said sharply. "I'm bisexual. I am attracted to and capable of having feelings for both men and women. Being bi doesn't mean I have to lean further one way or another. Bisexuals aren't the seesaws of the rainbow."

"I'm not saying that!" Angel exhaled slowly. "Yeah, this is coming out wrong. I just thought you didn't want to date guys because guys are fucking trash most of the time, but you were still okay with casual sex. Does that make sense?"

Some of my defensiveness simmered. I relaxed again. "Okay, yes. That phrasing is better. And most cis dudes are trash, but you're not. I would never lump you or Ray or Chris in with faceless randoms. But you do have a point that I was more comfortable casually dating women. I trusted them more to not try to pressure me into doing things I didn't want to do. But it was still *casual*. I've never been compelled to get sentimental with anyone before now."

"Then why now?"

I slowly rewrapped the rest of my jerky in the plastic. With each motion, I took a deep measured breath. This felt like dangerous waters, but I waded in. "After what you said, can you blame me for choosing this day? I feel like you're always blitzing me with sweetness, and I get flustered and sweaty in response like a confused teenager." I ran a hand through my hair and leaned backward so my pose mirrored his. "And . . ."

"And?"

I blew out a slow breath, like a regretful leaky tire. Stalling. That's what I was doing. He knew it, and I knew it, but I couldn't stop. This wasn't me. None of this was me. I wasn't this girl. Which meant I wasn't the girl for him. That was the real kicker. Eventually, he'd find a woman who *was* his match.

"You said you wished you could fall for someone else." I ran my tongue over my lower lip, squinting into the distance. "And the idea was like a kick in the gut."

Angel rolled onto his side, face braced in his hand. "I've dated other people before."

"Never for long," I said grudgingly. "And I know you. If you get serious with someone, you'll fall hard. You'll end up married with—"

"Stop pretending you know what I want, Stephanie."

"Don't I?" I rolled onto my side as well so we were facing each other. "The problem between us is that you want something I swore to myself I'd never have. That I'd never want."

"I want a fucking relationship, not a wedding and you in a white gown," he growled, brows drawing down low over his eyes. "Do you think I don't know you?"

"Do you think people don't get into relationships pretending to respect what the other person wants but really having a secret goal to change them?" I countered. "It happens all the time. The whole relationship thing is a game people play because they want to lock someone down because they're afraid of being alone, and usually lie to each other about who they are in the process. And about what they want."

Angel's expression morphed from irritation to incredulous. He sat up, leaning over me. "That's what you think of Ray and David? Nunzio and Michael? How about your friend Ashton and his boxer—Val?"

"No, but just because some of our friends—"

"You can't just make broad generalizations and then pick and choose when it's applicable, Stephanie."

There was time for me to reply and defend my thoughts, but his flashing green eyes froze me in my place. His angry face was sexy as hell, and I loved it when he said my name in that sharp tone. The way he leaned down to bring our faces closer together.

"You always talk about people being narrow-minded and ignorant, but how do you sound acting like everyone in a monogamous relationship is an asshole? Or boring? Or deluded fucks just spending their lives pretending they want something they really don't?"

"I didn't say all that, and you know it." I pushed myself up, arms extended back and palms flat on the ground. When we were closer, his eyes automatically dropped to my mouth. They stayed here. "My entire point is that people tie all their hopes and dreams on one person because they're afraid of being alone and that sounds *terrible*.

It sounds fucking exhausting and like a letdown waiting to happen. All because people *need* companionship."

"And you don't?" he asked, voice pitching lower. "Maybe not need. But you don't even want it?"

The no nearly leaped off my tongue, but it didn't feel right. The shape of the word was clumsy in my mouth, and tasted too much like a lie. Wasn't me wanting companionship how all of this had started in the past week? Not with any random person out of a sense of desperation not to be alone—but with him. Specifically.

Me wanting Angel to go places with me—first the party, then the retreat. Me wanting to parade him in front of my coworkers because of the flush of pride I felt when they liked him so much. Me wanting to be close to him because our bodies fit together like puzzle pieces, even though I'd sworn all this time we belonged in different boxes. And me wanting him for myself. Wishing he'd just up and wake up one day, and be like me. Capable of having sex with people without all the feelings, because the idea of him being in a serious relationship with someone else . . . It killed me, even though I didn't think I was capable of giving him the type of relationship I'd always thought he wanted. But now I wasn't sure what he wanted. Maybe I'd never known. I'd never actually asked.

"Be honest with me, nena," he whispered. "It's just you and me here."

"And the moon and stars?"

Angel looked up at the sky. Dusk was giving way to night, and the moon was clearly visible above us. "Yeah. The trees too. Probably some dumb animals."

Leave it to him to dislike animals while enjoying roughing it. He was as contradictory as I was, as unlikely as this entire conversation, but maybe that was why we worked. Neither of us made any sense unless we were naked and pressed together, sharing breath and time with our bodies connected.

"What do *you* want?" I asked. "I know you said you want to be with me, but . . . how? What does it look like to you if it's not marriage and kids?"

"Honestly?" Angel smiled faintly. "I just want to be yours. Yeah, the only one you want to sleep with, but I also wanna be your go-to person. The one you call first when something happens, or when you get good news. And . . . I want us to live together one day. When I'm pining extra hard, I have these stupid daydreams about moving in to your place after letting Tonya take over the lease for our apartment. I think she and Mere would appreciate the privacy anyway, since there's no way Tonya is ever gonna live in that fucking mansion. And Mere seems to hate the idea of ever going back for long periods of time."

My heart had begun to pound halfway through his quickly spoken admission, and it was partially because I'd thought of those things too. I'd had fantasies of waking up with him on Sunday mornings, the raw ache between my legs and in my muscles following a night of sex, and then him whispering for me to stay in bed while he made coffee. Or the winter days when neither of us ventured out from the covers because body heat was more delicious even than caffeine. The look on his face when he watched me get ready—affectionate and infatuated. The way I ran my hands over his chest through a T-shirt, still a little shocked that the boy I'd known for so long had turned into this tall, solid man.

Cooking in my underwear and watching TV with him. Leaning against him and knowing he'd support me. Trusting him with everything from the confession that my parents had abandoned me and Vic to get high in a housing project in another neighborhood, to him helping whisk my brother away after Kings Park had exploded in gunfire and blood.

My lower lip trembled, my stomach flipping over. After so many years, it shouldn't affect me so much. None of it should. I'd spent years forging steel around those memories, but the return of Victor had melted those barriers like butter. Now all I could do was remember the past. Shielding Victor from the sight of our parents getting high in the kitchen when I was only ten. Waking up to find him crying in the middle of the night because they'd both vanished, and it was just me and him in the dark basement apartment we'd lived in until getting kicked out. Crawling through the window to run down the street in my nightgown, to the house with boarded windows, to ask the big men inside where my mom was. The look of loathing on her face when I begged her to come home. It had been that moment when I'd known she'd never wanted me. Us. Later, when we'd gotten older and she'd tried to pick herself up as our father fell further down, she'd said it out loud.

"If it weren't for you two, I wouldn't be here with him. I'd have finished school and had a real job. I wouldn't be fucking trapped."

Then she'd started using again. And she'd left.

"Hey . . ." Angel put a hand on my back. "Let's not talk about this."

"No, I'm fine." It was the worst lie, because my voice was thick and my eyes were wet. I felt so stupid, but there was no shame deep in my bones at him seeing me like this. It had always been okay for him to see me cry. Only him. "I don't know what's wrong with me, Angel. Ever since Victor came back, I keep thinking about our parents and how they'd never wanted us. And that day when Shawn got shot. How the kid who killed him didn't get caught, and I'd see him around the park knowing what he'd done. I used to wonder if he'd kill Victor if he ever came back from Chicago because he saw it all."

"That guy is in jail now for something else," Angel said, still running his hand up and down my spine. "He can't do shit to Victor."

"I know, but I keep thinking about it all, and I get so fucked up." I wiped my eyes, pulling in a shaking breath. "And the more I think about us, the more those memories bombard me." I could tell he had questions, but he just stroked my back and watched me. Waiting for an explanation. Not pushing me like he was afraid he kept doing. "I had to be a grown-up before I had all my adult teeth. My first real thought about the future was that I didn't want to end up like my mother. Trapped with some man and letting him control my life. Then, later, when I had to lie to everyone to keep us out of foster care, that promise was all I had that made me feel like I had control of my own life. I made my own choices. I fucked who I wanted, never letting anyone stake a claim. I picked my friends. I picked my high school. My college. Every decision about my life was made by me and me alone. No boyfriend. No girlfriend. No one to try to steer me one direction or the other. I didn't even want to go to the same college as you and Chris."

Angel stopped rubbing my back for half a beat. "That's why you refused to apply to City Tech instead of John Jay? I figured it was because of the law thing."

"City Tech had a decent legal studies program too, but I wanted to be on my own. Not always . . . depending on you guys to make me feel like I had my squad nearby."

He nodded slowly, searching my face as if he'd never seen it before. I could sense things clicking together in his mind. Realizing this went far beyond monogamy and sex. It went far beyond him.

"So what changed?" That question again. He did not intend to stop asking it, I could tell. "You don't want to depend on anyone, and you think being in a relationship is the ultimate sign of dependency—I get it. But then why are you acting different lately? Sometimes you treat me more like a boyfriend than a fuck buddy, but then you refuse to admit it's true."

I lowered my eyes, but he tilted my chin up. Not cutting me any slack.

"It's not just me, Stephanie. Ever since we started playing this game this weekend, I've been getting the vibe that you're enjoying it. You like pretending to be with me. A lot." When I gnawed on my lower lip and didn't disagree, the tiniest smile ghosted across his face before vanishing. "And I see how you get when someone else pays me any mind. You're as possessive as I am. You don't want me with anyone else. You don't even want me to fuck anyone else."

It was selfish, but it was true. Before Meredith got with Tonya, she'd looked at him a little too long on more than one occasion, and jealousy had taken hold of me fast and strong. I always talked about his jealous fits, but I was just as capable of them, though I was better at hiding it.

"I don't know how to answer." I collapsed against the ground again, looking up at the darkening sky and the faint pinpricks of light from the stars. "I'm not lonely. My life is going great. The only thing that changed is that in the past year, I only want to sleep with you. You're the one I want to talk to when I first wake up and before I go to bed. And since Victor came back . . ." I shut my eyes. "You're the only one I know I can talk to about my family, because I feel safe breaking down in front of you. I feel safe around you in general. Like . . . comforted by your presence. Happy in a way that doesn't happen with anyone else, really."

Angel settled beside me, his fingers brushing my hand until I relaxed my balled fist. He brought my palm to his lips before holding it against his chest. I could feel his beating heart beneath cotton and flesh and bone.

"I'll be real with you: I think we would be good together." Angel rubbed his thumb against my skin. "But I understand why you want to stay solo and unattached, more so than I ever did before, so I won't push you anymore."

There was no small amount of trepidation in my voice as I asked, "What does that mean?"

"It means now more than ever, I realize I need to respect your decision and not try to push you. I shouldn't have been pushing you before. I need to stop hoping that if I'm patient enough, you'll change your mind."

There was a finality to his tone that made my stomach churn and my breath hitch. I knew we couldn't sustain this forever, I knew we were just hurting each other, but the reality of it ending *for real*, was stunning. It knocked the wind out of me.

"Are you going to try to move on?" I asked softly.

"I have to, Stephanie. Even though I keep telling myself that I can settle for this thing we're doing now . . ." Angel tightened his hand around mine, squeezing so tight it was nearly painful. "I know it's only a matter of time before this starts hurting a little too much. After this weekend, I'm going to try my best to reset things."

A chill cut through me now that the sun was gone and the wind was picking up, blowing cooler ripples of air off the water. "And for the rest of this weekend?"

Angel exhaled slowly. When he spoke, it was in a much lower voice. "I get to pretend you're mine."

CHAPTER EIGHT
STEPHANIE

S'mores were pretty awesome until you got melted marshmallows in your hair. Maybe that was what I got for trying to go for three marshmallows at once. If there was ever a metaphor for wanting too much of a good thing and making a fucking mess in the process, this was it.

Angel didn't try to hide his delighted laughter as I scowled and muttered in Spanish and trucked down to the water to do a quick wash before it dried. I'd planned to punish him with all kinds of sexual teasing. Making him suck chocolate off my fingers, sit on his lap so I could feel his dick against my ass—typical Quinones/León shenanigans.

Except, when I returned to find him setting up our shitty little sleeping bag back in our tiny tent, I was suddenly exhausted. Not even s'mores could breathe enough life back into me to keep me alert once we were snuggled together. Weariness from lack of a real dinner, the hike, and the conversation, settled into my bones. I fell asleep hard and fast to the rhythmic feel of his fingers combing through my hair. When I woke up, the early-morning sun had turned the sky a very pale blue.

I watched daybreak through the slit in our tent, and marveled at how comfortable I was, even though the ground was hard beneath the sleeping bag. Angel's face was pressed against my neck, and he was hugging me like a stuffed animal.

The left side of my body was falling asleep though, so I wiggled out of his grasp. Considering we were zipped together, it didn't work. I sagged on the floor for a second, regrouped, and then undid the sleeping bag just enough for me to escape his clutching arms and sit up. If the marshmallows had been a metaphor, what was this? Him holding me tight while I tried to escape.

Laughing humorlessly, I rubbed my hands along my arms and watched him. Still breathing softly, he'd rolled onto his back. He was a way prettier sleeper than I was. I snored, drooled, and kicked my way through the night, but Angel just looked like a more peaceful version of his strikingly handsome self.

The first time I'd laid eyes on Angel had been in high school. It was entirely possible that he'd been around the block or handball court before that, but the image of him striding into my ninth-grade Biology class was engraved in my mind. I'd already zoned out, wishing I'd had a cell phone, when suddenly this tall boy with dark-blond hair had strolled in wearing a bomber jacket over a Nas T-shirt, and Timberlands. I'd only looked up from my out-the-window daydream because I'd heard Raymond's voice in the hallway—he'd dropped Angel off before allegedly going to his own class—and had quickly found a random reason to speak to the adorable creature sitting next to me.

"Hey, blanquito. How do you know Ray?"

He'd looked at me with those light-green eyes, froze in place, then mumbled, *"From the park. Handball."*

Fourteen-year-old Angel had quickly averted his gaze, staring straight ahead at the whiteboard as if it held the mysteries to life, while I'd studied his profile. He'd slowly reddened under my rapt attention, and I'd been so charmed. His shyness had been a total change from catcalls and "Hey Mas" and corny little boys talking about my tetas until I wanted to knock them out.

We'd ended up having like three classes together, and had become friends despite me knowing he had a hard-core crush on me. He'd been too sweet, and respectful, to tell me about it.

In some ways, Angel was still that same sweet boy.

In some ways, I was still so fucking charmed.

I leaned down, brushing my lips to his. He didn't so much as stir, so I did it again. That time, I ended the press of mouths with a slow lick. Angel might as well have been a stone. His deep sleeping was a challenge I couldn't resist. Us being in nature did not change my desire to get my greedy hands all over his golden skin, or to wake him up in exceedingly pervy ways.

It took some effort to get him in the position I wanted—sleeping bag unzipped, legs pushed apart, and his briefs skinned down—and he *still* hadn't stirred beyond a pucker of his brows at all that skin being exposed. I barely noticed. I was all about the happy trail leading down to his groin, and the light-brown hair at the base of his dick. He was semihard from sleep, but already wilting from the cool air. Unacceptable.

I kissed his stomach, and looked up to see a smile flicker at the corner of his mouth. "Stephanie . . ."

I leaned down to take him in my mouth with no finesse. I grabbed his thick base and went straight for deep-throating. There was no point in wasting time.

Angel released a low sound, half groan and half whimper, his hips jutting up. I hummed around him and closed my eyes, enjoying the solid length of him in my mouth. His dick expanded and grew so hard it was now pulsing.

"Steph . . ."

A hand found the back of my head, fingers sliding through my messy hair, but he didn't push my face down. The only time he went full caveman on me was after a lot of foreplay or a long dry spell of us not touching each other. Or when we were so pissed that all that energy exploded into sex so intense it was nearly frightening. Like when he'd pulled me away from the ballroom on the QFindr cruise, pushed me against a balcony overlooking the ocean, and hiked my dress up. I'd been as enraged as I'd been turned on, and I'd slammed back on him as some crewmember likely watched the cameras. Angel and I had growled at each other after, before stalking off in separate directions.

In our little tent with the sun barely rising over the lake, there was none of that intensity just yet. There was only peace, quiet, and the knowledge that for this moment, we were playing at being engaged, and I could get away with a lot.

I pulled away with a wet *pop* of my mouth. Saliva covered the column of his dick, wetting my fingers. "You fully awake now, mi caro?"

The endearment came out in a low purr, and it hit the note I'd wanted. Angel hissed out a breath, his feet sliding against the now-askew sleeping bag so he could bend his legs at the knee. I liked him spread open in front of me.

Angel dragged the tips of his fingers along the side of my face. "Very awake, mi vida."

My heart stopped. It was the worst timing to get misty-eyed and shaky. Turning my face down, I pressed a sloppy kiss to the head of his dick.

"Yeah," he murmured. "Treat me real nice."

After tracing the veins in his shaft with the tip of my tongue, I suckled his weeping crown once more. I could taste his pre-come, so I sucked harder. The sound he made, half growl, half cry, was probably heard across the lake and in the lodge, but I wanted to hear more. Seventy-five percent of the time we spent in bed was with him making me come repeatedly. When it was his turn, he could be stoic. There would be none of that this morning.

I took him in my mouth, still gripping his root with one hand. I slipped the other down to his ass, pushing him back just slightly so I could trace the crease with my fingers. Some guys might clench up or pull away at the hint I was throwing, but Angel just groaned again and rocked against me.

Pegging had been part of our games early on. As soon as I'd shown him a delicious series of Tumblr gifs portraying a guy having his prostate stimulated by a woman, Angel had wanted in on it. My adventurous sweetheart had looked at me with dilated pleading eyes at the very idea of having an orgasm that hard. I'd been so ecstatic. So fond. Maybe him digging butt play had been the first real sign that I would fall in love.

I pushed my two spit– and pre-come–covered fingers into his hole and found his prostate easily after so many months of practice.

"Ahh . . ."

I hooked my fingers up, and massaged the little notch inside of him. When he rocked on my hand, making agonized sounds, my pussy clenched. I squeezed my thighs together, overly aware of how wet I was, and sucked again. This time, he clutched the back of my head with more force and guided my face so I could take him deeper into my mouth. My eyes teared a bit, but it didn't stop me from working his prostate with more purposeful movements.

"Ay Dios, Stephanie." Angel's voice hitched. I opened my eyes just in time to see him grabbing up the sleeping bag with his free hand, squeezing it in his big fist. He'd dropped his head back, hair hanging over his face, and only the damp sheen across his mouth visible as he panted. "Por favor, no pares."

Groaning, I bobbed my head and the tip nearly brushed the back of my throat. All the while, I felt myself rocking against the air and clenching around nothing, wanting very, very badly some pressure against my clit. To get it, I'd have to stop touching him, and that wasn't going to happen. I wanted him on the edge.

When I shoved a third finger into his ass, Angel seemed to hit his breaking point, and sweetness switched to demanding.

"Yeah, Steph," he growled. "You suck that cock."

"Mmm . . ."

He fucked my mouth so hard my eyes teared again. I saw spots dancing before them, the world dimming just slightly at the edges, but I didn't pull away. I reveled in him finally losing control, but my body was an inferno. I was so overheated and turned on that it was nearly painful.

"You want to taste my come or feel it in your pussy?"

My hips jerked forward, and for a second, I thought I was going to come from the question. God knew I was close enough. Breathing hard, I pulled my mouth off his gleaming dick and stared at him through a mess of hair. There should have been no question about what I wanted. I'd been on birth control for a decade, and we'd stopped using protection with each other months ago. He knew I loved feeling it as he released. Not only the way he clung to me and said my name in that low worshipful moan, but the pulse of his dick inside me.

"What do you think?"

Angel swept his tongue over his lower lip. "Ride it."

It wasn't smooth as I fumbled out of my underwear and climbed atop him in the small tent, but I managed it in seconds. I positioned myself above him, squirming as he tapped his cockhead against the hard nub of my clit.

I rubbed myself against him. He had a level of restraint that I didn't possess. At least, not when it came to him. Angel loved to tease me, to draw it out until I was drenched and aching. Sometimes, I just needed him in me. Now was one of those times.

"Angel."

He dragged his tip along my slit and watched me from beneath his eyelashes. "Pull your shirt up."

Impatiently, I yanked it off. I had all kinds of tan lines from the combination of my tank top and sports bra, but he sighed like he'd just set eyes on a work of art. I leaned forward so my breasts rubbed against his shirt, my nipples taut and stinging from the friction, and kissed him hard. I kept kissing him when he was sheathed inside of me, and only stopped when his steady thrusts ripped my breath away all over again.

My knees dug into the hard ground on either side of him as he clamped down on my ass with one hand and gripped the back of my head with the other. We stared into each other's eyes as he moved inside of me, and I rode him as much as I could even though he had me locked in the position he wanted.

A thousand sensations went off in my body like mini explosions. The sensation of my clit grinding against his groin, the angle of his hardness inside of me, his breath on my face, a hand tight and possessive in my hair, and then . . . the sudden pressure of his finger against my anus.

I bit my lower lip, so close to coming it was agonizing, and reared upright. He smacked my ass, as if chastising me for ruining his plan. He smirked, but it turned to a hooded look of pleasure when I began to ride him in earnest. One hand braced behind me on his knee and the other between my legs so I could frantically rub my clit.

When it hit me, my orgasm was loud and messy. I was so wet that I had a distant fleeting wondering about how we'd ever hike back down to the lodge around other people. The concern was blighted from my mind once Angel shoved himself up to press his lips to my throat. He bit lightly and surged inside of me, coming with harsh, breathless gasps.

I wrapped my arms around his neck and my legs around his waist, keeping him inside of me. "Nice try, León."

"Mmm?"

"The attempted DP."

Angel snorted into my hair and smacked my ass again. "Does one finger really count as double penetration?"

"Yup. After the other night, you're getting greedy." Snickering at his exaggerated pout, I pulled off him. "I need a bath. We both reek of sex."

"There's a problem with that? I like having you all over me."

"Ugh, stop being so . . ." I waved vaguely at his flushed face. "Stop making me want to fuck you again immediately."

"Give me like ten minutes, nena."

I smiled broadly, then forced myself to shake my head. "Nope. We need to get down to that stream before the rest of the normal people wake up and see our unprepared naked culos."

"Is your culo being unprepared the reason for no fake-DP?" He dodged a swat and sat up on his knees, snickering. "Fine. Maybe later."

"Maybe."

We fumbled in the small space to gather our clothes. I grumbled that I had nothing to change into, and he silently presented me with an extra tank top and a pair of shorts. My eyebrows hiked up.

"Those are mine."

"Good eye, Sherlock."

I poked him in the side. "I thought you'd planned this little camping trip to be solo?"

We'd just fucked each other's brains out and joked about butt play, but Angel flushed like my sweet boy all over again. "Well, I guess in the back of my mind, I was kind of hoping you'd stay out here with me . . ."

I stared at him. He tried to duck out of the tent for a quick escape, but I grabbed him and dragged him back for a kiss.

"I love you, fiancé," I whispered against his mouth.

Angel held me to his chest and released a shuddering sigh. "I love you too, Stephanie."

CHAPTER NINE
ANGEL

Angel: *I'm fucked*

Chris: *???*

Raymond: *Literally?*

Angel: *I'm not joking, man. I don't know what I'm doing.*

Raymond: *Be specific or I'm putting my phone in my locker and going to work*

Chris: *What happened?*

Angel: *This whole pretending to be Stephanie's fiancé thing happened.*

Raymond: *I told you you're an idiot. Or a masochist. Not my kink but hey . . . more power to ya*

Chris: *:/ What happened, bro?*

Angel: *We made this deal to just . . . live out this weekend like we're really together, pretty much enjoy the game, and then move on because I want to be w/ her and she doesn't want to depend on anyone enough to be with them in a relationship.*

Raymond: *That sounds like some shit I'd have done with David tbh so I can't even make fun of you*

Angel: *FML dude. This entire thing was a bad idea.*

Chris: *Let me guess: the whole enjoying the game thing just made you want her even more and now you're stressing over the weekend ending and going back to jacking it all the time while thinking about her?*

Angel: *Yep*

Angel: *Except now it will be even more depressing because she told me she loves me. So basically . . . I'd have a shot if all of these circumstances I can't control were different. It would prob hurt less if I didn't know she felt the same*

Raymond: *WHAT*

Raymond: *She SAID she loves you??*

Raymond: *Hold up hell just froze over*

Angel: *Shut up man its not funny*

Chris: *There's no chance of her changing her mind?*

Angel: *I dunno. I'm not going to pressure her. She has good reasons for being the way she is, but it just fucking makes me feel like I want to rip my heart out. Or move away.*

Raymond: *Move away? Dude this ain't eat pray love, calm down*

Angel: *I'm serious tho. How the fuck am I supposed to ever move on if she lives right up the street? I see her all the time. I want her all the time. Just imagine David having told you he loves you but can't be with you and he's just . . . ALWAYS THERE.*

Raymond: *Ok yea that sucks my dude.*

Raymond: *Idk what to tell you*

Chris: *The only thing you can do is try to move on? Date other people and try to find someone else and don't spend every date comparing them to her. I tried that when I was trying to forget Jace and Aiden, and it sucked.*

Raymond: *Or you could start sucking dick. That would distract you*

Chris: *Omg Ray shut the fuck up for real*

Raymond: *What? Am I wrong?*

As much as I loved my boys, Raymond trying to distract me by making me laugh wasn't going to do the trick right now.

I'd gone from being on cloud nine while hiking back to the lodge with Stephanie, hand in hand and bumping into each other like a couple of kids who'd snuck out for the night, to descending into a depressed cloud so thick I was shocked people couldn't see it around me. Everyone was in a great mood while cooking and chattering about the last day's activities, and I was trying my best to keep smiling, but my brain was stuck.

It'd been stuck as soon as I'd sat down on the bed we were sharing and realized tonight was the last time we'd share a bed. The last time I'd make love to her. Maybe tomorrow was the last time I'd kiss her. Maybe this morning was the last time she'd tell me she loved me.

All things considered, as emotional as I could be, I tended to suck it up. I angsted to myself, but rarely to other people. Except lately.

And I hadn't cried since my abuelo's funeral in San Juan, but the idea of ten years of longing being officially over, with no more hope, crushed me. If smiling through suffocation was an art form, I'd be winning awards. When I kissed Stephanie on the cheek and told her I was going to shower, she didn't seem to notice anything was off.

Good.

The last thing I wanted was for her to think I was guilting her.

I turned on the hot water in the bathroom, flipped down the toilet seat, and sat there staring at my phone. Chris's words glared up at me.

Move on. Date other people.

My automatic response was to say it would never work. No one could replace Stephanie. I'd tried before, and it had failed. They'd known I was preoccupied. That I wasn't invested. Or had I only been preoccupied and uninvested because I'd been comparing them to Stephanie the entire time? Had I spent the last ten years sabotaging all potential attempts to get over a girl I would never have?

The possibility was terrifying. What if I did that for the rest of my life? What if I never got over her?

My mind supplied two options: get over her or gradually pull back and cut her off.

A shudder went through me. I felt sick at the thought of not seeing her anymore. We'd spent years being solely platonic friends, and I'd watched her hook up with or date different people. None of it had cut as badly as the idea of putting our friendship somewhere in the back of a junk drawer. It wasn't an option.

Chris was right. I simply needed to move the fuck on.

As steam billowed into the bathroom from the shower, I redownloaded Tinder. By the time the heat from the water had turned the small room oppressively warm, I'd swiped a few faces and already felt the mind-numbing disinterest of finding someone to date for the sake of dating.

STEPHANIE

It didn't take a mind reader to figure out that something had changed as soon as we'd returned to the property. Angel turned inward almost as often as I sought escape in partying with Meredith and going out, and he was definitely internalizing something right now. Like the end of this trip and whatever we'd become over the past year.

It was an unpleasant thought. Frankly, a horrible one. In an attempt to escape reality, I held my breath and dunked my head beneath the water in the pool. It was the best place to seek refuge from my coworkers. Retreat or no retreat, I had more things to think about right now than their team-building games. And they'd have a hard time suggesting I pop in to join them if I was wearing a bikini and drenched.

Most of my coworkers' partners had the same idea. Dee in particular had been camped on a floatie since early morning, and was idly swiping at her phone while sipping on a beer.

I broke the surface with a gasp, trying to throw my hair back like a Norwegian Sun commercial and probably looking more like I was about to take someone's eye out. After smoothing wet hair out of my face, I peered through the patio doors and saw Angel sitting by himself in the sun room.

I swam to the edge of the pool and braced my arms along the side, watching as he sat in a recliner and pulled out his phone. Random things about him caught my attention and drew me in these days. The way he sat up straight all the time like someone had beaten the need for good posture into him at a young age. How he held his phone one-handed as he rubbed the back of his neck with the other, a simple motion that made his biceps bulge beneath his T-shirt.

But mostly, I was caught by his expression. So pensive. Always worried and thinking. It looked like he was doing both at the moment, and I was dying to know what was going on in his brain. We'd had such a good morning, but things shifted fast between us on a regular day, let alone on a day when we'd fucked, said *I love you*, and made a semi-promise to . . . leave this all behind starting tomorrow or the day after.

"Are you staying out here for a while?"

Dee's voice drew my attention away from Angel. "Yup. Why?"

She raised an eyebrow and peered at me through her pink cat-eye sunglasses. I loved Dee for primarily this reason. Well, for several reasons. She was like Lana Del Rey but short and curvy and did not give a fuck what anyone at the law firm thought of her. You had to love a girl who wasn't going to waste her mini-vaca pretending to care about team builders.

"Just curious."

I swam away from the edge, went under the water to kick my way across the pool, and popped up next to her float. She jumped, startled, and I snickered. It turned into a full-on laugh when she sniffed and rubbed her now-damp phone against her bikini top. If it weren't for Angel, I'd probably be all over her. Then again, I'd said the same about Meredith before she'd hooked up with Tonya, and every other person who'd almost sparked my interest lately. My "that could be interesting" flag would half-heartedly go up, then wilt almost as fast.

"Because," she drawled. "It'd be nice to have some company. After the first day, everyone is focused on work-related things."

"Yeah, I'm here because of work, but I don't plan to talk about work." I swam around her floatie, being careful not to splash her any more. "Are you having any fun?"

"There's a pool, free booze and food, and I'm out of that armpit of a sweltering city. So yes." Dee turned on her side so she could peer down at me. "You're the first person to ask me, by the way. I think I've been dismissed as Kip's arm candy."

I stopped swimming and hung on to the end of her floatie with one arm. "That's shitty, but you're probably right. This—" Maybe it wasn't the best time to go off about the sexism in the firm. "This weirdly doesn't seem like a venue conducive to getting to know new people? Everyone is cliquing up."

At her slow nod, I glanced over my shoulder again but could no longer see Angel through the doors. I'd been so preoccupied with him that I'd barely hung out with anyone else.

"So, Dee, why don't you tell me about yourself?"

"My name is Diana." She wiggled her toes and got into a comfortable position again. "And I'm a nurse."

"Oh, nice! When I was applying for colleges, I was torn between the nursing program and the legal studies program," I admitted. "But I had a specific interest in the law."

"Why didn't you go to law school?"

She asked like it was the most natural thing in the world, and I'd somehow overlooked it. "I didn't have money for law school. I put myself through undergrad." I swam backward a little and looked up at the sky, feeling my hair drifting around me. "Besides that, my primary interest at the time was understanding the law. Specifically, my rights." And Victor's. I'd been preparing myself for a lifetime of having to fight for him. "I was disappointed about that reality when I was younger, but I'm happy with where I am now. My work matters, and I feel successful on a regular basis."

Dee, or Diana, made a satisfied sound. "Good for you, girl."

"Thanks." I pushed through the water again and ran a hand through my hair. "I'm going to head inside and get something to eat. Do you want to come?"

"I'll be in soon."

"Cool." I started to backstroke my way to the edge of the pool, but something about her expression threw me off. The way she twisted her mouth and glanced at the patio doors, then back at me. "What was that?" I asked, laughing. She pursed her lips, expression going serious, and my smile faded. "Are you okay?"

"I am, yes." Another pause, another glance toward the doors. "And it's not my business."

"What are you talking about?" I followed her gaze, and my eyes fell on Angel. He'd started pacing in the room. Something he only did when agitated. "Does it have to do with me?"

"It has to do with him." This hesitation was shorter before she said, all in a rush, "I was on Tinder, and his profile popped up for me. I don't know what your situation is, or if you guys are open, but—"

"Wait." I held up both hands to stop her talking. "You saw *Angel* on Tinder?"

Dee stared at me silently, which was all the answer I needed. My body went on autopilot, swimming to the edge of the large pool and dragging me up out of it before my brain caught up with my actions. Water sluiced down my body as I walked quickly across the patio. A large fan blew a surprisingly cool breeze that should have sent a chill through me, but I didn't feel anything but anger.

I jerked the door open and slipped inside, startling Angel into fumbling with his phone. The guilty way he shoved it into his pocket spoke volumes. As did the way his fair skin flushed red.

"You couldn't wait one day?" I pointed at him, and was hit with déjà vu. Wasn't this how all of this had started? Me yelling at him while half-dressed? Him looking at me in confusion like he had no idea what my deal was? I was so fucking sick of the pattern. The way he gave me that 'Who me?' look. "You were on Tinder. Just now."

His brows crashed down, eyes narrowing. "How the fuck do you know?"

"Because Dee was on, and she told me!"

Angel inhaled through his nose, but deep breathing exercises weren't keeping him from reddening further. "Look—"

"Why couldn't you wait one more day?"

"What difference does it make?" The incredulity on his face was killing me. "Mira, nena, we just said last night that this is over starting tomorrow. It was my idea, I know that, but—"

"So why couldn't you give me one more fucking day?" My voice was too loud, too shrill, too goddamn angry. And there was no way it had gone unheard by anyone in the vicinity, but I couldn't stop the rage that was contorting me into a version of myself that I hated. The one who let people know they'd gotten under her skin. Judging by his slack-jawed expression of surprise, he knew all right. "You think I have no feelings because I've never been in a relationship?"

"What?" Angel shook his head quickly. "No, of course not."

"Then why couldn't you wait?"

"Because I didn't think it would matter! It's not like I'm going to meet a new girlfriend—" He stumbled over the words at my flinch. "I mean, my . . . whoever I'm looking for." Angel cringed harder. "*Fuck*. Stephanie. I wasn't seriously looking for a girl in Lake George, okay? I was just . . . preparing myself."

"To find your new girlfriend," I repeated bitterly. "I guess that's on tomorrow's agenda. Maybe the bus ride."

He lifted his hands and buried them in his hair, closing his eyes and taking another deep breath. It made me want to shout at him, because I hated this act. Like he'd done nothing wrong, and he was dealing with some irrational, out of control person. Or maybe that was just how I felt? How the hell was it possible to tell anymore?

"I told you I loved you, and you respond by . . ." I looked down at his pocket as if I'd be able to see his phone. Or his Tinder profile. "By immediately looking for someone else."

"I responded by trying to do the only thing I can think of to save myself from pulling way back from you," Angel said roughly. "Because if I don't move on, I'll end up staying away from you, and I fucking know it. I'll put up a wall between us because it will be too hard to see you."

My stomach sank, so I crossed my arms over it as if that would help the sick feeling. It didn't, but the anger seeped from my body and dripped onto the floor like the water sliding down my skin. I was suddenly very aware of how ridiculous I looked. How fucking stupid I was for charging in here and demanding anything of him after I'd once again asked him to do something against his own best interest— coming here and pretending to be my lover. My fiancé.

"I'm sorry," I whispered, looking away from him. "It's none of my business. I have no right to be jealous. Or angry." Angel made a sound low in his voice and took a step toward me, but I held up my hands quickly. "Please don't. Just let me be sorry. Let me feel like an asshole."

"But you're not an asshole." He maintained his distance for a moment longer before taking two steps closer and pulling my wet body against his dry clothes. My back straightened, and I wanted to pull away, but instead I tilted my forehead against his chest with a sigh. "Mamita, if you'd been out there flirting with some dude so you could hurry up and move on, I'd have cracked his skull open on the side of the pool. For a hot second I thought you knew I was on Tinder because *you* were on it, and I got instantly pissed. How fucked up is that?"

A hysterical laugh burst out of my mouth, but it borderline sounded like a sob. Bringing my hands up, I clenched my fingers in his shirt and squeezed my eyes shut. "Why are we so bad at everything?"

Angel kissed my forehead. "We're bad at trying not to be in love with each other. That's it."

He was right. He was so fucking right. The truth of it cracked the dam inside of me, and tears welled up in my eyes, spilling onto his shirt. I sucked in deep breaths, trying to control myself, but the tighter he held me . . . the harder it was for me to hold myself together.

"Let's get the fuck out of here," he said softly in my ear. "We can get a taxi to the nearest car rental, and go home."

"God, that sounds so good." I pulled away, gazing up at him miserably. "But it would look really—"

"I'll kill off a relative. My tio Ivan."

Another wet laugh escaped me. "You'd kill Ivan for me?"

"I'd do anything for you."

Forget Ivan, he was killing me, my resolve, and all of my rationale as to why this would never work for me. Why promises I'd made to myself as a kid still mattered today in the face of someone I'd never replace. Someone I never wanted to replace. Someone I didn't want to lose.

I bit down on my lower lip, and he kissed my forehead again.

"We're leaving. Ivan's toast."

He was trying to make me crack another smile, but I was all smiled out. Instead, I nodded wearily and let him leave the room to make our excuses while I dripped all over the floor.

CHAPTER TEN
STEPHANIE

We got stuck in traffic almost instantly. As much as I told myself I didn't believe in signs, it sometimes felt like I was presented with one example after another that they existed for real. Case in point, us leaving the lodge so we could get out of the unfortunate position we'd put ourselves in, just to get trapped on I-87 in a complete standstill.

Angel drummed his fingers on the steering wheel, slouched in the driver's seat, trying hard not to look annoyed by the situation. He occasionally sighed or sucked his teeth before muttering under his breath too low to be heard over the warble of the radio, but he kept his irritation to himself. Maybe because he'd wanted this ride back to be low-key, or maybe because he knew aggressive drivers put me on edge. Driving in a car with Raymond was an adventure between one explosion of rage and the next.

After twenty minutes of not moving an inch, I unclipped my seat belt and extended my legs so my feet rested on the dashboard. Angel glanced over, eyes skimming my legs before returning to the road.

"You're still allowed to look, you know."

His mouth quirked. "Yeah?"

I shrugged, going for nonchalant. "I'm going to keep admiring the goods."

"'The goods,'" he repeated with a laugh. "Which goods are those?"

"Hmm." Smiling slightly, I rolled my head to the side so I could give him a long exaggerated once-over. "The shoulders for one. And your ass. I love a guy with a bubble butt."

"You like a guy who doesn't mind having his bubble butt pegged."

My smile widened. "Damn right. I love that sound you make when I play with your prostate."

Angel scoffed, but heat was already rising up his neck. "I barely make any sounds."

"Lies. You moan really loud, then try to hide it so it comes out like a growl." At the sight of his flush turning a deeper shade of red, I lowered my voice and mimicked the sound. "*Mmm . . . Ugh. Oh fuck, St—*" Angel reached over to cover my mouth, but I dodged him, laughing. "Don't be embarrassed. It's hot."

"Yeah, but I don't really want to think about fucking while I'm trapped in this tiny vehicle." He made a grumpy face and shifted in the seat. "Me being horny is a waste of energy when I can't do anything about it."

On a usual day, I would have zoomed to discussing all the things we could be doing if we weren't in a car trapped around hundreds of other cars, but now my enthusiasm dimmed. I slumped against the seat, legs still stretched in front of me, and toyed with the frayed hem of my jean cutoffs. After a beat of us sitting in silence, he shot me a worried look.

"What's wrong?"

"Nothing!" My voice came out too loud and bright. Cringing, I dialed it back. "Everything's fine. I'm fine."

Angel continued to observe me from under the brim of his cap. "Don't be weird."

"I'm not being weird." It was a complete lie, and judging by the way he kept giving me the same dull stare, he knew it. "Fine. I'm trying to act normal."

"Nothing about you trying to sound super upbeat is normal, babe." He poked my side, smiling when I inched away quickly.

"Don't even try, León. I'll kick your ass right here."

He pretended to poke me again and laughed outright when I nearly threw myself against the side of the car to escape his fingers. "So ticklish. Remember on our senior trip when you snuck into my and Chris's cabin?"

I rolled my eyes. Our senior trip had been notable primarily because Raymond had been banned from all field trips due to one fight too many, and Tonya had not gone to any of them in solidarity.

The senior trip had been me, Chris, and Angel getting into shenanigans at a weird dude ranch. And me ducking my other school friends to hang out with them the entire time.

"Yes. You got drunk on that shit Crystal snuck in and made the mistake of tickling me."

"Yeah, you kneed me in the balls, and Chris nearly pissed himself laughing."

"I told you not to tickle me," I said, smirking. "But you were so dramatic and pathetic—"

"Dramatic? That shit *hurt*!"

"I offered to kiss it better," I reminded him, grinning. "And then *you* nearly pissed yourself. Chris was so ready to watch me blow you."

"Yeah, because Chris couldn't get anyone to blow him," Angel grumbled, as if the memory still annoyed him.

"No. He was just a baby smut muffin who didn't realize he was poly as fuck even back then."

Angel made a low sound in the back of his throat that was half laugh, half incredulous grunt. "You know, it's really weird how I can look back on all of this minor shit that happened when we were kids, and see signs that were always there and that I never noticed. Chris and Ray didn't change, they just became more confidant in who they are. And stopped being afraid of what they wanted."

"What specifically do you mean?"

"Everything that's happened with our friends in the past couple of years." Angel shook his head slowly, squinted at the traffic, then shifted the car into park. He arched his back. "Chris being queer and poly, but also Raymond. I was all shocked when I realized he was bi, but thinking back . . . it was pretty obvious. I'd catch him looking at guys sometimes, but he was so . . . Ray-like that I never thought twice."

"'Ray-like.'" I snorted. "Meaning, he was like a prettier version of my tough-guy brother, and tough guys don't like dick?"

Angel rolled his eyes. "I know it's stupid, but I was a teenager. Teenagers are stupid."

"Especially teenage boys."

"*Especially* teenage boys," he agreed. "I spent so much time wishing and worrying and fantasizing as a kid that I let a lot of experiences pass me by. But it's easier to think of what we could have done in retrospect, right?"

The words hit close to home, so I only nodded.

Right.

I watched him twist and stretch and roll his shoulders until the car filled with the nerve-racking sound of everything popping. I knew he was probably sore and uncomfortable from being cramped in the tiny car we'd rented, and I itched to rub his neck and shoulders. Before this trip, I would have without a hesitation. Even when we were in our "off again" stages, we didn't hesitate to casually touch each other. He wasn't wrong for not being sure of how we were supposed to act around each other. I played it cool like I had this all figured out, but I didn't have one clue who we were if we weren't the Stephanie and Angel who'd carried not-so-secret torches for each other for years.

It didn't seem possible to go back to being *just friends* when we hadn't been *just friends* since we'd met. He'd said it was easy to see things more clearly in retrospect, and in retrospect, I now realized I'd always been infatuated with him. Since that first day when he'd walked in wearing a Nas T-shirt, my eyes had locked on him with laser focus.

Not only had I been charmed by him, I'd wanted him to notice me. To see me. Later, I'd *loved* that he'd had a crush on me without ever confessing it in some stupid text message or passed note like all the other boys in school. I'd loved that he'd been kind and sweet to me without expecting anything in return. It was partially why I'd kept us in that place—never acknowledging his crush or my own developing feelings. I hadn't wanted to spoil it by making us like all the other couples who inevitably crumbled to dust, and I hadn't wanted to lose his unconditional sweetness.

Now, as I nibbled my lower lip and gazed into the hazy distance, I realized this was why I'd felt so threatened by Crystal. All she'd done was want him. Want him, tell him she wanted him, and they'd wound up together. That simple. I'd seethed and hated her for it, thinking she should have somehow known he was off-limits because of my weird thing about him, but in reality . . . I'd just resented her for doing something I'd not allowed myself to do.

And it was going to happen again in adulthood. Me wanting him, holding myself back, and . . . losing him to someone else. And maybe this time, as adults, there would be no second chances.

My eyes slid shut, and I took a shaky breath.

"You okay?"

I inhaled again, slow and deep, and wrapped my arms across my stomach. Angel touched my cheek, those callused fingers rubbing gently against my cheekbone.

"Hey. If you need some air or something, we can—"

"I want us to try," I blurted.

Angel's hand stilled, but he said nothing. I covered it with my own and opened my eyes, trying to convey calm while shuddering from the storm waging inside me. There was a push and pull of what I wanted versus what I thought I should want, and in the middle of it all was the part of my heart that had always been reserved just for him.

"Try . . . to get some air . . . jointly?"

An incredulous laugh burst out of me. I smacked his shoulder. "*No*, pendejo. Don't ruin this." He kept giving me the same bewildered look, so I forced a tremulous smile. "I want us to try being a couple."

Angel's light-green eyes were unblinking, his face creased with worry. "Are you fucking with me, Stephanie? Because it's not—"

"I'm not fucking with you." I turned sideways in the passenger's seat and leaned across the center console to touch his thigh. Every muscle in his body was drawn tight with tension. "I want you. I want us."

"But you said you don't want a relationship." The confusion didn't leave Angel's expression, but his breathing grew faster. "Last night when we talked, you said—"

"I know." I reached for his hand and squeezed it hard before releasing it. "But I keep thinking . . . about the what-ifs. What if I stick to my guns because I don't want everything to fail, and for us to ruin each other, and the only thing that gets ruined is my chance to be with you? What if this time I lose you for good?"

"Steph—" Angel's voice was strained. When he touched my hand again, his own was shaking. "Nena, are you serious? Is this for real?"

"I want it to be for real. And, look—" My words started coming out in a rush, tripping over each other and blending together in a panic.

"Maybe it won't be perfect. Or maybe I'm bad at being a girlfriend. Maybe we'll fight just as much as a couple as when we're upset over *not* being a couple. Maybe—"

Angel grabbed the back of my neck and drew me into a kiss. It wasn't harsh or demanding, but it wasn't gentle either. It was a firm, seal-the-deal type of kiss. A we're-a-fucking-couple-for-better-or-worse type of kiss.

And it was exactly the type of kiss I needed.

When we broke apart, he smiled against my lips. That little-boy smile. The one that was hesitant and excited all at the same time.

"We're really doing this," he whispered. "You're sure?"

"I'm su—"

A horn blasted behind us, and Angel jerked away. I blinked, looking out the window, and saw traffic had begun moving again. The horn blared again, longer this time, and Angel unrolled the window, his face flushed with anger.

"Hijo de la gran—"

"Angel," I said, laughing, and pulling him back to me again. "Fuck him. Look at me."

Angel swung his angry gaze back to me, and his face instantly melted from the hard glare into a searching stare.

"I love you," I said. "And if I'm going to change my mind for anyone, it's for you. Now let's get the hell out of here before that dude rear-ends us."

"Yeah." Angel was nodding but not driving, still staring at me like he couldn't look away. Or like he'd never seen me before. "Okay."

When a series of horns blared behind us, I covered his hand with my own and put it on the shifter. This time it was him who closed his eyes for a second, like he was saying a prayer, before we shifted together and put the car back into drive.

"We've got this, Angelito," I said softly. "I promise. And if we fuck up, we have a whole bunch of pain-in-the-ass friends who will try to help us fix it."

Angel snorted out a fond laugh. "I can hear them now."

"Me too. And I can't wait to tell them."

This time the smile that crossed Angel's face was broad and proud. As he steered us back toward the five boroughs, one hand on the wheel and one hand holding me steady under the sudden weight of this new reality, "Real Love" by Mary J. came on.

Maybe signs were real after all.

Explore more of the *Five Boroughs* series at:
riptidepublishing.com/titles/universe/five-boroughs

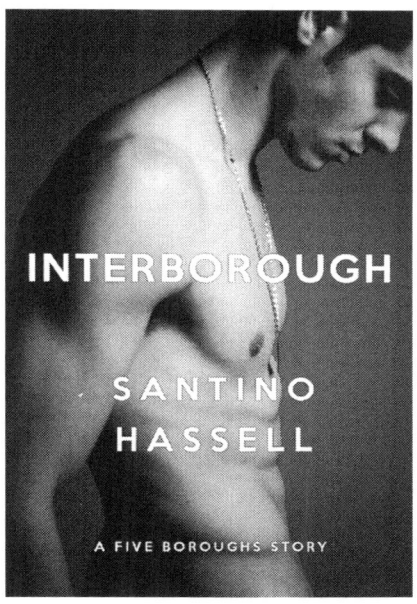

Dear Reader,

Thank you for reading Santino Hassell's *Citywide*!

We know your time is precious and you have many, many entertainment options, so it means a lot that you've chosen to spend your time reading. We really hope you enjoyed it.

We'd be honored if you'd consider posting a review—good or bad—on sites like **Amazon, Barnes & Noble, Kobo, Goodreads, Twitter, Facebook, Tumblr,** and your blog or website. We'd also be honored if you told your friends and family about this book. Word of mouth is a book's lifeblood!

For more information on upcoming releases, author interviews, blog tours, contests, giveaways, and more, please sign up for our weekly, spam-free newsletter and visit us around the web:

> **Newsletter**: tinyurl.com/RiptideSignup
> **Twitter**: twitter.com/RiptideBooks
> **Facebook**: facebook.com/RiptidePublishing
> **Goodreads**: tinyurl.com/RiptideOnGoodreads
> **Tumblr**: riptidepublishing.tumblr.com

Thank you so much for Reading the Rainbow!

RiptidePublishing.com

ACKNOWLEDGMENTS

This book would not be possible without my Five Boroughs fans. Since book two, readers have been asking to know more about Stephanie, Chris, and Angel (then Sharky). And since book three, readers have been asking for more of Jace and Aiden (Jaiden). It's amazing how characters in this series who started with minor roles became not only became important reoccurring characters, but people who needed their own stories as well.

I especially want to thank my patrons for motivating me to write about the Queens Crew. Every month for the past year, I've polled my patrons to ask what short they wanted that month, and several times they voted for more Chris, more Jaiden, and more of the Queens Crew in general. Without them, the threesome short that sparked my realization that Chris is much queerer than I anticipated would not have been written. I've only been allowed to explore and flesh out this series due to Patreon, and for that I am thankful.

We have two more books to go in the Five Boroughs universe, and I am so excited for you guys to read! Thanks for sticking with my 5B squad for this long.

ABOUT
THE AUTHOR

Santino Hassell was raised by a conservative family but grew up to be a smart-mouthed, school-cutting grunge kid, a transient twentysomething, and eventually transformed into a grumpy introvert and unlikely romance author with an affinity for baseball caps. His novels are heavily influenced by the gritty, urban landscape of New York City, and his desire to write relationships fueled by intensity and passion.

He's been a finalist in both the Bisexual Book Awards and the EPIC Awards, and was nominated for a prestigious RITA award in 2017. His work has been featured in *BuzzFeed*, *Huffington Post*, *Washington Post*, *RT* magazine, and *Cosmopolitan* magazine.

You can find him at santinohassell.com, in his reader group on Facebook—Get Hasselled, on Patreon, and on Twitter as @santinohassell.

Enjoy more stories like
Citywide
at RiptidePublishing.com!

Whiteout
ISBN: 978-1-62649-512-8

Seasons of Love
www.riptidepublishing.com/titles/
universe/seasons-love

Earn Bonus Bucks!

Earn 1 Bonus Buck for each dollar you spend. Find out how at
RiptidePublishing.com/news/bonus-bucks.

Win Free Ebooks for a Year!

Pre-order coming soon titles directly through our site and you'll
receive one entry into a drawing for a chance to win free books for
a year! Get the details at RiptidePublishing.com/contests.

Made in the USA
Columbia, SC
11 November 2017